MW01195358

Fables

Other Books by Alexander Theroux

FICTION

Three Wogs
Darconville's Cat
An Adultery
Laura Warholic; or, The Sexual Intellectual

FABLES

The Schinocephalic Waif
The Great Wheadle Tragedy
Master Snickup's Cloak

SHORT FICTION

Early Stories

POETRY

The Lollipop Trollops and Other Poems
Collected Poems

NONFICTION

The Primary Colors
The Secondary Colors
The Enigma of Al Capp
The Strange Case of Edward Gorey
Estonia: A Ramble Through the Periphery
The Grammar of Rock: Art and Artlessness in 20th Century Pop Lyrics
Einstein's Beets: An Examination of Food Phobias

Alexander Theroux

§

Fables

TOUGH POETS PRESS
ARLINGTON, MASSACHUSETTS

Some of these stories have previously
appeared, in modified form, in *Antæus,
Boston Monthly, The Iowa Review, The
Massachusetts Review,* and *The Mississippi
Review.*

Cover artwork by Brian Froud.

ISBN 978-0-578-30423-6

Tough Poets Press
Arlington, Massachusetts 02476
U.S.A.

www.toughpoets.com

For
Sarah
"Non sine sole iris"
and our
beautiful children
Shenandoah, and Shiloh
with
all my love

Thus far, with rough and all-unable pen,
our bending author hath pursued the story . . .
Shakespeare, *Henry V*

Contents

The Schinocephalic Waif

Outside, it was 1554.

A waif named Gremlina, who wouldn't even smush an ant, desperately walked over the blue snows of medieval Russia on her little printless feet, seeking justice.

She had a head shaped just exactly like an onion.

Cheated by nature, Gremlina further suffered the anomalous problem of being both fat and thin-skinned. O what a swift, what an awful circuit! "O Lost!" she cried at the grave of her parents in the potter's field and wrung her arms. Should she hurl herself into the River Bug, and simply have done?

Instead, unloved Gremlina nightly flung herself with knotted hands at the stoop of the steepleless Monastery of Our Lady of Spaso-Yefimev and humbly wailed, "*Xitler, Xitler!*" Meaning?

No one could say. Orphans are riddles.

But the ears of God were surely filled with sobs.

Even her little sister "Zizi," born Eupraxia, was gone, having injudiciously, one cruel frost, poisoned herself by eating some phosphorus matches she found in the way.

Meanwhile, the mighty czar, Ivan the Terrible, had sent

a decree far and wide in the realm that all architects instantly come to the Kremlin and show him their new designs for the steeples of Russia. They trembled. "I am sore afraid," said one.

"What is to be done?" screeched the Czar. It was the age-old Russian question.

The Czar was around the loop with anger, kicked cushions, and gulped villainous cups of coffee, for none of the architects could answer. Heads rolled. Some were mercifully eradicated by official fire.

Everybody in court had the sullens. Even the jester, Grock the Sequesterer, cowered, having failed to amuse the Czar with his musical swinet, fulsome bellshakes, and whipt tops.

One dryasdust functionary presented his plan, with a church steeple shaped like a mitten. The question now was, would it wash?

"Twaddle! Artificial rain! Lesions!" howled the Czar and flung out of the throne-room, greatly disappointed. Unhinged, some said. Gone asiatic, said others. And some, absolutely bats.

Time passed. By day Gremlina cruised past the quays and wistfully watched the oarage of birds' wings.

At night she wandered and with a lump in her throat searched the gutters of this exitless world for umbles, lollies, and discarded suckets, too afraid to sleep which caused bad dreams innumerable.

Of nixies, monopods, dangerous wishniks, yelpies, archdruids, onocentaurs, kraxen, thwitchets, snools, pea-and-thimble men, and crazed boars from the Urals, horned, tusked, hoofed, bristled, and befanged.

Or the Frost Giants who roamed the icebound mountains.

But her worst dream wasn't one. It was real. It was her head which was shaped just exactly like an onion.

Once, a gentleman, clacking his loose wobbly dentures, set his cap at Gremlina in a dark alley, rubbed his hands, and, approaching her, likerishly whispered, "O Nymphadora, my love."

It brought a blush of shame to the cheek of modesty—until he spotted her head and, recoiling, cursed his fate in no uncertain terms.

Then one rare (i.e., sunny) day, the unhappy Czar rumbled forth past the crowd in a carriage drawn by prancing coursers, emplumed, and suddenly noticed a strange shadow cast against the snow. It was the lengthened shadow of Gremlina's head. "Halt!" he cried, in Russian. "Halt!"

People were agoggle. Through the carriage doors a regal finger was pointing directly at little knurled Gremlina.

Immediately, mustachioed guards in huge shakos lifted her aboard and swept her off at a gallop to the chambers of the Kremlin where she proudly sat, fresh as an apple, while the Royal Architects (those who remained) scratched away at their drawing boards night and day, repeating, "*Littera occidit, spiritus vivificat.*"

The steeples over all Russia from that day to this, modeled on Gremlina's head, were henceforth shaped just exactly like onions.

Gremlina, now famous and loved by all, ate buttered rockbuns, owned swans, and even went for walks in the button-garden of the Czar, who sometimes held her hand. One afternoon, she was created a duchess. She became a bequest to the nation.

The Great Wheadle Tragedy

It was opening night!

The sleepy hamlet of Spritz, Germany, had never seen anything like it. Each canvas had been pegged, roped, and yanked aloft, catching the wind with a report like a gunshot. Pennants flew.

The colorful Great Wheadle Circus, famous throughout Europe, tweedled out under the big top, lit by gaslight, to the sound of quail whistles, water jars, citterns, buzzers, friction drums, sackbuts, and finger cymbals. It was every thing the puffs promised. "*O wunderbar! O ausgezeichnet!*" came the cries.

"*Hey ho numbelow, rumpopulorum, per omnia sæcula sæculorum,*" sang the prinking clowns, goofy, turning handstands, and tumbling along in red bulb noses, masks of white bismuth, immense pockets, baggy breeches, fright wigs, and brightly rouged triangles on their cheeks.

But isn't someone somewhere always heartsick? Think.

By the aura of a penny candle in her tent crouched Anonyma, the sweet little rope-dancer, who, alone in her frillies and nursing in her heart a great ache, spilled tears on the pages of *Mercy Philbrick's Choice,* her sole companion now and a book she wouldn't give away for a wilderness of monkeys.

Existence to her now was as the shake of a wrist to a kaleidoscope.

Tragedy had struck only two days before in Caux when her tiny twin, Aer, having been forced to throw the acrobatic triple her too few years couldn't as yet manage, missed the catch and, *con precipitatione*, plunged headlong into a Lucozade stand up near rows Y and Z. Inquiries were made.

Whys, wheres, whens, hows—even suppositional ifs.

Conspicuous among those questioned was the girl's brutal uncle, the rake Truculento, a dashing trapeze artist with mustaches who drank swipes, smoked the fumes of simples, and was said to have a secret life.

This prince among winepots, confronted by the constabulary, merely shrugged and claimed that there was no purchase in the swing. It ought to have been oiled.

"Does ought," moaned Anonyma (at that time coincidentally sitting on the other side of the thin canvas), "imply is?"

At the end of her tether, she took up a quill and silently wrote, "My makeup kit wants a burnt umber."

Suicide notes are almost always insignificant.

But then she asked herself, would Mercy Philbrick do that? So she ripped up the note and just moped and moped. She began nightly to dream of octopi, sinister brownies, hobs, monitor lizards, Jotuns, autochthons, kleagles, Lapiths, bonicons, and nests of ninnies.

A sneaping frost crept over her heart. But of this anon.

Many of the performers in the Great Wheadle were famous and could already be counted on the bead-roll of circus history: Fatima the Panpsychic; the Flying Negritos; Mother

Crambo's Human Candle; feetless Mr. Cickle; Charlotte Russe and Her Magic Dogs: world renown King Zog the Midget (a millionaire); Drede the Rubberoid; Grissini, Who Stood Upsidedown on a Breadstick; and, especially, the great hydraulic exhibitions of Faucit, The Man Who Leaked from His Elbow.

But all of the Spritzians gasped in awe when the spotlight fell upon (drum roll) the lost illustrious star of the circus—

Vittoria ("The Flying Maleficaria") Carrambona, she of the quince-flower breath.

Over whom Anonyma, sallow as boxwood, was frequently wont to pine, whispering to no one, "Why amn't I so beautiful?"

Now, the maltworm Truculento had long harbored an insane and dreadful passion for The Flying Maleficaria, and, inflamed by several glasses of jingle, stumbled into her dressing room after her act, where, flinging off his Benjamin, he knelt abjectly and once again made his declarations.

"You silly twisted boy," ruefully laughed the beauty, who wanted bright city lights, the gay life, and reckless abandon. She wore a proud Parnassian sneer and coolly continued her game of foot-scent. But he wheedled. He fawned.

So, rising, she stepped on his hand and casually reminded him of Anonyma, his other niece. For, of all things, The Flying Maleficaria detested children.

"Cowpox!" muttered Truculento in high dudgeon, who then betook himself hastily to tiny Anonyma, his copesmate on the high wire. Tonight, he decided, she would throw the triple!

A plan quickly hatched in the foul nest of his heart—to smear the trapeze bar with doses of wintercream. *O blush! O cry havoc!*

The center could not hold. Mere Truculento was loosed

upon the world. Recalling the past as he tied on her wedgies, Truculento (moistening all with pleas and promises) reminded her again of how he had found her a mere conjuror's stooge in rags, jack-flipping for farthings in end-of-the-pier type work, and parentless utterly (her papa died from an ungallant disease, her momma became a professional *fille de joie*). He promised her a pouncet-box, whistling bottles, gum.

Anonyma shock-absorbed his faithless kisses. "My misery beggars description," she wailed as he left.

The crowd howled. In her little irreproachable tights, Anonyma climbed the ladder to the high trapeze, true to type— with a jest on the lip, a tear in the eye. She then bravely performed her vegetable dance, a preliminary in which she simulated a swaying leek.

Came the climax. Truculento waited menacing behind his black vizard. Anonyma rosined her *adductor pollicis,* and then—

The trapeze swung forth, back, forth, back.

A fingerlock, all saw, failed coming out of the third spin. Fate took place.

Afterword

Briefly stated, The Flying Maleficaria went to Rio shortly after with rich little King Zog the Midget. Truculento went crackers.

And the circus went belly-up.

The Wragby Cars

At the edge of the wolds of Lincolnshire, looking vaguely plutonian, stood the Soeur Scholastique Seminary for Girls.

Figpeckers flew past frequently.

These little Exempta, there a schooler, numbered among her friends, along with a still as yet unidentified pet which she kept on a warm coal shovel in a pantry amid a jumble of oddments. It went, "Yick. Yick."

On Community Presentation Day, few parents came. It was too far.

Exempta won the award for deportment, an antique volume of poems, D. J. Gynt's *Smoak and Crowquills* (soiling of prelims, foxing to title, joints cracked), which, now long defunct critics averred on the dust-wrappers, smacked racily of the soil.

She'd have preferred, confiding it to no one, a book on Crisis Theology (which speaks volumes anent the presentee).

Her pet, she saw one morning after its collation, had gone west. She dreamt that night of fearful wiggings.

Idly keying out plants, Mr. Pfuel stumbled upon Exempta alone and feeling glum in the school orangerie and, unplugging his faithful biro, generously inscribed her book, "Up, socks!—

Mr. P." Goodness, she treasured that.

Mr. Pfuel, venerable author of *Massachusetts Drinks* and *The Inch, the Foot,* taught her Latin verbs and prooves in the Fifth Form from the thirteenth-century scholars Thomas Sprot, Trivet, John of Shepesheved, and Adam of Nutzard.

Several dark rumors had lately been bruited about that Mr. Pfuel and Headmistress Wyvern were spied twicycling together in the direction of Dogdyke and Potter Hanworth last autumn with only one hamper of food.

And that he sometimes, past midnight, ran flashing to and fro in the upper rooms in nothing but his braces and socks howling, "*J'ai le vin mauvais! J'ai le vin mauvais!*"

Headmistress Wyvern—O vanissima! O emptiest of women!—was jealous of Exempta and, secretively husbanding her candle, stole nightly through the ambulatories, looking.

And spoiling for evidence.

Or clues.

Contriving, she saw fit to implicate Exempta in plots. Whippings ensued, than to which anything was preferable.

Exempta, as scandal rent the chaste silences of Soeur Scholastique, was turned out, but not before she had been shaken down for the three silver butter knives and the embroidered tea-cosy cover filched from the refectory only days previous. Clean this time, was the verdict.

Night fell. Exempta feared exceedingly in thought, word, and deed.

She headed into the Cars of Wragby where, legend had it, one was sure to meet with trooping fairies, ghosts, bogies, hekatoncheirs, pixies, norns, and the Tiddy People. Some had even seen bird-headed men, who cawed.

The Cars of Wragby, since drained, weren't then—but showed pools black with frogs, ditto geese, and things rumored malevolent.

Exempta somehow felt her heart burgled. She sat on a stone and bravely shined the tips of her now fraying shoes on the backs of her legs, though she bucked up when she thought of wonderful Mr. Pfuel, whose book she still carried.

Prooves, it suddenly came to her: the plural of proof! She smiled sadly.

Day came; followed night. Exempta, smudged and wandering, thought of her classmates enjoying sippets and tea by the open hearth or whispering in the close dark about Anthropophagi and men whose heads do grow beneath their shoulders or sharing bags of boiled sweets, sherbet dabs, mint imperials, licorice bootlaces, toffee knobs, and jelly babies. The moon came up.

Now would she have danced for a mere rusk of black bread.

"What a grip of fingers, Fate!" said Exempta out loud, put in mind, by contrast, of past times, happy times: of the day when she led the descants at chapel; of hoopball; of the neap tides; and of loyal Phthia with whom alone she shared especial aspirations to be steadfast, moral, and true—and who would now at last have her rock collection and her bottles.

Had she only a fruit jumble!

A week passed and her raffia was found jettisoned in a dark dingle.

Deep in the Cars, much deeper, Exempta was found dead but clutching in the small grip of her hand the title page from her award book, come unsewn, upon which just faintly could be read: "Up, socks!"

Epilogue

It was announced not long after that Headmistress Wyvern and Mr. Pfuel would be married on Boxing Day next.

Master Snickup's Cloak

One morning, it was the Middle Ages.

The sun shone down on the foundling home at the end of Duck's-foot Lane in the quiet little dorp of Sleutel in the Netherlands. The year was 1307 (by Pope Hilarius's corrected calendar, of course).

Master Snickup, a tiny ward there—wearing the black and red uniform of the home—gleefully played punchball against the cobbled wall beneath a yew tree near the town weigh-house.

It was a feast day: the Pardon of St. They. Cattle were blessed. Children processed. You heard litanies.

"*Wat is uw naam?*" asked a new little orphan girl who suddenly appeared at his side, smiling, plum-cheeked, and wearing a chaste wimple. Her beauty put to shame the roses of Paestum.

Superfecta—for this was the name of the flax-haired frokin—immediately stole Master Snickup's heart away.

The two children, thereafter, spent day after day playing games of noughts-and-crosses, ducking mummy, backy-o, all the winkles, stickjaw, egg-in-cup, stich-away-tailor, and skip-rope, when they frisked and jumped to the jingle:

Do you love me,
Or do you not
You told me once,
But I forgot.

Happily, Master Snickup even did her chores for her, scowring cups, dipping tallow, and decoding the squinches; he even did the wash pots. She played the dulcimer.

A decade passed, just like that.

Superfecta, who had bloomed into indescribable loveliness, now drew smiles from each and all. There is no potential for permanence, Master Snickup told his heart, without a fear of threat.

And so, they were betrothed one day at the shrine of St. Puttock of Erpingham—and swapped gifts: he gave her two white pigeons and received from her a wonderful blue cloak.

Now, there lived on the verge of the village at that time one of the richest burghers in all Gelderland—the ill-living Mijnheer van Cats, an unctuous cheese-gobbling fat pants who smoked a clay pipe and wanted sons.

But who'd be his wife? A purse of 2000 gulden was put up.

In vain, however, did the merchants of the guild offer up their daughters, a group of off-sorts who had pointed noses and pointed caps.

"Knapweed! Hake! Twisses!" screeched van Cats and hurled other unprintable names at them. Modest pious folk covered their eyes.

One winter dusk, it so turned out, the orphans were given a special dispensation to go to the Haymarket to watch the "illuminations." Mijnheer van Cats, in attendance, sat up high on the balustrade of the guildhall, whereupon his gaze fell—fatefully—upon Superfecta. That little *boompjes*, thought he, will soon be mine.

An ouch of heavy gold was hers the day following; his, a sealed envelope, which he slit open with his pipestem. What could be the decision?

"Yaw, yaw," guffawed the fat Dutchman.

A record of the wedding can be found to this day as a small entry in the old chronicle of Nuewenburgensis. You will do, as the diverb has it, what you are.

Master Snickup, disedged with grief, took up scrip and staff and, wearing only his blue cloak, set out to pick his way across Europe. He sought the antipodes.

Hither was yon, yon hither.

Mountains were climbed, mazes thrid. He crossed a sea that had no motion on the ship *What Is Pseudonymry?* and came to a desert where he said penances and fed on caper buds, dormice, and lentils. Still he pilgrimaged,

Reading the footprints of geese in the air,

To reach eventually the Black Sea where, living alone on an uncharted shale island, he chastized himself with thongs and subsisted only on air and dew. Rain fell on his blue cloak, which he sucked supplying himself with vitamin B_{12}.

Swallows sang upon his wrists.

"*Sero to amavi*," whispered Master Snickup to God—and prayed constantly with perfectly folded hands, a shape best fitted for that motion. Small furious devils hated that and visited him in a variety of shapes and torments: six-fingered Anaks, freexes, nasicornous beetles, chain-shaking kobolds, sauba ants, red-eyed swads, sorcerers who could disconnect their legs and flap about like bats, and pinheaded Hippopods, with reversed feet, who leapt instead of walked.

Master Snickup soon fell ill. But who could help? For ships in sight there were none.

The town of Sleutel, meanwhile, rang with news. Superfecta van Cats was delivered of a son. "A witty child! Can it swear? The father's dearling! Give it two plums!" boasted its sire, butter-balling it with his gouty feet.

But hear of more. Mijnheer van Cats, now fattened on perfidy itself, had turned syphilitic and even more hateful than before. He sang curses against his wife in the taproom and, roiling and hissing, streeled home drunk. He locked her nights in the black windmill. He chased her through town slashing her with timothies.

Sadism and farce are always inexplicably linked.

The orphanage, in the meantime, closed down—without so much as two coppers snapped together to prevent it, despite the bulging wallets of all the snap-boilers, razor-makers, brewers, and guilder-grubbing rentiers who lived thereabouts. O events! God could not believe man could be so cruel.

Winter settled hard over the Black Sea. The soul of Master Snickup now grew pure—a hagiographical commonplace—as his body grew diseased. He never washed his bed save with tears. The tattered blue cloak had become infested with worms and rotifers, which also battened on his holy flesh.

It snew. And on that desolate shale island, since fabled, Master Snickup one day actually looked into the heart of silence, rose and—with a tweak-and-shake of finger and thumb toward the sky—died. Rats performed the exequies.

The moon, suddenly, was o'ercast blood-red in an eclipse.

Thunder rumbled. Boding?

III.

A rat flea, black in wing and hackle, flittered out of the shred of blue cloak and flew inland—as if carried along by destiny—toward the Crimean trading port of Kaffa. The infamous date was 1346.

Stinks were soon smelt—in malt, barrels of sprats, chimney flues. Physicians lost patients in spates.

"The plague! The plague!" squealed the chief magistrate, biting his thumb, his fauces black, the streaks of jet vivid along his wicks and nose, and then dropped dead as a stone. Fires were lighted. The harbor was sealed.

But it was too late. Ships, laden with produce, had already set sail in the pestiferous winds and headed out along the trades to Constantinople, to Cyprus, to Sardinia, to Avignon, and points beyond—

Sleutel, among them: a town that, recently, had expanded and grown to the clink of gold in the guilds, the crackle of flames in the tile-kilns, and the mercantile sermons in the new Dominican kerk.

Why, there was even entertainment.

The town brothel, formerly the orphanage, represented the major holding of a certain Mijnheer van Cats who lived alone with his sort, a dissolute half-wit seen once a year moping into town to paint its shutters and touch up the wooden sign out front that read *De Zwarte Hertogin*.

It became famous. Merchant sailors, visiting in droves, always wept with laughter at the idle boast of its madam, that she had once been the village beauty.

Or was Time, indeed, the archsatirist?

For the place was run by an ooidal-shaped sow with chin hairs, a venomous breath, and grit-colored hair who always carried a ladle and trounced her girls. They called her "Mother Spatula."

The legacies passed on by the sailors were worse than the legacies they received. It began with the "sweats."

The town of Sleutel was soon aflame with flews, black spots, boils, pink eye, and the stinking wind that broadcast one to another. Lost souls screamed aloud to be crimped with knives like codfish.

A whole Arabian pharmacy could do no good.

Nothing could stop the contagion, neither chanters nor flagellants. The townsfolk spun into dancing fits, cat-concerts, and fell to biting each other and frying jews. Men castrated themselves and flung their severed genitals into the hopeless sky to placate an angry God.

The Black Death struck, and struck, and struck. Bodies fell like the leaves of Vallombrosa. It beggared rhetoric: recorded only by historians as the worst disaster that had ever visited the world.

Mijnheer van Cats, staring upon his son's flapping tongue and hopeless insanity, waddled up high into the black windmill, took of his clogs, and—pinching his nose—stepped past the revolving vanes and cowardly made his quietus.

They both went to their accounts impenitent.

But more. Mother Spatula ran into her dank room, made mouths in a glass—and shrieked! Her drazels, horrified at the telltale nosebleed, held to her lips a little statue of St. Roch, the Plague Saint; but she went deaf as a beetle to their pleas, curled up into a fork, and died, notwithstanding, the fact that to her black feet—in order to draw the vapors from her head—they had applied two dead pigeons.

She did not seem to attach a good deal of importance to them before she went.

The Oxholt Violin

Adolf Wurstwängler, a young man of sixteen, was raised by strict German puritans, grandparents who loved him and instructed him according to the strict rules and tenets of a strict Luthern belief. He was brought up in the legendarily lovely town of Rothenburg ob der Tauber in the southern part of the forested country overlooking a blue river where the tall evergreen trees are fantastically formed.

The lad yearned to be famous, and not remain a goat-keeper, which was one of the chores he had taken up to save money in order to marry. The girl he hoped to marry, however, he had yet to meet. He had limited schooling, and in the classes that he attended he'd proven dim. He worked for a time in the flax factory down by the Tauber but had stolen a hammer and was fired.

It was a mere peccadillo in his mind and one that had been forgotten after he had been assigned to pay a small fine. But he was a covetous young man and sought to win the yearly village pail races and earn the coveted purple Tauber cheese-wheel award ribbon. His ambition was part of the need in him to feel worthwhile in the ranks of the world he read about in books of fable. But not above having rewards he felt due him, he at times pilfered things that were not his. Still, he occasionally helped himself to items—jewelry from a church table, a set of andirons, leather harnesses for tethering—which he kept in a malt house behind the back of a goat shelter.

An old metal barrel stood by a slatted fence in which he kept a fire always burning in order to dispose any of any evidence connected to certain stolen items or to discard anything no longer wanted, lest he got caught with them. Occasionally he would burn off goat hair from bones that he liked to throw at odd targets.

It was widely rumored among the local townsfolk that he was abnormal. He walked oddly and appeared to have a morbid need for self-punishment. He once munched some ants in a schoolyard, showing off to some classmates. He threw small gunpowder pellets at passersby. He performed stunts in public, did cartwheels, tumbled, and attempted contortions, acrobalances with his legs outstretched like the spokes of a wheel, and slacklining.

Food held great intrigue for him. He once wolfed down an entire Westphalian German tart in order to make himself faint, a clownish act he performed so needy was he for attention. Boys hooted, and girls turned away in utter disgust. *"Adolf des habgierig"* they called him for his cravings.

His soul was thin and mysteriously empty, a vacancy that was paradoxically energized, *not* exhausted, by its own sense of greyness. Most of what he felt or did was ruled by impulse. His law was to try to rule over what he needed from what he saw and grab all he could to fill a hole inside him.

With a view to growth, he took violin lessons from old

Herr Falk Kreindler, a gaunt, angularly tall and other-worldly figure, a wild-haired martinet when it came to the exacting requirements of instruction but a gentle oldster who, living above the town alehouse for more than half a century, invited considerable respect in that region and yet was disposed to teach any students who came his way and were willing to learn his art. Kindness was a key for him that opened most doors. It was mainly at the prompting of his grandparents that young Wurstwängler was signed up. The lad from the first admired the venerable old rooms. An old lithograph of Grünewald of Christ's resurrection, along with an Altdorfer landscape of Regensburg, hung on the wall.

One day his teacher returned to the wall the workaday violin and bow, for the lesson of the day had concluded—alas, as usual, with little progress having been made—and, opening a cabinet, took down an old black case which he opened with great delight. He took out a rare violin.

The instrument, a matchless one fashioned in 1742, was an exquisite, unique, and incomparably rare Guarneri *del Gesu* violin, the "Oxholt," one of the most valuable musical instruments in the whole world.

A faded label could be seen inside, as old Kreindler raised the frail stringed body, lifting it to eye-level and canting it, to demonstrate that it bore the initials *IHS*, which reverently stood for *"Jesus hominem salvator."* All Guarneri violin labels after the year 1731 incorporated the *nomina sacra* and a Roman cross.

"A great violin is a living thing," Kreindler told the young man, tapping a fret with a bony finger. "You can see the wood is incandescent, feel it vibrate, and resound with the radiance of sunlight, the ringing echo of arboreal wetsap in its soul.

One can divine in its deluxe shape the glorious human figure itself, which inhales, exhales, inspires, expires—it breathes. A violin is organic, wood not metal, a biology lignified with volts of dynamic energy stirring in the heart of its xylem vessels. Its soundboard was born in the untamed weald and transubstantiating wild. Feel the nap. Go on, touch it. It has as silken beauty. The top plate of the violin is made of spruce, the back maple. Matching densities of the select woods give them an edge in terms of a resolute stiffness and sound-damping qualities which of course aid in producing the tonality of superior musical notes. Wood is like a skin that bears the history of its soul, imbedded there." The old teacher seemed almost tearful. "I never play this instrument without having the sense of evoking the many artists who have caressed it and played it before me."

He placed a hand on the lad's shoulder. "Do you understand? Their memory sits in the arrangement of my fingers, their thoughts in the frail beauty of this form, their hopes in the very chords I conjure."

I would cherish this very rare thing forever, was Wurstwängler's one prevailing thought. *I feel a hunger for it.*

"The sun comes out," exclaimed the young admirer, gasping. He regarded the golden beauty of the exquisitely varnished maple, sunned to perfection, its matchless buff gently tiger-striped and seasoned over the centuries with a mixture of rosin oil and balsam fir varnish. "Fat over lean—more oil on the topcoat, see," pointed out his teacher. "Too much varnish?—it will hurt the instrument acoustically and roughen its appearance. Good initial preparation means the maker can get away with less varnish but still manage to polish the surface the way he wants. It is probably better to leave the varnish thinner, and the surface a little more textured, than to keep adding coats of varnish trying to level and polish it all out afterwards. A good ground coat helps there, and this is why it was common to use a ground that was high in mineral content—particles help plug and fill the very small pores and smooth the small surface imperfections. You see? The alum in the propolis ground helps to do just this."

Wurstwängler smoothed his hand along the ribs and back, sliding up to squeeze the scroll as if he owned it. Closely watching, old Kreindler noticed how, while in a strange and anomalous juxtaposition the chubby boneless hands inconfidently pawed and stroked the elegant shape, his pupil had not the slightest physical gifts for a good violinist. The young man with his damp pale skin, had a groundhog's torso, dumpy with mid-belly rolls, to which his drooping shoulders added nothing to correct. His hair was mouse brown, limp but twisted at the top into several incorrigible cowlicks. He walked in a slouch, hard-heeled, sloppily, abdomen forward, and was hesitant in conversation, an obvious misfit.

To the teacher nothing seemed sadder in his hapless pupil of his than the mottled yellow pointed shoes he wore, bent like those of a medieval dwarf-goblin. The tubbiness of the boy, his clammy hands, disheartened the kind man, as well, and his fat dimpled dependence on his need of help.

Knödel, thought Kreindler. Dumpling.

No teacher, no lesson, struck fire in him, and no subject stirred his interest. Music as a subject balked him completely. Covetousness alone seemed to thrill him, that and eating and doing zany cartwheels in public. All that he ever claimed for himself was that he did fairly well at being able to open his mouth—

pulling it wide as a window—and, to the shock of disgusted onlookers, ingest whole in one shoving gulp an entire bierock meat pocket.

"I tell you all of this by default and only as I manage to imagine the way that the genius violin maker fretted away over his instruments," said Kreindler, "his workbenches covered with the sawdust of maple and spruce, his loyal apprentices handing him saws, spool clamps, measuring tools, reamers, shapers, knives, all sorts of calipers, when later in another room, completely spare of wood dust, clear of any particles or powder, he fussed over his many pots of lacquer, shellac, japan, glazes, polishes, oils, resins, and miraculous waxes." He paused and bent to look closer at the boy.

"Consider what had to be accomplished before with a reverent heart, as I envision it, the master pasted in—never varying the wording, making no alteration on it throughout his career—the cipher—"

"I.H.S.," put in a bold Wurstwängler, making the proprietary observation with a confidence he had never shown before. It was as if in his hands the violin had imparted by its own majesty and grandeur such self-possession.

"Do you know what the letters signify?"

Wurstwängler stood dumb.

"*Jesu Hominum Salvator*, in Latin. Jesus Savior of Men. It's a Christogram."

No response.

Observed Kreindler patiently, holding up two and then four fingers. "The other figures you see there—look—were always well formed, the '17—' of the year always *printed* in the characters of the period, the other two numbers added by his own hand by way of an ink pen, bold strokes, you see. Notice? No one has ever come across a marginal note, or even a line of Guarneri's handwriting."

He might well have been speaking to air.

§

It was a bright sunny morning, and the lessons were finished. After due deliberation, Kreindler was resolved to offer his student a surprise. Stooping, bowing, shuffling about, the old man in his faded green tailcoat and ancient buckled shoes took up his instrument, paused, and, eyes closed, proceeded to play part of the Brahms Violin Sonata No. 3, its melancholic splendor sweeping the air with sweetness as the heartbreaking notes sang through the pores of the golden wood, the slant of sun in the room reflecting on the violin its geometry, its lustrous shine of glorious wax and polish like a rapturous piece of furniture from God. The vibrations—the sound radiation—was perfect. No echo the youth had ever heard seemed more profound, its lilting reverberations, a celestial richness that called up enchanting, unearthly tones as if answering to some heavenly counterpart well past the azure skies and beyond.

The trembling voices of the violin soared, as the grand old man coming to the end of his bow left, as he always did, just the faintest anticipation of a tone, offering a touch of dramatic expectancy in a hiatus of ringing sound, as if expressing a thought spared the indelicacy of utterance.

Spellbound, young Wurstwängler applauded. The old man smiled and carefully set aside the instrument. He took his pupil aside by the bench there and, opening a crank window for air, for breathing came hard to the maestro, with a dramatic but gentle narration told him the story, as he knew it, of the instrument's creator, Bartolomeo Giuseppe Guarneri, whose label he had shown him. An Italian from Cremona, the luthier had had a mercurial temperament and, at least according to legend, was a tough, restless brawling non-conformist, a man highly contentious, unhappily married, without children, and who died rather young, at the age of forty-six. Rumor had it that one proof of the man's impatience and explosiveness was that he was once imprisoned for killing a rival, one of the Lavazza brothers from Milan. The Guarneri trait was extreme passion.

It is so valuable, thought Wurstwängler, staring at the violin.

"Pick it up," urged Kreindler. "A story goes that much of the art of his violin-making was actually the work of his German wife, Caterina Roda, who apparently returned to Germany after her husband's death in 1744." He guided the boy's fingers. "Feel the wood," he said. "The woods of his violins are poorer than the Strads, some say. Caress the back, here feel it, stroke gently down the spine to sense its power. Treen! Wood is delicate—hygroscopic, you see—it absorbs water as a vapor through the lumen of its fragile cell walls. Touch it. Feel it. See? All wood, so very delicate, has a moisture content, do you see? As it dries, wood contracts and expands in different ways, in directions of the growth rings and in direction of the grain, a phenomenon that goes by the name 'anisotropy.' Wood can warp as it dries." Kreindler's profound love for the instrument endowed in him an infinite patience to explain its intricacies. He had his pupil Wurstwängler lean in closely to listen to the punch and expression of the instrument as he lifted it and played passages of Debussy's lovely "Reflections in the Water."

"A violin maker's wood is the key to perfection."

"You play fast, then you play slow," muttered his pupil, scowling, confused, a slow resentment rising in him.

"But that is the surprise. Music in its capacious glory is never predictable, dearest boy. Franz Schubert in his *Trio No. 1 in B-flat Major* for piano, violin, and cello has a slow movement in D flat going along just fine but then with a sudden twist—lo!—ends up in the unrelated key of E major."

"But—"

"No, no, it is the *unexpected* effect that makes magic. Delight is diminished by what is anticipated." He smiled benevolently. "There are different glimpses of ideas in a piece, just as there are different kinds of wood."

He sat the boy down to instruct him.

"Heartwood is always drier than surface wood, which can make the act of making a violin a challenge. Anisotropy and the internal tensions of any wood are also caused by its warping as it dries. The moisture dynamics of wood for a violin—which may cause, for example, its frame to skew or bend or wobble, even crack or split—must constantly be taken into account as it is made. The fine tuners are delicate, look here, the tailpiece exquisite as a young princess's index finger, the pegbox carved by love. Those are original pegs, as is the bridge. See? As I play the instrument, I can sense on the chinrest by the lower bout the devoted feel of my predecessors, as the long bow rises and falls, can actually feel an ardor transferred, a leap of civility, the stirring of their souls. From scroll to endpin, there is majesty. Still—"

"Still?"

"A flaw is evident—was it intentional? Consider the f-holes.

In a Guarneri, you will find it is often gouged as if measured solely by the eye. Curiously, you will see, a stain or sap mark parallel to the fingerboard on both sides appears on the bellies of many of his instruments, as if almost—given its creator's deep regard for the Savior—with an intent to leave a holy stigmata. Was Guarneri thinking that only God is perfect? Artists have for millennia deliberately *introduced* flaws into their works, only to remind themselves that defects are an integral part of being human. Imperfections we have inherited from Adam. Blemishes describe us, faults define. They bless us, in a way. Artists and craftsmen of all cultures have done the same."

The boy shifted, waited, was exasperated.

"An Arab rug contains a mistake," continued the teacher. "Navajo rug weavers will always leave small snags and kinks along the borders of rugs in the shape of a line called *ch'ihónít'i*, which is translated into German as 'spirit line' or 'spirit pathway.' Natives there understand that, when weaving a rug, the weaver entwines part of his or her being into the cloth. The spirit line allows this trapped part of the weaver's spirit to safely exit the rug." He took a hard breath. "My very own weakness speaks of my deficiencies."

What deficiencies had he? wondered Wurstwängler. How could there be faults in such a grand and talented old man? Can everything be broken like me? There must be some secret trick to what he says. I know about tricks myself—and secrets.

§

Time passed. Adolf Wurstwängler continued with his lessons, month after month. His grandparents asked him how he could continue to afford to pay for such instruction. His reply was that most of the time now Kreindler would take no fee. One day the old man sat down gasping, he was so tired. But he was always willing to answer the boy's questions about his rare violin, which, obviously paramount in his mind, inflamed a great hunger to know more. "Niccolò Paganini himself owned a Guarneri. A rich count lent the teenager his Guarnerius but was so impressed by his playing he refused to take it back. It is now called *Il Cannone Guarnerius*. Other owners of Guarneri violins were Baron Vitta, Huberman, and Rappaldi. . . . but no," added Kreindler, rethinking himself, "these names will mean nothing to you, and then why should they?"

He smiled gently. "I have decided to bequeath the 'Oxholt' to our Rathaus here," he explained, by which he meant the ancient Rothenburg town hall, a Renaissance building, the rear Gothic part of which dated from as long ago as 1250 and served as the seat of government for the city-state during the medieval ages and for the city since the formation of the federalist government now functioning. "Once the instrument has been donated, everybody in our city will have the occasion to come to view it and enjoy its fame. Have you ever climbed the tower?"

But Wurstwängle was only half-listening as his eyes gleamed with greed, surveying the marvelous wooden gem that sat before him, but he managed to offer, "The strings themselves seem to be throbbingly vital."

Kreindler bent to pluck a low G string. "Widely referred to as 'catgut.' '*Gut.*' Slide your finger down the string. Maybe for kites. But never from the intestines of the cat. Most violin strings are made from the intestines of sheep. The English poet Shakespeare asks in his play, *Much Ado About Nothing:* 'Is it not strange that sheeps' guts should hale souls out of men's bodies?'"

Don't steal it. Do not.

"Usually, the older the string, the yellower and drier it is. Fresh gut looks translucent and feels soft and flexible."

Kreindler kept talking but eyed his pupil. The young man seemed preoccupied or was not interested.

"Do you live by the Spitalgasse? No? Oh, near Burggasse. Yes? There is another violin to be seen there! You do not have a bloodthirsty disposition, I don't doubt, but have you visited the gloomy vaults of our medieval Criminal Museum? On display there one can see the 'shrew's fiddle' or neck violin—we call it the *Halsgeige*—that was used in medieval Germany and Austria. It is a variation of the yoke, the pillory, or rigid irons, whereby the wrists are locked in front of the bound person by a hinged board or steel bar. It was originally used in the Middle Ages to punish wayward women who were caught bickering or fighting."

"I have indeed heard of it, Herr Kreindler."

Added the teacher, "A bell was sometimes attached to this portable pillory, to alert townspeople that the victim was approaching so that she might be mocked and otherwise humiliated. Another version was a 'double fiddle' by which two people could be attached together face-to-face, forcing them to talk to each other. They were not released until the argument had been resolved."

Lessons with Wurstwängler were uphill always. Mistake after mistake. Select pieces were chosen for simplicity but also as a challenge. He was the laziest pupil he ever had, never practiced at home and the main impression his teacher derived was of the waste of time and money. Wurstwängler struggled badly with Edward Elgar's *Salut d'Amour*, of which he learned but a part. It went no better with Henry Wieniawaski's showpiece, *Légende Op.*

17, written for solo violin and orchestra, to which Herr Kreindler accompanied him with a piano reduction as a substitute.

On another day, trying to reach his pupil with the pure beauty of sound, Kreindler took up his violin and played Massenet's dramatic *Elegie*, the brief, simple, but haunting piece, but nothing worked.

The pupil's efforts that day were weak. Wurstwängler who was lax nevertheless seemed to manage his face in shaping a merely a feigned interest in basic techniques. He dawdled. The specific steps to coordinating tempo, dynamics, and rhythm were lost on him. He remembered nothing of what he repressed and so reproduced what he played not as memory but as a series of blunt actions that, when called upon to be repeated, wholly evaporated. He would not track his practice habits. Routine bored him. Double-stops confused him, as his mind wandered. Asked to play a scale with a quarter note for each note of the scale, then two eighth notes on each note, then four sixteenth notes on each note, exasperated him, and he gave up. His bowing was indifferent and always off the "highway."

Wurstwängler was maddeningly uncharismatic and plodding. His open seams buzzed, he would sullenly claim that his sound post was placed wrong or that his bridge wobbled or a G string was loose. Sounds like air-raid sirens, birdcalls, and erratic high E-string action fairly scored the air blue. His posture was dreadful. He was rarely ready to play and when a metronome was employed to help him resume with a steady beat, it only had the effect of him going stiff and unnatural, as if he were walking in place. Kriedler was resigned and even-tempered up to a point, but when his pupil's scraping attempts at even the most basic of violin sallies, such as "Lightly Row" and Bach's easy *Minuet No. 2*

—with each of the efforts culminating in the *doink doink* noises of a honking Chinese goose—it became too wearisome.

Pausing, to check the time, Kriedler took out of a vest pocket his "Bürk Patent" watchman's stopwatch and saw it was late.

The teacher stood up. "But I am tired now and must rest. Our lesson is over." The following question was hard to ask. "I will see you again for our monthly tutorial?"

A willing compliance is required to learn any art in the sense of practical imitation, but conformity is another thing entirely. Submission must never be resignation, imitation never a slavish adherence to mere rote. A cipher always finds himself at variance with the laws of learning. In his heart Kriedler could see that the lad was unstable. Damage done to him in childhood must have been immense, thought the old man, inculcating that strange temperamental mix of dreaminess and rage he seemed to grow up with. But it was his hope to instill rather than thwart ambition.

As the young man walked off, he habitually never looked back. It spoke as much of a lack of passion for music as a want of accord with people. Looking on with a forlorn wistfulness, Kreindler sadly reflected on his lack of talent: *er ist ein Flötenspieler mit Überbiss.*

He is a flute-player with overbite.

§

Weeks passed. Wurstwängler, who had often dreamt of the Guarneri, longed to see it again. What pretty girl would not have been proud to see him play it—watched him shoulder the rare violin! In the meantime, he tended his goats along the flat passes and green rolling hills of the old walled town with its many clay-red rooves and half-timbered gables. Not a day passed, however, as in the meadows he sat brooding over the grazing animals, when he did not harbor a sense of loss in what he felt deprived of and defeated by his lot in life, especially when, coming home, he would pass the many wealthy people of the town in taverns eating and drinking.

What nagged at him was the beauty of an object, the Guarneri. The paradoxical effect of finding something so bewitching was that it made him sad, the very same way he felt when a beautiful girl passed him on the street, inducing a sense of loss, an abandonment of striving. You cannot have it, he heard echo in his ear, this object is not for you and never will be. It stung him. Compared to that violin he felt he was literally nothing.

At each visit, Wurstwängler would fairly plead again to see the Oxholt. To please and satisfy the lad, while both instructing him as well as acknowledging the power and beauty of the instrument, Kriedler by way of dramatic movements would bow up a gentle berceuse, a frisky zapateado, a mellow cantilenas, a soothing meditation, a chubby prelude, an inviting imaginative polytonal czardas.

The music made little impression on the crude, inattentive, generally distracted pupil who seemed more caught up in the rarity of the instrument, its value, and, before it was put away, he would trace a finger, often too roughly, along the center bout, chinrest, and venerable old fingerboard.

Herr Kreindler was a very wise old man. He could see the young man's need. It was clear to him the boy, being raised fatherless, was not only sheepishly suspicious of authority, doubtful at bottom of its worth, but evidently at odds and ends with himself, his concentration insufficient to master the instrument in which, after a suitable period, he had demonstrated small headway. His lesson-master saw damage in the dubious fingering alone. Wanting in certainty, he had no faith. Trust begins early in life. Wanting any early experience of deep trust, the teacher knew, one can become convinced it is not there and crucially does not look for it again.

On his next visit, when Wurstwängler came to the room, he took his instruction. But on this day the teacher took the occasion to sit him down by a sunny window-seat to say, "The 'spirit' achieves freedom when the subject"—finger to chest—"finds itself in its own object, so that it is at home with itself in its own safe conviction, as such. Do you understand? What I'm trying to say? You must accept with overwhelming insight that to be at peace one has to accept what is given—what is *there*."

What was he telling me, wondered the boy. *To steal?*

Having looked for the chance to let his talentless pupil down easy, he had found it. "One must sacrifice—to 'make holy'— to learn what one can achieve, and if to find nothing achieved, accepting is the noblest sacrifice of all."

To feel free to take what I want?

He generously took the poor lad's face in his hands. "Will you please ponder these words?"

The young man in his slowness was like an elephant. But according to medieval lore, that ponderous beast was associated with chastity, of simplicity, of modest unaffectatiion, even iconographically of the Blessed Virgin, and Kreindler, smiling, knew beyond a doubt that he had to let him go.

Determined, Wurstwängler, hearing nothing, only asked again to see the Guarneri. Had the youngster heard what he said, wondered the old man, and would he be advised? No guidance or suggestion ever seemed to register with this particular pupil; it seemed blocked by a dissembling inattention, fed by what he saw as contemptuous self-appraisal, the refuge of a lost soul. Of course, Herr Kreindler obliged him, again carefully extracting the black case from the cabinet, unsnapping the clips, and lifting the lid to reveal the irresistible glory. This time without asking, his pupil confidently lifted out the violin and held it up to his eyes, glowing.

Where talent is a dwarf, self-esteem is a giant.

From noble forebears, Kreindler had been well-born, *Hochwohlgeboren*, his progenitors, grandparents, great-grandparents, even before that, long ago, having been government ministers and soldiers in service to the crown, but down through the centuries, through stages of peace and war, it was the fate of the family to have come down in prestige. Germany had suffered much. But traditions held, and it was through the good offices of his maternal great-great-grandmother that he had inherited the "Oxholt," the rare Guarneri *del Gesu* violin, personally passed down to him as a living responsibility to husband carefully through the time his tenure.

How could it be mine?

Kreindler explained, "Fewer than two hundred of Guarneri's instruments survive today. The *del Gesùs* are rare." Kreindler pointed to the Crucifix that he kept on the wall there and then tipping the instrument at a slant—to his very own surprise, even Wurstwängler had not let go of it—with a thumb indicated the cross inside the body of the instrument. "It is a holy instrument, considered, as I say, equal in quality to those of Antonio Stradivari, his Cremonese neighbor and rival, and many experts claim them to be superior, the most coveted of all. Guarneri's violins often have a darker, more robust, more sonorous tone than Stradivari's.

He stood up, slowly. His back hurt.

"They are all violins, although one cello bearing his father's label, dated 1731, seems to have been completed by *del Gesù*. The quality and scarcity of his instruments have resulted in sale prices in excess of millions of marks."

The master again refused to take his due fee that day, as several times over the last months he had also done. He stayed the youngster's hand with a gentle pat.

"No, no, give the money to the poor and pray instead for Bartolomeo Guarneri and this *del Gesù*, the instrument he wrought—*Jesus hominem salvator*—and for the music that through it that he gave us. Pray for me, and I will pray for you."

§

It was on Easter week, unpredictably to all, that old Kreindler died of old age, alone in his rooms. The funeral took place on a windy and blowing very rainy day in April in Franziskanerkirche. The much-loved man was to be solemnly buried in the old cemetery in Rothenburg, located on the eastern side of Erlbacher Strasse. When this event took place, as a group of mourners dressed in black gathered at the main gate located at the corner of Ansbacher Strasse in order to process to the grave, young Adolf Wurstwängler, who had been standing in wait under the pavilion roof of he Rathaus, crept into the dead man's lodgings and stole the violin.

The rooms were dark, ghostly quiet, and smelled of oil and wood. There was nothing on the table but an inkhorn and several pens and the "Bürk Patent" watchman's stopwatch. Wurstwängler checked, to ascertain he was alone, slipped the watch into his deep pocket, took the instrument, and fled.

Not a soul had seen him commit the crime, he saw to that. It had been a plan over which he had long brooded, and so, taking advantage of the funeral being held by the river—it was perfect timing in the coming and going—he sneaked out of the rooms above the town ale house, and, lest anyone see him, went home by back alleys in a roundabout way, past Sign of the Fish Street, crossed Pulp Steps, past the Bootham shacks, ducked behind St. Athelstans's Fountain and Street of the Lantern, and looped around through Mad Alice Lane, old St Saviourgate, and headed by narrow alleys to the malt house behind the back of the goat shelter to hide his spoil.

Was it simply out and out theft?

Not at all, he reasoned.

Why else had Herr Kreindler, even as he was ill, taken the time to show to him alone, of all others, that sacred instrument? To stand forth and play it for the special pupil he was as he had done for exactly no one else? To make an effort to rehearse for him, for him alone, the fabled story of that instrument time and time again? Wurstwängler understood that he above all was the old man's star pupil, and a friend as well, not merely some smelly goatherder wasting his time on the jumpy slopes of the Rothenburg hills. Had not the master explained to him that one's "spirit" alone achieved freedom when the subject finds itself in its own object, so it is home with itself in its own otherness? Had he not *found* that object? Was he not the subject who must actually discover itself in its own object? Who could deny it?

Exactly no one, he concluded.

Since Adolf Wurstwängler thought music proof against contamination, it fit in with his warped dream, born of an obsessed craving he could scarcely explain to himself: to hold, to have—actually to *own*—the rare Guarneri in hopes that owning it would absolve him of his own sad failures and through a snatched fate redeem him from himself. How the girls would then love to see him play it!

Before he did anything, he took out the stopwatch from his pocket. He shook it. He put it to his ear. He smelled it. He decided he didn't want it and indifferently pitched it into the burning barrel with a loud clank.

Now, the great moment had come, however. In the back shed there that dark afternoon he slowly took out the instrument and bow. He hunched over and looked at them with glistening eyes. He then began to play it. His hands were trembling, but he also felt an exhilarating spur of boldness within him. As he began to bow, it seemed odd. The violin suddenly seemed too light, too thin, too breakable, almost insubstantial as he held it to his neck. Too vulnerable. What was wrong?

Nothing, he insisted, as he bowed up some of the amateur pieces he had already practiced. What was wrong? He raised the violin to smell it, to breath it, inhaling its woody essence, shook it a bit as if better to control it, but asking himself with increasing wonder what was happening.

Whatever, he saw proudly it was none other than Adolf Wurstwängler now holding the exquisite, incomparably rare 1742 Guarneri *del Gesu* violin, the peerless "Oxholt." He shook fright from his hands and throwing aside any and all second thoughts began again to play, as if out of habit like some demented prelate who had lost his faith but continued to pray to a God in whom he no longer believed, simply because he did not know what else to do with himself.

He badly wanted someone to see him.

§

Dark thoughts now began to rise in Wurstwängler's mind. Was it the heavy rain? He looked out and peered up into the filthy clouds in the sky overhead and nervously jerked the bow fractionally. His fat hands moved awkwardly, his shoulder incompetently moving, as he knew by past lessons, it should not. His bow movements madly angled. Was the bow poorly cambered, or could it be him? He swerved his arm, straining to remember Kreindler's caveats, hearing the echo of his teacher prodding him with directions. *Let gravity do its job.* He then tried the "baroque" bow hold, holding the normal bow farther up, where, instead of using the thumb on the frog and index on the leather, the thumb is on the leather, the index on the metal.

The violin began to speak. But then what was it saying? His wrist and lower arm seemed inharmonious, with no sense of détaché or legato. When all should have been seamless, it was nervous jerks at every bow stroke. *Too heavy on the martelé.* What had once seemed easy seemed something to be dreaded, as if looking into a mirror with the expectation of seeing his normal face but finding a disheveled mess. *You hear the jumping arpeggio? You're breaking chords.*

As he continued to play squawks, it was as if the instrument refused to obey him, as if in rude counterpoint the tentative voice of the violin went from white to black as a personal insult by way of mockery. He began to fear what he hoped but hoped for what he did not want to know. In his rude, incompetent, cacophonous scraping, he heard *uncertainty*. Then, *falsehood*.

Innocent of decency, experienced guile kicked in. Black guilt was what he felt. To possess such a valuable object was to be possessed by it, mere ownership its instinctive retribution. What did he hear as he played? He listened to an ear echo and heard despair in the sudden reverberations: "*You must accept with overwhelming insight that to be at peace one has to accept what is given—what is there.*"

But nothing had been given at all—only stolen! Conscience took hold of him with such a grip it seemed it would throttle him. The violin was actually teaching him who and what he was, object lessoning subject. Frozen, he realized with a raw glare of grief what he had done. It came to him all in an instant. His hunger to know was not a cognitive act but compulsive and insane overreaching.

His hunger was only greed!

The driving rain never ceased. It sluiced off the roof of the malt house in a high wind. Wurstwängler pulled the fire barrel under a roof by the goat shelter. He sat in the shed, soaking wet, a knot of frustration for a heart, hating himself outright, realizing how despised a creature he was. He stared at the Guarneri violin. *This* was the object in which he, the subject, was to find himself! How, just how, exactly how—how had his spirit achieved freedom to be at home in its own otherness if, in having the thing, he had not found himself? There the object was, he the subject. Where was the release or liberty if he was still at home, alone, hungry for love, in a shed being pelted with rain, with a box of pilfered items? Was this—

All at once he experienced, in a small epiphany as if it spoke, a moment of abandonment of striving!

Was this to be the freedom Herr Kreindler spoke of?

It was instantaneously that he glimpsed exactly what he must do, resignation, acquiescence, a compliance by which to achieve the fruit of a yearning to encompass the paradoxes of existence, matter and energy, life and death, pleasure and pain, himself and all creation in one harmonious purifying whole.

He grabbed the neck of the violin, and, standing there in his yellow pointed shoes, with a small axe he chopped the instrument in two. He was so consumed, so he consumed—to make a sacrifice, to "make holy" an offering, an *oblatio*. He snapped the bow over his knee, brutally tearing off the strings apart, stick, pad, screw, hair, and frog. He bashed the Guarneri halves, tearing open the frail lacqured wood into splintered pieces of skin that in their thinness seemed as attenuated as paper. He ripped out the purfling inlay, savagely smashing the saddle, scroll, and sound post, and after fiercely prising out the frets yanked out one by one the ancient violin strings, like hair, wrapping them over and over into a knot bundle to throw away. Snap went the neck, fingerboard, pegs and pegbox, and then the tailpiece, all broken like sticks.

Volcanically, Wurstwängler's fire barrel, flaring almost with an uncanny growl—flashing with what seemed almost like electric bursts—went fully ablaze with all of the angry ignited wood spitting purplish-blue sparks and crackling the better for the varnish, resins, and oils freely feeding it.

He listened fascinatedly to the voice of its warping complaint, its snap-screams in the final immolation. Yes, he laughed, it does expand and contract in different ways! "I'm burning the water out of it! Pan-frying it!"

After hours, as night fell, in a final act of propitiation, with a claw-pot rake in one hand and an elongated spoon in the oher, he slowly pulled out of the charred ashes all that he could manage—bits and pieces so filigree fine that they crumbled like dust when stirring and swirling in the blowing gusts of rainy wind—amounting to a mush, a disgraced pomace, that, after Wurstwängler's slow and deliberate acts of extraction, he packed into a bowl with flour and pounded to cook into cakes.

Seeking to accept what was given, the better to know himself, slowly, patiently over days devouring, ingesting, and swallowing each piece, including—especially—the initialed label, for that sanctioned the act, he was at last content.

There was revision but no transfiguration. A transformation had nevertheless occurred. What he had taken away by dishonor, he had put on by greed, what he once held as a value in a mockery of victory had vanished.

He had eaten the violin.

St. Winifred's Bells

The bells of St. Winifred had been silent for over a hundred years.

There was still the belief in 1206, during the reign of King John, that a terrible curse had been placed on the bells many, many years before, but whenever the villagers determined to do something about it—as now, for the Feast of Pentecost, they wished to do—panic by sudden reports, dangerous bruits, and open hubbubs broke out and made them fearful. Would you like to know why?

A wicked crone named Gagoola, an old hag with a face like sudden night and a hook for a hand, lived nearby in a pawnshop and wove spells. She wore boots, drank vinegar, and lived in utter secrecy—

—except for her sole companion, a fierce black falcon with scarlet red eyes named Mousemeat.

There was a dreadful paradox in the relationship of the two creatures: no one ever saw the old crone and her falcon at the same time. It was almost diabolical.

An ancient legend, however, passed from generation to generation, had long left the villagers hopeful. It was so told: "A bow alone will break the spell." Priests bowed, merchants bowed, pilgrims at the church door, all bowed—but, alas, to no avail. The bells were still muted.

Now, it was common knowledge that the ruinous old scold Gagoola hated the bells of the church—that, in fact, she'd been alive when first they went silent—and each and every time that funds were sought at the mayor's request to replace the clapper, missing over a century, the evil old harridan shut up her shop, snap-fastened the window hasps, and with a thunderous echoing noisebanged the shutters to, lest anyone try to pawn a value. She would suddenly disappear—

—which, curiously, became the occasion of the evil bird always appearing high in the dark belfry overhead, its eyes glittering and imperscrutable claws reddened with the blood of innocent doves.

To climb the steeple then? Instant death!

At the best of times, the grim little pawnshop, its thatch gone dry and black, was a blight to the village, and whenever children-with-hoops, monks, or nesting cranes came near it, she ran out waving a metal cane and screaming, "*Wurstfatz! Wurstfatz!*"

Was she ever merciful?

Not by half. Gagoola lived in the darkness, slurped soup, kept to herself, and took the villager's valuables only on market-day when, unrolling the tiny wheel-window but a crack, she took in whatever piece of *vertu* was offered and, giving small return, threw out a few old shillings.

This continued.

One day, however, Prince Alexander, a nephew of the King who was young and handsome, happened by those parts on a pilgrimage to the Holy Well. He suddenly saw by the way a beautiful girl whose face, in the westward lamping light, seemed sculpted of new-sawn ivory. The gleaners, of whom she was one, were kneeling at prayer in a field, but she was holding a dead bird and singing softly:

Si - lent fell the rain On the earthly ground

Wherefore, asked the Prince, halting, did the workers kneel—could the Angelus have rung and he not have heard? And wherefore did they all bow? The maiden, coloring, pointed to the distant wimble of St. Winifred's and recounted the story of the muffled bell. She repeated the legend: "A bow alone will break the spell."

And who was she and wherefore did she weep?

"My lord," she gently replied, "I am only the simple maiden Patricia, who once happily, but no more, fed this sweet dove from no less humble a shrine than the perch of my finger."

The Prince's eyes grew luminous with that special excitement of mental sympathy that can bring tears from something deeper than passion.

I trow, he thought, no more hallowed a shrine.

It was then tearfully explained to the noble Prince that the poor people of the village lived under the spell of the venomous old witch, Gagoola, and her dark familiar, the black falcon Mousemeat, who perching where he did constantly prevented access to the bell.

"She have likewise killed this innocent dove," she confessed, lowering her eyes, "and many another as innocent."

Apprised of all this, Prince Alexander continued on to St. Winifred's Well where he spent days piously bowing—with a view to fulfilling the legend—and after a sennight in prayer returned by way of the village.

It was the very day of the Feast of Pentecost (although the bells never tolled it) when a fair was traditionally held in the cheap—a celebration, with roasted mutton and stoops of beer, of juggling, ballad-singing, cock-fighting, ringums, skimble-skambles, bowls, dancing, split-your-forefinger, and on the green archery butts had been set up for the annual contest.

All the greatest archers from the countryside round entered the competition, and the Prince, having decided to join them, was soon in contention for the red rose after his first two arrows—*thap! thap!*—hit the bull's-eye. Everyone gasped in delight as he took up the third—

—not the least of whom the maiden Patricia, whose blush-worthy cheeks now seemed to pale. Following her gaze, his eyes slowly moved upwards to the top of the church steeple where, menacingly, the black falcon crouched in a shadow of the parapet.

The legend! He understood it now! It meant not a humbling bow, but rather an archer's *bow!*

Prince Alexander, whispering a prayer to the Holy Spirit, drew out the massive bow—his arm trembled—and turning fired his last shaft high into the sky overhead.

The falcon Mousemeat turned around, disgusted, and plummeted to the ground with an arrow straight to the heart!

A piercing shriek simultaneously came from the old pawnbroker's house where, when the villagers ran in, they found the hag Gagoola, glassy-eyed, lying twisted in death in a pile of dirty feathers.

Justice in sentence, celerity in execution.

A joyous shout went up, for the village after all these years was at last rid of the evil curse. The people, dancing, quickly retrieved the pawns unfairly taken from them, pooled their money, and soon set to the restoration of the bell—the clapper for which they used Gagoola's hook.

The death of what is, is the birth of what's to be.

Prince Alexander and the maiden Patricia, deeply in love, were subsequently married in the church of St. Winifred, and when the bell pealed, flourishing out a flock of doves, everyone agreed it was the most beautiful sound ever heard in the realm.

They rode away together under its holy reverberations.

The Loneliest Person in Scituate

for Dorothy Day

On the coldest night of December
At the wintry turn of the year,
When the hearth threw out not an ember
To assuage my increasing fear

That I was a creature whose friends
Had diminished with passing time,
Although I had money to spend,
Accrued in a lifetime's climb,

I was living—I can't explain—
In a house alone on a hill
As if in a black kind of rain
That rarely left my heart still.

I heeded little of others
And cared little more for myself;
I reckoned no man my brother
And ignored them with conscious stealth,

For more than my own profane
Way of living, if selfish and small,
I considered that, even if vain,
Next to others I somehow walked tall.

I paid my way and walked on
And scarce bothered a soul I met;
Anyone's pain I looked upon
With infinitely little regret.

For the poor, the gimp, the benighted
Living on scraps handed out,
Any social reform so blighted
Increasingly raised my doubt.

On one night rainy and grey
When it meant not a whit to care,
A truth I could always relay,
A stranger seemed to repair

From a doorway (it gave me a fright)
To pick me up from the ice
Where, slipping, I promised to fight
With every last legal device

The office of public works
In the Scituate offices where
Pretty much everyone shirked
Any strict obligation to care.

I rose but quickly released
My hand from his with distaste,
For I saw that he was a priest,
Inveterate symbol of waste.

A coin from my greatcoat I offered
Him there in the low archway light
In exchange for the help that he proffered,
But waving it out of his sight

He touched my arm with concern,
And he looked me deep in the eye.
What in me then started to burn
As if something started to cry?

Not a word did the stranger utter
Yet a voice I heard all the same.
Did I myself simply mutter?
Was someone calling my name?

Was he perhaps putting a curse on
My hand as he squeezed it so tight?
He said, "Pray for the loneliest person
In Scituate Town tonight."

Advice seemed never so stark
As I finally regained my feet.
I walked wordlessly on in the dark
Along the empty and desolate street.

I felt it but fair to the bums,
To the prostitutes covered with lice,
To the widows and beggars in slums,
To follow the prelate's advice

And just for once give them the pity
Of the coin I had managed to save.
What's a line from a pious ditty
A priest conjures under a nave?

And do you know something? I prayed
For the thing that he asked me to;
Even if somewhat dismayed
I did what he asked me to do.

A silence suddenly dropped
In the midst of what I had said.
My heart, fast beating, now stopped.
My feet became painfully lead.

Is prayer in utterance echo,
The cause of what we must hear?
Does what we ask somehow beckon
Our personal ghost to come near?

Can absence be suddenly presence?
The whole forgive somehow the part,
Whereby is supplanted the essence
Of emptiness in one's frozen heart?

Like the world I was suddenly cold,
I was the beggar, the whore,
It was I now friendless and old,
The old drunken sot on the floor.

I'd become the souls I'd rejected
The drifter, the friendless whelp,
The lost, the scorned, the neglected,
The creature in sore need of help.

Tears for what I'd forsaken
Scalded my eyes almost raw
For in the single look I had taken
Was something deeper I saw.

You see, in my plaintive call
I was never prepared to see
The loneliest person in all
Of Scituate Town was me.

Captain Birdseye's Expedition

It was England, 1889.

J. C. Birdseye, M.C.B., C.S.I., D.S.M., the famous explorer, had long since removed with his wife to the village of Drowsimere after having sustained a fateful wound in the Sudan that put an end to their domestic bliss.

He did nothing but read the *Times*, which he considered a patriotic duty. She knat, furiously.

Margot soon grew bored. Her husband's preoccupations—botany universally, orchids in particular—kept him frustratingly aloof. Wouldn't he at least join her in a game of dot-boxes? Drawing-room archery? Squalls, then? No answer. At first, she wept, pitches of suchness that soon drove him to galvanic belt treatments for nervous exhaustion.

Always a bit too previous, she now began to throw his incapacities up to him, often by making up small but vicious facetiae about his dear Queen ("another widow," she sneered) with whom, for her own Irish origins, she was fully out of sympathy. "Some orchids attain larger dimensions, I am told," one night she declared out of the blue. "On the other hand, is it not so that they have no organs for nutrient absorption from below? I believe you once claimed—a rather rum prospect, I daresay—they are characterized in a rather wilting way," she chortled, "by a need for rest after the vegetation period and require less moisture in cooler periods."

It all came to an abrupt head when one evening, as she was peering into a lenticular stereoscope and remarking on a well-endowed kaffir pictured on a slide that they had taken in Namibia, he to change the subject quietly commended the Queen's potato embargo, which made her snap at him.

"You don't feel," she asked, slowly lowering the optical device and smirking, "that the bill went further than public opinion warranted—or was justified in the case of a private member's measure?"

He peered over the newspaper, querulous.

She snickered—

—and packing her trunks that night, she flung out the door without so much as a by-your-leave and took the fastest train to London.

Having sardonically made the constatation that there wasn't then a noble thing left to do in life but write the memoirs that sought to prove it, he took himself upstairs to the windowless library and sat day after day at his dwarf Sutherland sipping pints of old-and-mild, unconfidently scribbling away.

Nothing noble left to do? But wait.

One day, it so happened, he unexpectedly received in the morning post a commission from Westminster notifying him that—a distinctly rare honor—he of all others had been voted a bursary by Parliament to secure for Queer Victoria, the Widow of Windsor herself, a certain gift (the existence of which, however, was questionable for none had ever been seen, none ever found) to be subsequently offered by her in memorial for the deceased Prince Albert, he of the chain.

The Queen, who loved flowers, apparently wanted, yearned for more than anything else on earth, a black orchid. But did one exist? Not a soul in this history of floriculture had ever seen one.

It was a miracle, thought Captain Birdseye, the chance at last to redeem himself and by heroic act to win back his wife, who at the time, unbeknownst to him, was living in concubinage in Lisle Street with two Maltese ponces. Upon being invited to a formal dinner at Frogmore with the Queen, he was thereafter all zeal. He threw himself at the task at hand with perhaps an over-burdened conviction, a fevered zeal that supplanted the warmth and affection denied him. He began by accumulating, in order to study, small groupings of Cryptanthus Black Magic, exception-ally beautiful plants and easy to grow, a genus in the botanical family Bromeliaceae, subfamily Bromelioideae, from the Greek "cryptos" and "Anthos." He examined coir sands, perlite, various propagation, drainage, and various strains of ebony color.

Orchids lilt and love and lollygag, he knew, but as to color they eschew dark colors. Black? Possible, but rare. *Brassia maculata* hints at it. And sullen *Bifrenaria*. And the narrow-leafed *Masderallia*.

Before anything else, however, he went to his library and pulled down to read, sitting up late many nights, Charles Dar-win's great botanical, entitled, under its full explanatory head-ing, *On the Various Contrivances by Which British and Foreign Orchids Are Fertilised by Insects, and On the Good Effects of Intercrossing.* It was the Captain's proud boast that he owned the 1862 first edition, a jewel in his shelves. It was wonderful on the subject of exotic and foreign orchids.

When he was a mere lad, he well remembered, Birdseye found them in late September gloriously dotting the upland pastures with their little spirals of white flowers. One day he spied a bird's-nest orchid in a local beechwood and, taking it home to inspect its stringy roots, discovered he had a friend, bonding with it. It was a delicate plant, needing much care and taking as long as nine years to reach maturity. He never did see the ghost orchid, that rarest of all native plants in Britain, which is almost always mysteriously hidden out of sight, down below ground, feeding on mycorrhizal fungi, rarely seeing sunlight. But he always made sure to keep a weather eye out for the fig sphinx moth, *Pachylia ficus*, since it was the first insect to be scientifically described as pollinating *Dendrophylax lindenii*, the obscure, almost supernatural ghost!

No man is too great to be willing to be little.

Nothing little is too small to love.

No love given is ever wasted.

§

An expedition for South America was immediately organized. He got out his maps, mugged up on his botany, attended several travel lectures, swotted up on matters of bushcraft, and then proceeded by list to gather and to load his supplies: a mallet; waterproof bags for carrying water; several penny cyclopedias; arsenical soaps; Keating's Worm Tablets; an eel ferret; an Ulster cape-rug; a spiral abdominal belt (for a late indisposition); tins of jerked meat; antibilious pills; ropes of treacle; Boots' multivites; Rouser tabloids; Freeman's chlorodyne; three pairs of stout puttees; lunar caustics; tartarised sodas; 1 cwt. of pressed vegetables; a blunt-pointed bistoury; twine; protractors; a classic *navaja*-like Laguiole pocket-knife, originally produced like no other in the "knife-city" of Thiers in France; a bottle of Mrs. Winslow's Soothing Syrup; two tins of Shippam's fish paste; a Huntley & Palmer's Dundee Cake; packet samples of the Wyeths' Compressed Chlorate of Potash Tablets (5 grains each); chloride of ammonia, dialysed iron, and pepsin; scowring drops; ginger rock; common salt; a packet of sewing needles; three of the eleven volumes (first editions) of Alexander von Humboldt's *Personal Narrative of Travels to the Equinoctial Regions of the New Continent* (octavo, bound in three quarters morocco over marbled boards); six stoneware jars of J. Sainsbury's Bloater Paste; Epp's Cocoa; Bird's Custard Powder; quinine; eyewash; glass beads to pay porters; pannikins and spare boots; a snake-proof helmet; one Watt's hymnal; two mattocks; half a ream of paper for drying plants; an aneroid barometer; and many rolls of mosquito netting by which he hoped to set legions of them at defiance.

After all, he was a Gemini, Third House, a house of transportation and active learning, people curious by nature, no quit in them, bright, energetic. "You will find us playful and intellectually curious, right?" he cooed to his beagle, roughhousing his head before sending him off to a kennel.

On the day of departure, to celebrate his allocation, Captain Birdseye, having removed to his library, lit up a rare, expensive, handmade, tightly rolled, highly aromatic, middle-ring-gauge size 48 Hoyo de Monterrey Double Corona, the flagship of the brand, which had a beautiful draw.

He sat back in his favorite leather chair, studied the cigar, rolled it gently between his fingers, inhaled it deeply from plume to foot, cut the cap, leaned back, lit it, stretched out, and puffed away, confidently.

§

It was raining in South America.

Captain Birdseye, with a handful of beads, enlisted several dusky little bearers, whose chief qualification was that they had no family ties. It could have been the Congo, for they were black, many of them Saramaccan maroons, descendants of runaway West African slaves, he was told, the lot of them pagan "animists" who spoke Tongo or Auken, Fongbe, Gbe, all sorts of Creole jingo, gibberish, and they believed in spirits. The equatorial tropics should always be entered by way of water, the sea, where the approach is smooth, gentle, almost imperceptible. The rain stopped, but it was as if the torrents had given birth to suffocating humidity. The heat was intense. He was in and out of a volcano town before he knew it, where women now became shapeless, bandy-legged, old, and wore at all sorts of ditzy angles Q'ero hats, *ch'ulhu*, woven of alpaca wool with twisted rainbow-colored tufts hanging from each comic earflap.

The scorching sun was boring in, the jungle steaming, the snarl of the bush in the outskirts of Suriname so dense, so roaring green, shades of green that he had never seen before or even imagined, that with its snaking rosary of unnamed, undocumented, and unidentified rivers, he saw why this place stood among the most forested areas on the planet. They set off through the overwrought vegetation, at first through a long savannah and then whacking away at palms, lianas, and rainforest grass when things started to go badly wrong. Again, it began to rain javelins. The entire food supply went awash at thirteen degrees latitude, crossing the River of Doubt. At one point, he thought he saw a blue crane winging westward.

But it was merely a mirage, only one of many. There are no cranes in South America, not a single one.

As they trudged in, the porters proved vile. They spat incessantly, brazenly engaged in acts of buttock love, and filched a brooch. It was all frustration. He had taken aside one of the lankiest, blackest of the bonzos—he taught him to salute—whom he taught to cook, but then the boy got hungry, one night whacked up a pig in a self-styled abattoir, ate parts raw, and died of sarcosporidiosis.

And then one lead boy, mindlessly micturating one night, peed on a lit Tilley lamp—and it exploded. They were all without light.

The expedition had sailed by bumboat into sky-blue Marajó Bay, up to Santarem, pushed into the zone west of the Essequibo River, and headed north, when Captain Birdseye got his first glimpse of dynamic peaks. Gasping with delight, he took out a pad of paper and drew a series of sketches of them. At his feet he also took notice of many rare primitive plants perfuming the landscape. It was heaven! He snatched up his binoculars and raced to look everywhere, sweeping the landscape, up, behind, and around, for, surveying the delta, he knew that he was at last inhaling ancient Pre-Columbia. It was the Lost World!

In the tropical Amazon region of rainforest and grass-lands, the Roraima—or "Parrot Mountain"—where Venezuela, Guiana, and Brazil met—there stood a group of huge rectangular plateaux called, locally he learned, *tepuis*, which meant "house of the gods" in the native tongue of the Pemon, the indigenous people who inhabited the Gran Sabana, a rude landscape rising above the clouds, isolated, time eroded into flat-topped mountains in the Guiana highlands of southeastern Venezuela. There on high, veiled by steam and tall shadows, stood the peak of black naked rock, sheer walls soaring vertical, almost mythical towers and uncanny dark shields, consisting of Precambrian sandstone, buried beneath Phanerozoic strata, towering over surrounding viridescent rainforests by up to 1,000 meters or 3,280 feet.

Waterfalls dropped from its grand heights. Around the headwaters of the Orinoco there, flourishing on the mesas, he was told were at least 30 different species of orchid. pre-fossil if anything.

"Relict fauna and flora!" madly sang out Captain Birdseye, dancing his hands over his head, flamenco-style, like a passionate *bailaor*. Mushrooms two feet high. Pitcher plants. Bladderworts. New and rare species to be discovered, amazing vicariant speciation all created when, over a period of geological time, the mesas there had fragmented, creating sinkholes and crevices that at such exotic heights, with heavy rainfalls, had become completely isolated from the ground forest below, turning them into extravagant ecological savannas with strangely different climates, all fostering a growth of rare plants, even a different world of animals, endemic flora and fauna, through evolution over millennia, cut off from the rest of the world. Santa Elena de Uairén, a grassy little dorp near the Brazilian border, was their jumping-off point for Roraima.

Would he find the black orchid here?

Frankly, he was doubtful, so scarce it was. But, who knew, maybe with a bit of good fortune he might very well manage to stumble across a Curled Odontoglossum or Giant Ansellia or the rare Rothschild slipper orchid with its sweeping side petals that look like outspreadarms of a dancer. Why not? No artist or sculptor had ever created an object as beautiful as these!

They hastily broke out their rooftop tents, unzipping the covers, opening them up, unfolding the ladders, and attaching the rainfly rods. Squinched into his sleeping bag, damp as a cave, Captain Birdseye gathered notes from his *Contrivances*. Some tepui sinkholes contained species that had evolved in these "islands within islands" that were truly unique, large numbers of plants not found anywhere else in the world. The adventurer Sir Walter Raleigh, who had come across this remote peak in 1595, had called it a "mountain of crystal" but declared it impossible to climb. Darwin had skipped the place. Two strong, flat-faced Pemón porters, who spoke not a word of English, conveyed to them by signs, that an ascent into the cloud forest to the summit of the flat peak above was at least a seven-day, six-night trek and for a handful of *reais*, carrying their own gear in woven baskets strapped to their heads, led the way.

All the expedition bearers stayed below, except for one bearer, as they would only get in the way. It was a wet haul up through tropical vegetation and icy waterfalls, steep slopes, a vertiginous sprawl upwards, an enormous black wall, now green, then yellow, springs trickling out of fissures and crags, a huge drop below, its bottom no longer visible, up, up, up the gigantic walls and across suddenly steep and slippery boulders, inexplicable diagonals that opened up to bewildering paths, but when they did achieve the top, Captain Birdseye, discovering a grey creepy outcrop, faced the kind of roaring winds he had once felt standing in a howling gale on the very tip-top of Table Mountain in Cape Town.

The summit of Mt. Roraima, across which blew fierce winds swirling in a milky panorama, was a desolation of freakish rock formations, surreal outfalls of stone balloons and caricatures of megalithic tombs and dolmen, incongruous ziggurats, distorted boulders like lorries and nutty lampoons of teapots and tortoises and other incongruous and unexpected objects, ancient remnants of two-billion-year-old layers of Precambrian sediments that had eroded into a black landscape that stretched as far as the eye can see. There was not a sign of an orchid.

A bearded bellbird had merely squawked at him, a stone cluck, with a voice like Margot's, as if telling him to leave.

§

Months passed.

Food became precious. There was minor pilfering, depredations—snaffling—that Captain Birdseye preferred to ignore. He was forced to hire several bearers, dusky noirs of God-knew-what origin, for whom anything packaged thrilled, and of course, just as night followed day, cribbing followed.

At times, they fed off the land, hacking at shrubby cassava trees for the long waxy tubers, a fall-back resource—manioc—which they peeled, sliced, and roasted or boiled with turmeric, a staple they gobbled for meals, which, still, had the disadvantage of having an extremely poisonous juice containing cyanide that had to be gotten rid of before consuming it. They ate it in chips, they sometimes grated it into pulp; at other times they pounded and crushed the cassava leaves and boiled them in water as an efficient process for the removal of cyanogens. Some indifferent bearers—crude warlocks, dark coolies, and hottentots born for munching root crop—ate the knobs of *yuca* like a Goya cannibal, black spots and all, and farted for days.

He had tried to put names to his porters and bearers, to distinguish them—"Lumpy," "Ratcatcher," "Gums," "Cabo," "Westminster" (who had manners), "Skylark," "Turtle Bum," etc.—but, for the cheekiness it gave them in the way of proud identity, they began sloughing off, and it didn't work out.

They penetrated deeper and deeper now into unchartered territories, most of it filled with loopy vegetation, humped hills, and primordial black lakes, swollen with algae. As they thrashed their way forward, cudgeling brutal grass, he suddenly saw the striking foliage of star-bright red-tipped bromeliad pinguins, balansae, and humilis, scarce to come across in that they only bloomed once throughout their lifespan. The sight of the rare but delicate, fertile flowers heartened him with general possibility and hope.

Suddenly Captain Birdseye became abstracted and stood stock-still in a sharp attitude of listening. Drums. He heard drums, the thumping wireless of the unmapped jungle! Worried, in need of a restorative, he munched two mineral-rich health wafers, took a Beecham's pill—he believed in progressive pharmacy—and washed it all down with a large cup of Eno's Fruit Salts in water. *Always a pill*, he thought, *never a comfit*. The vibrations of the insistent drumming—strums, booms, thrums, and throbs—actually seemed to animate the huge broccoli-green foliage, that actually wigged and wagged. He also took a tablespoon from a bottle of Mrs. Winslow's Soothing Syrup and hastily mixed a "bumbo," a concoction of rum, sugar, water, and nutmeg, fuscous in color, which he gulped down in hopes of feeling better. Just fashion becoming irregular in the bush! The pulsing sounds that they heard unnerved even some of the bearers—Rat-catcher, spooked, fearfully made devil horns—as they halted in their tracks their big lips opening in frighted apprehension like the flapping flews of a bloodhound.

What would his end be like? the incessant drums seemed to be asking. Would he and his expedition be decimated by mosquitoes and curare-laced arrows like Vasco Núñez de Balboa in 1513 exploring the interior of Hispaniola? Pecked at by slaughtering and maniacal natives or trapped deep in hot jungles teeming with deadly snakes, spiders, cockroaches, lizards, chiggers, and jaguars like the Aztec-murdering Spanish conquistador Hernan Cortes in 1526 when he penetrated the mysterious interior looking for the Lost City of the Monkey God?

It was always the same, jungle green succeeding jungle green, skylights rudely closing overhead, the screams of monstrous blue-and-yellow macaws, flapping wings, and, persistently, no end of worries pelting the roof of his mind like hailstones.

It was a palaver to have to keep stopping, removing backpacks, as they were required to keep moving and in doing so doing so quickly. Willful and intractable bearers, confounding any logic, made it impossible. A military "hard routine" was called for—minimal noise, no idling or gadabouting, no fires, certainly no cooking or riffle-rifling the bushes for pepino or pitahaya. They set up camp. Captain Birdseye pushed out a pirogue from a grass plantation, crossed the Cottica River, and waded ashore near Mocha, where he got the shivers watching the swirls of piranhas, stingrays, and electric eels swarming in the murky waters gorged with water hyacinths.

Now shone the sun, then it was hammering with rain. Often, both happened simultaneously. Captain Birdseye, licking droplets of rain from his chin, squinted into the waving trees overhead, savoring a delight he felt should be shared. Calling the porters' attention to the phenomenon, hoping to keep their favor and jolly them along, he noted, speaking slowly, "In South Africa when there is rain and sun at the same time"—here he performed a touching little mime for them—"the Zulu people call it '*umshado wezinkawu*'—a monkey's wedding." It did not have the effect he had hoped for, if the response was to be reckoned. One bearer grunted, another bent over and insolently showed him his bum, and all the others went off to begin snatching coca leaves from plants they found, snapping at them, which they munched by the handful, jumping up and down like crazed squirrel monkeys. It was disheartening but merely a spot of bother. His occupations were strictly elsewhere and otherwhere. Protestations—cavilling of any sort—was not within the remit of a Victorian explorer worth his salt.

It was not always an uphill battle. Once at the far edge of a mangrove forest by tumbling water, Captain Birdseye's heart leaped with delight, coming across a precious "Queen of the Andes," the largest species of *bromeliad* to be found, its trunk seven yards tall, with a rosette of leaves and leaf spines. The inflorescence was lovely. A whole plant may reach as much as fifteen meters tall, and a single plant can produce between 8,000 and 20,000 flowers in a three-month period. Enchantment. Magic. Endless appeal. Charm.

But it was not the black orchid.

One of the bearers came running up to him wildly waving with expectation and proudly holding up two fistfuls of gigantic hogweed, grotesquely spotted with a purple stem and filled with toxic sap.

"No, no," said the frustrated Captain, taking it from the sorry man, recalling Edward Lear's nonsense botany—*Piggwig-gia pyramidalis.* Speaking clearly and slowly, he lessoned the boy, "This. No. Good. The orchid has three petals, you see, usually green, but sometimes brightly colored like the petals, two of which might be considered normal forms of petals. These two, you see, flare out at the sides and are called 'wings.'" He pranced about a bit, flapping his arms for effect. But it was useless. A few of the new, ogling, half-naked bearers he had hired to replace some of the lost Saramaccans apparently spoke only the Arawak language, Chamicuro—or Amuesha, he wasn't certain—and they began all of them giggling and, covering their mouths in crazy glee, squealing, "*Molota! Molota!*" which he found out later meant woman!

Sighing, Captain Birdseye gave up. What to do? He asked his lead bearer to try to interpret what he was trying to describe in hopes that might help. "The third petal is the queen. The showy one, see? With fringed edges? It may end in a lazy spur, or it may resemble a trumpet, or a bulbous sac, which is called the 'lip,' It may be found in a range of colors, rose, purple, lavender, brown, pink, but never red, see? Now the little hood of an orchid can easily be taken for one of its beautiful petals, but it is in fact a stamen, stepping out as a solitary. The stamens conjoin together with the pistil to form a column. That is the orchid. Now the black one—"

"*Molota! Molota!*" they hooted, laughing, and stuck out their bums, as round as moons and as black as pitch.

§

They trudged through brutal heat and humidity, watching bats flap, and faced the green wall of the jungle rains. At unexpected moments sheets of a blue rain commenced, then abruptly stopped, then began again. Captain Birdseye could smell Mesoamerica! In the dark of night noises of drums and rattle-gourds could again be heard penetrating the darkness. It was unsettling to try to read the variations. Birdseye fixed another bumbo, mumped a cocaine throat lozenge, and forthrightly tramped on. Was not this the land of the world's last pre-Columbian tribes? Would they now be encountering ur-creatures wearing blue macaw feathers, raw stark-naked men and women with half moons in the septum of their flat noses and freakish lip discs? The endangered Piripkura? Kawahiva of the Rio Pardo, Mato Grosso? The uncontacted and potentially dangerous Awá, or Guajá? Marauhas with wooden plugs stuck through their bottom lips? Bum-biters all stenciled up and down like freaks? How would they engage the inhabitants, they wondered, by offering gifts of fish, scissors or safety pins, and singing pious Anglican hymns?

"Give them strips of red cloth," he had been told, by which to barter. Aborigines believe red to be a kind of gold—the color winds them up, makes them go giddy! He was sure he'd read that was what von Humboldt did. What was the alternative— was he supposed to do what his Spanish and Dutch predecessors had done, slaughter every poor Indian nig-nog he stumbled upon? The damnable thing was, a person never quite knows with autochthons and abos. The Tahitians stole Captain Cook's own leggings while he was using them as a pillow! Naturalist Joseph Banks was brutally stripped clean of his stop-watch and hanky while he sat down feasting with them!

Certain of these peoples, Birdseye well knew, were savage and would not hesitate to burn outlanders alive or shoot them with arrows tipped with curare. Many of these bush people, when they had not been killed by the British, had been historically persecuted or, possibly even worse, approached down through the years by zealous glad-handing, Bible-thumping evangelists. They never forgot it. Birdseye had read his Henry Walter Bates, his Fritz Müller, and the famously missing Percy Fawcett. The aboriginal Indians instinctively feared and despised anyone in uniform. If they spied an individual in such regalia walking along, they would kill him on the spot. They had no sense of property, except for the hunting trail, where, with expert eyes, usually in one desperate yank, they could swiftly bring down out of the overhanging trees marmosets, snakes, tamarins, and screeching howler and capuchin monkeys, none of which they would hesitate to gobble up. But this was neither here nor there.

He was looking for his black flower. The color of an orchid can change the meaning of a flower, red, white, purple, and they all conveyed passion. At one point the Captain thought that he actually spotted his incandescent beauty in its wee grassy homeland, the specific *bulbophyllum* he sought, and he went leaping at it like a Rappenspalter after a pfennig.

But it was not to be. The petals were free from each other and smaller than the lateral sepals, the labellum predictably fleshy, curved and hinged to the base of the column. Neither ebony, nor sable, it was only dark purple. He took his compass in hand instead, straightened his shoulders, and stepped off.

The expedition headed southwest. Deeper into the jungle they penetrated. They heard tom-toms, scary rhythmic beats from afar, summoning god knows what. The only thing worse, however, was *not* hearing them again, which indicated how far afield they might be into nightmare territory. The Captain was disconcerted, having discovered a blue rash on his ankles, which left a maddening itch. A torrential downpour set in lasting for three days.

Fungus began growing on everything, turning them blighted, musty, and spoiled. Leather turned white, metal green, their jackets transmogrifying into stiff stand-alones, all with a damp and decaying nap. Two of the volumes of the rare priceless first editions he had brought along of Alexander von Humboldt's *Personal Narrative of Travels to the Equinoctial Regions of the New Continent* had turned to a gummy mush. (The other as he later found out, with curses, the ignorant porter, Ratcatcher, had stolen and been using as toilet paper, page by page by page.) Skin turned splotchy with red spots, and the sweat on their bodies now felt as slick as oil. Green mold—*cladosporium*—left olive-black streaks on all of his woodwork and cloth, mattocks and water bag canvases and cape rugs. The metal on his whistle, barometer, needles, and machetes were corroding with rust and oxidation. Jungle environments do not respect brightwork.

Soon were heard the lethal grunts of jaguars, terrifying noises, one of a few animals that can mimic the sounds of hapless prey, like skunk pigs, hairless dogs, and peccaries. He heard jungle fowl, coos and cacks sounds so liquid that in his thirst they reminded him of bubbling streams. He smelt hair tonic in the bay trees.

Two bearers also fell out with loud complaints of stomach cramps. They also shared on their ankles and legs the blue rash that had been plaguing him. He checked his medical dictionary and saw they were suffering cluster bites from the poisonous Vinchuca bugs, that can both fly and crawl. Was it Chagas disease, known as trypanosomiasis, a tropical parasitic infection spread by insects known as Triatominae, or "kissing bugs"? He applied a deep salve to his limbs which he shared with his boys, an embrocation that in the rubbing—a viscous balm wholly new to them—gave them a taste for it, which they began lapping at with grinning delight.

Rain, rain, rain. It never stopped, hammering black sleet rains that soaked everything through, blankets, boots, canvases, coats, guns, and backpacks. Everything was waterlogged, sopping, wringing wet, drenched as if with blood like the corners of the altar! The humidity which became so oppressive brought on clouds of mosquitos which in numbers and ferocity could exsanguinate a wild pig or a capybara or a white-lipped peccary

Captain Birdseye had mad waking dreams of Ténéré and the sand sheet of the Sahara, a desert within a desert, of all places the single most sunlit place on Earth, more than four thousand hours of it a year. He dreamt of building a hut in Fachi or Bilma and live bone dry, soaking up the medical warmth of God!

So, would he resign the job and cowardly bow out?

If such you thought, you do not know an Englishman, the citizen of a nation with the most intrepid determination.

Queen Victoria who loved Tennyson's poetry had invited that man to read to her. She had asked Edward Lear to teach her to draw. She wanted to have a black orchid. How could he not oblige Her Majesty the Queen? He would never let her down, not a chance, even if she had asked for the lost cratons of Gondwanaland! Thinking of peevish Margot and her scowl on his promise to find the black orchid, the words of Benedick in *Much Ado About Nothing*—a man who by the way vowed he would never marry—

came echoing out of the mephitic air of the jungle and he quickly thumbed through the copy of the Bard's plays he brought, only to read:

> "Your highness, will your grace command me any service to the world's end? I will go on the slightest errand now to the Antipodes that you can devise to send me on. I will fetch you a toothpick from the furthest unch of Asia, bring you the length of Prester John's foot or fetch you a hair from the Great Cham's beard, do you any embassage to the Pygmies—anything rather than exchange three words' conference with this awful, screeching woman . . . O God, sir, here's a dish I love not: I cannot endure my Lady Tongue."

No, it did not redound greatly to Margot, he thought.
But the Queen was his Sovereign.
And a vow was a vow, nothing less.

§

Captain Birdseye forgot the rain. Championed in mind by the force of new-found resolve, feeling a rumble of success within him, he ignored the jungle noises and the sounds of the tom-toms and his rude bush boys. He opened his bespoke travelling case and took out his portable flatware to enjoy a dinner, alone. It was fiendishly ritualized, he saw to that, a meal of cold grouse, orange jelly, and chocolate sponge. There were sides to sample, as if he were home by a fire. Menager's Pickle. Bengal Club Chutney. Promising seemed possible prospects. He sat by a hillock in the wild and spotted some beautiful storksbills. Were geraniums too serviceable a flower to send to the Queen? He wanted to give her a simple red pelargonium. Maybe a jaguar bone for Dashy, her pet spaniel. But send where? To Frogmore? Remote Balmoral? Windsor? Osborne? Buckingham Palace? By way of post to the duchess of Atholl, her friend? But send how—he yanked out a map—by raising a lucky telegraph station in Posto Awá? Iquitis? Tabatinga? Itacoatiara? Some village in the Tapajós river basin? He munched his grouse.

He favorably recalled his one dinner with the good Queen. He had brought her a bouquet of primroses, her favorite flower. "Of all the flowers, the one that retains its beauty longest, is primrose," the sycophant Disraeli had told her, he knew, lavishing Her Majesty with chaplets of them. That ambitious Conservative parvenu was a scheming and arrant flatterer, of course, and she was taken in, so much so that she allowed that man actually to *sit* in her presence, an unheard-of privilege.

They had dined on a saddle of luscious Southdown mutton, with croquettes of salsify and celeriac. The Queen just barely nodded her head with authority and a bottle of rich tawny vintage Port was poured for them. They started with a pale consommé, he remembered. It was her favorite soup, and to perfect this hard-to-make broth, her royal chef had to clarify a veal stock using a cracked eggshell and minced breast meat mixture, with meats like venison, marrowbones, brawn, and beef. Nobody ate peas with more efficiency than the Queen. Her hands were tiny and dimpled, and beringed her chubby fingers. For dessert they had a chocolate and blue cheese crumble tart. A centre-piece was composed of dessert fruit and delicate quince blossoms in specimen glasses. He knew enough to wait until she began to eat and to stop eating exactly when she had finished.

Her Majesty was a trenchant but joyless eater—it seemed to be a matter of concentration—and despatched the food very quickly, nose down, hands expertly in play, being all business. Margot had once uncharitably put it that she gobbled her food and did not pause between courses and wore large underwear and had a 49-inch waist. But the Captain would hear nothing against his Sovereign. She ate with gusto, concentrating on the food. At 70, she still loved a good lamb chop for breakfast, or so he'd heard, and had a weakness for potatoes. She brought food with her whenever she travelled, with confections created by her chef de cuisine, Charles Elmé Francatelli, good tidy "light" dinners in woven baskets filled with baked ham, tongue, game, lobster salad, cold chicken, plovers' eggs, sandwiches, patisserie, jellies, and creams.

They had three rare wines. Port marries well with Stilton. The Queen who had a discriminating taste in cheese loved a ripe Stilton, the *ne plus ultra* of cheeses, as did the Captain. A cow in Notts drinking Rutland water and chewing Spring meadow grass and clover—*never* fodder or or patent "cake"– imparted to a Stilton's matchless nutty taste and salty finish, he knew from past experience. A good Stilton should be creamy, not white, with thin delicate blue veins, and its famous crust showing as bright and saucy as a field of gold. Acrimonious difference of opinion may have been Margot's way but not his, thankfully, and for such as those who preferred a different kind of cheese, any choice from whencesover it may come being welcome, the Captain freely and open-heartedly accepted. He personally enjoyed a stick of celery with his Stilton, in the way that radishes go well with a Gorgonzola, but at the royal dinner none appeared, which was fine and they nibbled water biscuits cooked right there at Windsor.

The Queen barely spoke at dinner. Had she been preoccupied? The Battle of Toski had just been fought in the Mahdist War, and the Anglo-Egyptian troops had proven victorious. The troubling Dock Strike, a fret, had just begun. The recent Ripper murders might have been weighing sorely on her mind, as well. (The Duke of Clarence, "Eddy," the very grandson of the monarch, a fellow who all through his life had been suffering from mental health issues, some argued, actually might well have been the grisly serial killer himself! And what a burden to bear!) The longest bridge in Britain, the Forth Bridge, was about to be opened.

Captain Birdseye, who cast about for subjects to discuss, luckily had read *Leaves from the Journal of Our Life in the Highlands*, the one book his Sovereign wrote and illustrated. "In Auchmore, Scotland, I noticed, Your Majesty planted two fir trees and an oak with Lady Breadalbane, as companion, who is a third cousin of mine," he offered. "Your Majesty loved the glens, the hills of Cruachan, saw flights of ptarmigan in Blair Athole. I marvel at your sketches. The depiction you did at Pembroke, sailing in the '*Fairy*,' of Welsh women with their high-crowned men's hats? Remarkable! Oh indeed, yes, frightfully good, and the drawing of the 'Dutchman's Cap' in the Treshinish Isles—such splendid renderings, your Majesty."

"Bertie shot at the ptarmigans. The blessed man missed more often than he brought one down, the dear soul." she said wistfully of her dear husband who had passed away in 1861. "How I miss his good company. We lost him 28 years ago." She faithfully wore her mourning dress right to the end, a fine ensemble comprising of a bodice and skirt made of black silk taffeta and embellished with layers of black silk crêpe. It was a grievous loss that the very earnest woman never quite got over. Wettin, changed to Windsor, was Prince Albert's family name, as distinct from his "House" name, a full one, of Saxe-Coburg-Gotha. A formidable monkey-puzzle. The Consort, her dashing husband, endearingly, called her "*Liebes Frauchen*." Victoria, however, always disliked her family associations with the immoderate Hanoverians, of which house she was the last crowned monarch in Britain. As monarch, she much preferred privately to identify herself instead with her more remote descent from the ancient house of Guelph. Rather than the House of Hanover, the surname that Her Majesty considered more appropriate for herself was Guelph D'Este of the House of Brunswick.

The Widow at Windsor could be fussy—she hated cats, forcefully disallowed smoking of any kind in any of her palace rooms, disliked dull and tiresome clergymen who preached in surplices, and, being finicky about her tableware, used her gold plate solely in her own dining rooms at the castle, nowhere else, and woe betide the servant or footman who mistakenly set them out by mistake. On the occasion of his dinner, Birdseye had properly worn a black dress suit with an open waistcoat and white neckerchief. Guests of the Queen invariably wore double layered stockings in deference to her taste, for it was bruited about she was scandalized by the fact that, when British lawyers wore silk stockings, she could still see their leg hair sticking out of the tights! In modulated response, she had imposed a royal dress code: all barristers had to double layer their stockings, and that rule held ironclad and never wavered.

Gracefully, the Queen tendered Captain Birdseye as a parting gift a rare coin, the newly minted Golden Jubilee Crown in pure gold showing the Sovereign in profile on the one side, stern, with down-turned mouth, and on the reverse side, helmeted St. George, the Patron Saint of England, slaying the dragon.

The memory was sweet. The pickle and chutney did the trick. The grouse meat, in the leg area especially, was gamey and mild. The blue rash on his ankles had faded. He climbed into his sleeping bag, the nap of which he hugged like the soft feel of fragile memory subject to no erasure.

The moon was high.

He went to sleep smiling.

§

Trekking inward was exhausting, and there was no end of unpredictable experiences. More mountains loomed in the distance, Captain Birdseye saw, climbing high into a cecropia tree, only to notice at all points of the compass a grim, unwelcoming uniformity, the depressing sameness, of the isotropic and homogenous jungle spreading widely and brainlessly below in every direction, only this time with boring, undifferentiating sameness and so a kind of dread. The tree in which he sat like a trembling fakir, all alone, frightened him, after an earlier ophidic accident, when a five- or six-foot-long spotted bushmaster silently dropping from an adjacent tree, making a lethal strike, killed one of his bearers—goodbye, Cabo!—with a single toxic bite. That grim death was only one of the discouraging mishaps encountered on this questionable adventure, but, needless to say, it was sufficient. They watched the man's dark, beady eyes panic, sunken beneath their projecting supraorbital bones and bulging almost prehistoric cheekbones, and then turn to a fatal grey.

They saw orange/pink/purple potatoes, munched pink corn, breathed thin air, witnessed left-handed waves in the ocean, drank coati dung coffee, climbed a rainbow mountain, slogged through salt ponds, sucked *camu camu* fruit, unearthed ancient burial food, were chased by the ugliest dogs in the world, and ate virtually raw chunks of meat from alpacas hung up to dry. What a comedown from the delicious pork shoulder butts that he and Margot shared of a Sunday, slavered with mayo, mustard, cumin, treacle, and rosemary, and then slow-cooked all day!

He entertained long reveries of home, a spot of tea, a wander down the road among the lupins, a glass of port in his gazebo, of the warm confines of his paneled library. Would that I had my books, he thought. Such old and dear companions they were. He missed them. He was in error not to have carted one or two of them along instead of a lump-pile of anti-scorbutic foods, far less worthy company. They would have helped his progress, as well as buoyed him up: Fleming's *Quadrupeds*, Davy's *Consolation on Travel*, Caldcleugh's *Travels in South America*, Paul Scroope on Volcanoes, Burchell's *Travels*, Conybeare's geological book.

He missed absent Margot and the camararderie she gave. Guilt confused him. Had he not ignored her moodiness, as best he could? Or should he have put his foot down and, taking umbrage at her occasionally challenging remarks, shouted, "You want me to be a Signor Baldassare Castiglione's lute-playing minuet-dancing equestrian swordsman swashbuckling Renaissance courtier?"

A spell of depression faded when he noticed a round-headed bird peering at him with a smile. It was a resplendent quetzal, of all things, with its red belly and iridescent green wing coverts, back, chest, and head, the "jewel bird" sacred to both the Maya and the Aztecs, whose priests proudly wore their feathers on their headdresses. The birds can sprint, walk, and swim, as well as fly, loved fruit and the high mountains, and belonged to the 'Trogon' family of birds which is the Greek word for "gnawing," which is a distinctive trait to these birds.

The sight of the bird reinvigorated him with a feeling of reinstated good luck, especially when he found one of its feathers.

As they stomped through wet grasses and soggy bush, battyfanging through sopping overgrowth, Captain Birdseye came across lots of bulbs—*monocotyledonous geophytes*, to be scientifically precise—cool begonias, dahlias, cannas. Not items for his mission, he dismissively referred to them as "foozlers," although at moments he would stop to finger one or two of them simply out of botanical delight, many of the fetching eucomis, hardy hippeastrums, tender lilies, lovely speckled nerines, and tigridias, bless their hearts, most of which dove underground for winter, not tethered by nature to colder latitudes north of the equator.

But it was the black orchid that he sought, nothing less, the perfect flower bang up to the elephant, stark, perfect, complete—no compromises. He wanted no fake skilamalinks and would not be sold a dog.

What did hearten him was coming across some large stanhopeas (*Stanhopea tigrina*), a fragrant orchid, found mainly in Mexico, fine specimens which live on low tree branches in the shady parts of a jungle. Captain Birdseye gently fingered a bract. He loved them: fragrant waxy blooms, last only a week, love shade, direct sun easily burned the broad foliage, backbulbs leafless. A characteristic of this orchid was the way the flower came from the bottom, growing directly downward. How fitting for me, he thought—how characteristic of my topsy-turvy journey!

He raised his canteen—he lifted the nozzle to the sky—and with a long pull drank a toast, "A salute to the Right Honorable Philip Henry, 4th Earl of Stanhope, president of the London Medico-Botanical Society 1829 to 1837."

But troubles soon emerged. The Captain had a mishap opening his trusty Laguiole pocket-knife with its "half-lock" on the blade where a small projection at the end of the backspring (*mouche*), exerting pressure on a corresponding indent in the blade heel, snapped and sliced open the fleshy thenar eminence of his palm, when he tried to extricate a blooming *Encyclia cochleatum*—Belize's national flower—with its filigree bulb-like stems and fetching clam-shell-like valves with showy purple veins. He not only had to forego the flower, plans began collapsing everywhere.

It was monstrous! Method was all. Attention to be paid. Program and system. Failing to plan is planning to fail!

Change, however, was the only certainty. No terrain was ever the same. Rainforest gave way to thick jungle, deep canyons to small high-altitude deserts, and in the far distance with towering cones, staggeringly vertical, thorn-pointed, as deeply blue as cyanosis and so terrifyingly steep they could literally stop the clouds. The top spur was lost in a swirling mist. The bearers were alternately cold and hot, sleeping now on canvas cots in small tents and in the brutal humidity on straw paliasses under netting. Rifles—bolt action Lee-Metfords—were ever at the ready.

Captain Birdseye with unexpected horror slipped and fell hard on his groin while climbing an intractable mud-cliff and put on an umbilical truss which gave small relief and so to stem

ALEXANDER THEROUX

the pain, after consulting a copy of Dr. Lionel Beale's compendi-
ous *Disease Germs* that he had brought along with him, slathered
all over himself with Portugal oil, general gum salves, and gobs
of Holloway's Ointment ("The Soldier's True Friend"), and, after
looping battery-charged brass and zinc wires around his upper
body—as prescribed—and after splashing himself with vinegar,
having no access to a water-cure spa, he wrapped himself up tight
like an Egyptian mummy in sheaves of sopping wet sheets, and
went to sit in the hot sun until he began to frizzle and almost
faint.

It was always being supine in the darkness of night,
mentally excavating his heart, as constantly he did, feeling vulnerable over his abrupt departure from his wife, that Captain
Birdseye, with a constant throb in his groin, heard in the gusts of
the snarling Peruvian winds the sound of Margot's cruel estima-
tion of him with the phrase, "*Weeping meringue, weeping meringue.*"

He remembered their wedding in St. George's Church in
Hanover Square, so long sanctioned for society nuptials when his
mother had uncharitably whispered of his new wife, "She is no
oil painting."

Visual morphs flitted in his head. He smelt water, meth
odors. Had they penetrated the Urubumba? Were they in Cusco?
Several indigines, discovered babbling, suddenly leapt howling
from a tree and skittered off in fright. What dialect was that?
Not Spanish, surely. Had he heard mutters of Huinchirim or only
imagined it? A Chibchan language like Moisca? Maipurean?
Tucano? Panoen possibly? "I have just seen three hairy bonobos
gibbering," cried Birdseye. Was it the rant of some Olmec script
come alive? A kind of Mayan cacophony found only on colorfully
painted stelae? Nothing, felt Birdseye, was more disorienting

than gabble!

Nights now, fearful, he slept within an outstetched grommet of rope, piled high from his fear against pumas. Winds in the tropics always blow from the east, and the incessant currents in the heart of which he constantly heard his wife's cesses and hexes and maledictions seemed an endless curse.

Independent of all these mortifications, still, there was ever his belief in himself and the cause of his undertaking. If the tour answered well, and, in truth, not a single night passed when fondly he hoped and prayed, please Providence, it would, why, any and all acclamation and honor would redound to Her Majesty the Queen, all honor and glory being conferred to her, not received.

All glory to Alexandrina Victoria, Queen of the United Kingdom of Great Britain and Ireland, by the grace of God, Empress of India, Defender of he Faith, "Drina," the Grandmother of Europe!

§

The group kept on moving, not to be deterred. They crossed high above a pongo on a long, scary, swinging *ichu* grass bridge woven by the pastoral Incas, masters of fiber, curious people from the ancient empire of Tawantinsuyu, who actually *communicated* in fiber—developed an exotic and impenetrable language of knotted strings known as *quipo*, which has yet to be decoded. They seemed to lose their way a every turn. Was it the Huachuma they'd eaten, the psychedelic San Pedro cactus with its sense of detachment? Coincidences seemed to repeat themselves. Clouds piling up in the west, Birdseye found, came to resemble the clockwise whorl in his own hair! Chills married muscle action to no consequence. Wind played at the dominant side of his face as if mocking caresses even deeper than memory's past of lost love.

Too many of his bearers, peon-crude, proved to be detestably designing and unprincipled men, causing him no end of setbacks and an endless host of vexations. The Captain was furious. What a bobbery it was to wake up one drizzling morning only to find that a food tent flap had been slit: it turned out that the goobers had burrowed into one container like thieving rats and eaten all the mangoes, dried apples, even drank the lemon juice, and rifled no end of sixteen canisters of Kilner and Moorsum's preserved meat, a favored specialty of his. What a pretty pickle!

The nogs needed to be sidetracked, redirected, put right.

He decided to try to divert their attention, to turn their minds to busy-making tasks to keep them honest.

The Captain tried to teach his bearers rope work. To secure tents. As belay anchors. To connect slings. So important were knots to their fate! The Inca's only "written" language, he knew, was a system of knots tied into necklace-like "documents" called quipus, or "talking knots." Gorillas knew how to tie knots. So did weaver birds. But not these bongos! He would take the bitter end of a rope, the working end, and wiggle-waggle it to show the "feel" of it, the "hand" of it. He tried to be patient. "A *hank* is a looped bundle of rope, see," he said, shaping the lead line into a mountaineer's coil. "A *bend* is a knot that ties the ends of two ropes together. Get it? A *hitch* attaches a rope to a fixed object, such as a tree or a shackle, or a loop, or a boulder. A short section of slack rope that does not cross itself is called a *bight*. If it crosses itself, it's a *loop*. Twist a loop and you form an *elbow*. Do you see?"

But the giggling nincompoops and twits only wagged the ropes in front of their groins as simulated codpieces and, loudly whooping, cavorted and leaped about like the crazed barbarians they were, draping the ropes around their stuck-out behinds, towel-wise, Halfwits! Clods! *Cabeza de chorlito!*

§

The explorer and his bearers climbed higher and higher, spying into misty gorges, and saw various *cattleya* waving in rocky crevices. The flowers often hid perversely like tiny self-effacing but flirtatious imps or elves in a magical toyland. Orchids oddly flourish at heights but are well-equipped for coping in harsh and even impoverished environments. At the reaches of many inaccessible pinnacles and elevations, growing like willful children, they were immature, and, being callow, mulish, soon found they lacked the moisture that sustain the bromeliads at lower altitudes and so had to collect nourishment in other ways, with some dangling their roots in mid-air to try to absorb what moisture they could from the humid atmosphere, and others spreading their roots over branches in order to collect drops that trickled through the leaves.

Hanging at precarious angles, magnifying glass in hand, Birdseye was agog with appreciation at the flora and fauna. How beautiful were the flowering Arisaema with their damson cobra-headed inflorescences, their hooded spathes rising spookily, faintly sinister and fabulously seductive, as well as the rich purple 'Ostara' hyacinths pushing up between clumps of blue-flowered polyanthus! He was thrilled in finding large pink-white *drosera*, or carnivorous sundews—Charles Darwin performed much of his early research on *Drosera*—odd to find there because rich varieties of carnivorous plants such as *drosera* and most species of heliamphora, as well as a wide variety of orchids and bromeliads, were usually found on the floors of mesas which are poor in nutrients.

He wanted to stay up on the mountain longer. But, due to delays, he had no time for poking about or gawping at lesser flowers. One hare-brained bearer fell off the mountain, idiotically limbing backwards with a rope. Another, trying to bite open a knot with his mandrill-like teeth, managed to do so, but, inadvertently swallowing a mouthful of hemp, badly gagging, he went coughing into the bush on a frenetic run to stem it and suffocated to death.

"Mind the grease, mind the grease!" Captain Birdseye would snap intolerantly, brushing past them when anyone of the idiotic groids, jungle bunnies, or Hottentots that he had hired came dopily running up to him, full of expectation—and possible reward—like the button-headed children they were, to show him nothing but simple grape hyacinths, mere blue-spiked *Muscari armeniacum*, or unimportant purple irises of rich gentian blue.

Pointless! Once, one wide-mouthed porter with a bowl haircut came expectantly drooling up to Captain Birdseye with a flower of rose-colored petals and a frilled-lip of crimson and yellow—but, no, no, no, *no*, it was only a stupid Dendrobium, lovely, but *not black!* The reverse might have been said of Peru, thought the Captain. But in fact is that where they were? Who knew!

Captain Birdseye's mind with intense colors nightly began to turn to food, and he began dreaming with longing of spitchcocked eels, salted and basted with bright Irish butter!; Halibut Pondicherry; a fat braised goose with lobster sauce and a side order of marrow toast; a Rassolnik soup filled with choice kidneys; a fresh bowl of Water Souchy, followed by a Belvoir pudding, some flead cakes, Renel buns, and a Singin' Hinnie—the real "fatty cutties," with buttermilk and currants; a mince pie; a crispy puck of bubble and squeak; a bowl of buttered neeps and tatties; a ham and pease pudding stottie; fig strips, large stacked pear baskets, with all of the fruits shiny and hard; warm, baked, filled chestnut and mushroom pithiviers; several trays of *feuilletés aux épinards et au chèvre*; buckwheat cakes with creamy leeks and baked eggs; and lovely silver goblets of chilled clove sorbet. Whelks. Cockles. Yum. *Yum.*

Winkles, even. He opened a bag of them and began with a pin to flick off the operculum, the shelllike trapdoor that covers the opening, and root around to nail the winkle and pull it out. He heard someone say *"They are narrow and fragile towards the end, so you have to go very, very carefully to get them out intact,"* then he woke up and realized that he was all alone in crisis undergoing a mental fugue and that the sounds were only his mother's frail voice jabbering away, and instead of pinning lovely winkles, he was instead rooting into his own ears!

They were hungry in the extreme. It was especially difficult to negotiate the difficult terrain on empty bellies. But Captain Birdseye had a cache of supplies waiting up ahead. Meanwhile, they learned to grind meal from mesquite pods, cut from woody desert plants—genus *Prosopis*—pounding the pods into meal, then sifting it into flour, which they sprinkled with water and shaped into cakes to leave out to dry. As the dampness turned them mushy, they were barely edible. How dearly he wished he were back home with a plate before him of hot floured whitebait—blue anchovies—with lemon wedges and a tall glass of pale ale! For a drink, however, they made a crude *anapa*, a beverage they devised by grinding *algarrobo* pods with water and straining out the pulp for a cool drink, with the carob taste in the juice adding something of a boon to their increasingly parched throats. They came down from the heights.

Stalking plants to eat made them indiscriminate. The Captain, who experienced increasing spittle, soon began throwing up after indiscriminately eating handfuls of yew berries and, following Beale, he washed himself all over with carbolic soap, popped some meat lozenges, took several large tablespoons of phosphorized cod-liver oil, and then hastily gulped down a mixture every few hours of a bitter concoction of Condy's Ozonised Fruit Water composed of tinctures of bismuth, opium chalk, and carbonate of ammonia, which only made him fart rainbows. A fatal mistake two of the less intelligent and self-indulgent bearers made was cramming down bracken, not "fiddlenecks," not the young stems, but munching the full fronds of the adult plants.

Young stems were quite commonly used as a vegetable in China, Japan and Korea, Birdseye knew, but the big leaves that these yobbos were eating by the fistful produced hydrogen cyanide! Its spores had been implicated as a carcinogen by way of the cancerous compound called ptaquiloside or PTA, which, when it leaches from the plant into any water supply, may explain the noted increase in the incidence of gastric and esophageal cancers in bracken-rich areas. In cattle, bracken poisoning can occur in both an acute and chronic form, acute poisoning being the most common. In pigs and horses, bracken poisoning can induce vitamin B deficiency. What fresh hell was next?

Nothing was normal as to weather. They were either freezing or roasting into disintegration, sopping wet or dry as dust. Rain brought out squamata. One night a lizard slipped up his sleeve, and, shaking it out, he hurled an imprecation at it with a burnt-out light-bulb look in his eyes.

Visuospatial dysgnosia, linked with topographical disorientation, overtook Captain Birdseye who in a fit threw his hat at a tree! He thrashed fitfully in his sleeping bag that night. Over and over, he felt an increasing need to report—something, anything—to Windsor. But what of value had he to report? Birdseye now began to have heroic dreams: of flying; of conquering death by way of the spirit; of carrying a message to the Queen with an invisible fluid written on his skin made with cobalt chloride or a baking soda solution or red cabbage water.

§

The expedition was deeply off-track now. The Captain's handdrawn maps, woolly with erasures, showed how hidebound he had been all along by constant and havering indecisions as to proper routes. Quags of stagnant water and decaying vegetation brought on intermittent fevers. Ticks twitted invasively, itching him to beat the devil. At night, a strange silver light exaggerated the weirdness of every bivouac. Sleep which came fitfully prompted despair, until, looking up through a grateful fissure, he managed to get a glimpse of clear bright heaven again and the holy sparkling stars which gazed down on all poor earth-trampling men.

Soon they were lost again. Birdseye now began to curse his fool compass. It was an old Negretti & Zambra (London) with a silvered bearing ring and a smart brass manual transit lock and finger brake on one side, measuring 50mm in diameter, with a heavy beveled crystal. But, dammit, had its leather case gone and *leaked*? As with his telescope, a plumb bob, and a trumpet that he had brought along (to blow—how vain! how ironic!—upon success) in the relentlessly sticky, watery, sodden, maddeningly irriguous climate there, meant for snakes alone, the brass of the once proud compass had turned part turquoise. Ammonia badly interfered with and played havoc on any brass everywhere, a hazard he should have foreseen. Thaumarchaeal ammonia oxidizers in tropical rainforest soils are well known. It was something that *he* should have known as a competent leader.

He chastised himself in failing to husband his equipment properly. A cursed compass reacts weirdly near geomagnetic anomalies, he realized, works poorly in vehicles when not adjusted properly, becomes virtually useless when proximate with steel, and boggles near igneous rock. He harshly rubbed the open face of the compass with a large green monstera leaf and shook it. So enfeebled was it, he wanted in his wrath to bite the useless gizmo in half! He rattled it, hard, cursing, "Stinking pelorus!"

A magnetic compass, it dawned on him in his grief, is nothing but a greatly overrated navigational tool. Stellar navigation worked so much better. Even the wily Vikings did not depend on such contraptions on sea travel but wisely used sunstones, which could track the sun even on dark, overcast days. Huffing an inhalant of despair, Captain Birdseye wound up and, with a panfurious half-volley like an overpitched cricket ball, went flinging the feckless piece of equipment into the middle of a desperate demon-black tropical lake while screaming out loud so maniacally into the high rims of a bustling forest—a green hell of sopping wet cacaos, kapoks, rubber trees, freijos and jenny-woods, balsas, and açaí palms—that flocks of outraged great blue turacos went flapping angrily into the disarming boom of the echo and kept on flying.

What can I depend on now? he asked himself. Confabulate with the tropical and sidereal zodiacs? Consult Raphael's *Ephemeris*? Peruse some grimoire like Robert Cross Smith's *The Philosophical Merlin*? Get down on my knees and, forgetting all my dignity, kowtow to Apu-punchau, the Inca sun God?

Should I divide the horizon into thirty-two points, as the Arabs and Polynesians did, he wondered, crucial points that were derived from fifteen significant stars which rose at approximately equally spaced points of the eastern horizon? The setting points of these stars on the western horizon gave them another fifteen points and north and south brought the total to thirty-two. But the sky down here was murk, mist floated through the jungle like a spray, and drizzling clouds let nothing at all be seen.

"I will henceforth proceed by dead reckoning," vowed the Captain, chin out, eyes diamond-crazy, "which does not depend on any outside force or signal. I will follow the heat of my beating heart. I will navigate by the brain of my raised thumb! 'Cease, cease, wayward Mortal! Shall I unveil,'" the Captain whispered, misquoting Percy Shelley, while choosing a bleak interlude to play with words, "'The shadows that float o'er Eternity's vale.'"

He stared pathetically at his hand and the slubbered wedding ring that faithfully he still wore, now a victim of raw-water, its alloys also leached by dezincification, corroded and reductively left a porous copper shell that barely retained its oval shape—a zero, a cipher, nothing, nil, naught. It alone seemed to mock his futility in the worst way and stood as a stark parallel to the loss of his one small photograph of Margot, framed in Benares brocade (inscribed "Jeremy Mine"), that, splitting, abrading in the first weeks, he chose to scrap, as it had turned to wood samp.

By now he had stopped shaving. He took his once gleaming trusty Mappin & Webb straight razor, ground in Hamburg, friend in the morning and on this perilous expedition as much a counted-upon pal as ever he had in his entire life, and, with a sigh, set it passively down on a nearby rock. It was a symbolic act in which he embraced the unknown. He then walked, step by step, into the uncertain future following his shadow, desperado of his unshaven self. The mesquite flour or meat lozenges he had been eating all along began moiling in his innards and now as a last resort he had to fall back on using wild rhubarb as a laxative.

He spied by a stream bed a deserted cayuka laden with scrap rubber and, taking some, carved out rubber flanges in an attempt to make crude flaring shoes for the bearers for tramping across scarred black ravines. *Pour comble de malchance*, they put them to no use whatsoever. One nincompoop biting the rubber tried to eat it! That was not odd, as utterly unwholesome articles—bugs, moth pods, even the fierce, aggressive, predatory foraging marabunta—they greedily devoured. Other bearers yanked and pulled pieces of rubber over their heads or wagged it in front of their groins like codpieces with loud guffaws of derisive laughter and, bouncing, squealed, "*Caucho chota!*" "*Pipi!*" "*Cabeza de gato!*" "*Pinto!*" "*Paronga!*"

Loyalty had flown. Birdseye's perpetual banging on about the black orchid impressed the bearers not a whit anymore. They had all become a cluster of buffoons and, having grown rebellious, completely undependable. The captain's temper grew short as a candlewick, and where formerly his fortitude had given balance to their trek, now it was all impatience and restiveness. Looking into the heads of these Hottentots to ascertain the nature of their psychosymptomatological disorders was beyond him. It was too exacting to try to probe such staggering stupidity.

§

Down now into a green valley, they stumbled unwittingly upon a bald and elfin creature in rags, a likely dement— at least the fellow looked half barmy—who leapt back in sudden fright. Captain Birdseye, himself wary, had a hand on his knife. A Gemini, he knew, will die by making friends with the wrong person—readily insisting he has excellent intuition, his trust is often misplaced. The man seemed unstrung merely to see people at all and, backing up out of fear and anxiety, began mewing, making fluky motions toward them. "Are you a *Strafexpedition?* A punitive excursion—come to punish me?" he managed to utter as he shuffled even further rearward into a tree, which he fearfully back-clutched. He was of German nationality, it turned out, wore a cone hat, and was living all alone in a hut in the jungle and apparently working on a dictionary of a previously uncontacted Amazon tribe called the Asháninka. He kept medicine bundles. Around his neck, he wore a pouch containing a bag of coca leaves. His long probing fingers were black with dirt. He had been in the process of slurping up with a scoop from a poorly hewn bowl what looked like a ghastly concoction of tidal pool ceviche, wiping white foam from his mouth. He had been munching on some flowers, as well.

There were the rudiments of graves on a hill. White ants had eaten most of the crosses, now covered with wild jungle overgrowth. Turtle skulls lay about, the empty carapaces and whacked plastrons of the poor beasts scratched, their broken scutes and peculiar bones lying about everywhere. It was an abattoir. Knives of Bengal bamboo lay about, shaved into diamond-hard points.

The old man havered at the interruption, blinking as if in disbelief, holding out a flat hand as he peered fearfully through the slants of light.

But Captain Birdseye had turned his attention elsewhere as he gazed about to discover with no small amazement and epiphanic delight many rare plants and species—love beans, sinister sundews, fat dragon lilies, one a scarce variation of sugilite-purple *Dracunculus vulgaris* whose abrasive, mordant, caustic juices he fully believed contained a tuberculosicide—amazing!

He sniffed the air roots of the beautiful flower and delicately fingered its graceful nodes and stakes. Hybrid plants are sterile when they have the incorrect number of chromosomes, which results from polyploidy. If a plant has an uneven number of chromosome pairs, it cannot produce balanced gametes—egg or sperm cells—and will not be able to produce viable offspring. The explorer leaned to kiss the inflorescence. "You exhibit a unique reproductive strategy, don't you.my child?" he whispered, smiling. While most flowers spread their pollen to other plants, an orchid is extremely exclusive and only mates with itself. This method of self-pollination, which comes in handy when blowing winds are clement or light or insects lacking, adds to the variety of mechanisms flowering plants have evolved to ensure success.

But this was not his mission, sadly, that was not his goal. He had strictly one objective. Anything else would be to him as pointless and as purposeless as trying to feed hay to a goose. He was not even tempted to consider worthwhile or give more than a glance to one rare orchid he saw, genus *Dracula*, which, abbreviated as "Drac" in horticultural trade, consisted of 118 species native to Mexico, Colombia, Ecuador and Peru, and which in several species showed long spurs of the sepals—unfortunately, a blood-red color.

He knew from scientific recall that no such flower had been listed in Darwin's *Contrivances*, so it was rare, but, again, much as he loved to find that gem, along with so many glorious six-petaled, star-shaped orchids all beckoning to entice swirling clouds of nectar-mad hawkmoths, sphinx moths and sap-feeding butterflies, his hunt was for something entirely else.

Poor dear gentle man, he stopped to tickle the engaging spiral hoop of a slipper orchid, smiling, as he sang with a lilt,

> *"Tepals and sepals and petals*
> *all my aching heart unsettles . . ."*

for well he knew the segment of the outer whorl in a flower has no differentiation between petals and sepals.

Looking closer, he could not help noticing by a stool a pile of gorgeous purple-and-white karma orchids, along with a hibiscus or two, those along with some sweet sentimental amaryllis bulbs, all edible he knew. "We are harmless explorers in search of the rare black orchid," explained Capain Birdseye to this odd creature in the pointed hat, trying to disabuse him of any curious notions. "*Schwarze Orchidee? Sort orkidé?*" He helpfully wangled two fingers under his nose to imitate the joy of smelling. "*Orquídea negra? Orchidée noire? In Swahili, nyeusi orchid?*"

The solitary man was way ahead of him and knew what he meant, as he held up one of the karma orchids. He then timidly offered the Captain water from a scoop. It was the carapace of giant shelled yellow-footed tortoise. Said the bald man, "I've seen one or two *im Becken*, um, in the Basin, *ja*."

"Yes?"

"*Sechszehn* sixteen or so years ago," he stated, removing his cone hat and nodding agreeably. Green scutes were the spoons he was using. "Orghids *und* bromeliads," he clucked, "egploit twees *und* plants to zeek *Sonnonlicht, verstehst du?* Zey gwow *hoch* hanging onto ze branches *oder* twee trunks *mit* aerial roots, not as parasites—"

"—but as epiphytes, I understand, I know," interjected Birdseye, impatiently. "But where are they, man, where the deuce *are* they?" Chastened but trying to be helpful, the man offered some turtle meat, extending a shaking hand that held an object dripping green sludge. "Try a gobbet?"

The Captain gracefully forswore the offer, hoping soon to link up with the stockpile supply awaiting them. The expedition relied on depot-laying. A cache of tinned food (dry sauces, soups, puddings, etc.) was to be waiting for them at Los Islas de los Monos, along with—he had expectantly kept the list in his pocket—a case of dietetic sherry; Pouley's malt-bread, Leslie's Patent Plaisters (in a caddy); boxes of Blanchard's Iodide of Iron Pills; Aerated Lithia Water; Young & Postem's Bismuth, Pepsine, and Steel; Hartin's Crimson Salt; bottles of Aroud's Ferruginous Wine (with Cinchona & Extract of Meat); a favorite ventilated waterproof coat that he thought he might need; and no doubt an escalating pile of mail.

It turned out that all the goods had all been stolen, except for a case of carbonated fruit drinks in cobalt-colored Codd-neck bottles under a bush the thieves overlooked. The type of bottle had a closing design based on a glass marble which is held against a rubber seal, which sits within a recess in the lip.

Unfortunately, while Birdseye slept that night, his bearers, taking the glass balls for rare fruit, opened the bottles, poured out the contents, and were found in the morning sucking the marbles and clicking them in their cheeks and grinning!

A last hope had been thwarted. He almost broke down looking at the broken wooden case and several empty hampers. How all along he had relished the growing idea of having one great breakfast. Was that asking too much after all of his travails? He closed his eyes and reverted in memory to a vision of a groaning breakfast table—a well-filled egg-stand, a small steaming bowl of frumenty. Bloaters! Buttered eggs aux crevettes or poached eggs à la crème, hashed mutton, roast larks, plates of cold galantines-in-aspic, some fresh devilled kidneys, or, better, a sheep kidney split in half, some pickled walnuts—although Margot always raised a hornet's nest about their odor—oh, and a marvelous Bradenham ham, recognizable for its coal-black outside, which he relished for its exclusive sweetness. (His wife, on the other hand, typically preferred a Wiltshire ham, which, he knew, was technically gammon and didn't last long as other hams.) And what about a delicious game pie?

He looked wistfully at the hamper—bare to the wainscot.

So much for his dreams.

He was as thin as an empty apology.

Once into the depths of the interior the Cholo halfbreeds grew restless and began ominously murmuring. "*Wiwi!* *Wiwi!*" one of them screamed, bouncing in a squat and pointing desperately to a chain of distant smoke-holes. It was the Valley of the Inca Kings, a place where, while supposedly cursed, orchids yet profused. But when the Captain trekked in—

—the frightened bearers all bolted, except one, but in his extreme hunger he had mistakenly partaken of something foul and, clutching his neck, he jumped headlong and fatally into a driving waterfall. What had he eaten, physic nut? Devil's apple? Castor bean? Diseased ceviche?

"Shagbags!" railed Captain Birdseye. "Spit-dribblers! Low-bred, smelly-bottomed, arse-grabbing quisbies I was given!"

Tears came to his eyes, for the first time.

§

Captain Birdseye, now all alone, got lost in an intervening swamp and was virtually bitten blue by bushmasters, termites, and motuca flies in pursuit of what turned out to be merely common twayblades and pegonias, grasspinks and arethusa, specimens that could be had for a tuppence from any florist in Cattrick, Portwrinkle, or Elmers End. Anteaters with hideous worm tongues rumble-scuttled past his feet looking for prey or sanctuary. But who was it who exposed the creatures? The poor Captain it was who, when idly overturning a log, believing that he had spied scuttling underneath a rare *Ophrys ariadnae*, uncovered an angry army on the march of fierce bullet ants, small club-shaped *hormiga* so predatory and fiercely unflagging that they will furiously snap-bite even into the flame of a match until consumed by it.

One of the enraged pismires stung him, inducing immediately such a hot crippling agony, the toxins blinding him with fierce, shockingly purple-electric pain, that he instantly fell over with an outrageous howl and lay trembling, utterly nauseated, and sweating as he started to drool white. The toxic venom alters voltage-gated sodium channels in neurons, causing the nerve cells to go haywire. The expedition was long out of bandages, he found. He employed instead bog plants, the fluffy material of which when dried absorbed twenty times their weight in water. But he suffered two full days of pain and an index finger on his left gand that had turned red as burning coal.

Most ants inhabited the world of the jungle, he knew, where in teeming horror there are almost 2½ billion to the square mile. He knew very well of the insect sting and animal bite. He had previously been bitten by an agouti, its front teeth chisel-sharp, when he was trying to grab a Brazil nut that had fallen from a towering bertholletia tree, but the ant pain was worse. His finger trembled as he tried to shake off the ant that got stuck by its bite, fanning the red-hot pain.

Captain Birdseye checked the map. There was portentously only white space, where no one else had gone. He ran his throbbing finger down various coordinates. Sheer pain. All open area. Unpenetrated jungle. Virgin territory. Was he in the area of cannibal headhunters? Nori carnivores? Yora anthropophages? Uncontacted Matsigenka? Sacrificing priests outfitted in macaw feathers and beads who tore out the hearts of living bodies all jumping rabid to eat the still-thumping meal they called "precious eagle cactus-fruit," only to dance in the victim's flayed skin? What about black caiman, electric eels, wandering spiders, poison dart frogs? Steel-toothed piranhas, which have one of the most forceful bites among all living vertebrates?

He fought through layers of bush, walked under rainforest canopies, and threaded his forlorn way in and out of meandering dark forest floors, as sunless as tunnels, at which point he could proceed in no way without his machete, negotiating a waist-high pandemonium of vicious barbed lawyer vines, climbing cowhage, and creeper vines. The wound on his groin began to ache in the relentless dampness, but he fully refused to give up, for his manhood was at stake.

Dry beds that he now traversed told him that he had taken another wrong turn, four days wasted looking for what he imagined to be a valuable cut-off, and in a long peninsula of desert he discovered with the bite of the sun that he had filled his canteen with foul water. He found and sucked dew from some pitcher plants, careful that he ingested no sap that was milky, red, yellow, or bitter. His finger badly ached. He smashed some roots into a pulp, which he strained through one of his socks filled with charcoal from a fire he made to sterilize it but collected little moisture. He cut back into some greenery to try to find some bamboo to cut open for even a drop.

He became desperately thirsty. He found a few sticks of wild celery he sucked but still felt parched. Where no water was to be found, he knew foliage in the jungle is largely made of water, so he slit some vines and tongued them for some relief and then twisted some leaves to funnel out water drops and then patiently sat and drip-drooled water drops off some cinchona leaves he pulled down and lapped at and even sucked the bark for quinine. As moisture from the earth will condense on the bottom of viscose silk, he took the time to set up a container under such a piece as he slept, which helped. As he trekked on, he found running water.

Snap to! he thought. Had he not read how, facing an open wound, the dauntless Humboldt, prompted to do so, rejoiced at the opportunity to dip his fingers into his blood and draw figures on his skin? Fine, except that the Captain's right forefinger was still frozen with injecta from insect poison.

It was his luck in the deepest interior where it seemed no human had ever penetrated to come across—out of the blue—a crazy-wild shaman with gristle-green needlepoint eyes sitting up in a half tree who, in exchange for a dirty bedroll and one shiny bullet, served him up—what was it, banana beer? Some sort of sacred masato? It turned out to be cups of iowaska, or *yagé*, an entheogenic brew—and spiritual drink—made out of the *Banisteriopsis caapi* vine and other drug ingredients that were used in ceremonies among the indigenous people of the interior Amazon. This may have been a mistake, one of his gravest, for the drink was mixed with the leaves of the *Psychotria viridus* (chacruna) or *chagropanga* or *mimosa tenuiflora* rootbark. Top-heavy high, Birdseye began crazily nipping ayahuasca vines, which for portability he looped around his arms to carry as he went wandering about helter skelter, eventually threading his way through a ghastly nightmare that lasted a full week, his having come to, shivering, pale-white with a lapsed memory, only after being ministered a sip of black tea—he turned yellow and his stomach was washing about like a snipe-bog—that was concocted from ilex (holly) leaves and some other herbs to induce vomiting.

Months went by.

Soon, he had come into higher elevations, where temperatures fell. He was often shrammed to the bone from cold, his shoes split, and colocasia leaves now had to be used for eating, clothing, and, now, absterging the podex, a last resort, for in matters of anal hygiene he had already been driven out of desperation to employ the last stiff pages of volume three that he had managed to save—with only scraps left—of Humbolt's *Per-*

sonal Narrative for such use. Captain Birdseye was only a shadow of his former self. His thin grey arms looked like two broken pencils. Look at me! he thought, He saw himself an open-mouthed fool, realizing that, along with optimism, a Gemini is passively directed, with a spirit never fully mastered.

Winds blew fiercely at night, watering his eyes—or were they perchance his own remorseful tears?—and inexplicably bringing to him the faint sounds and echoes of shoveling—was it for his grave? Should he kill himself? It seemed extreme, but had he not once read somewhere that suicide consecrates character?

At one point, so hungry, he mouth-gulped a moth that had fluttered onto his knuckles, failing to recall that Charles Darwin had once almost died by putting an insect in his mouth. Amazonian butterflies and bees, he knew, drank the tears of turtles. Were there moths that feed on human tears?

He was starving. In a haze of regretful memory, he recalled a vacation in Ness, Scotland, when a young boy, visiting an aunt, she had served him a meal of young gannet, which in those parts are called "guga," and how cruelly he had petulantly refused to look at it, never mind eat it. Oh, the folly! The fateful foolishness! Would he start losing his mind and, crackpated, find himself doomed now to go munching grass in the fields like the demented Babylonian King Nabuchadnezzar?

Constipated, Captain Birdseye's attempts to evacuate made his rump raw and the heat worsened it. Unguents might have helped to relieve it, but he had none. He tried slippery elm as an emollient, echinacea. He needed glycerine. A humectant. He attempted pressing a stone into his intergluteal cleft, but it hurt.

Finally, to cool his buttocks, he took his Golden Jubilee

Crown and carefully pressed it in. It brought some relief.
No queen had ever been embraced so well.

§

His only food now was bread kneaded with rainwater. No more butter upon bacon anymore. Realizing that he was going belly-up, the wistful captain opened up his trusty coromandel, took out a Beaconsfield crystal goblet, and drained a refreshing glass of absinthe, neat, an act called "smothering a parrot." The intoxication gave him relief. Except that he drank nothing: he had merely imagined it. It was a hallucination. He sat down on a piece of corrugated iron, pondering how little it had served a remedy for his woes.

The undertaking had by now become iniquitous. For sanity's sake, he set himself the task of doing difficult sums in his head. What for instance, he asked himself, was the square of 365,365,365,365,365,365?

133,491,850,208,566,925,016,658,299,941,583,224, it occurred to him. (He was, alas, one figure shy.)

Sitting in trees by night, he once peered over and, in all seriousness, proceeded to ask a proximate jackdaw, "Are you the orchid?"

That was normal?

At Puerto Maldonado, some time later, he shakily wrote in his journal with the tip of a wet lucifer, "I love the delicacies from Fortnum and Mason that the blessed angel sent to me." This was the first actual sign of his incipient derangement. Madness came upon him like the shadow of an uncalculated eclipse over an ill-prepared and unsuspecting planet, the fearful sweep of an inexplicable black wave across empty space darkening down under the gloom of calamity the mind of a good man. There was nothing to eat anywhere, except for a spoonful he found left in his jar of Shippam's Bloater Paste, which he gobbled down, although it had long gone eerie. He found himself one morning amorously rubbing a tent pole, smooth as poplar, as if it were the limb of a "charity girl" from a Blackpool music hall. Curiously, the human brain itself is the only organ we possess that does not tell you that it is malfunctioning.

He then began to suck his thumb and do unpredictable things—

—wandering the sky-high slopes of the tortuga-green mountains, crazily skipping about, and singing evangelical hymns at the top of his lungs. It was suddenly at 23,000 feet above sea-level when he saw it.

But wait—

There over his head just above a mere inch of ledge on the side of a deep precipitous gorge, affixed indifferently to a bare rock and fluttering in the wind, was a single velvety variation of *Coelogyne pandurata,* its calyx, corolla, and sheathing leaves of uniform color. A gleam of pardonable avarice shone in his eyes.

He could see, it loved shadow and even cold temperature. It was three-petaled with a fertile stamen and looked almost suspended in mid-air with an inricate, fluttering pouched lip— like God's chin! How had it come to be? Had it been somehow cross-fertilized? Irradiated by a meteor?

Captain Birdseye, goggling, sat there unable to move. Finally, looking down, he had to tell his fingers one by one: let go.

The orchid was as black as your hat.

He began giggling and slapping at his mouth. He swung out on a manual traverse and inched along by his fingertips, his feet dangling above the vast emptiness below. He paused a moment when it was at nose-level, reached for it with a shout of brief, but manly, triumph—then ate it!

It tasted, he thought, like vanilla, but it wasn't nourishing enough by half, poor thing, for him to keep his grip.

§

Queen Victoria, just before she died, knighted him *in absentia*, and as the only remaining family, his wife, who had been tendered an annual stipend in perpetuity in his name, while accepting for him a posthumous C.B.E., was also allowed to add a crocodile and hippo to their coat of arms. If the *Times* obituary of 1894 wrote down his last doomed undertaking to an excess of eccentric optimism and an uncommon if off-center sense of determination—explorations in general having led him, as indeed they had led other brave and intrepid late Victorian visionaries and adventurers before him, into the extremes of danger and, indeed, death—let the world judge him indulgently as one never cowed by a want of imagination.

A stalwart, he braved no end of mystery and allowed himself few self-deceptions. In his honor and with seemly probity, Margot commemorially had planted on a rising hill overlooking their largest pond by a hexagonal pavilion in the shape of a monopteros, a Roman temple, a crape myrtle (*Lagerstroemia fauriei*), widely acclaimed for its upright habit, ranging from ten to thirty feet, and also for its rich foliage that matured by clockwork from reddish-bronze to green, then to red and yellow in fall.

With its stunning bark, it was known to send out a riot of roots reaching in all directions, and in that it seemed particularly fitting for a noble and intrepid man with an out-stretched grasp. Alas, it died to the ground that winter.

A monument to the explorer, in Drowsimere, was later erected. Margot, in weeds, cut the ribbon.

A Christmas Fable

It was the very dead of winter in England, the Advent season, in the year of our Lord 1861.

Little Nicholas Bell, forlornly watching from a high barred window of the orphanage as snowflakes fell, wiped a tear from his eye as he thought of his dear mother lying in the cold London cemetery.

There had been no joy in her all-too-brief life after her husband was shot in the Indian Mutiny in 1858. The family estate, virtually falling to ruin, might just as well have, for another man appeared in her life suddenly, one who despite her Catholicism (which he loathed) coveted her money—her gentleness and her extraordinary beauty perforce being only subsidiary factors in the calculating courtship that eventually led to the brief marriage in which, it turned out, she proved less durable than he cruel. Upon her death, flatly refusing any further responsibility for the boy, he had sent him away to a school specifically chosen for its remoteness.

Several years passed.

Now it must be understood that all institutions in those dark Victorian days seemed hard and empty, for it was an age, at bottom, informed by disbelief and doubt, when the hollow doctrine of faith alone turned its back upon the necessity of good works, and the result allowed for the continuance of brutal self-interest, economic exploitation, and the smug supremacy of conduct over charity—the century's last firefly flicker of hope. And so it fell out with our little hero.

He was a beautiful boy—a mere twelve years old—who looked like a younger version of the *Athlete with a Strigil* by Lysippos in the Vatican Collection. But now he wore rags and his hands were whip-thin.

The Thrupenny School, in mood remindful of a catafalque and in fact a huge fairly windowless Gothic manor rising to three turrets with iron-roof cresting, sloping dormers, several crow-stepped gables, and large chimney pots, was a solitary workhouse in Goose Green, Yorkshire—an orphanage of the rigorous and severe type, Methodist in persuasion, with no escape beyond a wide cobble-stoned courtyard and severe grounds surrounded by high-walls and one large forbidding cast-iron gate by way of entrance. There were roof parapets where owls perched. It was a large, ugly monster of a building-pile built of unforgiving whinstone, dark-colored rock, standing at the far end, miles away, of the solitary bleak road that led to the place through a lost dark forest of forbidding black locusts, unlovely silhouettes, with no symmetry, only a timberwood of dead, ragged shadowy vestiges like troops of an old and unnatural alien army, its grim soldiery bent with gnarled fingers, thorny in bark, their buds sunk into the very bark of the twigs as if afraid themselves.

Water meadows across the hills were grey. Tidal marshes which flooded and ebbed twice a day, gave off an odor, and its fumes rusted the broken gates and kept the slates greasy. A blind man sweeping a white cane before him supposedly haunted the top floor. Rumors abounded about him. Was it a ghost? A mad uncle who was a former owner? A dead Gypsy?

There was an enclosed schoolyard, a tiny compact field of century-old mud-grime packed hard, where on very rare occasions the boys were allowed out for free-time to play games of "hailes," a cross between shinty and lacrosse, when the roistering upper bullies in the name of fun beat and mauled the lower boys. It bothered him. He was physically timid and broomstick thin. Sometimes they had rope-tugs and pulls, with high injury risk, or matches of slam-daddles or maffeking, which became punching outings, and in surly cliques they even sang songs like

"Up the close and down the stair
But and ben wi' Burke and Hare.
Burke's the butcher, Hare's the thief,
Knox the boy what buys the beef"

and

"The school's your mother
like father, sister, brother
Don't go looking for love
But to the blue sky above"

A set of bleak outlying wooden sheds, roofed with staggered shakes, housing old rakes, spades, trowels, and hoes sat out back as if deserted. A reminder that there was a larger world came twice a day, at five o'clock in the morning when the dustman's horse cart came noisily rattling through the single arched front gate to pick up the rubbish and later in the day, as it rumbled back to drop off the empties, whence came the creaking sound of a handbrake and the frenetic noise of the many barrels being punted off. It was a bleak time. Weather seemed often precarious. Mizzles or light mists in the morning always gave way to sudden bursts of rain, torrents, pouring down buckets, slashing onto the ragged roof slates, racing out of the gutters, a ravesdrip here and there, battering the windows and sheeting down into the dirty streets.

A colportaging group of zealous Bible distributors, the Society for Open-Air Preaching, also occasionally stopped by the orphanage with the purpose of leaving copies of the Bible, which the Grottlesexes used—stacking them up—for seats for the smaller boys toward the far end of the long greasy tables. They could not have cared less about having them read or understood or heeded.

It was an unlighted network of corridors inside, a great box-set of dark stairways, forbidding rooms, long passageways, rotten floors, and coffin-black work desks set in rows under a thick hammer-beam roof in the lower hall. None of the chimneys had been swept. Hall passages were as cold as icy caverns and black with age. Tall windows were shut tight, a fetor in the rooms fuggy from old coal fires. The dark, hooded refectory was composed of one long extended room, scoped along each length with long trestle tables and rows of benches. A broadsheet framed in black wooden struts ominously hung by the refectory door enumerating the school rules along with a list of terrible punishments awaiting any such transgressors who should choose to brook them.

A stark wooden staircase with a series of ribbed and twisted turns, square newels, and wide black steps, its creaking wood never lit with so much as a gleam of polish or a hint of style, rose in weird spirals to several private rooms which the orphams, banned from any ascension, never saw. A steep drop of break-neck stairs led below to a dank, drippy basement that reeked of mice, damp, and the sour odor of gas like bad cabbage.

In a bleak side room off the main hall, a horseshoe figure of chairs, with an Anglican hymnbook sitting on a raised lectern at the open end, stood, awaiting any who entered the prem-ises there. Held here were biweekly Bible readings. Sometimes hymns were sung in the early morning, to stave off hunger, when through high broken windows above one could manage to see, looking down with pity, the cold moon in the sky. Subterranean juniors revolved around the room handing out hymnbooks.

Religion was not be discounted there. Its guidelines were ordinance, its tenets mouthed at every turn. Whatever was not compulsory was forbidden. Rules were binding, promptness mandatory. In the refectory, at table, part of the grace, a Victo-rian entreaty, was invoked by the boys:

> *"Look thou be curious standing at meat,*
> *And what men giveth thee, take and eat,*
> *And look thou neither cry nor crave;*
> *Saying that and that would I have!*
> *But stand thou still before the board*
> *And look thou speak no loud word."*

Over the arch hung a sign in fading black letters: *Peace on Earth, Good Will Towards Men.* The words to most of the poor boys seemed peculiar, for the place was run by a black-hearted couple called the Grottlesexes: she an evil-smelling, havering old woman with fists like powercats—she always had a drop at the end of her nose—and he a great drum-bellied bully who was given to clawing at his lampshadeish hair and forever screeching, "I'll snap their noses off!"

He despised the orphans.

The distaff half, even more so.

The two barged to and fro about the ice-cold rooms, Grottlesex often with trowels, shears, and twine, his wife in a wide black apron that seemed to girdle the woman like devil wings and her ugly slat-bonnet with its deep brim and long bavolet like a curtain at the back that seemed to function less as a protection of her face and neck from the harsh elements than horribly to keep them within. The old wife, who had hideously red ears, perennially hideously red ears, harbored a strip-jack-naked craving to beat to the nines any of those children who might balk at any order gave. Hunger was commonplace there. She had several spy holes and was forever racing from one to another to collar someone taking an apple or licking a smidgen of sauce from a used bowl.

Subservience was the school rule. Once she discovered Nicholas standing halfway through a doorway, lost for all the many rooms to be negotiated. With her battered face armored shut, her eyes fierce and wary, and her red ears judding and alert in their pointed way as close to nastiness as she could make them, she lashed out and execrated the young boy, howling, "You, again, charity boy? You thieving octopus, you stink monster, you impish scag, what do you do there poking about"

Nicholas, terrified, went mute.

"Don't you hear me, you impignorating little scoundrel? Not a nail is driven here I don't see, not a single bap thieved!"

The boy quaked.

"Do you *heeeeed* me?"

"Yes, ma'am, please, ma'am"

"Wasn't I just in the kitchens, where the meat screens are filthy?" bellowed the woman from a big red mouth, flying into a fit of rage. She was a Scot and had a brogue and wielded a birch the size of a garden broom and ordered the boy to his trundle without dinner. Sometimes for extreme disobedience she much preferred to abuse a boy with a clacken, her long-handled bat with a flattened spoon-like tip. It mauled and could break bones. "But first go wash the fricandeau pans, see to the crusty gridirons, naphead, all of them! Then go scrub the bottle jacks and wheels, and if I see a spot of fat or grease anywhere, I will squirrel ye right up the arse with a filthy fishwhip! Clean the turbot kettles! The grip broilers! The milk jugs! The cutlery stinks of damp! Wemble the basins and saucepans! Succuss them filthy bottles of dirt and pissy grime! Deterge the toilets! Put ammonia in the mop water!"

The school's bustle was formidable. There was no end to the demands of work to do. Grottlesex himself would join in the harangues. "I seen ye blowing wax over the tables when ye put the candles out! I caught you paring a candle, like an arse monkey! Polish the pewter right! Scrub the table with salt! Brush 'em! Use silversmith's rouge on Mistress Grottlesex's silver, you stinking malapert, not plate powder! Ain' you git a brain? Mess up, I tell you, and I'll stew your own feet off you!"

Later, for his punishment, a wooden donkey's halter was hung around his neck as he knelt in disgrace at the refectory doorway during six consecutive meals while everybody passed by in procession, and they tawsed him with a thick leather strap.

Seeing him on the sill, Grottlesex bellowed, "Stick a dunce cap on the blighter for dessert. Take him to the tool barn and hang him from the brick lintel in the rain—will do 'im good!"

Sometimes they were sentenced to leave the school property—"to go to Brickendonbury Park," was the phrase—which involved being shunned. Across the way, to the side of a hill was the black expanse so named, half-field, half-thicket, although the park was purely notional. An old marketplace ages ago, it was now a deserted brick field, a chaos of rank grass, strewn with broken crockery, builder's rubble, and a tall split black fence that rose at one end with the look of a gibbet. Sentenced to go there meant a day of brooding and pointless reflection for a crime.

There were duties: molding candles, scrubbing sinks with lye, cutting hair, airing clothes, making green soap, handwashing sheets, polishing copper, gathering winter fuel, and having to pray incessantly in the ice-cold daily chapel during those long hours of kneeling forced on them for their small acts of ungratefulness Grottlesex invariably snooped out. He often gave an extra biscuit to the older boys who peached on the younger ones. There was Nailrod who was demented. And Tuckticket, who shoplifted baps and smoked birdwoods in the toilets. A mean boy named Abrumpo who, with a stone, put out the eye of Freddy Breadsauce.

The worst of them, Needix, a cruel boy with a dumbbell wit and bent shoes and nicknamed "Crocodile" for his wide mouth, especially reviled Nicholas, with whom he toyed constantly, even accusing him once to Master and Matron of making a Catholic grace (a papistical excess!) involving the Sign of the Cross. It was a harsh way of life in a very harsh world. At the time England was governed solely by the landowning class, five percent of the population owned eighty percent of the land. In the small foul-smelling towns, streets were filled with horse dung, sloughs of mud, and rubbish. Rain never fell without wet cinders, leaving infestations of heavy, dun-colored fogs. Everywhere were Dissenter's Chapels, ink-black canals, polluted rivers, factories belching smoke, coal mines, and squalid and notorious slums.

In the crowded dorm room, boys snored but Nicholas in his trundle bed never slept well, scrunched into a ball as he always was, thinking reverently of his dear mother and of his brave long-dead father. He was a sensitive and fully imaginative young boy, filled with moving dreams like high clouds, the only things left to him in his life, and by those personal visions of guesses and suppositions, beliefs, conjectures, and surmises was the way he shaped the world, in spite of the way life had fallen out for him. At night, he often heard rats in the eaves, chewing.

No end of fears crowded his mind. What of that blind man sweeping a white cane before him that supposedly haunted the top floor? Early every morning, he would jerk up from sleep, a pang of anticipation in his throat.

On his wall Grottlesex kept an array of favorite canes—rattans, malaccas, green ferrules, a rod, whipjacks, pliant sticks, rowan branches, several birches, witches' ashes, and a sharp menacing hickory. It was his hawthorn stick that truly made them howl. He even had a blackthorn stick he treasured for walloping legs. The whips all shone wih the implicit promise of unseen terrors.

"Make a back!" howled Mr. Grottlesex, who then grabbed a random boy and snatching his long hawthorn stick from the Mrs., who snickered. "Make a back! And you, you filthy Romish puppy—" With that, one boy bent forward and Nicholas, falling helpless over him, was unmercifully caned. Grottlesex licked his lips with every whack and stroke. As he beat children, his mouth always widened in the act of flagellation into a scary open howl like a machicolation. Perversely, he somehow knew when to go to the edge of pain. The victim was then locked away for this soul's health in the terrible Grumbler's Scrimmage, a damp root cellar at the far end of the yard. Closing his eyes against the sad reality that crowded in on him, Nicholas spent long sick nights in the darkness drifting, dreaming, through the Land of Counterpane.

Punishments, in fact, were often indistinguishable from games: furious encounters without rules or mercy. The smaller boys were always run to exhaustion by the same praepositors who barged into the dormitory at 4:30 a.m., kicking the rats off the foot pans and trundles (where the boys slept huddled two and three to a bed) and screaming, "*Surgite!*" If anyone hesitated even briefly, Grottlesex was at him like a great wild mad panther on a young stag, crying, "I should wallop your eyes purple, you crusty whoreson little untidy Bartholomew boar-pigs!" He ranted up and down the corridors. "Where is the stinking little nestor what bunged up the outdoor faucet? The eyebrow windows positively are slubbered with fingerprints, you buggers, and the turret railings black wi' grime! Who filched out the front downstairs newel post, only to riddle a face on it? I'll bibble his arse off who did! Coxybobbers! Stench bugs!"

"Send the filthball to Brickendondbury Park!"

This from a fat, untidy churl with facial spots named Eugene Tauro, who was always compulsively twisting his white bullish hands in anticipation of the many woeful beatings he was called upon to administer. One of the worst praepositors, he was older, in his late teens, and worked as a hired prat for the Grottlesexes. A savage with all his hairy Pelasgic strength, he had a hard, scowling, discontented face and walked arrogantly about with a Lochgelly tawse, a leather strap with thongs like a serpent's tongue. The whips were notorious for their strength and tang when released with a slash. They were made in Lochgelly, Fife, the most popular factory design there, and slang for it among the boys was a "fife." Belting a boy over his head and legs was his Tauro's specialty whenever a boy did not stick out his hand.

"Fatch him proper!" screeched the slattern who accompanied him in his loud forays throughout the halls. "Mew him into the attic, board the weevil up proper, that he might think on his sins!" She was his dumpy, orange-haired wife named Dropo, a baggage who slavishly did all of his bidding. "Where are the other scapegraces?" Tauro would screech, spitting white. One morning he caught Snouse, one of the smaller boys, munching a turnip tip. "You nit! You lice!" he screeched. "You get-penny of brazen no importance! You filthy sowball! I'll unjangle your innards and drape them around your consternating skin!" Whereupon with his whipping fife he beat the boy across his hands until they were raw and ragged and red. The meals they were given in a refectory of long tables was basically mush porridge, which the flinty Grottlesexes dosed with treacle and a sulfur brimstone which had the advantage of both spoiling their appeties and being much cheaper than a lavish breakfast or dinner.

The lads went off to chapel one morning—all but Needix, who was sent out to cut down a Christmas tree. He returned with one, but not before lurking hours in the woods where, sucking his wrist—*Pweeus!*—to make the sound of a wren, he found a small bird and throwing a stone killed it.

For it was Christmas Eve, over all the earth a holy night, except, perhaps, for such places where church ordinance had established a custom obsequiously followed by the Grottlesexes: the "visitation" to the school by the Bishop of Yorkshire—a corrupt, vainglorious miter, haughty and be-ringed, who gave a sermon each year on the joy of poverty in a windy, booming voice.

"We are in for a ministerial favor by a holy prelate," announced Grottlesex at a hasty assembly in the dark refectory before bedtime, "and if I should have the occasion to learn of any base behavior by any one of you crippled and stippled, barge-brown river crabs, any abruption by some stinking, unwashed peeweevil, I shall shove that haddock into a dark closet until he expires!"

Work hours trebled for the visit. Nicholas Bell was put to making bread, but the yeast wouldn't take in the cold, resulting in a batch of misshapen loaves with flying tops, breakaway, rope and sourness. He tried to begin again, proofing the yeast in ice water, but someone kicked the pan away. Nicholas looked up forlornly, only to see a cold, menacing face looking down on him. The boy had merely dipped into the rude water to taste it with a small probing finger. "Is this the Barsham Fair, you gagging, manky sloven, you filthy slagging pillock?" screamed Grottlesex. Other boys came running and jeered, as did the howling Tauros.

"You dweeb," bellowed Grottlesex, out of conrol, "you stook-buzzing, mudlarking, snow-gathering, cat-and-kitten-hunting idler!" Crazy Dropo, clapping her swollen hands in delight, giggle-screamed, "Cleave his ears! Abrade his flesh! Pend off his nose! Discuss his headball! Beat his livers into a whelksoup! Vex the weasel! *Bash the little bastard's soul open!*"

The Christmas tree was torn down as a penalty.

The boys, who dreamt of treats like fairy cakes, sultanas, glace fruits, toffee and treacle, creamy profiteroles, fig pies, cheese tarts, Winster Wake cakes, pigs-in-the-blanket, lovely small dishes of eating sweet carlings, or peas soaked overnight, fried in butter, and seasoned with salt and pepper, generally subsisted on watery slumps, flatbreads, and gruel (leftovers were usually drained off into large duck-ended tins to be reused)—sometimes hard swedes and jacket potatoes were donated by a town charity—and yet for the forthcoming ecclesiastical visit Mother Grottlesex, assisted by her favorite Slinger as dogsbody, cooked a specialty: neck-of-mutton stew. Eugene Tauro and Dropo marshalled the boys into line to pray a grace.

It turned out there was only enough stew for the few older boys on the front benches, so the rest, not without a few disappointed murmers, had to wait to be served while everybody else ate and were handed down some leftover bowls of fowl-jelly, a wilted fish stick each, and white bread made from bolted wheat-flour. The prelate picked up the grumbling. "'What meaneth this bleating of the sheep?'" he inquired, making a face and quoting Samuel I, 15:14.

The Bishop with great relish ate five bowlfuls of the stew, inhaling the steam which he luxuriously wafted toward his nose with a fanning hand, and felt afterwards so sated and sleepy, patting his belly, that of the school's many faults he remarked nothing. Sucking his teeth, which he then picked with wood, he leaned over to the headmaster and pomped, "To win the young" —here he raised three fat fingers in succession—"there is persuasion, there is compulsion, there is seduction. Preaching at them all day is a hook without a worm. You can cajole, 'You must volunteer.' That is a wall of brick. You can warmly express to them

'You are needed.' Ah, but spirits seem to fail there," he burped. "So, which do you choose?"

"There is not more than three?"

The Bishop looked querulous.

Grottlesex, rubbing his hands over and over, squintily leered and looking to his wife for corrorboration, said, "The flail." He paused, his eyes glowing with newer, even more perverse delight. "*The flail!*"

Smiling, the Bishop nodded, "That hardly ever fails."

O rigid virtue! So much more in evidence than flexible vice!

It was then time to remove to the large hall for the petitions, with the Bishop at the front in cold attendance, a sovereign sight in manqué and gold, and the malevolent Grottlesexes glowering nearby. But first the orphans interrupted the tenor of our story, entwined their arms, and with their white faces upturned, in beautiful tones by which a certain sorrow was released, sang:

> *"Wassail, wassail, all over the town,*
> *Our toast it is white and our ale it is brown,*
> *Our bowl is made from the white maple tree:*
> *With a wassailing song we will sing to thee . . ."*

"Enough! Bash it! Put the cork in!" cried Grottlesex, loudly banging his cup. He didn't think pig-tracks of music. He called for the onlooking bishop and bowed him forward with pious deportment.

For the good of the boys' souls, the Bishop also bowed and offered a small homily, concluding with, "Man that is born of woman hath but a short time to live, and is full of misery. Expect nothing free in this world, else where would we be in this society in which you find yourself well-provided? Are you sinfully content with your lot? What troublous days await the heedlessly ungrateful! Double bitterness awaits that wicked and benighted creature who, for worldly gain—whether for a sinecure at Westminster or a sixpennyworth of scraped beef—puts himself beyond the reach of amendment. Sentiments of contrition alone right the delicate balance between you and your Maker, dear chaps and little fellows, without which you are taking advantage of His goodness. Learn to spread light."

Pausing to twiddle his pectoral cross, he gestured to the candle on the table before him. "How far that little candle throws his beams / Like a brave deed in a naughty world," he said, quoting Shakespeare. "God's benevolence demands your faith! Do not be like the heathen lad who denied Him. Do you know the tale? Two young boys were strolling together along a dreary by-road when, upon hearing the lonely peal of church bells from the small village of Sharrow Vale, they began to discuss the existence of God, which the good lad promptly asserted but which the other willfully denied, that is until God terminated the discourse with a terrible crash of lightning, causing an oak tree to fall on the unregenerate infidel's head! Shall that be you? Shall your soul be put in jeopardy by backsliding ignorance?

"Accept what the Lord in His benevolence has extended you! Work is your redemption, obedience your special blessing. Do you think that life is all Lindisfarne fudge and beach balls? Chelsea buns and sugar pigs? Farthing everlastings and liquorice pistols? Caraway comfits and carousel rides? Oatcakes and strawberries? Pear drops and la-de-da rides on English ponies on the Brighton pavilions? Hard-boiled rhubarb and custard sweets?

Gobstoppers ain't life!"

He paused before his chastened and shamed little flock the better that his words might sink in.

"No," he concluded solemnly. "No—nay, never, no more. Be only watchful, my dears, lest some dire affront be taken wherein, in some neglect, you prove yourselves to be numbered in that army of demons that jangle the chords of refinement. Better that you prove noble in your duty by glorifying that England to which Scott points in *Scenes of Infancy* 'where Eden's groves again shall bloom / beyond the desert of the tomb, / and living streams forever flow.'" Whereupon, pleased, satisfied, full of good fortune, the Bishop clapped his hands and motioned for each boy to be handed the annual penitential sheet of paper: the petitions.

Smirking Needix was chosen to revolve about the room with long wooden pens. The boys sat waiting to write, but while Mrs. Grottlesex was distributing bottles of ink, she noticed Nicholas Bell with a moon on his face, haunted by his solitude and by the lost shapes of his parents. She pinched his ear red. "How's this?" she nastily whispered. "Or shall I give the shell another turn of a twist, aye?"

Nicholas scooped up the tears from his grey eyes, but could think of nothing to write. It was forthwith noted that of all the petitions collected, only one was missing, Slinger pointed and whispered, "He wrote nothing." Mother Grottlesex made teeth and cried, "Not a thing?" And Grottlesex shouted, "Nothing written? You with a face like a pudding bag—you think you are the Mufti of Jerusalem?" Eugene Tauro, Needix, and Dropo grinned at each other, relishing it in dramatic delight. All the orphans lowered their heads as Nicholas was summoned forward.

"Where is your petition?" inquired the lordly Bishop, peering at the boy.

There was nothing but silence.

"Speak up!" he growled.

Eugene Tauro raised his menacing white hands over his head and snapped, "Let me at the snipe!"

"Crocodile" Needix rose in his bent shoes, and "I will step on his feet and make him scream like a widgeon!"

Grottlesex squeezed his cane. The hall echoed.

"Shambles of beastliness!" screamed both Grottlesexes. "Ashcats! Slop kettles! I will crack your cheeks like walnuts! Turn you darker than blue stone! I will have the bones hot from your flesh!"

"I have composed a petition," said Nicholas, voice inaudible.

Everyone turned—where was it? He had written nothing and had nothing in his hand but a pen.

No one dared breathe.

Nicholas Bell, as if having wept, having thought and having said farewell, the great change within him constant now, found suddenly fashioned in his soul a tiny belief—one like unto the strength in it beautiful but small surprise of Him conceived so long ago in Bethlehem (a belief giving motion to a perfection as serene, though grown out of imperfection), and, finding the courage to do so, carried his stool to a spot beneath the refectory arch and then reached up as far as he could.

Silently he crossed out two words with his pen and, adding as many, corrected the sign there to read: *Peace on Earth Towards Men of Good Will.*

The Irresolution
of Rachel Scroop

A maiden there was of a willful bent
that lived in the village of St. Marquise
who was sent into the forest to find
among many tall, well-formed trees

the straightest, seemliest branch of all
and directed to choose, cut, and carry off
that selected prize whose magical thrall
sent her unwedded heart soaring aloft.

She might, if so pleased, wandering through,
hold off her selection to the very end,
except that retracing her steps was taboo
wherever it was she decided to wend,

and not choosing a branch was forbidden.
Yet options were hers, nothing disguised,
no trick was involved, not a thing hidden—
that which she chose was thereby devised.

One further enjoinment she had to meet,
her choice must be made in the forest there:
alternatives rendered the task incomplete.
Handpick your branch, fair and square!

The noble trees were handsome and tall,
with branches elegant, straight, and true,
as on she walked with a vow not to stall
and so miss selecting a branch she'd rue.

She discovered, did Rachel Scroop,
among a range of different branches
in such an an endlessly manifold group
an astounding lot of possible chances,

that for the hard ask of singling out
one among many perfectly straight
—the passing time? a fig to flout!—
presented a treat of endless debate.

She courted the embrace of the perfect stick
to grace the day for a marriage arraigned.
But soon the greenwood became less thick,
and the woodland aspect began to change.

Each stick felt honored to be her choice,
as on she proceeded without looking back,
still waiting to hark to some inner voice
which special branch to pick and to hack.

But limbs now seemed bent and cramped,
Twisted, gnarled, no single one straight,
scraggled with turnings as if devil-stamped,
not one of them matching the other's mate.

The headstrong girl thus ambled on,
feeling she'd find at each pathway's bend
the consummate stick as if newly born
before ever reaching the woodland's end.

"Charming you are," she'd whisper and point
to each limb, "but you—you're a fright!
You, you're warped at every last joint!
And you, sir, I only see warts and blight!"

At last, a final ugly, benighted wand,
the most deformed branch ever beheld,
a last alternative to fulfill the bond
as though a sad terminal bell had knelled,

was all that was left within her reach.
Her fate she damned for being perverse
with some inauspicious lesson to teach,
imparting within it some deeper curse.

She was forced in taking a crooked stick
to have to return with her hateful choice
amid the sneers of that timberland thick
and the taunts of each tall, wooden voice,

for by magic each had the gift of speech,
each tree in turn to speak its own piece,
in spite of what seems a logical breach
to warn against avarice, whim, and caprice.

She wept as out of the forest she walked,
regretful for her vacillation and havering,
her high hopes dashed, all fully blocked,
for finicky waning and fussily wavering.

Bitter's the pill of indecision and doubt,
understandable perhaps if borne of need
while chancing a hazard of doing without,
but it is always a folly in terms of greed.

The Curse of the
White Cartonnage

I.

Fatwana was thirteen years old and had grown up in Egypt of an old and wealthy family. Her mother was American, her father a Coptic Egyptian. Although young, the girl was wise for her age, having been raised with the confidence of being loved. Her father was a customs official, a scholar, and expert on artifacts. Theirs was a large mansion in the modern city in the Gezira district of central Cairo, connected across the Nile by four bridges each on the east and west sides. It was a place known for its exotic flowers.

After her parents had unexpectedly died of badly contaminated Nile water, poisoned, some insisted, by two conniving servants who had an eye on their valuables, she and her two sisters were sent far away to the town of Pole, Maine to be placed in the care of an older, retired uncle and aunt who ran an inn, the Columbine Lodge, a large white former sea captain's house with a wide deck surrounding it, a creeper-covered portico serving as an extensive colonnade with a roof structure over a walkway supported by columns extending from the period old stone dwelling, chastely set back from the road and surrounded by amorphous, untrimmed catalpa trees with long slim pods, old quinces, and hedges of four o'clocks, waist high.

A tall hulking temperance barn, slumping somewhat but with its original boarding and beams, stood behind the inn with a large main entry door on one gable end, a side one along an eaves wall, and a center aisle running the length of the old building. Crates of valuables had been sent ahead of them for safe-keeping. Their dead father, an expert on ancient obelisks, had accumulated a large body of artifacts over a lifetime, by way of his studies and lectures—valuable statutes, silver pieces, ancient flails, pottery sherds, bird models, faience, rare jars, amulets, even a board game or two.

It would feel so strange to be living in America now, she thought. The area to which they had come they had heard was very cold, located in very remote country that was covered with tall pine trees and thick woods and had animals called moose and beavers. Would there be wild animals, of the kind she had read about in old fairy tales? She dearly hoped not. The girls were packed off with many steamer trunks. It was a rough and endless sea crossing under an Old Testament sky, a white shroud boding ill.

The young girl fingered the gold amulet of Anubis that she always wore, a symbol of stamina, vitality, regeneration, and resistance to harm that was given to her, according to tradition, as being the youngest in the family. She had nut-brown skin, and her eyes were a soft mix and had for color that rare kind of curious blue-gray-white that is seen in tonic water. Her two taller sisters, homely Freya and Feroce, who envied and so disliked the younger girl, bore her ill will in general for also being the prettiest. They were tall, chinless, unkind, and, being older than their sister by a few years, craved to meet young men for husbands.

§

Prof. Drogue, an archeologist in his early thirties who taught courses at the University of Maine, was asked to tutor the young teens. The girls' aunt knew the man for having once sold him a rare diorite scarab that she had been sent as a gift from her sister, a sad reminder now of her untimely death. It could only bring bad luck to keep it, so felt the aunt, who wanted to give it away. She explained the circumstances of their parents' tragedy, requiring the three girls having to leave the Middle East with all of their goods. Returning home, he told his brother, Dreel, with whom he lived, about the foolish woman and what she virtually gave away and about a possible fortune that could fall into their laps, for the two were very much alike—he taught chemistry— each being as inquisitive and acquisitive as the other.

"I smell opportunity." "How so?" Spare, always playing it close to the vest, he gave no details to his brother, having also kept mum about his earlier purchase of the scarab. Dreel was doubtful. "Are you certain?" His older brother stood, looked at with unquestioning exasperation, and tapped his temple a few times. "When a blind man tells you that he's going to stone you," he said, "you know that his foot is on a stone."

He hung fire.

"Correct?"

"Ayuh."

They were always that cryptic, understated, hard to read. They trusted nobody whom they did not know, and those whom they did know they numbered among the untrustworthy devils they suspected they were.

"Who are these people?"

"Nobodies."

"From?

"Away."

"Far?"

"Ayuh."

"Loot?"

"Tons."

"Easy?"

"Praps."

"Likely?"

"Whole nother thing."

"Later?"

"Yup."

"When?"

"Hard tellin' not knowin'."

The archaeologist, a glum man, had a face that in its inimitable way could have been called gunpowderous. He had a reputation of being a cheapskate, wore a broad-brimmed hat and shad-bellied coat of a grayish homespun cloth, and walked through town like the wind lest he have to stop and talk to anybody. He had a head shaped like pear, the broad part a widening chin, and, because he suffered badly from hemorrhoids, he kept boxes of Feen-A-Mint laxatives in his pockets wherever he went to stave off electrolyte depletion. His trouble was that it was avarice that caused his constipation and constipation that caused his hemorrhoids and hemorrhoids that caused his foul temper. The two men were literally misers, had been brought up that way.

Cheeseparing was a way of life with them. They forwent basic comforts. It was all carl and churl with them. They lived stingy, side-hustled, never ate out, bathed once a week, took no vacations, and contributed nothing to the public welfare. They saved bottles, string, newspapers, wood of any size, and split the cost on everything. They contributed to no funerals, no weddings, no charities.

Their monosyllabic exchanges were a matter of economy, as well, tight-lipped and unforthcoming. A full spoken paragraph in Maine is eloquence. Virtually Demosthenic is that soul up there who will linger to talk to you in the street. A taciturn or brusque individual inevitably believes that in his silence something profound is implied of unvoiced depth, that in the brusqueness he is saying more, *meaningfully* more, that in the gruff and arrogant curtness he presents what is left unspoken indicates wisdom. It is an astonishing delusion, and a pretense, for that cold reticence sits nothing more than unbudging ego and sheer animal stubbornness.

They kept to a diet of mainly parsnips, eggs, and milk. In winter, hot sourdough bread soaked in lard did them for a full day. They dug clams, picked mussels out of the banks, and spread the roe of sea urchins on bread. They ate nasturtiums, munched dandelion leaves, and when wild hot mustard was in bloom, growing among the jetsam and high tide mark, they picked the leaves for salads. They chewed tit gum from spruce trees and, when they were kids, they hawked it by the roadside in penny sticks and—with their father's help—even sold balsam pitch to the town at $55 the gallon, as it was used by the Defense department.

It was also used by Indians in North America to caulk the seams of their birch-bark canoes.

As he tramped the woods, Old Drogue missed nothing by which he could turn a penny. *He would taste trees!* He knew about chemicals and with the possibility of trying successfully to market it was studiously looking into "retene," a hydrocarbon obtained from the pine tar, rosin oils, and various fossil resins of any and all resinous woods, usually prepared from abietic acid.

Nothing served as a better example in the world they grew up in of what could be had for nothing than spruce gum.

"You want free?" their old father would ask the boys, efficiently knifing resin off a woodland spruce tree. "Look!"

§

Old Drogue, their father, now dead, had been their tutor, guide, mentor, trainer, and coach all through their lives from the time they were inchlings.

"Thrift is your ticket to freedom," preached the old buccaneer. "I'm talkin' low-hangin' fruit. Take what you can that is free. There are gifts galore staring you straight in the face! Most of the dolts in the world are asleep. Be awake, I am telling you. Only a damn fool cannot live free in the state of Maine, vacationland for the open hand. It is all right there in front of you just for the taking—potatoes, lumber, bait worms, sweet resin, blueberries, ground elder, salt hay, cranberries, bog peat, apples, pears, Christmas trees, Jerusalem artichokes, firewood, alewives, ski trails, tallow, rhubarb, honey, mushrooms, sugar kelp and bladderwrack, acorns, fox pelts, beaver skins, rivers teeming with fish, otter hides, chokecherries, grapes—honeysuckle is nature's chocolate candy!—all shellfish, including clams, mussels, quahogs, and lobster, granite, and, let me tell you something, the best ice on the planet." Ice was his business. He made his money in ice. He would always nod and wave, passing a lake. "There's m' partner."

He was emphatic. "Trust in nature. I like this place and could willingly waste my time in it," he would shout in the forest and the woods. He would grab moss, yank up a mushroom, pick bee balm, snap a cranberry. "'My nature is subdued to what it works in, like the dyer's hand,'" he would add, for he knew his Shakespeare, or small applicable scraps and shards of him—exactly how, no one knew—"'Yet do I fear its nature. It is too full of the milk of human kindness.' Go to the source! Munch flowers—they're *best* eaten raw!—marigolds, nasturtiums, day lilies, squash blossoms, mint, borage." He would clap his hands. "Phytofinds! Now, there is a subject, lads. And I have not yet even broached the subject of healing plants," added the confirmed ethnobotanist, "feverfew for headaches, willow trees for aspirin, chamomile for spasms in the gut, basil for bad colds and bronchitis, and soursop, bayberry, and guajava for diarrhea. Have I mentioned blackberry thorn?"

The old man demanded that they listen, as did their mother who, upon the occasion of anything spilt or spent, strapped them for wastrelism.

"And should I not bring your attention to gold, silver, emeralds, *diamonds?* A volcano in the Bismarck Sea off the coast of Papua, New Guinea emits gold and silver! Ever hear of the blue lands in South Africa, me buckos? Diamonds in fact are as cheap as gravel—only the Jews with the particular cunning of that race know it. The rocks are not scientifically rare—they are *made* that way. Planned obsolescence!"

Object lessons were his forte. On a rare happy morning he would not shut up. "I was saved getting lost once on Bore-stone Mountain for three days"—he would fix them with a long, hard, studying look—"eating young green edible seeds, known as 'keys,' from the ash trees, *Fraxinus excelsior*, how d'you do! Look it up. Sometimes when thirsty, and the family well froze up, I resorted to eating snow, like a sled dog."

The old man, an ill-tempered if not tyrannical parent, demanded that his boys march in step. Born in Maine, from a family that went back six generations down east, he was a cur-mudgeonly original, a martinet prone to vituperate men he thought inferior to himself, which included more or less every-one he met. He threw himself into every enterprise with a will-power so intense as virtually to exclude the possibility of its ever changing. He spun on his own axis and listened to no one but himself. No one could hold a position or knock down a flimsy argument or ram a point home faster than Old Drogue.

His likes and dislikes were supported by a body of doc-trine which on its own assumptions could not be contradicted. He learned the nature of his powers by misusing them, a default as forceful as that hard old determined face of his that pointed in the direction of anything and everything that he could grab without paying. He was up and awake in the morning before the roosters, certain as sunrise, looking for an advantage.

One day he was deep in the woods setting out leg-hold traps for groundhogs, which he regularly caught and ate, con-sidering them sweet as pot roast—he knew every kind of trap, for the state of Maine never banned them, bite snares, body gripping traps, wire rigged traps, Conibear traps, deadfalls, spring-powered traps, steel jaw traps, rope traps, box cages, even glue traps—when abruptly a terrible thunderstorm blew up out of the dark threatening sky that sent a battering of hail crashing sidelong against the face of the forest, twisting and bending the tops of the trees writhing as if some mad, baleful giant were pissing on peasants below, and yet as one ferocious wind gust wrenched a huge limb from a brittle poplar tree and dashed it down next to Old Drogue, he never even looked up.

He walked straight as a yardstick. He had iron tenacity. Locals said they put a baboon heart in him. He built birdhouses, was addicted to long walks, concocted his own sarsaparilla, fried rabbit in a skillet mostly every night, loved Indian pudding, drank bottles of an old health tonic called Vegmato, and supposedly cried only once in his life, listening to a Robert Schumann song over the radio, which had the paradoxical effect of his never wanting to listen to it again.

He mistrusted government, never voted, did not believe in drivers' licenses, refused to pay taxes—"Taxation is predation," he contended—despised politicians, refused to have his road paved, petitioned to keep wild animals on his property, and refused to send his children to school, hating any and all public education ever since a day in fourth grade when he was held up to ridicule and widely mocked for having written in his homework "Moses went up on Mount Cyanide" and "The tycoon raged for two days" and "The banker's money was well infested." Fuel was only added to the fire the following year, terminating his school experience for good, when, after losing a school debate, "Resolution: Which is Easiest—To Cut Toast or to Cut Bread?" he was expelled after flinging an inkwell at—and just missing—his opposition. He was glad to be shut of school and would never again see a classroom. Liberals he called "crape myrtles" and "house mothers who live on Mount Fairy."

Nothing drew his hatred more than lawyers, the most despised profession in the world, not a single one of them worth redemption, all of them greedy, lying, crooked, pimp-like cackers who are by their very nature seedy, exploiting, slop-suckers, each one of them literally a trained-to-cheat bottom-feeding pleco, identifiable scum fish who tripfag though trash just to turn a fee. Not a single one of the 63 references to them in the New Testament is positive. "Every human being starts out as an anus—lawyers stay that way!" said Old Drogue. He would tap-tap-tap his palm. "The only outcome that interests them is income."

He virtually phosphored on the subject.

"Lawyers are money rapists," he fulminated. "Jesuit voodoo tricksters, cheats, the highwaymen of business, liars, and cutpurses! They are the original succubi—god lost! They stood on their toes like chinning capons and gelded roosters trying to cross-examine Christ himself! Why, Jesus declared thousands of years ago without equivocation that lawyers took away the key to knowledge—you can look it up—yet did not enter in themselves but hindered those who wanted to enter!" (Old Drogue repeated the charge every day, so often that the boys, becoming skeptical when they grew up, checked it out and he was right: Luke 11:52–54.)

Old Drogue was hot headed. It was his temperament that got him into trouble throughout his life. A latitudinarian, he was remembered in Pole as a deeply controversial figure, who at times seemed intent on taking a path in life that might lead to trouble. He called himself a "reformist" and "broad-minded progressive." Irony was his method, circumspection his manner, a resolute and ongoing suspicion his perpetual mode. He was taken to court in Augusta three times for tax evasion. There was also one public scandal. At age 76, he was arrested at a logging camp up in Hebron, where the State Police were investigating the mysterious disappearance of an unruly neighbor of his, which proved to be the murder of a local drunk and lay-about. At the time, Old Drogue had been walking around the immense wooded lumbering tracks and peddling burlap bags of Honduran coffee beans to outlying river camps and primitive log cabins with pot-bellied wood stoves, and isolated wood retreats up there in all those remote unorganized townships identified by range numbers like T4 R3 or TD P8.

Yearly, he canoed the Mattawamkeag, the Piscataquis, the Narraguagus, and the Spurwink. He had also been shooting partridge, wild turkey, and deer and fishing for black crappie and muskellunge, catching haddock, arctic char, and sole and then trading any fish caught for bags of Bay of Funday scallops.

When confronted with it by the authorities, Old Drogue denied out of hand any involvement in the killing, the victim being one "Swill" O'Rourke—a barfly and for years Old Drogue's personal nemesis with whom he'd had a long running dispute over property rights to a pond and whom he described to his sons as "a short, rat-faced, wine-bibbing Irish crawfish in a crapulent hat."

"All's I know he was a wind-sucker, a low-bred dog who plagued the town with the shifting shape of his evil shadow," Old Drogue told the police. He declared, "He was a scheming, reptilian, underhanded, weaselly, duplicitous, cross-grained, half-wittedly-low-in-the-frontal-lobe, dipsomaniacal shitball—no offense implied."

The dead man was named for his appearance. He might have been born Liam or Willem or William, no one knew, and none ever bothered to learn. A miscreant—he was the town toss-pot, a risible soak, the butt of the local children who with glee would watch him weave up and down the main street, three sheets to the wind—he was scary-looking with teeth angled backward like a tile fish, and you could smell his cloaca. He was cat-faced like a blighted tomato, spotted as if with fruit rot or a case of human septoria, with round sunken patches on his arms and cheeks, and always humid in the pants, both front and back. When Old Drogue saw this wobbling creature for the first time—big nose, bad complexion, huge feet in huge shoes—he morbidly exclaimed, "I predict a degringolade!"

In any case, the body of O'Rourke had been found, stuffed into a log, slain, with a sharp shard of ice stuck right into his heart. He had been jealous of Drogue all his life and owned a hefty court record, once having rolled a huge round cedar stave potato barrel down a hill into Old Drogue's truck garden. It was also proven that, while roaring drunk, he had set fire to his cork-insulated, cedar-shingled ice house. Worst of all, he had vindictively built a mill dam to siphon off water from Old Drogue's pond.

"Was this 'Swill I Am' creature a hideous stump about the size of a water hydrant wearing a toe rag on his head with a face porcine and indolent and pitted with craters, eyes like rubber knobs, mouth a strip of purple?" asked Old Drogue, who often found corroboration for his scorn in a person's physiognomy. "Nope, never saw him."

He denied any responsibility.

And nothing was ever proven against him.

"Must I be responsible for the death of every semi-cretin, jumped-up import, and irresponsible souse over here from BallyMcFuck who wears suspenders and walks down the street in flapping shoes drinking from a can?" was the question Old Drogue posed to the judge. It was his firm belief that the way it came is the way it will go.

There were many arrows in his sententious quiver.

"Wake *ready!*" he counseled his sons. He was a fund of gnomic phrases. The boys memorized all of them, proverbs that effectively constituted their education. "A jackknife is better than a hand." "The wolf has a thick neck because he does his job on his own." "Grief comes in waves, which never cease, learn to float on them and stay alive." "Accept no reality but yours." "Too much talk trims your advantage." "No doctrine for generosity can be taught by the laws of reason." "Miracles are lies, fully inconsistent with Nature." "A handshake is a handshake, not a promise." "The *non*-scenic routes hide the gold." "Old age and treachery beats youth and vigor." "The heart is the enemy of the mind." "Rules are dangerous!"

"Understand that the very moment that you allow the truths outside your own head to become public property," he told his boys, "they become immediately subject to revision, scrutiny, denial, mockery, and lies, and you?—you have rented yourself out to thieves and blackguards!"

Aggression was a pet theme of his. "Get in fistfights, it clears the senses." "Scar tissue is stronger than original flesh." "Disregard all bullshit." "A woman will always kiss you before she kills you." "Clergymen are all loafers." "Squeeze all pencil-neck geeks—width is invariably narrow on an isthmus!" "Be forever a bad loser." "Pain is just one form of information." "The immigrant Irish live to ruin and blacken New England." "Love is mainly sympathy, nothing more—check on this as you grow and prove me right—folks essentially care only by way of pity-petting, Attain success and you will be scorned—I know, for I have travailed in both weathers."

To keep the boys from any and all disadvantages was his determination, the foundation of a scheme that became his mission.

"*What you are made of, you are made for!*" he would cry, vigorously stepping on the accelerator of the bus at each iteration.

He was ever ready to tear a cat! Where did he dredge it all up? "Live where your feet are! Let ninety percent of what you say not be what you're thinking. Empty a bum-biter's fat pockets, and yet all the while with warm tears melt the snow and keep eternal springtime on thy face!" But was that consistent, the boys wondered, and did he do that with his own sworn enemy, Swill ('The Drinkweasel') O'Rourke in his fetid underwear?" Old Drogue queried his kids. "Betzalel or Shimri or Gad, that jumping mick? Stoplight Loosejaw, you mean, the dragonfish with pins for teeth and photon-emitting organs that emit red light? He was a wash-ashore like all the other coal-crackers and narrowbacks and no more belonged in Pole than fleas in an armpit. By merely walking by the sluggard, I infamonized the whoreson dog! Him with that spastic son, Knaster, sired by a milkman, and his grotty wife, Gneisspaws, and all those bubukles on his face! Characters in Shakespeare's plays with that name are comic, foolish or manipulative, but Swilliam—'swill I am!'—is another whole fuckball!"

§

Old Drogue's most important lesson—a paradoxical one—was simple: *listen to exactly nobody.* "Folks create an illusion of how you are supposed to live, or *not* live, and so infect you. You become real only when you cease trying to become real for others. Be a voice, not an echo. Only you are the you you are! Everyone else is either flattened by his own consent or against it. I have seen the housemothers of the world crushed like ducks! *Flow* into the who you are. *Seem* to be whatever you want to be, see? But *be* only who you are. Always remember that, never, ever be the you that others create."

Everything they knew they had learned at their father's knee. The grizzled old man drove a battered old black bus, which he had bought at a country auction. It would pull up in town, and out would step iron-jawed Old Drogue. He spoke to no one, simply went about his business, buying wire, beveled wood chisels for ice, serrated knives. He drove his boys on that bus, on what he called "take-ins," not for larks but for learning. He took them to the Lumberman's Museum in Patten, Maine. He took them over to Sniptuit Pond to teach them the geometry of cutting ice. How wild he looked, with his prehistoric head wagging, when he would jump and stomp his boot on the hard ice as if feeling for underfelt in a carpet. He could read the crystal arrangements in ice, knew grain ice from columnar ice.

He spelled out how ice is thickest toward the middle but how in the case of shallow ponds the underlying black ice melted first. He told them how the vast Antarctic ice blanket is on average about a mile-and-a-half thick—at its thickest about two and a half miles! "Solid ice," he would repeat for emphasis—and here he would stamp his foot on the gelid mass beneath him to make the point—"is classified as a mineral as long as it is naturally occurring, understand? Ice in a snow bank is a mineral, but ice in an ice-cube is not. Ice!" he would exclaim, "has different forms, faces, and formulations. Feel it! It can be as hard as a heart, rubbery as a nose, soft as quim, and colder than a gravedigger's shovel."

"There is ice to be had in outer space, sitting there on the hundred hundred thousand moons surrounding countless planets—stepping stones to salvation when Earth begins running out of water, which it soon will!" he warned. "Interdimensional hope! For you will be seeing vicious water wars in your lifetime!"

He would sniff the air like a basset hound or Belgian Malinois and clarify how fog was less opaque than mist. He defined *firn* (old granulated snow) and *iceblink* (horizon light) and *aggressive water* (soft, acidic) At such times, he would often slip a small flask out of his mackinaw for a long haust of antifogmatic.

He explained how crystal-clear glassy ice like sparkling diamonds fetched the best price from consumers buying blocks of it for their houses. "There are minerals in ice and treasures down on, in, and under the ocean floor. I'm talkin' rare, radioactive metals! he would shout with full conviction. He had snouted them out by reading, he said, and by spending time nosing around expeditions in the Athabasca Basin region of Canada, hanging out with ocean spelunkers.

"Ice shaped *America*," the old man said proudly. "It came like a rolling cannonade of thunder down through and over the continent and began where toughness conquered and crowned and you can even say created the natural world! Some say that, once frozen, water never recovers its original nature and that the clear, light, sweet part is separated out and disappears. They are wrong. Ice and stubbornness are the same, neither rises not subsides for a fool."

Old Drogue knew one poem, his own, "Ice," and for the benefit of his two boys often recited it as if he were standing on a stage:

> Shining its light
> as air puffs white,
>
> mirroring the sky
> a sheen but dry,
>
> and all the while
> with its icy tile,
>
> the water in tow
> by refusing it flow,
>
> bright as a pear
> blue in its glare
>
> a mineral mind
> as solid in kind
>
> as a gift of stone
> it stands a throne
>
> for a king to stand
> a promised land

The tutor in him also had a marketing need to validate his claims. He made his kids watch him power-jerk a 200-pound chunk of solid ice onto a truck with ice tongs and a hefty heave-ho.

He could saw it into 12" by 12" by 36" cakes in minutes. He created a frozen vault of ice to draw from all year, utilizing saw dust to pack the heavy blocks that he stacked wall to wall, earth floor to ceiling, perfecting the insulation of storage.

They watched puffins, dug for clams, ice-fished, sledded on toboggans, set out willow and grig-wheel traps for eels and osier traps to catch trout in the roadside streams, and panned for gold in the Swift River. He drove them to the top of Tumbledown Mountain to swim. He took them to Baxter State Park to see the wetland birds. He trekked them through wilderness and the deepest of Maine's puckerbrush to promote the finding and eating of nature's wild foods. Here he pointed out the American chestnut ("The rarest tree in North America, and endangered!"), loons—"They walk clumsily on land, how they got their name, and they do so uneasily because their legs are located far to the rear of their bodies"—and he called their attention to a dark green plant with shiny three-leaves. "It is called *Rhus Toxicodendron*, commonly known as poison ivy—that is the plant that returns the world's scorn. Respect it." He brought them to Kenduskeag Plantation. "I want you to learn a raccoon from a baboon from a puccoon," he always repeated. "And soon!" Upon returning, they were each of them required to sit down and write essays on what they had seen. By candlelight!

The parents would raise hob if anything was wasted or too expensive. So Drole and Dreel grew up into men the way they were taught. They kept their clothes in potato bags and housed their flatware in empty baked bean tins. They chose kerosene lamps over electric lights. They used solid crates and wooden boxes for furniture They employed out by the back an old jack pine outhouse for use as a dry toilet, using the single pages of the annual Montgomery Ward catalogue for toilet paper. even if they had to go out in winter in the cold. They kept a cow, tied up outside. They mended their wares, cut their own hair, hewed their own water, chopped their own firewood in a common forest, bought only what was serviceable, researched acquisitions, amortized costs, and wasted absolutely nothing. In their frugality followed an old Yankee dictum: use it, wear it out, make it do or do without.

The two sons, like their father, never set out in the morning to return in the evening with less than they had upon leaving.

"Remember?" asked Prof. Drogue of his brother.

"*Cymbeline.*"

What did that mean? It didn't matter. They both knew.

Prof. Drogue—old Drogue's first born, although given the name Drole, always went by this scholarly appellation—was requested to come to meet the new pupils who had come from abroad. They formally met in the Columbine Lodge with the Egyptian girls, awkwardly, the day following their arrival. He took his brother along with him, as an adjunct. The upper room at the inn where they were greeted seemed pointlessly lavish to them, as they both severely reprobated waste. He took off his hat and smiled at the young women, Freya and Feroce, who seemed taken with the brothers. His was a hard, uninviting, forced, barely obliging, standoffish smile with no corresponding emotion. The men as they sat were offered drinks, which they took, and sat for the meeting, learning about the tragedy of the family, the will that brought them to the town of Pole, their goals. They sat silent, offered nothing in the way of chat. The professor, who sat pricing the furniture, took port. Dreel drank claret.

The spoke almost nothing. Unlike their father—and most

people in the state of Maine—they said only what was necessary, if that.

§

Pole, Maine, on a backroad was nothing but a tiny white wooden post office, a sleepy gas station, a Baptist church, an old road tavern called the "Chat Qui Rit," and a small outlying graveyard with a scattering of granite lump-on-bump grave-stones with dates going back to the early 1800s. It was a wood village, a *wald dorf.* A regional joke there, often repeated, went, "You are entering Pole, Maine—set your watch back 50 years!" All its inhabitants, remote and sour as rhubarb, early learned and never forgot the stark lesson that life was generally something that happened elsewhere. It did not much matter, People "from away" mattered little. There was no shortage of "No Trespassing" signs. Old houses stood, were built, at discrete distances. Doors were kept locked all the time. Churchgoing among the townsfolk was minimal. A trial might be held at the town hall when they would gather like eels, which a drop of blood will convene, and no scandal. "I am Yanko Goorall," he would unregretfully tell his boys, looking out toward the town. They never knew what he meant by that, and they never found out. "I am Yanko Goorall," he'd simply repeat. "I am Yanko Goorall."

The place was a dead end of sorts. It was a padlocked town, xenophobic, repetitive, meaningless, eaten up by malice. It inexhaustibly caved in on itself. When the real world is felt to be outside, those who live removed feel inadequate and fraudulent. Old Drogue liked to feel at home, but not paradoxically, where that home happened to be located. Pole was too limited and closed. "Quillback carpsuckers" was what he called the townies. He agreed with Thoreau that society is diseased, that one could never find health anywhere but in nature, which was right at hand—"the spruce, the hemlock, and the pine will not countenance despair," he would quote. The old man was a majority of one, comparing himself to locals. A fellow New Englander, the poet Sam Walter Foss once wrote in a jingle that he'd like to live in a house by the side of the road and be a friend to man. If he had been brought up and lived in Pole, he'd have considered man an enemy and shoved *him* to the side of the road.

"Do they serve coloreds here?" Old Drogue was once asked walking out of a feed store. His reply was, "Colored what?" One July two men flying just overhead in a hot air balloon, realizing they were lost, came jerking by his garden in Pole and yelled down, "Where are we?" Out hoeing, Old Drogue shouted back, "You're in a hot-air balloon" and smirked defiantly as they floated away. Whenever someone had a problem that needed to be fixed, he would tell them how *he* would have handled it, then walk away.

Folks in the small town who rarely saw his two grown sons called them the Bubble Brothers, because their noses were inflamed with red buds from alcohol. They only knew they were sharp as nails, and twice as spiky. The brothers drank mostly whiskey from spurred rye, their *own* rye infested with ergot—it was the cheapest, its fruiting structure, something about alkaloids, giving it a surprising boost. They kept a bucket on a rope in a well out back by the barn and kindling in a collapsing shed. There were farm tools lying around, spades, shovels, a rusty tractor, a drag harrow ("Look, the horns of Sekhmet," said Fatwana), a wheel-barrow, watering cans. They washed in hard water, kept chickens, had no mailbox. They paid their bills reluctantly, usually after solicitors called them on it. It was bruited around the village that even in private life, they deplored laughter which they said cost too much to expend.

Their habit was to drink at home. They concocted whiskey from raw alcohol bought from a Canadian grifter who came down from Jackman selling purloined goods from the back of his car. It was much cheaper and gave a bigger kick. Staying home was a Drogue rule. They avoided the low-brow *Chat* tavern with its clientele of grizzled Down East rednecks, forest peckerwoods, idling long-termers, and half-witted drinking trolls at the long bar there, jobless losers, lay-abouts, and local chawbacons from the underscullion families of the interior holt with names like Henchy, Zaider, Wise, Hartley, Holman, Uhle, Markley, Schreiner, Dice, Beatty, and a few banana-necked ex-lumbermen with the IQs of farm animals. It was in this very bar that Old Drogue had punched out pie-eyed Swill O'Rourke, the drunk later found murdered. The place got raucous on Saturday nights, when the stewed clientele, unrepressed, tongues loosened by drink, sang lewd songs, like "The Bloody Great Wheel "and "The Good Ship Venus." The rest of the week they sank back into their usual vague torpor.

No one in town trusted the Drogues. People had doubts about them, qualms and misgivings. Being men of mystery and understatement proved to be unpropitious for academic advancement. They were not loved at the university, far from it. The head of the paleontology department, their department, Ms. Christiani Mariani Pianigiani—a bitter Drogue rival—not only helped prevent him from securing an academic chair there but automatically voted down any stipends for any and all trips abroad, claiming that they were not only irresponsible fakers but that both he and his brother were as "gay as handbags." "He's an eagle without a cliff" was the way she superciliously put it, comically raising an eyebrow. She declared to the committee, "Auntie can pay his own way. While his brother, 'Whoops, Dearie,' can stay home and sew the curtains." It was this same department head who, knowing the men well and learning of their extra-mural tutoring, only groaned and pitied the tutees.

Prof. Drogue lived alone in an old house, until he got his brother a job teaching. He charged him for the room he lived in. It was an old Steamboat Gothic house, ancient and listing, showed not a line of ornament. The rooms inside, in which the old floor boards were 30 inches wide, were painted brown only to protect the woodwork but were so badly ventilated that the air was pestiferous. On moldy carpets, sat a few mouse-bitten chairs near a stopped-up flue. A zinc tub sat in a far corner, by a slate sink. There was a fireplace and sometimes they nailed shad to planks and broiled them over a fire. They often ate "strip fish," hake or haddock, caught, split wide, flattened, and left outside on a bench to dry in the sun—eating it straight, ripping off solid, firm, brown strips, "piecening," they called it.

Mostly, they cooked their frugal meals on a two-ring burner that was kept on cut gray slate piled on a wide deal church bench. Only one cabinet was kept down cellar, down cellar was dark, down cellar was hidden, down cellar was where they stored their money, with a single box of some rare scarabs, which they had collected. Egypt was a major fascination of theirs. Upstairs inside might very well have been a mausoleum, an empty tomb. The walls were stark, the ceiling tin. There was no molding in the place, not a single picture or a print adorned the walls, nor was there a vase or a statue to be seen. Not an ornamental shrub or flower showed outside, a yard flat and dirt-hard with no sign of tillage. The very street on which they lived, a meandering dirt path more than anything, was narrow and crooked.

The men were village oddballs, aloof, held in suspicion, known for the strange quality of their detachment. Mystery and solitude characterized their behavior. They lived behind pulled shades, crossed the street when they saw someone coming, acknowledged no one in the street or at the university. Prof. Drogue often carried a willow-switch. Even their walk was queer. Whenever they went abroad on errands, they strode along, hunched over and scowling at the ground, as if bound on some secret mission. And what other neighbor in Pole in a yard of sawhorse barricades had a sunken black bus, wheelless on cement blocks, every last window broken or cracked, sitting hopeless on his or her property?

Neither of the two had ever traveled to Egypt, but of course both knew all about the world-famous, internationally broadcast discovery of the intact tomb of the 18th Dynasty Pharoah, Tutankhamun two years before, which turned out to be the best-preserved pharaonic tomb ever found in the legendary Valley of the Kings. There was a small collection of scarabs, kept in a cabinet at the university, which Prof. Drogue admired, even coveted. The sacred scarab—or *kheper*—of ancient Egypt was the dung beetle, an insect that lives off the waste of herbivorous animals. It was seen as an incarnation of the sun god, Khepri, and its name was part of many royal monikers, including *Men-kheper-re* and *Kheper-ka-re*. Never had he ever had a conversation in Maine on the subject. Not once. People's conversation there was confined to firewood and how to keep warm in winter and to selling lobsters in summer.

No, in Maine few gave much away.

§

While the young girls unpacked their steamer trunks—along with their clothes, an antique lamp, hand-carved leather, some amulets, jewelry, pectorals—Prof. Drogue was in alert attendance, having been called in that day, at a fee, to give value-estimates of some rare artifacts, especially an ancient Egyptian ivory scribal palette and holding slots to hold reeds, that the girls' aunt might be willing to sell. It was worth a fortune. He held it up to the light and with a sour squint offered to take it to cover the cost of two months tutoring. "And this?" asked the helpful aunt, holding out a first-century B.C. faience kohl tube. The professor ostentatiously deliberated. "Let me see, oh, I should think it should well cover tutorials at least up to, say, January," he monotonously replied. He picked up another item. She saw only a scorched ball of iron.

He pocketed a rare Greywacke Late Period 26th–30th Dynasty (688–343 B.C.) scarab and with a nod explained he would take it for an added month of teaching. There was a violincello tone in his voice, but the charm never reached his eyes, a stare cold as ice and calculating with the steady whirr of machinery running behind them. An Egyptian glass inlay of a vulture, roughly third century B.C. she thought she would hold onto. *The bitch*, he thought.

Prof. Drogue had kept up through the years on new and recent findings in Egypt and had heard of the secret tombs of Saqqara, where crumbling pyramids and 4,000-year-old royal tombs were said to proliferate. Gilded coffins, animal mummies, bronze statues, cartonnage sealed with black resin, canopic chests!

He saw in mind shabtis, small alabastrons, a rare royal insignia Uraeus, a bronze cobra with flaring hood and bulging eyes, the curving body bent backward. How often had he seen such a rare object in a textbook! He noticed that even the ornate gold clasps of the trunks were valuable, each one 24-karat gold, he saw immediately, but he told them that, as they were most of them scratched and bent, their value was diminished. Gold of any karat less than 24-karat has little value to an Egyptian. Deceiving his young charges, the professor told them 6-karat gold was more durable. He nosed over the antiques as if sniffing them. What was that? A tomb cloth fragment. No, those. Saharan Neolithic arrowheads.

And that? An Egyptian carnelian amuletic bead depicting Bes, about 1550–1070 B.C. Prof Drogue squeezed his hands. And the, the, the chest itself? The chest was very old and carved from the soft trunk of a Judas tree. He palpated with passion a sleek bronze statuette of Bastet, the daughter of Re,

That was when his eyes, surveying the girls' possessions, fell not on the objects they revealed but on the unrolled strips of strange cloth in which several smaller rare items had been wrapped. How had he ignored this before now? Was that not ancient Egyptian linen he was seeing? Bandages of a sort fashioned by plant gum? Weren't they used on ancient coffins? Under plaster? Her fingered them but disclosed nothing of what he was thinking. He felt a binder of chalk powder. Was that gesso? What was that pounce? It was pulverized. Could it be "mummy powder"—ground and mixed with vegetable oil—a valuable medicine used in medieval times, a dust-like talcum powder, dehydrated, lyophilized, triturated.

It was then he had a sudden glimpse, within a mis-rolled bolt of that chalky linen, a pair of *wadjat*-eyes peering out.

Funerary cloth! *Cartonnage.*

He was certain of it.

Nothing rotted in the sun-baked sands of Egypt. The desert climate—dry, rainless, free of humidity—preserved everything. What parched it, protected it; what desiccated it, safeguarded and conserved it. Cartonnage was preserved like the high stone-faced pyramids faced with limestone. Bless dehydration!

He went to snatch a piece of the cloth to pocket it when the young people weren't looking but everyone was too attentive. He was about to say farewell to their guardians, explaining he would be needing to charge a high fee because he was an expert. Thanking them profusely, the professor with a wheeze claimed that, as he was nursing a peccant chest, could he wet one of the cloths to place on his heart, please?

The girls smiled.

"And may I ask, might I use this old piece?"

The girls turned suddenly serious, even embarrassed.

"There is a legendary curse to such linen burial garment. It hastens the yellow wind, what the Arabs call *rih asfar*, hot, dry, strong terrible east wind that comes blowing out of hell once in a generation, seeking out those who have performed cruel and unjust deeds and exterminates them one by one. Such fabric is guarded by Set, our jackal-headed deity, jackal, member of the wolf family, who presided over the embalming process.

"Anubis," softly voiced Fatwana, speaking for the first time. "*Anpu* in ancient Egyptian. He is the son of Osiris and

Nephthys. The golden wolf, but his head is solid black. The color symbolizes renewal, the restoration of life. "The fertile soil of the Nile River," said Freya. Feroce, the oldest and a bit of a know-it-all, added, "Also, the discoloration of the corpse after embalming. Anubis is linked with his brother, Wepwawet, protector in the afterlife, portrayed with a dog's head or in canine form, but with white fur. The two gods combine in the female Anput, daughter is the serpent goddess, Kebechet."

The aunt intervened. "The girls tell me it was all packed and sent in error. We are returning it all respectfully to the National Egyptian Museum in Cairo."

He pointed.

"Are—are—these, the sole goods you've brought?"

When they all turned to look, he quickly kited a piece of cloth whip-fast and instantly shoved it in his pocket.

"Some furniture sent along with us has been taken to the barn, where it is stacked by the stalls," added the helpful aunt.

"May I ask, is it *all*—wrapped?"

Was Dr. Samuel Johnson not correct when dolefully he declared, "Whenever there's a mystery, roguery is not far off"?

§

A man of mystery himself, Prof. Drogue found his mind spoiling with plans walking down the path, with the scarab, kohl tube, and scribal palette clinking in his pockets all the way to his house where in the privacy of his rooms he began waltzing around in circles, dancing with glee, capering like a jackanapes over his good luck. He quickly hid them away down cellar, seeing no need to tell his brother. The next day without further ado, secretly and with his private key, he betook himself to his carrel in the musty upper library stacks and immediately began close research on papyrology.

His heart skipped.

The material of which many Egyptian mummy cases are made consisting of linen or papyrus glued together in many thicknesses, he knew, are usually coated with stucco. Indeed, many mummy cases themselves were also made of such material. Cartonnage was also a type of material used in ancient Egyptian funerary masks from the First Intermediate Period, even to the Roman era. It was uniquely made of layers of linen or papyrus covered with plaster. Some of the Fayum mummy portraits, a subject on which he himself had presented several scholarly papers, were also painted on panels made of such cartonnage. Most of this he knew, but the museums in the major cities had none of it, shop galleries and antique purveyors less, and all the jasper, feldspar, schist, lapis, and Egyptian blue frit objects were as nothing compared to it.

As a gift, the following day, Fatwana ran to his house to give the hasps to him—some 23 of them—having spent long hours unscrewing the buckles. It was a unique visit. People never came to his lair, not students certainly, visitors never. He had opened the door but a crack. It was winter. Frozen fog—what the small groups of Native Americans up in that area called *pogonip*—brought ice needles to everything. On the way back, threading home through a pathway behind the barn, she was frightened by the sound of a dog barking at her. To calm her fears, involving nightmares on several consecutive nights, her uncle had an odd-job man spend a few days knocking together a fence to raise to keep any animals out.

Many a night thereafter, before going to bed, for protection she clutched the chain around her neck with the gold amulet bearing the face of Anubis. Whenever she went outside the lodge, for a walk or simply to play, just to be safe, she always patiently stood behind the waist-high hedges of four o'clocks to make sure no creatures were lurking about.

On the side of Professor Drogue, he saw the girl had a heart as soft as a warm quince blotted by frost. When she left, he ran stumbling into the woods and twirled in circles and opened his mouth wide as a fire-bucket to howl to the trees, "I who have had familiar heartbreak know the heart is strange! My heart now has heaps!"

They were the most words that in a lifetime he had ever said at once, except for his next utterance spoken into his collar,

"What boobs! What buffle-headed morons!" he snorted with contempt. "Apple-brained greenhorns! Credulous goddam imbeciles from diaperland! If I gave them a penny for their thoughts, I would be given change!"

II.

Schemes of all kinds were now afoot.

It was now of paramount importance for Prof. Drogue to relieve the benighted girls of what he could of their rare treasures, keepsakes the worth of which the poor foolish dolts had no reckoning, rare possessions worth a fortune. Who cared for scarabs and shabti now that he had come across rare cartonnage? He had quickly learned about cartonnage, swotting up on its history and various uses and applications. It was a term used in Egyptology and Papyrology for plastered layers of fiber or papyrus, invariably flexible enough for molding while wet against the irregular surfaces of whatever object it was used to cover. It became the familiar method that was used in funerary work-shops to produce cases, masks or panels to cover all or part of the mummified and wrapped bodies of notables who died. That they could last so long? Amazing. That they were now within his grasp? Prodigious.

The plastered surface gave an even ground for painting motifs with greater stability than was possible with, say, a linen shroud. They were surely of value, they *had* to be of value. The question remained of hawking such things. That would involve a great deal of wit and wisdom, but he had already begun thoughts of negotiating with museums in Boston, Baltimore, and New York.

Prof. Drogue knew how fresh snow insulates, absorbs and muffles sound, lowering the ambient noise on a landscape, wrapping everything in a thick white covering blanket, but while everyone else was reaching for mittens, skis, and shovels, he was making secret forays out to the Columbine Lodge barn at dusk to snoop, peeking through the boards to see if he could spot anything in the rumored hoard of rare artifacts. He thought he saw a mastaba tomb-shaped box. What did it contain? Pectoral jewelry? A vulture headdress? Decorative collars? Glazed urns and jars? Terra cotta dolls? Any of those disc-like headrests that traditionally dated to Third Dynasty in the Old Kingdom, around 2707–2369 B.C.? And that long box, could that possibly contain a miter—a rare pschent? A deshret? An hedjet? An atef? He began biting his fingernails in an anxiety of anticipational guesses. His excitement exacerbated his hemorrhoids, which began to make his anus throb, swelling the veins and making the ache worse, which sent him home to his zinc bathtub where he sat in a sitz bath, stewing,

Still and all, at no time in his life had he felt more validated in his objectives. He now haunted the ancient history library section, pulling down from the stacks huge, old, dusty volumes, Victorian ones mainly, to swot up on early Egyptian fabrics, even clothing fabricated from linen and supplemented by leather and reed matting. He read of looped-pile effects in weaving from the Empire Period. A particular fascination for him were books on the Archaeological Museum in Florence that he managed to fumble up which revealingly showed splendid 19th-century bas reliefs depicting formal ceremonies of ancient Egyptians wearing angular, formal starched linen garments. Neglected, he came to see, were fabrics discovered in the tomb of celebrated Tutankhamen, for there were many rare examples of embroidered fabrics and tapestry weaving and cartonnage.

At Hawara, south of the site of Crocodilopolis, he knew, grizzled and unkempt old William Flinders Petrie, lugging his tools and biscuit-tin camera in 1888 came across and excavated a late Egyptian royal tomb, unravaged, from about 600 B.C., and the hidden figure of Horuta in a huge sarcophagus of limestone containing three inner coffins of wood, all in sealed chambers, and found papyrus manuscripts of the 1st and 2nd centuries! What a discovery! Just to be there and see what was revealed in the unwrapping of then giant Horuta, how, as he said, "bit by bit, layers of pitch and cloth were slowly loosened!" Prof. Drogue fixed especially on the Old Kingdom, a time of splendor and glory that endured until 2270 B.C.—it was Egypt's Golden Age and embraced four dynasties, the Third through the Sixth. Maybe *he himself* would find a staggering quantity of relics, amulets, gold rings, vases, caskets, lapis lazuli statuettes, inlaid birds, beryl and carnelian wristlets, a wealth of talismanic armory.

Daily now he began taking journeys in his head, hallucinating in his incessant and throbbing ambition to strive. At night, it became even worse. On his hard iron bed, he thrashed, dreaming of kohl-dark *wadjat*-eyes. They peered at him in the darkness of his sleep, in the depth of his daytime dreams, and later even in the brightness of day as he sat in his back carrel in the top floor of the university library. They promised untold riches.

§

Meanwhile, the two older sisters, Freya and Feroce, late teenagers who felt they had been robbed in the worst way of the marriages that they had been promised—chances that not only their parents thwarted but that had been derailed by their abruptly having to leave the country—had grown even more cruel to their sister, Fatwana. They indifferently ordered her about, and, being the youngest, she waited on them and had to do their bidding. They never wept for their parents, as had Fatwana who of course knew nothing of the evil so long spoiling in their curdled souls.

Which marriage? Whose promise? What evil?

It turned out that the two homely sisters in their desperation all along had all been having affairs with the two conniving servants who had poisoned the parents with Nile water into which they had slipped lowly castor beans, the ricin in which, ingested, killed them in mere seconds. Fatwana was ignorant of the crime, and although Freya and Feroce had not wished for their parents' deaths, they readily accepted the fact, freeing them now to marry whomever they wanted, for the parents, having become aware of their daughters' passions had refused to allow them to marry commoners, specifically the two evil servants who, determined on stealing the family jewels, had promised—a vow made by, and sworn on, sacred oath—that they would marry two gullible frumps, which was of course a lie and, having been hanged for the crime, now impossible.

The stark country town of Pole, Maine, was as small and remote as its identifying monosyllable. Drogues had been living there for a century or more. People—old local families who went way back like the Sparrows, the Knapps, the Marbles, the Strouts, the Watermans, the Pendletons, the Bumps, the Swifts, and the Drakes—remembered not only their father and grandfather but went even further back. Drogue stones filled up much of the graveyard. A cold hard pitiless race of isolationists inhabited the villages way up in that heavily wooded region, where ten miles could separate houses and cabins, an isolated region where main road and railway branched away from coastal north-south routes. Natives there were a wordless, standoffish, unapproachable, disdainful, unhelpful lot, understated at the best of times and on all occasions, rigid and destitute of affection. Inbreeding had given many of the townsfolk almost identical faces.

It was a place not good for the liver. Shades went up in houses, shades were pulled. Doors were opened but a crack. Nosiness preponderated, indifference prevailed. If acceptance into one's local community was essential to happiness and health, it was noticeably missing in this village. It was a stumptown of disdain and disregard.

Settlers of New England from the jump had been, most of

them, as cold and unbudging as the rows of stone walls that separated their various farms and holdings, boulders uneven, black,
sharp-faced, uncemented, frost-flung, broken, and without bond.
Over the centuries, they lost the power of loving, in the same way
that abyssal fishes of the dark deep eventually lost their sight.
Suppressing their natural affection, it was if over time, they were
starved of the very emotions needed to love. A faculty unused is
always lost.

The strict blue laws of Maine once punished a man for
doing so little as kissing his wife and child on the Sabbath day. It
was as if following generations, having imbibed those proscrip-
tions, stubbornly persisted in the beliefs of a doctrine of eternal
reprobation that to this day hardened the heart of the working
locals who passed each other in the street wordlessly and without
the slightest sign of affection.

§

Flintiness was a Yankee vice. It applied to emotions
as well as to the pocket. The people there *kept* not only a tight
purse. Sin bent us all, and we all ate the darkness of our sins
even as we lived. Wherefore salute each other, when they had
to grapple with bleak fate? Why should a father or mother love
the child possibly doomed before its birth to endless perdition?
An old fable of New England thrift runs, "Son, have you watered
the rum?" asked the shopkeeper. "Yes, sir." "Have you sanded the
sugar?" "Yes, sir." "Have you wet the codfish and tobacco?" "Yes,
sir." "Then, come to prayers!"

They kept firm secrets, a distinct aspect of frugality and
scrimping. Secrets, never to be divulged, are an old New England

habit, isolationist and clever. Why be extravagant and share? Where are the best flats to go clamming? Which are cheapest ski trails? How do you find oyster beds? Are lumberjack camps ever open to the public? Have they flea markets in Presque Isle? What is the best diet for sled dogs? Do you need a license to canoe down the Allagash? Is an Old Town canoe best and how do you keep a canoe pointed, or stop dead, or pick a course, and can you use a pole in fast-running shallow water?

The answer was? Nothing.

Keep on walking.

We divulge nothing. Go find out yourself, I had to. What, I am going to tell you so you can broadcast it to the world? Reveal it, why? Blow the lid off, so you can go public? That's what secrets are for, to be kept.

Stubbornness is a kind of parsimony, as well. The father, being an old cantankerous river man, had both, in spades. No shrewder creature ever lived. He had no enthusiasm for public schools, no loyalty to the government, no respect for the state, and no belief in God. He knew the large value of small things and dealt with the world by truck and dicker. He made tar from pine knots—a valuable article of commerce for centuries up there—to send down to the West Indies for barter. He would send down to them by packets tar, rosin, and turpentine, all in direct exchange for rum, sugar, and molasses. He often traded—no cash involved—in iron, turpentine, horses, kindling, vegetables, and even leather (an actual currency in Old Colony days) just as his forebears had done for casks of blubber or, going even further back, in indented scrip, "codfish" bills, "hull-mint" shillings and Spanish-milled dollars.

No one took advantage of him. No one managed or even

tried to low-rate or even bargain with him. You cannot dicker with someone who had traded the parts off customers all over the known world.

Old Drogue was willful. Nowhere could be found a more premeditated man. He worked, always alone, in the coldest weather. He looked to none for advice, sought no help, heeded not a soul, for that was his main message to his boys: Do not be the you others create. He hand-cut his own ice in freezing weather, standing astride the solid blue-white sheets as if he owned them. No cross-cut saw was sharper than his, he made certain of it. He designed and made his own 24-inch folding oak bucksaw, perfectly designed to cut across the grain. So old-fashioned were crofters, yeomen, and countrymen up in those parts that new appliances for saving work were either shunned or overlooked but definitely not in favor. He would be up before dawn and be the first one out on the frozen pond, as if determined also to be the first to answer the Psalmist's question, "Who can stand before His cold?"—except that, having had no truck with religion, he would not only have not known the verse but scorned it.

There was only one verse that he did know, one that he had made up, and the only one that he taught his children:

"Cut the ice,
milk the pine,
pick the berries,
strip the vine.

Chop the wood,
farm the brine,

dig the ground,
the Earth's a mine"

The physics of ice explained history for him. It was the point of departure for the full panoply of cryogenics—surgery, electronics, geology, food, ecology, civilizations, the nature of ablation, structural materials, travel, meteorology, transportation, harvesting, insulation, thermal ballast, gravity, national defense, etc., and it was this very subject, pumped into them when they were as small as icicles themselves, that interested the boys in archaeology. He looked far past our own planet. In the Solar System ice is abundant and occurs naturally from as close to the Sun as Mercury to as far away as the Oort cloud objects. Interstellar ice pervaded the Solar System, in the formation of planets and icy planetesimals.

Old Drogue spent much of his life filling piles of rude notebooks that constituted an original manuscript (never published), explaining the connection between the size and history of world populations over millennia and the configural immensity of the universe, finding a distinct link with, he thought, mathematical certainty in the cosmic duplication, a perfect match in the tempo-spatial distribution between the two measureless magnitudes, expanses, and volumes—a eureka moment for him!—exact, unique, associated, parallel, corresponding, complementary, harmonizing, and absolutely inevitable. (The old rumpled notebooks were found in a pile in his attic, all of them tied with strings, after he died, the flyleaf mysteriously signed "Yanko Goorall.") And, of course, he had written his poem, "Ice."

The old man knew everything about ice. It was the sole

element he truly loved and about which he could disquisit all day. "Although dingbats don't know it, ice is a mineral just as much as quartz is! It is a naturally occurring compound with both a defined chemical formula and crystal structure You won't have heard of seabed mining—pulling up minerals from the seafloor mud, deep down the ooze. I'm talkin' the bioluminescent dark, the profound of the ocean floor past the hydrothermal vents into the mystery of the gaping unfathomable which is a source of rare nutrients. It can be done, and I will do it. Commercially. Extracting cobalt, nickel, and copper from way down, fathoms way, way past the sunlight zone—700 feet—the 'midnight zone,' the 'abyssal zone,' the 'hadal' zone—where, along with ghostly fish with eyes like lamps, blackness alone thrives." He would toe-kick the ice with each complaint. "Trouble is, you need *permits*." A permit, being a document, was a thing he despised. Licenses, warrants, vouchers, *certtfication*—all came in for a spitting dismissal. "Authorizations were not part of the original Republic" he'd grizzle, and kick the ice again.

He was cantankerous. The unruliness of life that he found beneath everything, its turbulence, challenged him. He insisted upon taming the lions, not sitting, but as they circled and prowled. He never brought the kite down safely.

"No primitive, straitjacketing complacents or nosybodies down in the abyssal benthic—only ooze until bedrock, and minerals! Manganese! Ever hear of it, boys?" he asked. "Well, it is nothing less than an essential element for all living things. The ocean is about descent! I am talking lower than the morals of lawyers, those apex predators with corrosive souls and runt brains with a nose for the stink of lost and struggling man, except that the pelagic sediment is uncontaminated and pure. Manganese is a critical component for the diet! Other jewels of the sea? How about lutenium, hafnium, and francium! Francium—look it up!—is found in uranium. It has never been seen in bulk! It is radioactive—it can kill you! Would I lie to you? Look it up! I could be a rich man mining the stuff, for, I promise you, it is among the most expensive natural elements on the planet. The only trouble is it has short half-life—it decays so quickly it cannot be collected to be sold! People swim on top of the water but never look down. We are talking about the jewels of the sea, gullions and sea gems, part-and-parcel of minerals, that are found in rare-earth, like yttrium and scandium and a yellow brown ore called xenotime. *We could own the world if we could get down there!*"

Old Drogue was electric. "In pure form, they react with steam to form oxides, and at elevated temperature—like, say, 400° C—ignite spontaneously and burn with a fierce colorful pyrotechnic flame! They are used as additives in alloys, increasing their strength. I would happily spend summers investigating the reductive dissolution of manganese oxides trapped in ice at minus 20 centigrade under dark and light irradiation. I understand freeze concentrations and any and all liquid-like ice grain boundaries!"

In the ice house, he would chip off pieces from a chunk with an ice pick to have his boys suck them for flavor while he regaled them with all the facts about ice—ice being free, of course, its best and primary virtue. Afterwards, on ice-cutting days, he would always treat them to his home-made Indian pudding. "Around ten percent of the planet's land surface and roughly seven percent of our oceans are completely covered by ice. Chunk ice." He would heel-kick it in a friendly way. "Sea ice is frazil. Brash ice is floating, wreckage of other ice. Nilas—

thin sheets, level, in fact darkest when thin. Dry ice is not made of water—it is frozen carbon dioxide." He knew the history of everything. "Cutting ice is the Republic's oldest business. Glaciers, slouching, moved as fast as forest animals walk," he said.

He adored the subject of glaciers, read about them, studied their origins, their etiology of growth. "They are formed by snowflakes and time," he said. "Some glaciers are sixty miles wide and 300 miles long. A single glacier ice crystal can grow as big as a person's head. Almost all archaeological finds are made in alpine glaciers. The last ice age which began thirty million years ago, ended just fifteen thousand years ago, look it up, blanketing almost 30 percent of the land on this planet with a reach as far south as Virginia. You want ice? Take it! Snatch it!"

Anything is free you that want!

Name it and claim it!

It is all up for grabs, everything, just for the asking—but you have to act!

"Time passes," he said. "Nothing is stable. Rifling is a way of life. What spancels your enemy's neck? Simple. What you decide you want and no pussyfooting, that's all. The shepherd-crude Hyksos from the north swept in to capture a weakened Egypt, Alexander seized the whole world, the Huns overtook ancient Rome. Look it up. Talk about free? Civilizations begin on rivers. Rivers are free! What created Egypt? Nigger mud brought up by the Nile along its 600-mile length, flooding and engulfing the delta of its own accord, overflowing the valley banks every July and bringing fertility! It was the mud from Ethiopia, brought north in bountiful floods of fertile mud, allowing for villages to prosper, and then civilization! Canals, reservoirs followed—surplus waters. Free! Egyptian sun did the rest. Crops in abundance!

Fertile topsoil from rushing waters spreading over the banks! Any seed would sprout!"

Old Drogue was a fragmentary man who jumped in whole hog, a wayward genius of sorts who had an affinity with unpredictable Nature. He saw rainbows only in icicles and snow-glint and gelid slabs of pond. He lived by will, not in the euphotic zone, and gave not a thought to helping a neighbor. *A neighbor?* That was easy. He was an eavesdropping, disapproving subspecies who lived next door who exacted uniformity.

"And what is uniformity?" he habitually inquired of his boys, well-trained to know as they reported bouncing on the bus.

"*Habits,*" they sang out, "*are that which augment a limited personality and diminish any possibility in a vivid one.*"

§

The boys had imbibed most of his facts by the age nine. They shot up as willing pupils on uncompromising right angles to their father's turbulence and adopted his knowledge. The world's oldest ice is at the bottom of the ice sheet down on Antarctica. Ice is a window to the past. Most of Antarctica's secrets are locked away *under* the ice. What made glaciers and ice caps grow is snow. Antarctica is extremely dry, however, strangely, with *little* snowfall. "Since there is so little snowfall on Antarctica, one millimeter or one centimeter covers a long time period, whereas in Greenland each layer covers a shorter period. Ice reflects 90 percent sunlight, or its albedo, as the 'eggheads' call it. Ice plays a crucial role in the climate due to its ability to reflect sunlight. It is basically about how much sunlight is reflected and how much is absorbed as heat, see? Put on your old black jacket there, which has a very low albedo, and it will absorb all of the sunlight and become hot and uncomfortable on a warm summer's day," said their father. Fog—he hated fog—fog was worse than sun for melting ice, he complained, almost always at this point taking a long pull of his antifogmatic.

Eggheads! How they irked him. Liberals, all. It was eggheads who permitted all the new building in Maine. He hated liberals. It was liberals in town who gossiped about his trial and, as he always said, they were every one of them quillback carpsuckers! "Loons," was how he referred them. "Rafts of loons!" "A waterdance of loons!" "An asylum of loons!" "A cry of loons!" He had all the words. Each was a legitimate collective noun for them.

The old man put up with nothing, tolerated little, and took nothing lying down. Might it have been in such a mood that he slew the rummy O'Rourke? Vilified his half-crazy wife, Gneisspaws? Impugned their idiot son, Knaster, sired by a milkman? He told them that George Washington murdered many Indians, that the great baseball player Babe Ruth once punched an umpire, that the painter Caravaggio fatally stabbed a man over money. Once, on a contracted job, Drogue floated a huge raft of cut ice 54 miles all the way downriver. When he didn't like the price that the bum-biters offered him, he poled the entire load all the way back to maroon it spitefully on a sand lip to drown in pools of meltwater in the hot sun. They found him, half-drunk, four days later, sitting by himself on the shore of Lake Chemquasabamticook, frying a pan of togue over a fire while blowing into a whisky bottle to call a bull moose.

Father and Mother Drogue, in their eighties, had their children late in life, and it was inevitable they would not live much longer. A first wife died young. Her place was taken by a demented, hare-eyed crone, Mrs. Mewshaw, whom he referred to as "The Sewer" and who in her ferocity so horrified the family that her first name was scrubbed from history. A dumpy harridan with the fat face of grice and iron hair sharply parted in the middle and pulled severely around her head into a dreadful no-nonsense helmet, she was a bat from hell. She sucked pickled limes and wore boots and never spoke to anyone without an ironic snarl. His third wife had died from a life of smoking cigarettes, and, toward the end, he himself in his ruin recognized his own old age, often wistfully repeating, "I am a spent bullet."

"Pity the orphans," a cold-hearted neighbor once said over their heads.

Orphans they would soon become.

But, also, apples, which never fell far from the tree.

The Drogue brothers spent as little as they could and withheld as much as possible. Opportunity to them was fortune's right hand, frugality its left. They looked for what they wanted, kept what they found, protected what they bought, guarded what they had, and gave nothing away. If the righteous gave without sparing, they concluded, so much the better for us. Their own dispositions were shaped to possess, greed and avarice be damned, with a willingness to strive to avoid any and all emotions that questioned their reach. Inconvenience to them in any shape or form could only be gainsaid by comparative profit. If anything was so much the worse, they sought for so much the better. Whatever could be gotten was fed with pathological nurturance. Sharing was an ideal of which they had not the slightest conception.

"I sized the pile," said Prof. Drogue.

"And you calculate?"

He had often been down by the barn, nosing about. The

brim of his hat was wet, with his clothes, fermenting, giving off the odor of bituminous coal.

"Loads."

"Truly?"

"Honkin'"

"Easy to nobble?"

"Like a tree falling through cobweb."

"Remember?"

"*Cymbeline.*"

"Risk?"

"Negligible."

"Prospects?"

"Likely."

"Site?"

"Clear."

"Hazard?"

"A bumbler's worry."

Dweel grinned and nodded.

"Yet?"

They agreed.

"The longest pole knocks down the persimmons."

§

A severe Maine winter had come and gone. The right time, however, had not presented itself for Prof. Drogue to look into the barn, snow piling up high everywhere. The Bubble Brothers had waited months to do so, prepared all along to use any excuse freely to poke around in the old hulk and take a look around. He had asked the aunt if she wanted him to shovel off the roof. That was not necessary, she replied, explaining how when Spring fully broke plans were in the offing to have the entire lot evaluated for a public auction. The dark heart of Prof. Drogue misgave. To hear that made his hemorrhoids flare up, when he reached for his box of Feen-A-Mint laxatives. They hurt. He considered he might have to go on opium suppositories and would have done so before except he feared becoming dependent on them. The entire plan they had devised was now to go up in smoke.

That was when Drole and Dreel began to socialize, to a degree, with Freya and Feroce, the two sisters having been convinced that they were being courted when it involved only the odd soda or a picture show. They got dressed, after a fashion. Prof. Drogue wore a crumpled suit of inferior cloth, trousers that were too short and sleeves too long, and creaking shoes. Dreel with untended fingernails flounced on an old tie he found at a yard sale for a dime.

"Which one do you want, long nose or jutting chin?" Prof. Drogue asked his brother. As usual, the two devised their own patois, critical, with code. "You mean 'Slats' or 'Slivers'?" "Right." "I favor the youngest." "Me, too." "Too young." "Tell me about it." "Talks soft as a moccasin." "Still won't wash." "Easy to shape, control." "Ayuh." "I prefer the child myself but will go with either one." "Who cares?" "Slats—a big talker, long nose." "Eyes like gunstones." "Slugs." "Lead." "Slivers? Flap-valves runnin' all day." "Ayuh." "Bulb-baster breasts." "Peculiar." "Kettlebottom— she duckwalks."

"Dumb."

"As buttons on a fur coat."

"Shall we take them to the Chat Qui Rit?"

"Nope."

"Why?"

"No point—"

"—in being seen?"

"—with them."

"Or anyone."

"Right."

So, they went to Bangor with their dates. They had to spend money for these forays, two times. But it was for the good of the cause. They singled out a side-street near the waterfront to find a small rum café and suggested going Dutch treat, to which the young women were openly agreeable. They splurged on haddock pancakes and a pot of "plew"—tea. The men sprang for wedges of pie plant and, on sale, two egg puddings. "The sea air in town?" "Aye?" He pointed his spoon like a dart. "I can taste it in the custard." They had long developed a capacity not to enjoy themselves. A farcical meaninglessness pervaded all experience. They finished their meals without delay and left before satisfaction turned to surfeit, but not before Prof. Drogue, chafing at the inevitable moment, fumbled behind for his wallet, and, clamping his lips into a razor-cut line, stood up and, turning his back to the table, bent forward with a sidelong glance and tightly pinched out several crisp dollars.

Freya picked a winged insect off his coat in thanks. Her sister paid out four dollars of their own money. Dreel parceled up three Parker House rolls to take home for a late-night snack, then emptied his pockets onto the café table, swept off all the coins, and on the recoil flung down three dry dollars, while his brother, walking by a telephone, was fingering the spill tray of the coin return for change left behind.

"Yours ponied up."

"Scary—"

"—as Mrs. Mewshaw—"

"—with her underarm—"

"—batwings of flesh, ayuh."

It was an inexpensive treat later to walk down along the fishy-smelling docks to feed slags—cormorants—crumbs from a bag. They saw two movies at the cinema over the course of two weeks, *Forbidden Paradise* starring Pola Negri, Adolphe Menjou, and Rod LaRocque, and *Open All Night* featuring Viola Dana. The men would spring for neither candy nor popcorn. To what good? They had the souls of herrings.

The Bubble Brothers were critical. Taciturnity is another feature of parsimony, in the way being morose plays a significant role in being aloof. The young women from Egypt were dusky and suspiciously unfamiliar, out of the ordinary for being imported, exotic creatures—clearly non-natives—to be found in that part of the world. "Slats stahtin' to peeve me. I finding I'm right out straight for patience," muttered Dreel. "I want to take my-un to the Little City with the Big Ships, Bahth—and float her *awaaay.*" They could not wait to get home to drink their rye whiskies, not wanting to waste money that way on their dates. Prof. Drogue intercepted their glances and saw a flicker of interest in their dark eyes.

By earlier plan, they went to the men's room.

"Nose's eyes devour a man."

Dweel muttered, "Chin is more on edge than a nearsighted roofer."

"Yup."

"Dull."

"As a froe."

"Or hoe."

"Raccoon."

"Baboon."

"Puccoon."

"Swap?"

"Nope."

"Why not?"

"'Why?"

They spoke that way—the paratactic touch, short simple sentences. Phrases, as brief as possible. Nods sufficed, even grunts would do. Give nothing away. To them only the flamboyant were flannel-mouthed. Percentage in Maine by which the length of the average conversation differs from the desired length? Low, below ten percent.

Words were a confession, nothing less. Disclosure. A laconic person spilled no beans, ever. Never. Rambling on brought its own defeat. Faces alone gave exposure. The brothers were keen on always low-rating other people's faces. It never occurred to them that their own pear-shaped heads were unattractive, wide and weird. Two cheerful middle-aged ladies in a lot were selling Christmas trees. "Look like a couple of crabs," said Prof. Drogue. "Going sideways." A religious zealot went to hand them a pamphlet. "Crooked," said Dreel. "As a green snake," said his brother. The city of Bangor was full of pan-handlers. They had the *maladresse* to be rude in front of the women, *which charmed them*. "I need some bread," asked a begging student on the street, holding out his hand. "Then, go fuck a baker."

Walking on the way back to the car (they were being chauffeured in the Columbine Lodge jitney), the two men looked into every single ash barrel that they passed on the sidewalk, an old habit that they never broke. Prof. Drogue at one point thought he saw something. He stopped to reach in to pick out and hold up an object. "Worth anything?" asked brother. He shook his head, negative. "Pot warp," he muttered.

§

Acting fast now became paramount. There was no time to shilly-shally. There were no locks on the barn door, only holes in the cedar planks. He secretly checked one night after making one of his many house calls, visits he weekly made by insinuating friendship. He peeked through the high faded barns slats into a darkness that slowly ebbed. What he saw in storage were chimney stacks of trunks and boxes, a stockpiled hoard—"A pyramid," he whispered to himself, smiling. In his mind, it might have been 1922 and he, English archaeologist Howard Carter in the precious Valley of the Kings with a kerosene lantern held high about to break through a mud-brick door, revealing the passageway that led to Tutankhamen's tomb!

One evening in early April, the girls, alarmed, went racing up onto the porch, across the portico, and into the inn, running past the small front garden on the rising ground where pretty bearberry or kinnikinnick gave way to small tight bushes of lodgepole pine mixed with spiraea and juniper and a large aspen stand. They heard something growl—was it a dog? Quickly Fatwana jumped back inside and squeezed her locket, closing her eyes tight to hold her thoughts within a tall forest where virgin trees, blooming, protected her.

Her uncle sought her out to console her. Her heart was battening against her ribs. He took her hand and, pointing to her amulet, kindly offered. "You trust a jackal and not a dog?" Fatwana quickly disappeared to her room only to return with a nature encyclopedia that showed pages of photos of ferocious animals.

Rural Maine was wild, especially in the Penobscot region. Foxes barked at night. Fatwana who had seen moose, loons, even bald eagles and hawks soaring high over the woods, was fearful of animals. Weren't there black bears about? She never walked out at night. Always, and even during the day, on a pathway in passing through a dark dingle she clutched the sacred amulet around her neck for protection.

"That's not a dog—it's a wolverine," clarified her kind uncle, chuckling.

Their uncle had a big belly, and their aunt reminded them of a busy hen. Both were lovable. Uncle blustered. "Fatwana—scared? When Egyptian art portrayed pictures of so many hawks, snakes, beetles, lions and other wild creatures?" He patted the sofa on which he sat and had the girl sit down beside him.

"It is a *carcajou*, as the Penobscots call them—'injun devil,'" he kindly explained. "Now, *they* are fierce. They are the most despised of all the Northwoods animals, the most vicious, aggressive of all creatures. It will attack a bear, tear apart a team of Alaskan huskies, eat a porcupine, quills and all. Its fur will not accumulate frost, even at sub-zero degrees, and will not mat and freeze to the skin. Eskimos use it for trimming parka hoods and wristlets. Its very stink is nasty. It's teeth as hard as silver will almost outcrop on a bite! It possesses in an almost evil way a special upper molar in the back of the mouth, sharper than a pirate's cutlass, that is rotated 90-degrees, towards the inside of the mouth. This special characteristic allows wolverines to tear off meat from prey or carrion that has been frozen steel solid."

With a cold chill, Fatwana peered at its teeth.

"Its brain is, well, sort of thixotropic—stable at rest but becoming fluid when agitated, whereupon it goes berserk. It scavenges carrion. Nothing is off the menu, from bison to rats, moose to moles, goats to gophers, including birds' eggs, roots, and seeds. Look at its powerful jaws, claws like a harpy's, eyes that become lightbulbs in fury. They call them the 'glutton.' Carcajou, as I say, or quickhatch. And they are not misnamed. They bite and eat anything. They won't let go."

He gently shook his head. "No, no, no. it is the two-legged creature that you should fear, dear child. You are safe at the inn. The world in its odd way fears animals pointlessly," he said. "No truer friend to man walks the ground of God. Whatever goes on four legs is a friend. Who was it said, 'All men are enemies, all animals comrades.'?" He didn't tell her that Maine has more black bears than any state east of the Mississippi, but they were gentler up there, in part because there were no grizzlies up there to attack them and make them ferocious.

§

April blossomed, as Spring finally broke. Prof. Drogue, claiming to be unworthy—over the amorous protests of the Freya and Feroce—encouraged the girls that there were any number of eligible young men at the university whom they would charm, continued giving lessons in science and history. The glorious season, with re-greening everywhere, had given them an idea with mercantile possibilities. Why not have a dance in the barn? Wouldn't that be fun? Folk music, violins, a caller for jigs and reels? He also suggested that he could use the barn as space for his experiments. Fatwana who hadn't a thought of boys spent most of her time trying to improve her English by beginning to write about the parents she missed in a daybook. Freya and Feroce, who spent all their time dreaming, foolishly invested in the old legend of the Dumb Supper, in which young women silently prepared a meal backward, by which they hoped to see a vision of their future husbands in an empty seat. It was typical of them, thought the Drogues. Ninnies. Geese. Nitwits. Ding-dongs.

All along, the Drogues bided their time, banking on the cutthroat psychology which has it that someone in need of some-thing can only have it by specifically pretending not being in need of it. Tenacity involves guile, guile preparedness. All ants crawling on a rubber rope can reach the end even when the rope stretches much faster than the ant can crawl. But ants still crawl.

They were the ants.

Nothing could quite scamper like they could. Or bur-row. Or claw. Or tunnel. Or scrape. Or grub. Or dig and delve. But for rare sheets of cartonnage, what fool would not scratch and claw, frag and ferret? For rare items like objects endowed with the magical Eyes of Horus? It was a matchless nonpareil, the symbol in ancient Egypt—Early Dynastic, Old Kingdom, Middle or New Kingdom, and whatever intermediate period, it didn't matter—representing protection, health, and restoration. Designed to resemble the eye of a falcon, it was also called the Eye of Ra, which represented the right eye of the Egyptian falcon god, Horus. As the *wadjat*-eyes represented the sun, the mirror image, or left eye, represented the moon, and Tehuti, or Thoth, the sacred god of the pen, the male counterpart of the goddess of balance. The bite of Ibis! You want balance? How about retribution, retaliation, reprisal?

Revenge! He was not his father's son for nothing. He would show that rude and domineering, skoliosexual, switch-hitting, carpet-munchng dago, Ms. Christiani Mariani Pianigiani—or the "CMPG," a.k.a. Complete Pig, as he called her—how to suck eggs! He remembered only too well a muttered slander against him overheard by his brother at the Spring faculty meeting ("Frilly boy? His view of heaven is a row of pink tents!") and how she had refused a stipend that prevented his joining an expedition to Armant in Egypt, an integral site for the worship of the war god, Montu. It would have made all the difference.

Now? There were going to be some changes made, he revengefully thought, bet on it, weevil breath! He would be resurrected. And she, the sniping crone of the university department? In his mind, the baggage had already been hauled off her plinth like a corrupt tyrant and desecrated!

Prof. Drogue haunted several museums that winter. He took four bus-trips down to Boston and back to tour the Egyptian rooms at the MFA and, one week, even those at the Metropolitan in New York City, where rubbing his hands, he stared goggle-eyed through the glass cases at the many rare objects they contained—*he had seen no examples of cartonnage!*—torn between owning them and loving them. Regarding antiquities, it occurred to him, how could a rational choice ever be made between two outcomes of equal value?

No fear. It was not a question of Buridan's Ass. No fear. Prof. Drogue would resolve the dilemma by *selling* them. And it would happen soon. He had plans to visit the University of Pennsylvania Museum of Archeology and Anthropology on that subject. The way to solve a general problem that covers the specifics of a sought-after solution was by extracting yourself from the suspension by forcing the result! To fool most people, you had to get up early in the morning, as they say. To fool the Drogues, you couldn't go to bed.

You had to be very careful. Increases in efficiency lead to even larger increases in demand. The more product, the less interest. But he was wily. He knew the street. He fingered his few scarabs, their scored backs. The scarab beetle (*kheper*) was one of the most popular amulets in ancient Egypt, simply because the insect was a symbol of the sun god, Ra—an association that evolved from the Egyptians' misunderstanding of the scarab's life cycle. An adult beetle lays its eggs inside a ball of dung, which is then buried underground.

§

Prof. Drogue recalled with a sour chuckle how for gain many summers back, he had *made* scarabs, fashioned them out of his own devising, using the rare patterns he had studied in one of his insect books, carved the little creatures out of common clay and then hardened them in his college laboratory kilns, scored their backs, and sold them at flea markets in Fryeburg, Houlton, and Presque Isle as the real thing. It brought in money, added greatly to his teaching income, but he hated tourists—flatlanders, the worst being from New York. Vacationers soon bought property, sightseers then moving in. Out-of-towners! Built and brought the whole family. Caused septage. Screwed up the zoning codes. Land values soared, taxes rose. Uptick on crime. Traffic, congestion, noise. You found them walking on fragile habitats, even out in the willie-wacks leaving waste that washed into the ocean. Erosion. "Down street going all crowded with shops," their father grizzled. "Coming close to sixty years now, look up anywhere and there's a loud-mouthed Jew Yorker with his feet in your dooryard looking dumber than hammered shit—and guess what? A dollar chance the prick will soon be runnin' for mayor." Still, tourists were rubes, knew nothing, were open to all sorts of dodges, and fell for any scam.

You lookin' to scarf a lobster roll? Here, a few knuckles of meat with great gobs of mayo on a white bread bun. $17.50— thank *you! Come back soon!*

Prof. Drogue had already taken home that first strip of cartonnage. The task now was to find more of it and to relieve the family of all the wrapping pieces, the rare layers of dried material, fragments even if frayed still harboring its ancient spoors, touched with visible resin, delicate apron tracings and foot casings that only needed to be put under a microscope to determine their age and then to be sold for a king's ransom, for indeed the ransom would be made in the name of a king! His younger brother Dreel, something of a philistine and who was also the slower of the two, needed convincing regarding the nature of Egyptian art, even in museums. He exclaimed, "I don't think much of the art of a people who for, what, four thousand years have drawn cats in precisely the same way!"

Not so his older brother. He had the blood of his father coursing through his veins, and his blood was up. He was very much in the grip of *wedjat.* Eyes were the secret. There was more to know about the Eyes of Horus!

Rebirth! Healing! *Money!*

III.

It was moving day—

—moving all the crates, valuables, treasures, and cartonnage out of the barn that they could.

Like a scarab, Prof. Drogue was himself a natural accumulator, a pinchpenny, a niggard, a skinflint, a hoarder, and a remorseless magpie. He and his brother had been brought up that way. Their mother, a cankered crusty soul, told them in that voice of hers that was always thin, unearthly, and troubled that, according to an old tradition, rue grows best when it has been stolen from another's garden. Pretend nice up front, but in private, she warned them, show them how the cow ate cabbage. The frugal mother earned money by having acquired an electric needle and for added income learned to remove moles with it, charging the neighbors for each blot. The boys had been raised to believe the riches of earth were all in, on, and under the ground—they spent much of their childhood dowsing—yours only for the devising, which is why one son became an archaeologist, the other a chemist.

They had been schooled well. Their doctrinaire father taught them from the earliest grades that life was divided, not between Republican and Democrat, nor between one nationality and another, not between New Hampshire and Maine, not between pie plant and Indian pudding, but only between the will and the imagination. Be the force of *will!* he exhorted them. Follow the paradox of entailment—inconsistent premises always make an argument valid. Confuse them with lies, and you will grow rich.

No small boy in the Drogue family, by means of the strict

dedication of his hypothecating parents, was ever wanting in the knowledge of frugality or the ways it paid off nor ever failed to find in his pockets the fiat currency they coined and minted—nothing in real money, of course, only the vigorous promise it would come.

"*All* men don't want money? Do not be fooled that only some men do. Regarding acquisition, 'some' is a cowardly eulogistic synonym for 'all.' Sentiment is a purely subjective factor in determining value. Screw the scroungers, beggars, and moochers!" He would turn to his boys sitting in that battered old black bus of a classroom, much of it gutted, as they bumped along old out-of-the-way forest roads on one of their many take-ins and quote, "'I'll gladly pay you Tuesday for a hamburger today,' declared fat little soup-slurping J. Wellington Wimpy—he was a cartoon character in the funny papers who was always broke—'I'd like to invite you over to my house for a duck dinner'—except what did little tubby add?—right, 'you bring the ducks!' No, folks were right when they muttered, 'He should be killed to death!'"

Old Drogue on a roll scarcely took a breath.

"But that is the way of the world. Be a who, not a whom, see? Lead, don't follow. Do not be a slave—never, ever be—to forces compelling you to act simply as they command," he commanded. "Pay no attention to fewtrils. Look it up. Nature in itself is healing—it is man who is the virus, trash of little value. Don't go in for all those leftward lawyer's lies. The self is *not* an obstacle to human understanding, as those liberal 'crape myrtles' insist—you know, the 'house mothers who live on Mount Fairy'—it is the *only* key to understanding! Safety is found in the *absence* of feelings." The boys listened mostly, occasionally munching apples and chattering like finches among the reeds of a waterside, but if their attention ever widely wandered, he would come down like thunder upon them.

His tirades could be intemperate, his ravings scary. Were they born from all he suffered from creepy Mrs. Mewshaw and all they'd heard of her knowing and adept brutality? Or was it his abiding hatred of lawyers whom he dismissed, saying, "They are the kleptopredators of the world who will steal your meal, and then eat you, too"? What sharpened that thorn under his saddle?

Had it anything to do with that enigmatic remark of his, whatever that meant, the one that he was always repeating, "I am Yanko Goorall"? Or did it begin, wondered the boys, with his living contempt for that bog tramp, Swill O'Rourke? His insane gorgon-haired wife, Gneisspaws? Their hopeless son, Knaster, the droolie sired by a milkman? One night he actually *did* wake the boys up, screaming as he sat up in bed, waving a small gun, "I smell a taig and a stinkin' mick toe rag! Where is that pogue, that narrowback spud? Get that filthy mick bog trotter! *'Here you go, shamrock nigger, bite this icicle!'"*

The bus would be singing through forest and dale, as the old man went into his rants. "The empirical self, look it up, is nothing but a bundle of adaptations, cravings, longings, instincts, and impulses. Do not even let *yourself* be exploited by your *own* desires without a free and inner open-hearted personal consent, do you hear me? Altruism is a temptation. No diseased conscience should talk you out of your rightful gain. Have the strength to be free to withstand false piety to fight the derivatives of any so-called reality that weakens resolve. I have told you repeatedly and will tell you again—the heart is the enemy of the mind! Ideals and ideolog have been a curse of mankind since the Garden of Eden!"

The boys were not allowed to interrupt, which he considered *squandering* advice. These were important lessons, guidelines to survive.

But he would interrupt himself, often, asking them to repeat what he said, saying, "What have I asked you to be?"

They would sing in unison, "Do not be the you others create!"

"Again?"

"*Do not be the you others create!*"

"Louder!"

"DO NOT BE THE YOU OTHERS CREATE!"

"Look at history! What have ideals down through the millennia brought but war, famine, starvation, and misery? Liberal ideals, nationalistic ideals, republican ideals, pacifist ideals, religious ideals, state ideals, class ideals, bourgeois and proletarian both, should all be heaped up, *heaped up high*, into a gigantic pile in the middle of the town square come Fourth of July and be blown sky high into smithereens!"

He would angrily double-bang the steering wheel of the bus.

"Be cold to mystery," cried out the bold father. "Choose reason over wisdom. Logic has it all over what the simperers and merchants of fairy call truth. I impute to moderation a lack of desire for life. The only life worthwhile is a life of plenty. Death in life means an empty pocket. Amputate all humane and tender feelings to give, which only borrow from yourself. Neither have dreams, nor feed idle longing. Crave to have to get to own, both feet on solid ground where gold grows and shining silver sits. The crooked timber of human nature tends by default look it up to give in toward forces that transcend themselves. Adventure is not within man, as mealy-mouthed meliorists insist—look it up—it is *without*, hard as coin, crisp as currency." He would tap-tap-tap a knowing forefinger to his eye. "Newcomers, strangers, outsiders, and immigrants will pull out your eye-teeth to sell them back to you."

Old Drogue mistrusted all foreigners.

"They smoke dung in their cigarettes," he complained. "They swim with rubber wings. They have no speed limits. They never use soap. They wear berets. You have to pay for the suit-cases that you take with you on their buses. They carry loaves of bread under their arms and sell it naked. They wear weird underclothes. Their wines are too sweet. They eat sausages in the theater and make you tip the usher. They serve vegetables as if it is a food. They piss right outdoors in urinals in the cities and talk to passersby as they're doing it They point by wagging their whole hands, have shitty telephones that never work, take entire hours to drink a cup of coffee in midget cups, close their stores all afternoon while they sleep during the day, and haggle all the time without saying the price!"

Wrath increasingly characterized his monologues. Was it having missed out on never having made his trek to the bottom of the ocean floor? In never having never found all the treasures he imagined were there for the taking? All the lutetium and haf-nium and francium pullulating in the abyssal benthic?

Almost driving off the road, he would continue his rants.

"The self, *you*, the sole object for the knowing subject, is—*is*—only as it *owns*," declared the scowling father, "its sole appro-bation, and answer to the faculty of reason!" Wasting anything, even as little rogues, got them severely beaten with his ox-hide razor strap. "Experience concludes nothing universal except the principle of pleasure, which is to own! The word *right* in the bare state of nature is a person's freedom to do what he would. An individual's driving force is the will to survive. The deepest inner nature of everything is will—endless striving. The intellect is an attribute of the will, which necessity drives forward."

He spoke to the boys, especially as he grew visibly older—a later period when he began nightly going down to drink at the Chat Qui Rit—with a sort of strained, pinched ol' John Brown-like intensity, wearing the startling look of a hovering kestrel. Was that his fire-scarred memory talking? "People act in daily life of necessity. There is a deceit bandied about, a lie which buries its own ruthless logic deep inside the norm, that greed is bad." Sometimes he carried a ferrule. "Are you listening to me?"

§

Crusty Old Drogue took no man as a model, flatly refusing such idolatry, but for his cleverness and unsleeping vigilance and unappeasable greed probably his only exemplar was the merchant, John Jacob Astor, businessman, real estate mogul, investor, and, no small thing, the very first multi-millionaire in the United States. He was a bastard and a picaro and a good-for-nothing reprobate like all the robber barons, but he made killings not only in the fur trade monopoly and by smuggling opium into China, but also by shrewd investing in real estate in or around New York City. The unheard-of profits he scored in China sending fox pelts, beaver skin, otter hides, textiles, scarlet-dyed cochineals, and North American ginseng roots (which they treasured as aphrodisiac), and brought back by ship silks, satins, nankeens, taffetas, fans, nutmegs, cloves, porcelain, and choice souchong teas which he then sold to retailers and, again, re-exported to Europe! The buck reigned. He ignored jingoistic passions while remaining attentive to the money to be made on disasters, economic reversals, even wars.

"Greed is the motor of acquisition. All prosperity is married to greed. Greed is need. True need in greed, however, hardly ever lurks. Never wait for need to be impelled to take. Enough in greed is the opposite of more. I have told you many times, '*What you are made of, you are made for!*' Grab all you can!" insisted their father who all through his life had never ceased to be stunned by the credulity of others; their gullibility to him truly passed all comprehension. "Be lily-livered and you lose out. You want to be mashed by the world which it is only ready to do in spades? Mashing is crushing food until its original form is entirely lost. Make war for gain! A long reach constitutes a jurisdiction!" In the matter of unrestrained liberty, Old Drogue was never wanting for rhetoric. "What is it they say, peace comes never to sit, but to brood? They are correct! *Store up*, as the Egyptians did in their granaries, and you will never know famine. Thrift is revenue, diligence a cash cow, good will folly, and life as it comes a mercantile enterprise, the proceeds of which are very far from covering the cost of it."

There was a way to life and a way to lubber, which was the easy of the dumbbells and the dullards and the dolts.

"Free? My pappy showed all of us how to glean fields, for while there is plenty of food harvested, tons more is left behind simply to rot, putrefy, and crumble. You want to sit back on your fat asses like all them welfarites and government drones and hucksters on aid relief with their gerbil-on-the-treadwheel existence, going *squeak squeak squeak*? Them big motorized farm operations don't scoop everything from the fields, trust me. Ain't economical, see, for them big-scale farmers to trundle back aiming to scour acres of harvest before the frost sets in. So, go, help yourself, no need asking the farmer. Why bother? There's your breakfast, lunch, and dinner!" He told them, "Shake a leg!"

"No Maine winter ever challenged the wood pile of an intelligent and self-sufficient upright human being who is *awake!* You can find more to feed on, in, and among the fir pines and the beckoning woods than in any goddam general store, and the state of Maine is 92 percent woods, you hear me, little fiddleheads? Get lost on purpose! Christ, you can snatch a salmon from a stream like picking out a cabbage at a farmer's market and grab a goose right out of the air with a good reach. Think like Maine loon! Harvest time!"

He would point right into their young faces. "Music is a joy only when cash sounds the song. Knowledge is an analogue for gain. Look it up. It is nothing less than a distemper of learning—a lost, crippled, squandered, self-scuppering sabotage—not to take or to give things away. Make things *you!* Stealing is merely adoption. My motto is 'Fortune brings in some boats that are not steered.'" He would look quizzically in their direction.

The boys looked bewildered.

"It's from a play," he told them. "*Cymbeline.*"

§

The lessons took. Thrift animated their souls, rapacity becoming the vehicle of their hallucinating imagination. Without their inborn overriding obsession with parsimony and penny-pinching, they would only have haunted the ramparts of

the world as disembodied shades. Not a day ever passed growing up in the Moosehead Lake region when young Drogue and
his brother did not wander poking through ash barrels, walk
through neighbors' back yards to steal grapes, pilfer ice from the
ice wagon or coal from the coal truck, sneak vegetables from the
market trundles, steal kerosene balls from road worksites, or fail
to visit the town dump to search for throwaways, bicycle pumps,
old bottles, chains, old books, picture frames, trash brass, lamp-
shades. Prof. Drogue still ate dandelions he picked. He sold any
kind of brummagem at flea markets. He several times pilfered
a church poverty box. If he could not find cartonnage, maybe
there were mummy masks. He wanted all the cartonnage! Proof
of this was his perennially watchful eye. No one else had such an
eye?

Except?

The Eye of Horus! The professor had done all the research
he could on the subject—with exhaustive delight studying that
stylized symbol with its distinctive markings and as it appeared
in all of its many varieties, on rings, steatite cippus, on diorite
bowls, on glass cartouches, on beads and Coptic wood combs, on
a bronze oxyrhynchus fish statue, all with its watchfulness representing healing, well-being, and protection. Protection? laughed
the professor, sitting up in his carrel at the university. (Scholars
in adjacent carrels whispered *hush!*) It derived from the mythical
conflict between the god Horus with his rival, Set, in which Set
tore out or destroyed one or both of Horus's eyes and the eye was
subsequently healed or returned to Horus with the assistance of
another deity, such as Thoth. Horus subsequently offered the eye
to his deceased father Osiris, and its revivifying power sustained
Osiris in the afterlife. The Eye of Horus was thus equated with

funerary offerings as well as with all the offerings given to deities in temple ritual. It could also represent other concepts, rebirth, growth, the waxing and waning moon, restoration on a thousand fronts and in a thousand ways—

—including an empty purse.

Mummies were often turned to face left, suggesting that the eyes were meant to allow the deceased to see outside the coffin, and so in a studied lateral way the pair of eyes of Horus were mainly painted on the left side, meant to warn and to ward off danger. Painted on the bows of boats, they were meant to both protect the vessel and allow it to see the way ahead. Eyes of Horus were also sometimes portrayed with wings, hovering protectively over kings or deities. Stelae, or carved stone slabs, he knew from research, were often inscribed with the eyes. In some periods of Egyptian history, only deities or kings could be portrayed directly beneath the winged sun symbol that often appeared in the lunettes of stelae, and Eyes of Horus were placed above figures of common people. The symbol could also be incorporated into tattoos, as demonstrated by the mummy of a woman from the late New Kingdom that was decorated with elaborate tattoos, including several Eyes of Horus.

Why was such a symbol painted on coffins? On carved stone stelae? On the bows of boats? *On cartonnage?* Did it actually have protective magical powers? Who could say? Both of the Drogues believed it did, and they refused to be wrong. Why else was it one of the most common motifs in Egyptian art, remaining in use from the Old Kingdom (c. 2686–2181 B.C.) to the First Intermediate Period (c. 2181–2055 B.C.) to the Middle Kingdom (c. 2055–1650 B.C.)? Prof. Drogue knew that the eye symbol was also rendered as a hieroglyph (𓂀). Although some scholars disputed it, many astute Egyptologists have long believed that hieroglyphs, representing pieces of the symbol, stood for fractions in ancient Egyptian mathematics.

§

The last weeks approached for the heist. Every night in his house Prof. Drogue sat up scheming, while filtering it with his long tapering white fingers, he felt over and over the nap of the white cartonnage he owned. The thrill was matchless. With a microscope, he examined he delicate fiber and grain of the cloth. During mummification, mainly done for wealthy people as poorer people could not afford the process, the chief embalmer was a priest wearing a mask of Anubis, the jackal-headed god of the dead.

Although sometimes cartonnage is compared with papier mâché, there is no pulping of the substrate, he learned, whether papyrus or linen—no, instead, smaller or larger sections of linen were cut to specific shapes, and layered, and the white plaster applied over the top, a method of preparation preserving the sections, the reason papyrus cartonnage became a prominent source of well-preserved manuscript sections. "There are four principal periods of use of cartonnage," he read, "each with distinct ingredients and effects:

1. *In the early Dynastic Period (3150–2686 B.C.), plastered linen was often used for mummy masks; by the Twelfth Dynasty workshops fashioned longer masks covering the upper body, when wood was used for mummy-cases, enveloping the entire lain-out body.*

2. In the Third Intermediate Period (1070–664 B.C.), the innermost coffin of elite burials was replaced by a mummy-case, made in cartonnage (linen and stucco), with 'cartonnages' brightly-painted—by the Late Period (664-332 B.C.) no longer used.

3. In the Ptolemaic Period (332 B.C.–30 A.D.), from the reign of Ptolemy III, to the very beginning of the Roman Period when they took control of Egypt (30 B.C.), cartonnage elements and masks were produced from old papyrus scrolls; during this period, many masks and elements were also being produced with linen in place of papyrus.

4. In the Roman Period, mummy masks and decorated pieces placed on the mummies were being produced from thicker fibrous material supporting a thicker layer of plaster. The Romans ruled for over 600 years until around 640 A.D.

But enough of scholarship. The time had come to own what he coveted, what he deserved. Prof. Drogue had his knife, flashlight, a hieroglyphic dictionary in his back pocket, and a walkie-talkie. Dreel wore crampons for the roof.

They took long swigs from a jug of ergot rye and pulled on hats.

"Ready?"

"Wicked."

"Sure?"

"Yup."

"You?"

"Roof."

"Me?"

"Door."

"Side?"

"Ayah."

"Not back?"

"Same difference."

"Right."

"Take it all?"

"Both feet."

"Leave nothin'?"

"Not a scrid."

"'Chout."

"Course."

The inn traditionally closed on April 19th, Patriots Day, a celebration in all of the New England states. The uncle and aunts would be taking the young girls to a city celebration in Orono, they knew, where they planned to spend the entire day. Brother Dreel, with a hoist to lift heavy objects, would go up on the roof, right to the very cupola, past the soffit vents, up to the gable. The professor with a flashlight would simply slip through a side door and negotiate the premises, select what he wanted. A small truck that they borrowed, which stood by a back fence, they would fill to take back home all the cartonnage they could steal, no matter how small, no matter how much he had to cut away.

That was hard work? Nothing at all compared to their father back in his day setting out in harsh sub-zero temperatures with iron hammer, chisel, and saw—and sometimes a specially-designed iron plow—working from grid lines sketched on the thick, solid sheets of ice and kneeling to handsaw and harvest headers out of pond ice in the dead of winter, cuttings 20 inches thick, all tough dangerous work. No small gasoline motors—too pricey. He worked the second and third weeks in January mostly, floating rafts of ice to a truck, guiding them with long-handled picks, sometimes carting them by sled over snow pulled by a rented Percheron draft horse, eventually breaking it up with tool bars and then personally hoisting it all by himself into the ice house that stinking souse O'Rourke tried to burn down. He spent much of his life hard at it, taking millions of pounds of pond ice from a one-acre plot from which sloshed and sozzled O'Rourke with a mill dam sought to siphon off water.

And where was O'Rourke just now?

A full six feet under.

Planted.

Like a spud.

§

Prof. Drogue pulled up in the truck. It was time for the great appropriation. Climbing out of his seat, Dreel noticed right away that the fence that the old uncle had put up in a long circular surround against their girls fears of intruding animals, a protective but feeble sort of *chevaux de frise* that he had hoped no creature could jump over, had been worn down by wind, wet, wildness, and winter in a few places. Had it been breached? Doubtful. A bear would have battered the slats to tiny pieces.

Prof. Drogue knew that the pair of *wedjat*-eyes he had seen were hieroglyphic eyes allowing the dead to see. He was convinced that within the plastered lines wrapping the odd, oblong packages in the barn, in the heavily wrapped shrouded boxes, along with the valuables they contained, were *themselves* rare finds—who knew, priceless treasures, possibly even rarer than the artifacts that they contained! After mere months, probing about, it would be just as he thought, finding labeled maps that went back multiple centuries, rare written and pictorial texts from ancient body containers from nearly prehistoric shells that had been decorated with geometric shapes, deities, and inscriptions. During the Ptolemaic era—for he had checked—the single shell method was altered to include four to six pieces of cartonnage. There would generally be a mask, pectoral, apron, and foot casing involved. In certain instances, there were two additional pieces used to cover the rib-cage and stomach. Were these, he wondered, the rare items that the evil servants had so coveted in their brutal assaults?

There was no rush.

This is for you, Ms. Christiani Mariani Pianigiani, he thought, my luck a curse on you and all of your ginzo wop relatives who had no business being in Maine for holding up my allocations, he grizzled, for obstructing my advancement. He paused to take a Feen-A-Mint from his box of them. Nerves.

Prepared, greedy Dreel clambered up onto the high roof, ready with a long rope dangling to swing any treasures onto the truck.

In the barn, Prof. Drogue saw a pair of *eyes* peering out. His heart leapt to his throat, walloping in a burst of merrifying joy. He went closer, much, much closer. Another pair of *wedjat*-eyes? It was when he reached in to grab whatever it was when his forefinger was fully ripped off, before he could scream. His hand was then snatched and bitten—*and held.* An adult wolverine the size of a medium dog, its rounded head, black eyes, and short rounded ears, which more closely resembled a bear. was yanking him backward, kicking, with insane guttural growls, insistently swerving side to side, expelling a nauseating yellow oily spray, biting and kicking with each snarl, thunder-thumping the victim's groin with its broad, punt-propelling feet.

It buck-bucked, drooling white, spraying rat scat, skittering backwards on its short legs, madly scuttling while dragging the professor into the hay with its daggered teeth and large, five-toed paws with fierce crampon-like claws and that plantigrade posture enabling it, hump by stinking hump, to climb up and over steep cliffs, trees, and snow-covered peaks with relative ease, refusing in its inexorable hatred to release its grip. It hissed and spit and bit with its shearing canines, lunging for his throat while fastening its forefeet claws into him attempting to disembowel him with raking strokes of its hind feet, hoicking, jerking, and yanking.

Prof. Drogue was being rolled, spun, pinwheeling under the beast. There was nothing for shelter. He was upside down, enmeshed in snarling teeth, a welter of hot nacreous blood spilling from deep bites into his head, rupturing, and with snarls he heard himself howling from being eviscerated. He felt and heard his bitten cranium crack and snap shooting with pains of hot fire, a large swatch of bloody scalp being torn off his skull. The animal was shaking him in his teeth.

"O good Christ," he screamed. *"I'm being devoured!"* As one arm swung out wildly circling in a desperate reach for help, struggling, his own feet madly kicking, he blindly yanked the rope, unseating Dreel high above who pitched headlong backwards off the roof directly onto the rusty tines of an ancient upended drag harrow, where he was impaled, pierced through by spring-teeth even in part of his head, where he lay quivering and spouting fountains of blood, exenterated.

Under a back stack of boxes and crates, in a dark hidden

den, a lactating wolverine with its young had cached her food. Alarmed, discovered, armed with powerful jaws, sharp claws, a thick hide, and a ferocity and brainless strength out of proportion to its size and enough to kill prey many times larger than itself, the solitary carnivore, all muscle, its guard hair high and fur brittle as wire, was dug in and had Prof. Drogue firmly by the throat with its sharp ferocious teeth as serrated as a megalodon shark's for flesh-tearing. The animal, hump-backed, was actually red-eyed, fatally digging into the ground and crazed with each howling bite. It was Prof. Drogue's last realization as one arm was already chewed off.

There came one final crunch, the beast spit-groaning with the satisfying crackle produced by its teeth penetrating the hard crust of the throat, stringy ropes hanging from its jaws twisted like a kneck of rope.

When the uncle, aunt, and the girls returned from Orono, seeing the tragedy, they called the sheriff from Pole and waited for him to arrive.

Young Fatwana, shocked, stood concerned on the back porch of the inn. Clutching the chain around her neck with the gold amulet of Anubis for protection, she saw a mess of cartonnage in a pile by the two mangled bodies.

"I know what we can wrap them in," she said innocently.

Finocchio; or,
The Man with the Long Nose

"Hooooo!"

"Dry it again, signior."

Dry it, I thought with amusement. Dry it, say, with a handkerchief? I can't resist a joke.

"Hooooo!"

"Dwice," he said. "Dis de bowels of de erd."

"*Hoo-hoooooo!*"

I bellowed. The very cementum of my teeth shook. The shouts, which in other contexts would clearly have seemed a presage to knife-sticking, boomed through the Roman catacombs, where we stood—me, and Marco, my guide. Below the church of San Sebastiano, the passages, some obstructed by landslips, reached out all around us in a crazy chain of subterranean labyrinths, honeycombing, crossing and recrossing at all kinds of angles in a network that spoked out something like sixty miles in circumference. The low tunnels—once quarries, later Christian hiding places, and, so rumor had it, also at times the site of unspeakable orgies—had been explored for twenty miles. It seemed, however, as if we intended further exploration into the goetic and the dark. Me—and Marco, who had just relighted his seventh candle. I had earmarked several graves, or whatever, I wanted to see.

A ladder led to the tunnels, with several cubicles; here, the paintings of Jonah's cubicle, dating back to the end of the fourth century and depicting four scenes of the life of the recalcitrant prophet, excited me. The restored crypt of St. Sebastian houses an altar shelf replacing the former one (of which some traces of the base still remain) and the bust of St. Sebastian attributed to Bernini. We poked about. A lay-by, under which sat a sandstone cavity, intrigued me. In the lay-by rose three mausolea dating back to the second half of the second century, later reused.

I had done my reading, you see. Well, how much can a pamphlet tell you, right? "These were once mines," I tactfully observed to my guide. "Correct?" Marco simply farted and blurted out, "Watcha you foots!" But I was right, you see. Before its employment as a burial ground, the area we traversed was occupied by deep mines that eventually gave rise to pagan cemeteries, which were then taken over and utilized by the early Christians as burial sites and even covert meeting places. The graveyard of St. Sebastian was known since the third century as *in memoria apostolorum*, a toponym referring to the presence within the catacomb, for some time, of the relics of the apostles Peter and Paul. Other martyrs were interred there. I read that some of the sepulchers were hard to reach. I particularly wanted to see the grave of Eutychius. Nothing is known about this fellow Eutychius, but his grave was discovered during excavations carried out in the twentieth century in a crumbly area of the catacombs, and a poem dedicated to him by Pope Damasus I was displayed at the entry of the basilica, and it was that poem that moved me to want to see the latest excavation. Marco dampened my ardor. "This man nobody."

Our footsteps were the only footsteps.

"Dooms."

Marco wiped a finger across one of the *loculi*, a ruined vault upon which was inscribed under a film of mealy dust, "*Stercoria in Pace*."

"Dooms and glooms," said I, "heh, heh." The little squib cost me nothing, and, illogically, I somehow thought it might make us move on a bit more quickly. I had to go to the bathroom. We had been down there an hour.

"No, dooms. Holy dooms. Dooms for corpuses, to bury," squawked Marco. "Meat."

He drew a finger slicewise across his neck and, smirking, flapped the Sign of the Cross over his swarthy expositional self. Well, I am a Catholic, I recognized it, but the quick unrelated movements, blending, looked like some uncanny prelapsarian ritual, executed frightfully, in this instance, above the glare of his penny candle. Marco's eyes gleamed like a ferret's, black and snapping. He appeared to be waiting for something. He scrutinized me, comically. I looked past his shoulder, perhaps to distract him, possibly, who knows, to see in my mind's eye the, alas, no-longer-with-us salted away in the circle of vaults not ten feet away.

"Dead bipple," he waved.

Each seven feet, I had read, could accommodate ten sepulchral niches, and one could almost X-ray into the stacks of skulls and heaps of browning bones. And here I was finally seeing some of these who knew how many interred and reinterred saints (olive pruners? oxherds? henwives? who knew?), troweled in with great exactness that they may one day realize their comparatively simple intention to meet the Day of Judgment intact. I was going to say you had to give them credit, but, my god, what a helluva way to live, huh? I mean, how did they bathe, play hoop-ball, experience the extraordinary property of the Roman moon? (I know where I'd have been without love. Briefly, nowhere. Same with my wife. And have often pointed out to my maturer classes, explicitly with reference to Pliny, that the influence of the moon on love warrants further study.) These underground Christians, *sotteranea*—first declension, neuter, nominative plural—were photophobes, plain and simple. Look it up. This is what I always tell any class.

"*Bade bene, ancora*," he said, pointing to the icon of an anchor, briskly walking me along. "Maka da marka *i cristiani*." He kept walking, "*Bade bene, pesce*"—he nodded to a wall-scrawl of a fish. He pouched his cheeks like Harpo Marx. "Efish, sweem sweems." He helped out, prodding me, one hand on my bum, the other fishtailing in and out, "*Fatti dai cristiani*."

"Hooooo!" Just for the heck of it, I shouted again. I felt devilish, bladder aside. But, good grief, my echo sounded like the hellish voice of Virgil's Alecto. It was scary.

I don't mind creeping vetch and cypresses. But what irked me underground was the mournful penchant of these people for depicting death as a hideous skeleton with an inverted torch. And while we're on the subject, remember how St. Peter wanted to be crucified? Upside-down, that's right. And Pacuvius, speaking of the famous gladiatorial combats, indicates that the *premere policem*, the "thumbs down," meant—contrary to popular

belief—to *spare* the victim. Point being, was this the Roman way?
Everything in Rome was inverted! *Per*verted, in a way.

Well, not really.

The sexual excesses of the Roman Empire? That's a subject. People make too much of it. Oh sure, sure, I had read of the *spintriae*—Suetonius, on Nero—brothel tokens for those who, experts in libidinousness, sparked their lusts by rolling around on floors to whet whatever their depraved appetites conjured up and all that. But does a foul stem rot an artichoke? Poo, I say. Poo and more poo.

I teach Latin, you see. California. Right, sunny old. And, well, I honestly thought I could use a summer in Italy, partially because of my seminar in Roman Satire; partially because of a monograph I was writing, "The Chicken/Egg Question in Macrobius's *Saturnalia*, VII, xvi"; and partially—well, what does Virgil say?—*haec sat erit, divae, vestrum cecinisse poetam*, right? *Bucolics*, Eclogue 10, line, ah—wait—seventy, I believe. Or sixty-nine. No, seventy.

My wife would know. But she was in confinement back home, sixth month.

§

How I met Marco? It was an attachment, of sorts. Snaffling pages to my rather outdated *So You're Going to Italy!* (1925)—the nonpareil, I was assured, in the Clara Laughlin Travel Series—I had been for some time sitting alone in a pew trying to sort out, with as much confusion as alarm, the dreadful fact (footnoted, fine print) which had it that, from A.D. 235 to 252—the span, it was suddenly brought home to me, of my entire secondary education, vacations included!—no pope had ever appeared above ground. Can you fathom the claustrophobia factor? A certain Pope Liberius, further, doubtless cadaverine, has gone on record for it, the bookish little thing. Imagine spending a lifetime down there, crouchant, rampant, or dormant, and then trying to bandwagon his successors on the efficacy of breathing soft volcanic rock? The excess of it was borne in on me like an echo.

I am an American, used to fresh air, sun, rides. So then, sitting there, I glanced with understandable regret at the narrow aperture of the San Sebastiano main gallery which led to those deep adjoining passages, thinking to myself that, heavens, in spite of the rambles in the 160 catacombs Rome affords, there surely must have risen the occasional need for a swim, a mow of the grass, an alfresco do with vermouth and a few finger-foods?

Have I explained to you that I am an American?

To get on about Marco. Suddenly, I started. I blinked at that doorway, I tell you. Framed, as if by sudden magic, in the cubicula hunched a little hispid man, essentially nose, round as a dark circle, with a huge ring of keys dangling at his waist. Had he sprung up like a troglodyte from the undermining tunnels? He looked like a fragment of obsolete Tuscan legend ungummed from an underground wall drawing and furbished alive in greasy socks and a five-o'clock shadow. I had never seen such a creature. He had a nose like a *douille*, the tin nozzle of a pastry bag—his actually *had* a hole at the top!—that allows you to squeeze out cake decorations as the icing blurps out. His crown of disheveled shagbark hickory tree hair, tangled and unkempt, almost peeling, stood up like stooks. It is hard to forget repulsive things. Try it sometime.

He had begun crooking his finger amicably at me.

"Dake my hand," he had ordered. "I, Marco, make you the traveling dour of San Sebastiano. I am good, I am good."

"I haven't the time," I had said. "Really, I *haven't*." And, you see, I really hadn't. My heart, frankly, had been set on the Villa Borghese. Can you understand that, a concern for system? Maybe it's the Californian in me. Nor had I seen Hadrian's Column, that rugged monument of staggering proportion which, no matter how many times I had seen it during the school year in those old flat Bettman Archive black-and-whites in my Bradley Arnold, invariably put me in mind of Roman virility—the quintessential Roman virtue, don't kid yourself. Its tenant, in spite of the fact that he's after so many years now only a mere ouncelet of dust, I see as unique in his honest manhood, the which is only recapitulated, in my opinion, by the modern *carabinieri* in tricornes and white gloves, their black uniforms with red braid, trimmed with gold, and set off by a displayed sword, brother! Clearly not like the perfumed fops and dandies in male corselets at Pebble Beach, California, or the transgendered how-be-its flouncing around Venice Beach or the wimps in the wall drawings at Pompeii unselfconsciously postillioning each other like their real-life counterparts who, poor buggers, were even *found* that way in the excavated lava deposits. But not the Roman, pal. Not your Hadrians. Look at that column sometime: 165 feet of peperino and travertine rising up magniloquently and, for thousands of years, saying to we poor underlings, "I'm a man!" It's a great heterosexual poem.

It means something to *me*, anyway. I work out. My wife even comes to the gym sometimes, but not as often as I. As I say, I believe in system.

"Dis the candle. Dake," Marco had said. "*Sic natura jubet.*"

Isn't that Juvenal? Actually, yes it is. Not that it really matters. And so we padded in.

§

Let me be frank in telling you here that, once inside, the only comparison (in terms of ghastliness, depression) that came to me apropos the dark tentacular crypts and extensive burial vaults we soon encountered was to a vague sepia photograph of the Mormon settlement at Nauvoo I had once, for some reason, indiscriminately paused over flipping through an art oversize at a Junior Classical League meeting over which I happily admit I preside. We meet in the library.

With each successive alarm, apparently, the ur-Christian burrowed deeper and deeper into the narrow, winding, and absolutely black passages with molelike speed, which explains, one needn't much wit to see, both the frequency of anti-Christian comeuppances then and the fact that these catacombs can't be reduced to any plan now. System croppeth up again, take note. Well, in teaching Latin one doesn't just jerk up the book and begin with the laws of Ciceronian tmesis or the fineries of ablative-in-the-supine before he first explains just plain stick-in-the-mud declension, huh? But, taking it all together, why talk about *plans*, for the love of mike, when one is being chased, hunted, *tracked* underground all the way to Ostia by angry behelmeted schizopods and the huge Roman soldiers with hippocrepiform legs Tacitus frightens us in telling about—and then, what? to be ripped from the ground like shrieking mandrakes and impaled on sticks for Nero's living torches to illuminate the imperial roads?

Since I first heard that fact, by the way, I haven't eaten shish kebabs once. Veal, yes—in cutlets. Forgive the digression? My wife makes great cutlets, *alla parmegiano* incidentally.

Anyway, give me the twentieth century. *Ite, profanae!* Recognize? The fifth-century essayist Fastidius.

We were still walking, now silently.

"My wife makes great veal parmigiana," I told Marco.

Marco, out of the blue, then told me—blurted it out—that Romans in their day wore nothing under their togas.

§

If I didn't find a—well, my bladder was about ready to burst. But we kept on moving, no pause, threading our way, groping hands everywhere, and crawled past passages choked up with stones, recessed cubicles, subterranean chapels, vertical air-shafts, *luminuria*, escape hatches marvelously if inartistically hewn from the porous volcanic deposits of tufa through which, hand in hand—yes!—we burrowed, burrowed, ever burrowed. Our lights were frail. I wonder if Marco noticed my grip. I squeeze handballs, which is great for the wrist.

"Dis de bowels of de erd," I heard again. Marco paused, farted, excused himself. *This* was your Marco in a nutshell, farting—and even spitting. He also kept grabbing, *plucking*, the seat of his pants. I had noticed, by the way, special areas in Rome where one *could* spit, marked with signs, weren't they, that read *Vieta Sputare*. But, I mean, good god. I hate vulgarity.

Again, there were no footfalls but ours. Have I pointed that out? We paused at the most inauspicious places, where Stentor the Bellower exercised his craft, pausing after each howl for

ALEXANDER THEROUX

I don't know what, save, on *his* side of the ledger, some kind of childish amusement at the perhaps misplaced fear and suspicion any ordinary American might ordinarily show when his hand, already held, was patted! Smoothed like a glove! I put up with it, *ex comitate.*

Marco, not asking, grasped my hand whenever he could, you see, and when not clutching it, he went skipping around and around me in circles like some kind of diabolical black poodle. On the few occasions when he did let go of me, I mistakenly thought it was because I showed an uncommon grip—weight-lifting and such—but most of the time it was the result of his flinging out of the arms *á la romana* singing softly with a lilt whenever we came across the thousand empty columbaria which once held cinerary urns. His repetitious narrations on them proved, more than proved, his affection for them—with a vengeance.

"I see, I see," I kept saying, I kept saying.

Marco paused—was it possible we were now into our second hour?—before a murk of unexceptional wall inscriptions and drawings, and my now vivid sighs of exasperation did nothing to stave off his urge to pause, dissertate, and reflect upon pointlessly unrelated facts and *disjecta* (most of it common knowledge to a classics man) dredged up from who knows where: that resin was used as a male depilatory in ancient Rome; that Nero's real name was L. Domitius Ahenobarbus; that imported slaves were identified as such by the Roman chalk-marks on their bums; that Mussolini *Dux* had stomach cramps; that the Forum cats were annually blessed at the church of St. Anthony the Abbot; and that—I swear, it must have been the fifth time he told me—all Romans, nobles especially, wore transparent tunics.

"Dey show his bologna."

"Really," I said archly, looking away. He kept looking at me with that nose of his, Tin Man-horrible.

"*É vero*," he cackled and slammed the wall.

"*Trombare. Capisci?*" He giggled. "*Da giovane, ho imparato l'inglese rimorchiando le turiste Americane.*"

Coo coo crazy, I thought, *yuh*.

My dislike of Marco had now reached such proportions that merely his walk alone was almost enough to throw me into convulsions. At this stage, I would have given the world for another guide—anyone. Quintilian insisted in his *Institutio oratoria* (Book III, vii, 25, if you want the reference) that a speaker as a guide of men should be a "good man." Morally. And look at me, I thought, fobbed off with a—a lusty slob, a lackey. And as we bumped along—he fumbling, passing his hand along the rough walls, me more practically concerned with the scant light of my candle whose wick I husbanded carefully, fearfully—I was yanked, stooping, through a side tunnel and charged at a run I far from relished into a rather large, gray, triple-walled *arcosolia*, with its several niches spread shoulder-high around us,

"Subplots ramify," I said aloud, sarcastically. I mean, what the hell!

Marco dripped some tallow onto the shelf of a particular hollow and into it mushed his wobbling candle, I sat down, tired, gassed, on a grayish ledge. But it was cold, dirty, and brittle with stuccolike stones. My buttocks felt like a crupper. He wiped his hands on his coat. He took out his handkerchief, rubbed his brow, and then began knotting it around his fingers. He turned straight to me.

"You, um, like *ragazza?*"

"You say?"

"*Feminina*, for lady," whispered Marco, snatching at his trousers—a displacement activity, for what I couldn't say—or did not dare to. That we were wasting precious time and that my lower abdomen was expanding like a bloated rubber zeppelin, however, were facts not lost on me.

"Geerls. These you, um, you like, am liking?"

What the *deuce?* I thought.

"Well, shoot, of *course* I like girls."

"No like booeys? Mens? *Ragazzi?*"

What the—?

The guide's head looked like a wet Veronese peach or a cooking apple, hot, red, perspiring freely before me through the somewhat sheepish grin that is so easily taken for, because it often indicates, an apology. And was he pointing to his key-chain?

"You want like I want to dutch, mister man?"

"Dutch?"

"Dutch, like dis, signor."

He clapped his hand on my thigh, he looked up and smiled wetly through his brown juicy eyes.

"Oh, *I* see," I offered, shaking my head. "No, ho, no, no. You mean—" I, glad to be of use, crisply enunciated "*touch!*"

"*Si,*" he nodded, "dutch the body."

He wasn't pointing to his key-chain. He wasn't pointing to his key-chain at all.

"*Touch? The—body?*"

My ears rang. Can I actually have heard the protracted yowl down the tunnels I later swore I did? Were mine the dolorific lungs? If not that, I distinctly remember, and always will, those lips like rubber bands that dispassionately uttered one final line.

"You want dry it?"

Instinctively—I did tell you I was American?—I almost grabbed his *handkerchief,* just before I ran out.

§

A son was proudly born to us, my wife and I, in September just about the time classes resumed. We're all doing well, thank God.

Julia de Chateauroux;
or, The Girl with Blue Hair

One strange day in 1464, during the reign of Louis XI ("The Spider"), king of France, a baby was left abandoned on the door-stoop of a poor farmer and his family by the surname of de Chateauroux. His wife and four extraordinarily homely daughters, breakfasting on black bread, sour pickles, and vinegar beet-soup at half-past four in the morning, all heard the noise. The story soon became the talk of the entire village, for the child was different than any child who had ever lived. Her hair showed a glossy and extraordinary beauty and was cornflower blue.

No one ever learned from whence she had come or what villainy, if any, was the cause of her desertion. It was a complete mystery to all, but rumors were bruited about. Some whispered she came from the sky, others insisted the sea. A local priest snapped, "Sin has stamped her the color of catarrh."

It was a fallen world back in those days, Theologians with tall cone-shaped hats and long, flowing black robes superstitiously thrashed their cats, hanged heretics, and, screaming in long sermons that nature was evil, exhorted such husbands whose wives in their vanity were wont to dress their hair with crimple-crispings and cristy-crosties to pull them out, citing as a foul and repugnant example the benighted foundling child in their midst who was kept locked alone in a closet on Sundays as living proof of what trials and tribulations awaited any such wayward women, trelapsers in fornication, who weakly gave in to the extremes of vileness and vanity and walked about the streets like common trulls.

A terrible period passed, for Julia, as she was named, found herself as she grew into a young beauty constantly mocked and ridiculed out of envy by local boys and girls in the thoroughfares. They pulled faces, making wide mouths, pointing to her hair. Nor could the family daughters abide her, for her comeliness threw a shadow over theirs, which was already in ominous arrearage. It was decided that Julia be sent away to the nuns of La Trappe, in an isolated convent located in the far reaches of Nevers. Nature became her only comfort. She was lonely in the extreme, but a spirit of childhood and innocence always played inside her loneliness. She took long walks into the perfumed fields and old faraway hills that often spoke to her. The deep green forests alone were her consolation. A fat blue cat named Chartroux whom she met by the way became her one friend. Birds warbled on her finger. She ate mushrooms, whistled softly at webs, and on her knees made mimic boats of leaves gently to push in puddles. Back at the abbey were only hard black pews, cold cloisters, chants of death. She wondered, was death an awful thing or was it a release from pain?

Her reputation as a beauty spread far and wide. Folks marveled how her lustrous hair, with its blue softness and scent, fell in cascades as if in a dream waterfall. Her skin was alabaster. At times she seemed unreal, as often happens with people of extreme loveliness or excessive ugliness. Poems awaited persons properly to champion that shining face. How heavy her heart always grew when, at the sound of the tolling bells, she had to return to the church for the holy hours of matins, lauds, tierce, sext, vespers, compline.

Moonlight, which silvered her cell, had the eerie effect on her of both feeling hope and yet of instilling desires for leaving this world where nothing would ever hurt her again. Should she jump off a turret? She wondered: do we do what we are afraid of in order to deliver ourselves from it? Does suicide derive its prestige from the odd fact that it appears to us as the only means of escaping death by making use of it at will, by creating it ourselves? Is suicide an answer that solves a problem?

Julia instead went for long midnight walks alone, leaving her cell every night and seeking refuge in the dark secret gardens and dazzling forests, where in the moonlight her hair in its glowing incandescence appeared even more beautiful. She swam in mysterious pools through her reflections and, almost flying, swung from tree branch to tree branch, feeling in their strength and natural power a sense of comradeship. By hand she fed berries and nuts to the birds and squirrels and deer and spoke to the fish and played with them in silver lakes by way of her sweeping, churning, and loving hands. Chartroux, always by her side, protected her. In the deep green dells lived the strangest creatures: ungainly fly-winders, bulbous-shaped feistfists, weird manticores, jut-jawed griffins, even gigantic red lions with human faces and triple rows of teeth, which fit into each other like combs, exotic but sympathetic personages of a hidden world, all of whom cared for the girl as they vigilantly watched, including an aged confessor, a hermit with white beard who lived in a forest behind a waterfall, whose saintly appearance seemed to assure his piety, and who advised her,

> "Wings for shoulders,
> Flippers for feet,
> If the world mistreats you,
> From the world retreat."

The old hermit told her that to live in the world was to suffer, that suffering was inevitable, that you had to confront suffering, that from one's suffering emerged the strongest souls, that we are actually healed from suffering, that only by suffering, by accepting it, can you prove your love for God. Innocently, Julia asked him how he knew so much about the matter of agony and anguish, adversity and affliction. "My answer to you is that I know about it far too well. You see, I have caused so much of it."

When he turned away, she saw him weeping.

"I am the very worst of sinners," he mournfully confessed. He turned back, and taking her soft, smooth cheeks into his hands, looked deeply into her questioning blue eyes. "I once knew a child, and I betrayed her." Tears rolled down his face. "My guilt is such that the mere idea of feeling it within my soul seems too good for me. I don't deserve the honor of even speaking to you, dearest child. Suffering accepted with joy is the most authentic sign of love. I need my suffering to evoke—to reflect—my unworthiness. I await forgiveness from God and hope one day to know it by a sign."

Nuns in those days, many from well-born families sent to convents by arch and overly paternalistic families, hated their sequestration and instead of leaving became internally neurotic as a feeble escape. One day Sister Bedwide, a nun with a face like grey crottle, saw Julia talking animatedly to a wild pigeon at the window of the refectory and, citing Proverbs 31:30, ran to strike her across the hands with a hickory switch. Such was her envy that she later looked for a chance to report the mysterious girl to the bishop for engaging in communion with the pagan world. That lordly prelate visited the convent one day and, after being shown a tally of her faults, demanded of her, "What is the secret that the bird told you, what the fish?"

Julia, mute with sadness, could only answer nothing, not a thing, for their relationship was always of a silent kind, about the knowingness of innocence and good. There were penalties in the Chapter Room, in consequence. She was forced to clean piles of pantry pans, pots, kettles, all crusty, burnt, and riddled with grease, and also scrape tallow from all of the candle holders. She was to go without mixt for a week in penance. She had to shell peas, make pottages and stews, bake huff paste and turn out shortcrust pies, change the straw in the outhouses, and outside the cloister scrub clean the marble statue of ascetic St. Benedict, posed with an index finger to his lips, on the base of which was written the word *Tace*—silence.

The Convent of St. Thierry was cold as charity. The sisters of the cloisters there, who learned of her nightly excursions, brutally snipped her hair and set her to menial tasks. Nuns, sexless as teabags, judging her a sinner, went by in pairs, snubbing her. Sister Flatbord maliciously pinched her arms. Sister Coquatrix, in revenge for some slight offence, whispered it abroad that Julia was a cohort of the devil. Sister Grissim, half syphilitic, whom she had to spoonfeed, lied that she had stolen her orthopedic chinstrap. Sister Younghans, a orange-faced reprobate, fractiously walked past her in the cloister with gritted teeth. Sister Bose would maliciously fashion little *poupées* of her into which venomously she stuck pins. Sister Alvina Poussaint, a sawn-off little rocking horse of stupidity, viciously calumniated her with charges of meeting a Moor in the woods. And Sister Vibrissa, who once saw her sobbing in her cubicle, cramped with pain, screamed, "Offer your tears to the dead, you speaking harlot!" They treated her like a milkmaid and a scullion and a pantler and a kitchen wench.

Only small gentle Chartroux, the fat blue cat, was at hand to give her comfort. The nuns in the meanwhile, opportunistically discussing the blueness of her hair, schemed as to how to make money by it, while simultaneously ridding themselves of her presence, for Julia remained a constant curiosity far and wide. What could be done to their best advantage?

Fate circumadjacently ruled.

A traveling carnival came by. And a fat oily master-of-revels, a sinner with a furious mustache and beard named Repulisti, twisted and cruel, with promises to give her work, for which percentages would be given to them, took her from the nuns. An ungulate of uncommon ruthlessness and crudity, he devised schemes to extract money from gullible people. He took Julia in hand, fondling her hair, and proceeded with his plans for her. Her face was painted with make-up, and, given hoops, she became known as the dancer "La Tantarelle Bleu." A singer, she was taught to mime, and was outfitted in elegant gowns of crimson silk, with bows and ornaments and tiny buttons of oriental pearl. Her shoes were shaped like birds with pointed beaks. A long silk veil depended from her pointed headgear called a *hennin.* The caravan toured through Clairvaux and Romilly and Auvers-sur-Oise and eventually bumped along through the arch at St. Denis into the teeming city of Paris. All the while, her innocence protected her in the same way the sound of ringing bells is pure.

Soon famous, "La Tantarelle Bleu" was painted by artists who wielded long, thin brushes and exclaimed over her lips, her pale skin, but mostly her hair. Select pieces of her soft luxurious hair, tied with ribbons, were sold in swatches along the way, hawked from dumpcarts by the traveling company for folks to carry home. Bluer was her hair than the richest lapis lazuli, bluer than the veiling mist of Arabia, a cerulean blue of breathtaking depth and sheen, and her skin was whiter than the spuming crests of the ocean waves. She was so pure her fingers shone. The eye of the trained hawk was not brighter than hers, her chaste bosom snowier than the breast of a swan. Whoever so beheld the girl was filled to bursting with affection. Four white trefoils sprung up wherever she trod. And yet for all her comeliness, she still felt lost, in spite of the attendance danced upon her even by the court.

At one of her performances, King Louis XI himself made an appearance. Drunken, howling, surrounded by silken sycophants, he laid eyes on the bewitching girl and, being struck dumb by lust, instantly sought to possess her. He was thirty-eight years of age when he ascended the throne. Selfish, cunning, and cruel, false to all sense of honor and affection, he had crushed out the young life of his wife, the lovely Margaret of Scotland who, having been visited with a mysterious illness that might have been cured, in light of his cruelty refused medicines and was resolved to die. "The Spider," having a wife no more, at one royal performance lewdly wiped his mustache and pointed an arachnoidal finger toward the illustrious dancer with the blue hair and ordered that immediately she be brought to him. Repulisti, cagily rubbing his hands, was happy to sell her for a thousand gold francs on the spot.

King Louis, maddened by her beauty, became lavish with her. She was given collars of ruddy gold, on which were precious emeralds and rubies. He ordered tailors to make blue gowns for her. Ultra blue. Cerulean. Teal blue. He filled a walking pen by the orchard with electric blue peacocks that foot-strutted and screamed in what he took to be high euphonies of praise. He went so far as to concoct a blue wine in her honor, *Lividivinum*, and proclaimed henceforth the color be revered. Blue soon became everywhere the fashionable color. Houses were painted blue, windmills and waving pennants, sharpshills and shields, towers and tracking oxen. Blue corn, blue potatoes, eggplants, grapes, and borage, being blue, were sold at higher prices. Vendors even sold buns of blue as well as loaves and tiny cakes.

The King directly proposed marriage, although a forest wizard warned him against doing such a thing. Julia shrank back in horror. Again and again, the King sought to win her over. But again and again she refused to yield. One night he grabbed Chartroux and put a knife to his neck, screaming, "*Veux to la foie du chat manger?*" The furious cat, spitting, clawed the wrist of the King, who chased it into a corner with a raised fire-shovel, whereupon Julia on her knees pleaded for its life. Contempt was heaped upon the poor girl. "Iron-maiden her," whispered his privy counselor. Chief counsel muttered, "Whapple her." "Slunk her cheeks!" "Throw her into the mill dyke," snapped an attendant, "until she changes her mind." It was finally decided that, until she gave her consent, she be shopped up with her cat in the ancient stone tower on the lonely island of Mousehold, which was completely surrounded by a roaring sea, where she was given mere rusks and water to sustain her.

Comforting her, as well, were the remembered words of the confessor, the old hermit with white beard who lived in a forest behind a waterfall: "Affliction is the surest sign that God wishes to be loved by us; it is the most precious evidence of his tenderness. Embrace your pain and you will transcend it."

A day was meanwhile set for the wedding. Under the King's orders, banns were published, the local thoroughfares were ornately decorated. The archbishop was ordered to stand by with a blue missal. A crown was fetched for her to wear. Festivities were ordered. Still she was sequestered. The townsfolk wondered aloud: where was the girl with the blue hair? Weeks had turned to months with still no sign of her.

On the night before the nuptials, however, Louis XI fell gravely ill. The cat's scratch had poisoned his blood in a most unnatural way and left him raving with fever. He recoiled with horror at the thought of death, which he had inflicted on so many. He sought privacy. Shut up in his dark castle at Plessis, living in a suite of thirty rooms, the doors of which had been secured by six complicated locks, he never inhabited the same room for two successive nights, as it was his crude medieval belief that death was a literal ghoul that stalked the world with a scythe. The King roamed lamely from room to room, gimp and paper-pale and quite mad, howling into the dark hollows that Julia de Chateauroux would be his wife. He grew thin and his face turned yellow and he spit rheum, but still he gave the command that she be brought before him, even if in chains.

A troop of seven of the King's largest, tallest soldiers, bearing arms, sailed to the island of Mousehold, approached the tower in the havering rain, and by the aid of firecoal lanterns climbed to the top by the grey stone stairway to the highest ramparts where they came to that one dark cell. No response was given to their loud, importunate knocks. A silence held. As always, the door was coopered vise-tight. Hammering away the chains with thick broadswords, they pried open the door, with creaks, only to find the room completely empty. There was not a trace of Julia, nor a sign of her presence. There was only the pale and eerie whiteness of moonrise cast upon the stones. The girl had disappeared.

Screeching aloud from his sordid deathbed, or so it was reported, the King immediately had the countryside scoured. He sent guards in all directions and ordered the lodgings of the Chateauroux ransacked. Coming up with nothing, the guards reported their failure, and the King had the entire family beheaded on the spot. Vile Repulisti, dragged screaming by his beard, was forced to wear a dunce hat and paraded from village to village on a string. The maddened King then torched the convent, with all the nuns locked in it, and he set out to tear down the tower. Spiked from within, meanwhile, he ordered monks to besiege every saint in heaven to prolong his life. He weighed himself down with moldering relics. He even drank the blood of infants, to revive the failing current of his own. At last the end came, in 1483, and everyone rejoiced.

And Julia de Chateauroux?

Strangely, to this day no one knows how the girl ever escaped from the tower. Did she fly? Did she dive from its terrifying heights? Did she swim, and, if so, where? Some say she was taught to do both by the fry and fingerlings of the lakes in which she once swam and winged creatures of the dark forests that she had haunted as a girl, and some even said that they came for her in the night. The forest was only haunted by her absence like an echo of her last goodbye. She disappeared. Where, no one ever could say, but while those who insisted she had flown into the sky or fled into the waves of the sea, still others insisted it was she vanished into the mysterious place where sky and sea meet.

Only Chartroux seemed to know the secret, and, although growing ever fatter and living to a ripe old age, he never said a word, only because he himself was never seen again, except once, entering behind a forest waterfall.

Queen Gloriana's Revenge

Queen Gloriana of Albion, seventy-eight years old, was an imperious and domineering crotchstick of unexampled ugliness who, although having been married four times, remained nevertheless sex-mad, a matter at her age more of vanity than of passion, and every chance she got she sought assignations with likely young men throughout the kingdom. It was the year 1478. One particular morning, rising on white silk pillows, she yanked the bell-pull and with her snap-quack voice ordered Wheeldex, her servant, to come immediately to the inner chamber. She explained that she had dreamt of music and now knew the reason why. "Last night at the banquet there was dancing and a troubadour," she said. "Who was that lovely mandolin player?"

"It was young Vaillancourt," replied her servant, bowing deeply and setting down before her a silver spoon and a vacherin of berries and meringue. She gobbled it up and clapped her hands for her pet hyena, Slutswool.

She was often bored. She collected valuable old perfumes in bottles and made dumb art boxes with trifles placed in them. She wrote crapulous poems, which everyone had to like in order to keep their jobs. Whims dominated her aesthetic. In the past she had posted offers of large rewards throughout the realm, which never came to anything, for the creation by anyone of a blue food, chickens that could sing, and a sculpture that did not touch the ground. Her taste was exquisitely artificial. Fame was her sole profession, to appear young her obsession. On this morning she strode imperiously through her candle-lit, round-glass-object-strewn rooms with pounds of rejuvenating makeup on her crumbling old face recharged with new schemes to have fulfilled a lot of her new fantasies on the coming night. Several times, she insisted, that young mandolinist had smiled at her. Out of preening self-regard she was convinced in her juiceless near-dotage that he, as everyone, loved and adored her. Emotions have nothing to do with intellect.

In her mind she was the center of the world. Wheeldex was ordered that minute to invite young Vaillancourt to the castle. "And tell him to bring his instrument," declared the Queen, sniggering, who failed to know his heart was pure. Wheeldex, nodding, scooted out to tell his wife, the cook, but felt some dread. The Queen could be terribly ugly when she was fallible—and she was always vindictive.

Her cruelty was legend. If you crossed her, she simply made you disappear. It was well known that she had killed her five indefeasibly stupid brothers, who, each one colder and more ambitious than the next, had been scheming against her, in recompense whereof she had all of them locked into a tower with a starving Komodo dragon and the next morning found only a single femur and a swatch of hair. About her four husbands, very like the four shipwrecks of St. Paul, for which Holy Scripture, queerly, provides the details of only one (Acts 27:27–44), nobody in the realm knew a thing, except that all had been beheaded but the last, a weak ineffectual herbert who before he died from a brain aneurysm had given her two charmless sons, one of whom in his late teens threw himself off a cliff after a furious argument with his mother. She banished the other son, a sad cripple named Faucetwater who for his indisposition posed no threat. He took a job as a gravedigger. The Queen's heart was ice-cold. It was not in her interest to suffer fools. To extreme situations, to paraphrase Pascal, one must apply extreme remedies. Much of life is about what is missing.

Like freedom. Poor townsfolk there lived in poverty and were chattel to the castle. They swinged flax, ground wheat, chamfered wood, pressed curds, flensed blubber and braided seed corn. *Autres temps, autres moeurs.*

It was a beautiful moonlit night when Vaillancourt, brought to the castle in a carriage, appeared again at court to play his mandolin, singing ballads and plucking the strings to create salvation. But his music did not allay the amorousness it aroused. A feast took place while the Queen devised her plan. At midnight, after her dwarf Gropequeynt had tumbled for them and Creeple balanced ninepins and play-actor Justin, an endocrine dwarf with hideous muscles, performed some foolery and Dick Brodhead the eunuch sang "Die Nachtigall" dressed in a bird costume while fluttering his wings, Queen Gloriana ate a winkle off a pin and thought: I want to suck his lovely ears.

An endless array of unnatural acts occurred to her. She had love-whips, rumpswabs, scent-fans. Raising her shiny goblet, which held the smiling reflection of her face, her tongue resting lewdly on her lip, she slowly, confidently, walked across the gold room and whispered, "A whole hour has gone by and you have not kissed me yet." She lewdly flutter-tongued the *t*. Given a turn, the young man hesitated and with something of humor, generally the enemy of infatuation, could only say, but not uncharitably, "I—I don't even know you, Your Majesty."

The Queen coldly stared at him. "I see," she said with accusatory precision. Her fingernails were reptilian. The beginning is indeed half the whole.

Not that she gave up. Capitulation is neither an option nor an alternative for the monstrously vain. Encouraged to sleep over, Vaillancourt was given a large bed in a stone chamber, which he shared, he couldn't help but notice, with chained Slutswool, who glowered at him. Was he being guarded? Or, worse, locked in? That sleepless night he offered to the Blessed Virgin.

Night fell. The Queen, having redreamed hours about him there alone in that room, suddenly appeared like a ghost out of the darkness carrying a candle and a plate of Montepulciano plums. She was stark naked. Her face was slathered creamy-shiny in order to look young, her teeth were long and hideous, and her wide-nostrilled nose, shiny with luciflects, provided the only light. She believed she was enduringly young. She had always had her way. Her wealth and power had blinded her to her folly. She set down the plate and leaned forward, flashing her withered breasts. "I can arrange to be languid," she whispered, popping a plum into his mouth.

The young man sat up in shock, turned yellow as yarrow, and fled. The rumor quickly spread that he was in danger, and so his beautiful girlfriend, a lovely maiden named Childebrand, rowed him over the rough waters out to a ship which within that very hour set sail for distant lands, beginning with Belgium but reaching as far as to the city of Jerusalem. Is it not a legitimate truism that what you ignore is liable to kill you?

Vaillancourt, unlike the Queen, had been taught by monksand raised woth a reverence for the ascetic. Sex for her was born of mere whim. To experience it casually in cause and consequence was to separate it from sin and spirit at the same time and, not only that, but to mock the holy purlieus of intimacy.

"Fishpiss! Rotball! Snites!" screeched the jilted Queen, flinging about her rooms and growing entirely unforgiving in the wake of this unforeseen and humiliating repudiation. Out of monstrous arrogance she later then revised the entire story for anyone who would listen in order to save face. "I hated his hair," she stated to Wheeldex, who looked at his small wife, the cook. Both knew her well. "He was so common!" Several more looks crossed in the air. "Why did he always use those air quotes with his fingers when he was speaking with irony? It was so unattractive! And his playing! So florid—it, it, all of it needed editing! Anyone could see he lacked passion!"

Cutting him dead was not bad enough. He deserved far worse than that. With growing rue the Queen had revealed herself. He would certainly talk. The servants, quaking and bringing her a buttered toddy, asked what they could possibly do.

"Upstick asswards," she howled as she ran from one quaking servant to another, brandishing a stick like a sword and wagging it in a determined scold. "I will give anyone who rids me of him one quarter of a million in silver," she promised. A sullen group of pecker-faced brutalitarians with knobby overbrows, all well-skilled in assassination, were found and sent abroad to chase him down and kill him as a malefactor. They began to spread out with evil intentions. But not before one of the thugs creepy-crawled Childebrand's humble cottage where he proceeded to smother the poor girl, innocent in her bed, by means of placing a poison feather in her throat.

The Queen bitterly hounded Vaillancourt. She had him followed by her hired brutes across Germany, Syria, Egypt. As he walked, he thought: The more the universe seems comprehensible, the more pointless it seems. Under black threatening clouds and skies crucifixion-blue he moved and kept on moving. He traveled the guesswarps of the vast world in his exile, through deserts, ancient cities, the far-flung hills of the earth. The Adjacent Isles. Mount Richter. He traversed the Combs of Oyonnax and the Anteriors of the Choreoid, mauled with loneliness. His very own family, who never cared for him, forgot about him entirely. "A family is only tilth. It blows away," a wise man told him in the Mercenary Mountains. But he was too young to know that freedom is only a theory anyway.

As he passed from one land to another, he felt alienated. Aloneness is nearer God, he thought.

A year passed, then two. When Vaillancourt heard tragically that his beloved Childebrand was no longer alive, he returned surreptitiously to Albion to visit her grave. He finally found it, blessing himself, and devotedly scratched into the stone the following numbers, 1121790, and said aloud, "One follows one to one's heaven I know." It seemed impossible that she who always smelled like linen in the sun on a highland meadow was now gone. Then he knelt down by her gravestone, and taking up his mandolin he wept as he played,

What is that noise? wondered Faucetwater, who was sitting over the hill. A crow on a branch had called *ccr-rrr-ruk prukk* in the orange fog. When he saw who it was, the cripple took out a knife and stabbed the poor musician in the heart. He pawned the mandolin and, hoping for the large purse, he went, cap in hand, to the castle to collect his reward. But the Queen's barrister took the hapless gravedigger aside to point out to him a small detail on the royal proclamation, not without mirth, that if he looked closely he would see that a hyphen did not appear as written in the legal phrase "one quarter," that he would have been rich if the hyphen had been there, giving him one-quarter of a million. As it was, he was given a single coin.

As to the Queen, who was already in the extreme stages of myoma and a case of venal parametritis, she died in the queerest of ways. In an act roundly condemned by the Church, she had been savaged on the tile-floor of her boudoir in the process of trying to have carnal knowledge with Slutswool. As the result of being so polluted, she was thrown into the potter's field, the spot left unmarked. The Holy Church would have nothing to do with her. There were no exequies. Faucetwater danced on her grave.

All of her poems were burnt in high flames in the main square at the pump by a large gathering of townsfolk who, to wide rejoicing, formed a mummer's parade that has since become an annual event.

It was only proven true once again that since the beginning is half the whole, the other half is a period of which God's creatures should therefore make good use. For, indeed, the other half is the other end.

The Misanthropoetics of R. N. Thumbwheel

> Evil is unspectacular and always human,
> And shares our bed and eats at our own table.
> —*W. H. Auden, "Herman Melville"*

R. N. Thumbwheel, the painter and a man unaccustomed to happiness, woke up one morning, yawned, and without due deliberation—for a change of heart had been precipitated by a change of interest—decided to kill his wife. His work was odd, and he had been described in art journals as "a cryptic dauber of non-figural landscapes, grim wolves' heads with telekinetic halos, and pinheads emanating ectoplasmic auras." There were some collectors of his work, even a passionate few with strange, aberrated, and acquired tastes.

He disliked Nature but pursued Art. A penchant for self-contradiction he ascribed to his profession, for he seemed ever to be chasing himself, as opposed to pursuing the talent to which that self should apply. He was full of misjudgments and made morbid demands on and stipulations for himself he never saw to completion. He was given to abrupt reversals of a self-sabotaging sort and was missing a thinking heart. Was it not true that increases in efficiency led to even larger increases in demand?

In 1916, he had taken a secret lover, Rowena Ferripunch, a young woman typical of the faint water-colorish girls to whom his imagination often drew him and, for the first time in his life, a life that had been neither easy nor frankly very normal, began to create *figures* in his canvases. A new world opened up for him that he had long neglected.

He was a busy, pixie-featured man who wore spectacles, and, like Faust, lived in the condition of having two souls in his breast. His eyes which had the quick brightness of a cartoon character rested, it seemed, on two quite different planes and his one-line mouth showed a caustic looseness that revealed not only incapacity and little resolve but signs of a frightened and spoiled boy. There was no strict intensity of will in him, nor any empathy, rather a conformist selfishness stealthily employed for showing his better half in order to prevent the recognition of his worst. He had capacity, tenacity, audacity, fugacity, mendacity, perspicacity, sagacity, rapacity, pugnacity, salacity, and of course enigmatic opacity.

All he lacked was veracity.

He and Emma lived, precariously, on a dead-end street hard by a fish-paste factory in the Balls Cross area of Ladbroke Grove, a neighborhood of working poor, in an old structure beside a train trestle and high wall with an ambience of crumbled brick and peeling fire escapes. They had been married for thirteen years. A good deal of the disdain he had for his wife could be traced to his mother whose own husband, a Protestant, who decamped for a life on the road as an itinerant actor, the very day his own mother took one regretful look at him as a boy and thought *He's so dumb, he couldn't make a zero if he sat on a piece of paper!*

A schoolfriend had told Emma that good-looking men made bad husbands. But was the opposite true, which is to say, did ugly men mean good husbands? Not by anything she could confidently assert, after only a few months living with Redway.

It was his daily habit to wake at 4 a.m., drink a pot of tea, nip ginger-nut biscuits, and paint for the day. How could he— why would he—tell his wife that he had developed a passion for someone else? It was far easier to matinée his feelings, enjoy his Piccadilly Stem biscuits, and blithely proceed to work full time on his painting.

Why this change in him? Was his painting going poorly? Could he be secretly ill? His behavior was very like a knot of self-interfering patterns, going this way, then that, with his head the wobbly pivot. It was nothing Emma could put her finger on. His brain was like an aileron, but what winds it met, she couldn't explain—it only seemed she was dealing with a mind that could tighten or loosen arbitrarily, simply on its own.

His poor wife was thin, with diverticulitis, and on her grieving hands that bore an inertial dampness she often wept, hiding her face in a refuge of despair and shame, for her husband had begun ignoring her just when their only child died of left-heart syndrome. Thumbwheel who repudiated her woke up one day realizing he no longer cared. He who was at the best of times arbitrarily captious became even more belittling in his behavior to his spouse. He boxed the wireless because of her nocturnal listening habits. He claimed that she bore the musty odor of wallpaper—but it was from the emanations of grief. It was a cruelty from his point-of-view with which she dolefully agreed, In whatever way she turned, however, she could not get to the bottom of his restlessness, as her devotion blinded her,

She feared in her heart that she was not bright enough to handle the part of his personality she could not understand, especially lately when he seemed to be reassessing some deep conundrum within by borrowing this or that from the different— alternate?—sides of himself. Who was the emotionally damaged one, she wondered, who most plagued by unspecified anxieties and inexplicable unease, him or her?

Emma (*née* Whipday) had a history of mental illness in her family, which came from the area of Blackdykes, Angus, in Scotland. She was an identical triplet, among the rarest people on the planet. (Her two sisters, timid, died by means of their own hand in their teens.) Guile has a hundred faces, not so inno- cence. She would only sip spoonfuls of tomato purée and dust the rooms and weep.

He could read her expression in the offhand way his cold- ness forced her to behave, but she took him for what she hoped in her heart he was and loved him. He ostensibly feigned to care by trifling decencies. He would sit her down and read tender poems out loud to her that he never meant. It instilled a perverse joy in him, becoming something of a weekly, sometimes daily prank that subsumed his hatred and diverted his attention by way of funning with the woman he needed to prove a fool. Does good acting come from display rather than behavior—or was it the opposite? Secretly, he wanted her to disappear. He dreamt of ways to dispatch her. The murder seemed wrong only in the sense of his getting caught.

He was impulsive. He made it difficult for her to have serious conversations with him. He declined to let her depend on him. He was defensive and owned to none of his mistakes. He blocked her and refused to be responsible. He told those who did not even inquire he was married to "an angular old maid." Worst of all, he regarded the love she offered as a threat. Indifference is the womb of monsters.

Does anyone in this long, difficult, inexplicable, tattered life ever truly see anybody, look into their inner hearts, divine the real self, assay the truth, except through the flaws of his or her own ego? Doubtful. O, doubtful indeed.

When he first met his Emma, even then his mother disapproved of her. He stood firm that time, however, feeling he deserved some sort of answer. His mother suitably obliged, turning on him with a hard explicitness, peevishly to repudiate the young woman, saying, "Many a young girl without realizing it has schemed to have relations with a naïve gentleman and actually seduced him in order to be attacked, becoming thereby a victim of her own seduction, in accordance with her unconscious self-destructive desires."

Thumbwheel's mother, of a rabid religious bent, was that rare thing among natives, an English Catholic. She bore him late in life and, giving him far too much attention as any late mother would, he came to resent her even as a child and would later swear by the proverb: *If the devil cannot appear, he sends a bossy woman.* His mother was refined, meticulous, with dainty hands and feet. But her beliefs were extreme, severe, absolute, and were stubbornly held. Contesting her with any disagreement could only be met with dire peril.

She zealously took him to Mass in Ely Place, daily prayed the rosary on her knees, her little son being required to do the same, and never failed to put holy water into a humidifier as an efficient way of ridding their house of demons. She was ever quoting Zacharias, Christ's favorite prophet—his caveats always on her lip.

He had never gotten along with his mother. Quite the opposite, she strained him to depletion and left him ever culvert-empty.

She was elegant but a sharp-nosed and autocratic true believer who resembled Agnolo Bronzino's portrait of thin, tutmouthed *Laura Battiferri.* They crossed the water to visit Ireland, where his mother took him by way of pilgrimage to St. Kevin's Church at Glendalough in County Wicklow and to view the ruins of Valley Crucis Abbey in Llangollen and to pray at St. Patrick's Cathedral in Dublin, where he had to listen to a tour guide's longwinded fable—pious clap-trap, he judged—about an entranceway called, "The Door of Reconciliation," where two medieval feuding families ended a bitter feud.

She also dragged him at the unwilling age of eleven on a visit to the city of Rome to climb the staircase of the church of St. John Lateran, a twenty-eight-step staircase that, according to legend, was the very one that served the judgment hall of Pontius Pilate, and indeed one that supposedly Christ had climbed, its steps still stained with His blood. Since 850 A.D. the church had taught that if a pilgrim made the climb on his knees, then paused to pray, and knelt to kiss the holy staircase, his sins would be forgiven and he'd be granted a full indulgence in consequence. He believed none of it, however, and ever associated the word basilica—never an honorific with him—with that of basilisk.

Young Thumbwheel in the face of this straitening destitution suffered even deeper reversals than he knew. He was condemned to grow up a troubled, adolescent man—a painful case, immature, irresponsible, and unreliable, forever longing for more than he could have, to become in fact, more than anything, a fussy, indulged adolescent both to his maternal lover, Rowena (who referred to herself as "Boss") and to his accommodating but unstable wife who had no knowledge of technique and was deeply brain hurt.

A perpetual man-boy, he lived his life as infant and husband, a confusing fusion of opposites producing in its irreconcilable tension a mismatched human being who at bottom was too confused even to identify himself. He traveled mentally north the further he went physically south. He was an insolubly divided man.

Blind to consequences she'd not have heeded in the first place, Mrs. Thumbwheel in her hectoring and iron-handed way hurt him to the point of hatred and betrayed him into mistrust.

Was her child quelled like that of Lady Macbeth's own, in the way that she feared and so prevented him from being spoiled, in order to show him who was dominant in their own small unhealthy "marriage"? Was her abiding wish to command him, to stifle him, only a milder variation of Macbeth's wife insanely dashing out her baby's brain?

Domineering mothers figure largely in the life of all assassins. By making him afraid of himself, he became angry at her. When he complained about climbing the stairs, didn't she tell him, "Only weak people are befuddled by obstacles"? He looked for the chance to push her off a high-pitched landing when they were standing on the Vittoriano, the monument called the "Altare della Patria," but then, you see, he became *fearful* of doing so. In subsequent years, by way of diversionary tactics he could muster, he was able to cope with hatred and disappointment by covering up his emotions.

Was that healthy?

Religion nettled him. None of it made sense in the way his senses responded to what he saw. He labored no moral of the many his mother would have him draw by way of her faith. Hating her by way of her faith inured him against any fear of retribution by sharing exactly none of it. He was offended by the "scandal of particularity"—a "Supreme Being," creator of the vast universe, *arbitrarily choosing paltry times, locations, and persons?* Denoting a Sabbath as a day or rest, making one city holy over others, selecting one nation as chosen? It was, all of it, rubbish. The very faith itself was abnormal. "I wish that those who unsettle you would castrate themselves," St. Paul told us in Galatians 5:12. That was a good example of a good Christian attitude? Thumbwheel rejected it out of hand, all kit and kaboodle. God? A figment. Angels? Foo foo! Clouds? Fluff. In meteorology, there is no such thing as a cloud, at least as defined as an object with a quasi-permanent identity!

No, he belonged to that demographic of Romans 1:30 calls "haters of God"—a view shared by fully a quarter of the UK population.

In the meantime, the attractive model, Rowena, who had fully turned his head, quickly saw her power over him. He was smitten. She had long silver-blond hair, striking deep-set eyes, and pearlescent skin. He painted her wild beauty in fetching portraits, wearing old English fashions from previous centuries, several wearing hoods and poke bonnets, a paraphilia of his. She loved money and wanted to be entertained and asked for gifts. He didn't mind. For all his wife saw, he had become jaded to the bone, suffering from an existential despair and anger beyond his years.

At home, meanwhile, he could be merciless. There is a certain kind of sad sack that one occasionally comes across in life whose inadequacies are so pronounced that he seeks in turn to select by default something—one remarkable talent or a gift—that he can widely proclaim makes him special, unique, a standout. It very often comes under the heading of taste, for the best food, the presumption being that he is a gourmet. This mode of discrimination, his major claim, was precisely Thumbwell's. Whatever food his earnest wife lovingly cooked for him, he was always "disappointed." Fastidiousness made him demanding. Nothing ever quite pleased him. This fish was "just off," that rabbit "needed salt. "You had no time to buy fresh swedes, my dear?" he would nitpick. It was more than anything old womanish of him, even precious. "A good haggis should have a warm peppery flavour," he would carp—"yours, I must say, my dear, tastes perfectly dreadful." "Mutton soup two days old served on a hot August morning? Oh my goodness, no, no." "There is a squeakiness to this Halloumi cheese that puts me off—it has gone eerie." "Oh dear, lumps in the neeps again?"

But Emma seemed willing to forgive him anything. There was a long history of her trying to understand him—understand, and so forgive.

A trelapser, he had confided to his wife many years before on their very first date, as they sat riding the seating train at the Big Dipper in Blackpool, that he had completely lost the faith that he had all along feigned to his mother he had. "I have always hated God and felt angry at Him because, not merely content with frightening us by the law and the miseries of life, He still further increased our torture by creating the Earth alone, the sole planet with life, in the middle of nothing, just to bewilder us for thousands of years."

"'Be compassionate as your Father is compassionate'. Luke 6:36," his mother often quoted. "*Compassionate?* When God hadn't bothered to *appear* over the course of 2,000 years or more? It was all a vast nutty conspiracy.

Compassion was for rubberlegs! Caravaggio had killed someone. So had the Spanish painter, Alonso Cano. And what about artists Andrea del Castagno, Benvenuto Cellini, and the madman Thomas Wainewright?

Shakespeare himself maybe killed someone!

One of Thumbwheel's early friends at art school, Paul Fripp, who later became a painter, once confided to him that his own father, Rev. Edgar Fripp, a Unitarian minister and antiquarian who specialized in Shakespearean matters, discovered that in the great playwright's boyhood a girl by the name of Kathleen Hamlet had drowned in the Avon. It seems she had fallen in while trying to fetch water for cattle. Although suicide was apparently not ruled out by the authorities, disturbing questions had been raised. In his researches, the minister thought of Ophelia, for in his scholarly surmises, he felt that young Shakespeare had been much affected. A question rose, exactly what was his relationship to the girl, and had he been involved? One might go further, said Paul, which his father was too respectable to do. In modern times, suicide is the usual reason for a young girl, pregnant, taking such a course. Shakespeare was sixteen at the time, and we know that in a matter of months he got Anne Hathaway pregnant and had to marry her.

Later, he named his own son Hamnet, a form of the name

Hamlet. When that son died, the Bard wrote the play, in which the sexual relation between Hamlet and Ophelia is well-known, and sexual guilt a dominant theme.

But what had actually happened?

No one ever learned or seemed to try to find out.

After Thumbwheel went and got married, the complaints he raised against religion and churchgoing eventually increased to become the occasion of a breach big enough that he spent one summer, alone, in the Hebrides. Although timid, Emma, trying to keep peace, sided with her mother-in-law. "I feel it complusery to understand her, dear Redway," she wrote in a pleading letter to her husband, defending her position. "But, pleas, I want to stay married and not be devocied." It is a maxim that people prone to spelling errors are not really ready or eager to communicate. The need to reach out was only predominated by her inability to hope anymore. She had lost both of her sisters, and then her little son was taken away. Another crushing blow would surely have a deleterious effect on someone already so unstable. She became more and more dependent at the very same point he was drawing away. Emma was helplessly attracted to—but too guileless to understand—a person destined to destroy her.

Meanwhile, he went about, coy, with the secret air of a wisdom, undisclosed, he alone seemed to have divined but which he refused to share. What was most disconcerting was the incongruity—the dislocation—between the booming self-assurance he showed and the lack of core or substance within him. He was walking loose, with a mind that vitally confused imagination and the real world, freebooting yet unaware, with mercurial ungraspability, of the deep, self-generated conflicts and neurotic disorder within him.

Emma cut her hair short, mental patient blunt. She kept her sweet but wistful nature. When young, before marriage, she wore relatively fashionable clothes. Now, it was Mother Hubbard dresses that reached to her ankles and long aprons tied about her waist. She began to stay inside too much, became too neat, compulsively so, looked out the window, brooding, even became ill during thunderstorms

Her sad eyes, her hesitant, now often trembling mouth soon became for him, instead of the light-reflecting, delicate instruments of joy she had when they met, undifferentiated textures in a once sweet face rendered so by her indifferent husband's unheeding neglect and deadening lack of sympathy. She was not only beaten down with neglect, which created in her an unreachable sadness, but afraid of her failures and for her cowardice in not confronting them. She became rarely free from a sense of sin now and a fear of retribution so intense and immediate that it drove her to seek refuge in housework. That she was fading fast under the implacable force of his resentment mattered to a jot to him.

On the subject of murder, a victim often aids her executioner. One frequently illuminates the character of the other —there is often a mutual tie-in. The facets of murder are fascinating. Homicidal and suicidal impulses often become intertwined. Every homicide is self-consciously a suicide, every suicide in a sense is a psychological homicide. Are not both acts often caused by the perpetrator's lack of self-esteem?

What presumption, he thought, when posing such a question to himself!

No, he judged, his mother, was a muddled-headed fanatic. She used to prate, "I will take away the chariots from

Ephraim and the warhorses from Jerusalem, and the battle bow will be broken! Zechariah 9:10." What was that nonsense all about? She never had it right about Zacharias anyway—a name spelled wrong everywhere. Was it Zecharaiah? Zacharias? Zecharia? As many as thirty blokes appear with that damned name in the Old Testament! Was it Zecharah, a priest? Zechariah, the Baptist's father? Zechariah who sanctioned Zeruybabbel's goony temple? It appears that the Gospel of Matthew confused *two or three* Zachariases in Chapter 23, mentioning the ninth-century high-priestly martyr Zacharias—or was it Luke 11:51. Who cared? Not Thumbwheel. Thumbwheel cared not a jot!

Worse than secular, his paintings were all queer, puzzling, and even outlandish in consequence. Not for him the pious painterly religiosity of Raphael, of El Greco, or of Millet. He early chose to paint the canals of Mars, the rings of Saturn, and the moons of Neptune but then took up the subject of the foppery of the world in whatever he saw, using characteristically weird, rare, and outré colors—watchet, Modena, ochroleucos, fuscous, cramoisy, smalt, ponceau, perse, castoury, jessamy, eau-de-nil, and cinnabar.

In a rare moment, he struck off a portrait of Rowena, wearing a fashionable French style hood, a gable hood, allowing her to choose her own color for it. When she objected to the skulls on the surround of lace of the hood, it seemed fussy, and he upbraided her. "A work of art must never be a snuggle, a nuzzle or a warm scissor hug," he tried to explain to her. "If it no longer disturbs you, it is no longer art."

A man may fail many times, but he is not a failure until he gives up. And was it not true that those who cannot create begin to destroy? Thumbwheel who had washed all guilt from his soul was now intent to kill. Looking at his wife, he partially saw his mother. Who can explain the ley lines we walk and the whys and wherefores? Who explicate the shapes of our choices? The random points of reality?

Thumbwheel forsook design to choose death. It became something of a hobbyhorse. How many methods to murder! He studied up on various ways and means. The icicle as the perfect murder weapon was a cliché—far too fragile, can also slip in the hand. Poisoning? A perfect stealth murder weapon, but one had to come close. A knife? Silent, easy to conceal. How about the hard buttstock of a gun? Or his trusty maulstick? Brain her with a toilet tank lid? Drop a bowling ball on her head at the Ardmore Lanes? Bash her with a fishfuddle tree with which he cobbled his frames? Hurl her into the Solway Firth, 20 feet in neaps, 25 feet in springs? Cut her open nipples to knees with a parting knife and claim he went sleepwalking and took her for a hedge? Throw her in a sack off the Cannon Street Railway Bridge where his two sisters-in-law had years ago pitched themselves in a twin suicide? He gave any decision every chance to be.

Staying up late, researching the subject of poisons in old, old tomes, he thought of concocting a brew of pokeberry; arnica, or leopard's bane; deadly nightshade, with its shiny black berries; aconite, with its spikes of hooded blue; the fruit of hemlock, meadow saffron, and white bryony with its twisting tendrils, all lethal herbals guaranteed to kill. Why not deliver them all in a sponge, diluted with milk sugar, soaked in their juices to put her through in one slamming, swirling vertiginous gasp? Wait! But what if the evil potion by some perverse counteraction instead brought her around and *cured* the withered hen, indeed serving to cleanse, revivify, and restore her by some disgusting reinvigorating homeopathy?

Should he purchase a gun, take it for a wring out, then plug her when she was rapt listening to music on the wireless? Decerebrate her under anesthesia? Arsenical buns? Pump air into her ears? Dump a doorstone on her sleeping head at midnight? Bash her with a cold chisel? Jam a bite block into her mouth and inject her with succinylcholine? Tighten a cowhide over her head and squeeze? Rip saw her off at the knees while she was asleep? He had not the patience for the gnaw-on-her-ankle-'till-she-falls bit, for he'd done enough of that. There was of course the option of involving others. He was told by a weird Sicilian museum-guard acquaintance that he could go down to Dean St.—he helpfully wrote down the names—and find either a guy named Mondo ("Big Lollipop") Iliano or maybe "Rico ("Bath Beach") Magliocco or Otopo ("Clam Sauce") Pigafetta to do the job.

A pimp whom he met in Soho told him to inject her with heroin. "Give her the 'B-and-Q,' a mixture of bonita and quinine. Doomdust. A G shot. Half a yard of Mexican mantica. I will do the job for 20 quid. The creature will turn greyish purple and die under the influence of the *babonya*." Thumbwheel had to laugh. *Time* is of course the perfect murder weapon, *for us all*—but then who could afford to wait for old age?

What about playing music on the gramophone? Stravinsky's *Rite of Spring* ends with a girl dancing herself to death. Now, there was a thought.

To deliberate he went for a long walk in Hyde Park, by the Serpentine, which has only one bend, which is where he sat, thinking of doll-faced 18-year-old Rowena with her lovely deep-set eyes and round glorious form to whom he wrote racy notes.

She had a sweet disposition but was avaricious. So runs the world.

Reader, do you happen to know the story of the man who said if he had two pennies, he would buy bread with one and with the other a "white hyacinth for the soul"? No? Well, Thumbwheel did.

He watched clouds overhead, empty of symbol, scudding in the overhead sky. Why was he attracted to white hyacinth? White phosphorus.

Was this a foreshadowing of significance?

§

The fact was, indeed—and tragically—yes. For he came to see that all had been fated. The day before he took his constitutional around the Serpentine, he had called upon Dr. Pharmouse. MRCS, who for years had wanted to buy one of his paintings, *Fopperies of the World*, a triptych showing the faces of corrupt Popes. The two men were both members of the British Freethinkers League and found they had much in common. The doctor wanted to oblige his friend, whom he admired for his art, and offered, "How about death by bleach—it forms formaldehyde, a chemical with which cadavers are saturated to preserve them for medical school dissections. Or give her Vermin Killer. You can buy it in thrupenny packets. Polonium is good, a million times more deadly than cyanide. No antidote, lethal dose, around 0.0005 mg. The best route of entry? Ingestion. A very expensive method of assassination, however. not to mention that the only source of polonium is a nuclear reactor."

He touched a finger to his nose in deliberation.

"No, I opt for potassium. It is not complicated," he

explained. "When injected, potassium chloride can stop the heart and cause death by cardiac arrest. You can either feed her 1,000 bananas," he offered, reveling in gallows humor, "or goose her with a potassium shot, which will bypass both her stomach and intestines, trigger an irregular heartbeat, and she will be—as my old nanny used to put it—abducted by God."

Dr. Pharmouse, beaming at the work the painter brought, fingered a corner of its wooden frame. "No one will be the wiser. My son works at a chemist's. Hand over this painting, and I shall write the prescription. I have freakish and unwonted appetites in painting," confessed the slightly perverted doctor with a crooked smile.

He paused. "One caveat? The shot can induce in the victim high levels of pain and suffering if she is not appropriately anesthetized, otherwise she'll stay awake, paralyzed by the pancuronium bromide, to experience suffocation when unable to breathe. If the anesthesia remains insufficient, she'll experience excruciating pain."

Was there a moral basis for such a thing?

Indult is a term from Catholic canon law referring to a permission to do something that would otherwise be forbidden. How ironic it was—how fiendishly paradoxical—that he had learned of such a thing from his own mother. Thumbwheel remembered that in her zeal she had badly wanted the Latin Mass to be reinstated. She had often reminded him that many still-loyal English Roman Catholics held a deep and reverential attachment to the Tridentine Mass, the way that the Sacrifice of the Mass had been originally celebrated by the Holy English Martyrs of the Reformation and by all priests in the fanatical years in which the True Faith had been subjected to severe persecution by the six-fingered religious bigot, usurper, apostate, and adulteress, Queen Elizabeth I—a celebration of Mass in the old form, without any modern modifications or sops to the ignorant and the uninformed.

The English throne, which had been stolen from the queenly and more rightfully deserving Mary Tudor by her treacherous half-sister, according to his mother, more properly belonged to the true royal monarch, the Queen of Scots, until the obscenity of that demonic execution in 1558, as his own sorrowing mother often pointed out on the occasions of their frequent pilgrimages to the Palace of Placentia in Greenwich, where Mary, briefly Queen of France, had been born on February 18, 1516. "Pay no attention to the world's misanthropoetics," she repeatedly told her son.

It was a rainy Tuesday afternoon, and Thumbwheel was standing, with paper in hand, at a chemist's, across town in Clapham Junction.

"Potassium?"

"I need it for painting."

"Painting what?" asked the confused young pharmacist.

"The cold on mountains. Snow peaks. The sheen of ice sheets," came the reply.

Thumbwheel was duly covered here. Mineral colors are commonly understood to be silicate paints, which use potassium water glass as binder. He had read up on why as an artist he was to have it at hand, in case inquiries were made: all mineral paint contains inorganic colorants, and potassium-based alkali silicate (*water glass*), also known as *potassium silicate, liquid potassium silicate*, or *liquor silicium*, artists use. A coat with mineral colors does not form a layer but instead permanently bonds to the substrate material (silicification), the result then being a highly durable connection between paint coat and substrate. A water glass binding agent is highly resistant to UV light, and although silicone resin over time tends to grow brittle, become chalky, and even crack under such light, the binding agent will remain stable. The chemical fusion with the substrate and the UV stability of the binder are the fundamental reasons for the extraordinarily high lifetime of silicate paints. He expected the facts he read would cover his reason for having made such a purchase, if snooping inquiries were ever to be made, although buying it would have better applied if he had been a sculptor.

Surprisingly, at the moment of crisis, the skulking Thumbwheel began to suffer from purpose tremor, with all of his proprioceptors intense and alert, as if, in a maddening way, exclusively separate—of their own volition—questioning not only the action he was about to take, but indeed the courage to do it.

We hate whom we hurt, and we mistrust whom we betray.

The murder was a meal. It had to involve perfect synchronicity. Thumbwheel presented to Emma a brown earthenware tureen filled with greasy oxtail soup into which he mercifully sprinkled a powder to knock her unconscious. But he could not disguise his malice, and in the perfidious act, spoon still in hand, he saw her staring into his hard black intense eyes and the pointed face of a double-barreled shotgun with their hammers drawn back. Dying, her body got colder and colder. He injected her with the sound of a drawn-out kiss into the upper knob of her right shoulder. He watched the oval of her face with her beak nose. He thought he heard a single gurgle. Her forehead felt like damp cardboard. She was drooling white, into a pool of water on the floor.

He dropped his voice to a cathedral hush.

"Was the soup off?" he asked the sitting corpse, its eyes fully dilated and black. "Burning is a substitute for love." That was him all over. Do not some statements contradict the very conditions that allow them to be stated?

The room was cold, cold. She was going gelid, very faraway and unmoving, rising, it seemed, very like an offering on a frozen altar. Her skin turned as hard as the cephalothorax of a horseshoe crab. He cautiously touched the tip of her nose. The smoke of her soul, unbreathed anymore, rose as if a spiral and was no longer attainable. He remembered how the curtains of heavy, dusty maroon velvet made the room look like a charnel house.

Who was it said, the more I get to know people, the more I like dogs?

Murderers perceive their crimes as stories. Thumbwheel saw himself walking through a long black tunnel, blindly groping its walls, and emerging into bright sunlight. Of his victim in the story, he gave not a thought, merely of something remorselessly left behind. It was an adventure in success as well as a personal victory. Fantasies of true triumph, importance, brilliance, power, or victory in the narcissism of a child are standard.

Briefly, Thumbwheel's drab life was renewed. "Do you know the meaning of joy?" he would walk up to ask perfect strangers. He escorted Rowena to art exhibits and for Babychams at the local pub. They spent many glorious nights together at the music halls—they adored variety shows and comedians—listening to Lili Morris singing "Lardy-Doody-Day" and "Why Am I Always the Bridesmaid" and "Don't Have Any More, Missus Moore." They saw Joe Jelly juggle; and the magical Vaccaro, the Man with the

Disappearing Spindle and His Dog; and Mr. Akers sing and do a soft shoe to "Mother Kelly's Doorstep." They stomped their feet in glee listening to derby-wearing, cigar-smoking pianists, sweating at battered uprights and singing old tunes.

They especially loved the theatrics and acrobatics at the Alhambra and the St. James. They caught George Robey do his song-and-dance patter as "The Mayor of Mudcumdyke." Of course, it was a bit squeamish-making for Thumbwheel when he heard prissy old Marie Kendall sing "Did Your First Wife Ever Do That?" George Formby sang "Leaning on the Lamp-post." They saw the midget Little Tich do "The Gas Inspector" and Dan Leno as "The Railway Guard." Rowena's favorite of all was Vesta Tilley singing

> "When I think about my dugout
> Where I dare not stick my mug out
> I'm glad I've got a bit of a blighty one!"

in one of the last shows she ever did, a rare ticket!

Appeasing Rowena became the drapery of his dreams. She endeared herself more by disliking his mother. One week they took a side trip to Brighton, visiting the Royal Pavilion and having delicious fish on the seafront. They skipped down the streets, hand in hand, singing "Boiled Beef and Carrots" and "My Old Dutch." He hearkened to nothing of guilt. Someone died, a pity, give it a bloody rest. How? Anyone's guess. Who was it said, everything that happens doesn't mean something else? But, at the same time, who was that strange mysterious mustachioed man in a bowler hat and umbrella behind a newspaper who kept reappearing on the train platform? He loomed. Could he have been following them?

Would he be arrested? was his worry. Indeed, yes. How? It so happened that the young pharmacist with shock read in the newspaper of Mrs. Thumbwheel's untimely death and rightly concluded that a crime had taken place. That very day he went and placed a leaf of evergreen on the sod above the grave of the departed woman—

—then proceeded to the police station, confessing out of guilt as to the details about having sold the potassium.

Thumbwheel was sentenced to death. He was hanged at HM Prison Wormwood Scrubs on August 17, 1914. On the scaffold, aptly quoting the philanderer Byron, he declared, "I am not now that which I have been."

Allowed a last word, unperturbed, he took the occasion to recite a poem he had memorized from "A Warning for Faire Women:"

"Vile world, how like a monster come I soiled from thee!
How have I wallowed in thy loathsome filth,
Drunk and besmeared with all thy bestial sin?
I never spake of God, unless when I
Have blasphemed the name with monstrous oaths.
I never read the Scriptures in my life,
But did esteem them worse than vanity;
I never came in church where God was taught,
Nor ever, to the comfort of my soul
Took benefit of sacrament or baptism.
The Sabbath days I spent in common stews,
Unthrifty gaming, and vile perjuries.
I held no man once worthy to be spoke of
That went not in some strange disguised attire,

Or had not fetched some vile, monstrous fashion
To bring in odious, detestable pride.
I hated any man that did not do
Some damned or some hated, filthy deed
That had been death for virtuous men to hear.
Of all the worst that live, I was the worst.
Of all the cursed, I the most accursed.
All careless men, be warned by my end,
And by my fall, your wicked lives amend."

Strangely then, he suddenly burst into scornful laughter. "Wait a minute, wait a minute, do you half-wits think I am serious?"

Just before his head was covered, he offered to the executioner, "I have *painted* a hood like that—not black, however, but cramoisy."

And then he was sprung.

Mrs. Marwood's Spunkies

"Where you to?"

"Marwood's."

"Eh?"

"M-a-r," I spelled, hoping he would hear me in spite of the bite of blowing wind, though it was clear the old farmer was as deaf as cobbler's wax, "w-o-o-d. The bookseller." I pronounced the name a third time, loudly.

"Oh, Aye. There were a old goody as lived down to Exmoor way called that, who used to come up to market driving a push cart wi' her ever zo many books, zar. Aye. A old widow body, she were, bit of a thing 'oo 'ad 'eaps of books, aye." The two of us were both standing together at the crossroads there, a divergence where two old cobblestone roads met, I quite fretful, the Somersetshire cracker less so—although, for all of that, he was as deaf as a haddock. This near toothless thatcher in gumboots whom I had stopped for directions then extirpated the long stem of his peat-colored pipe and puffed a dungball of smoke at me, "Awwiver, down by Ebdon—"

The dalesman leaned on his rake. The Somerset mind is not inventive, nor swift to anticipate the answer you wish.

271

"No. No. No," I interrupted. I can be like that. Impatient. "The one in Batch. I specifically want to find the Marwood in Batch. I have been told that she lived hereabouts." I had, in fact, been told so—and, it might equally have been pointed out, told by a reliable source, an assurance that was solid enough for me, confidentially, for it was just about the only inducement possible that would have gotten fussy me up so early, dressed, and out on a glimmer train from London at six o'clock on a gray morning. A minor correction? The books I very much wanted were the main inducement.

It was getting too near dusk. I looked up. The sky was the color of rubber. Dark friable clouds. An east wind sloughed the trees.

"Aw-wiver, I zay," said he—and showing a like impatience he patiently closed his eyes—"she've a zizter, she, t'whom she be given the books years back, I've heerd, this just before she—died." As he spoke the word "died," he slowly lowered his ratty pipe and actually winked at me. On the irony of that, however, I had neither the time nor the inclination to ponder. "Backalong while, both they cut many a withy fer t' basket trade, I gnaw-knifed them down to the *stools.*"

"They made baskets?"

"Wurnt zent much for schooling—not a one them. Neither the type." He explained as best he could how she cut branches for baskets.

"The zizter Marwood what died"—correct, he winked again—"be not the zame, o' course, as she what 'ave a 'ouse here," said he, gesturing to a spot in front of him, the which, I correctly assumed, was to be taken as a metonymy for Batch. Then he pointed far past my ear, looking at me all the while through eyes like the dimples in old glass. "The zizter you want live past the four-wents there, crossed the hill, just out o' Batch proper on the road ye'll be following straight as a withy."

My Somersetshire friend thatched the directions in the air with his hand. I was about to set off. He paused, peered. "Be ye afraid?"

"Afraid?"

"Aye, that zizter Marwood be summat queer."

"Queer?"

"They zay she's gone eerie, like. Hafe daft. 'Twas never right, 'tis true, though is worse than ever now, zar. Eerie, be sure, be sure, eh?" He leaned into me and looked up with a wink. "Deals wi' hunkypunks."

"How sad," I said, dryly. I hadn't a clue what he was saying.

He peered suspiciously up at the sky and shivered. "Sright nottlin, rain. Cordin eye, g'woam."

"Yuh," I agreed. "Whatever."

You find that short of me? I found it difficult to be polite, frankly. You see, the Somersetshire accent—I am not going to lie about it—drives me out of my rubbers. All z's. Mouths twisting in haws and hoots. What an ugly accent! Just the memory of it alone, if I dwell on it, is enough to cost me a night's sleep, and often has. It sounds to me as if the speaker has had his tongue spliced in two like a jackdaw's! *Drone, bumble, whirr, fizz!* And nasal! There is always that irritating drone sound, a pinched, rhinal, adenoidal, I don't know, sound as if it were being sent out at a queer ventriloquial remove from a plastic horn and elicited in the pneumatically controlled head of whatever shovel-mouthed dummy is talking to you.

Have you any experience, say, with the musical instrument known as the oboe, played very poorly?

"Sad," I repeated, glad to be moving away.

The thatcher stopped me at the elbow. Wind snatched at his hair. He switched his pipe from hand to hand.

"Zad? Is the zame word what Mrs. Marwood's husband zaid, poor little zwipe, afore she went a-digging wi' a shovel a girt big 'ole one moonlighted night years back arter the vire and, a-blowin' and a-puffin', counted one, two, dree, and—*thunk!*—junketed the poor arfur right underground wi' the teddies." He re-winked. With pipe in mouth, his hands folding, swaddling each other, as if by imbricating a drama, he disclosed, "He were never zeen again, zar, not once."

I stopped short.

"Go on, now," he said. "Keep to the road, just out o' Batch proper. Straight as a javelin flying flamingo."

"Teddies?"

His tobacco was almost bleaching my hair. He slowly took the pipe from his mouth and muttered.

"Taiters."

"Come again?"

"Potatoes."

§

I am a reputable literary scholar. I had been tracing around for some time for matter touching on a new folk-motif index. Some time, did I say? Try nine and a half years. This particular person I was looking up, Mrs. Marwood, or so the poop went, harbored a trove of as-yet-undocumented books, all sorts of miscellany, rare volumes, manuscripts, all sophisticating right there in her attic, at least according to my sources. A London bookseller, to tell. There is little that the book merchants on the Charing Cross Road cannot tell you, I have come to see, although I secretly suspect they look down on Americans, among which of course I proudly number myself. Ohio. Cleveland, born and bred. Rubber. *Tires?* You name the brand! Hey, when you think rubber, think Cleveland, OK? How about the Great Lakes Brewing Company—Christmas Ale, anyone? Our symphony orchestra is the best in the land. I could go on! The Rock and Roll Hall of Fame Museum. The Terminal Tower. The West Side Market. Pierogies. Paczki. Buckeye Candy. Sweet corn. Listen, don't get me started.

President George Washington was a book-collector. But he always spelled the word "cat" with two t's. I always get a kick out of that, don't know why. Maybe it reflects an essential ambivalence in our profession.

Anyway, to clarify: one does not simply come to a limp decision, hail a cab, and go arbitrarily hunting books on a random afternoon in any old place. It is not just a holiday jaunt. You want to be a bit of a tartar. There's a rubric involved, a method. Processus? Same thing. So, what? I'm a book-collector—in the folklore line, have I pointed out?—and chuffed about it, proud you might say. We go way back in our family in the book trade. I had been in England, oh, I would say about a year—Somersetshire, I think, four times—hot, if I may put it that way, on the trail for antiquaria, special things, rare finds, the odd gem. Not the usual county collections, redactions, adaptations, jingle poetry. Good heavens, we'd had a wealth of that, hadn't we? With great scholars like Keightley, Charlotte Burne, and the divine Mrs.

Bray? They were good, still are, you'll get no argument from me. But I wanted real finds, you know?

You want to be a bit of a bloodhound.

An example, actually, was not far away. But first, for instance, what does Motif XIII.2; Tale 71 tell you? Nothing, I'll wager—and of course it shouldn't. But for me it's an entirely different story, believe me. For, you see, the deaf rustic from Batch whom I had just buttonholed for some information about Mrs. Marwood (she whom, not atypically, his type had been foolishly rumoring to be a loony and maybe a murderess) was an almost perfect XIII.2;71:"Deaf Peasant: Travelers Ask the Way." It was a find in itself, a lucky come-across. And he may very easily have touched on, so flexible are categories, Motif D1810.9.3.2; Tale 28: "Danger Warnings for the Future." Folklore. Documented. I think you may be beginning to see what I'm getting at.

I have often, just for the heck of it, taken a big box of Sun Maid raisins into my backyard in Cleveland and done absolutely nothing for the whole afternoon but run through my numbers. If you're in my business, don't—then see where you are.

Let me tell you something.

Nowhere.

§

Just about to leave, I stopped for a minute.

Before we parted, me and my pipe-smoking friend, a question suddenly occurred to me. "How could both sisters be named Marwood and simultaneously be widows," I asked the man. Legitimately, don't you think? "If they are widows, they were married, I mean, right?"

"Married, aye. Years past, were a vat podgy yellow 'ere-
abouts named Marwood what were courtin' the goody in Exmoor,
the one what—" He winked.

"Died."

"Aye, what died and were buried, astooded," he nodded.
"Zuddenly, they zays, Marwood come to Batch, married the zizter, he, and no zooner it were done than he wasted down, eerie
like, to nothin' but the zize of a rake." My friend worked up several flouncy, gratuitous gestures with an imaginary rake. Thinking, doubtless, I was a moron? Some kind of chuckleheaded rube?
Attitudinizing kills me, if you want to know the first of it. Enough
said. He continued.

"The old widow body be the only hobbler left around,
livin' in a old house, as I zay, wi' a chimmer window, but—"

"Look, thank you."

I terminated the conversation, and left him with his gumboots and oboe-like histories. Thank you, but no thanks. It was
indeed looking like rain, the wind was up, the sun long down,
and I had to get moving. Conspicuousness is the ABC of my profession, so don't think for one minute that I missed my friend's
explanation of the curious marriages, which, if he was not lying,
might fit perfectly into my book as sub-tales to Motif IX; Tale
46—"The Spying Widow"—or, possibly, Motif XXII; Tale 89: "Two
Sisters Who Work at a Loom." No, scratch the last one. No go,
I don't think it would quite fit. You see? You see how difficult
this can be? Complicated and what-not. You don't just turn over
a rock. This is not about finding lottery tickets.

I knew I was in weird country of course. The Mendips.
It was not necessarily bizarroville, but there was lots of mental
illness hereabouts. A cemetery by a watershed was peppered with

an array of odd-shaped stones, which, not rushed, I'd have liked to have read. I followed a dirt road along a shallow chalk stream and through hedge breaks opening to tableland saw long rolls of cornlands, where, past a patch of wood and a deep depression constituting a small valley, rose a church spire.

A view across Black Down from Beacon Batch, highest point in Mendip, alone could give anyone the creeps. Bell barrows and bowl barrows from the Bronze Age. Wanderers do not feel easy there. The name "Black Down" comes from the Saxon word '*Blac*' or '*Bloec*' meaning bleak, '*Dun*' meaning down or fort, but then also muddy, brown, grim. It could have been named for the old reeking ironworks that I also spotted, rising up like a black ghost at the end of a marsh of shinweeds. A great crook led up to a hill, a trivial swell at the top of a patch of spurs, carried the eye for 60 miles.

I had hoped to have lunch at a nearby inn, but was too late for the serving, and so instread had a small wedge of nutty Leicester cheese and watercress, eatables said to be made for each other, and a tankard of ale.

I had also stopped earlier by the old Wells and Mendip Museum next to Wells Cathedral to take a look at the infamous 1,000-year-old skeleton which, along with other fossils, had been excavated in the caves there way back in 1912, and of course I had come to learn, by way of much reading, about the old fables and legends of that village in the hills of Somerset there that the bones had been been traditionally associated with the legendary "witch" of Wookey Hole, although analysis of the bones later indicated that it is the remains of a male aged between 25 and 35.

The Witch of Wookey Hole! You had to laugh. It sounded like an old Hardy Boys mystery title! An old story goes that a man from Glastonbury was engaged to a young woman from Wookey Hole. A witch living in the caves there cursed the romance, which was then broken off. The suitor, after becoming a monk, sought revenge on this vicious hag who, having been jilted herself, of course, is dedicated to cursing and bringing down all loving relationships. The monk stalks the old witch in the cave, where she hides in a dark corner near one of the underground rivers, and then upon finding the old crone, he splashes blessed holy water on her, which immediately causes her to petrify into limestone, but she remains in the cave to this day.

It was all very charming.

But I had more important business.

§

So I clocked off at a brisk walk, trudging my way down a series of long A. E. Housman-looking lanes with hedgerows here and there. Mud. A well. I saw an old pulley to draw water. Hay rakes and harrows. Once in a while the smell of a piggery wafting through the night. Not twenty minutes after my first encounter in Batch, I looked up only to see a tiny feather of smoke on the near horizon, bucked up my walk, and in no time was standing on the front stoop of Mrs. Marwood's Bookery. A low sloping dwelling all in all, it appeared to be half seemingly a garden house and half clunch and tiles quarters but with a weird blackened roof-like apse which, incongruously, gave the place the air of once having been somehow intended, at least in external appearance, to be a chapel, for up an adjacent hill appeared a rockery of what looked mysteriously like small carved ecclesiastical fragments. The smell of a tobacco-like loam permeated the air.

I saw lots of hemlock growing in a roadside ditch—not cow parsley, which it resembles, mind you, but the real death plant, *Conium maculatum*, with its characteristic lean and lethal, hollow stems streaked with purple and finely cut white umbels of flowers that seem so harmless to the unschooled mind, naively ready to bite and suck it as a lark only to turn pale, gasp, and croak!

It was a poor dwelling, a fell-side house, to the rafters, dingy, quaint and irregular in shape, closely shuttered. A crooked half-aslant old sign swung at the edge of the grey porch. I looked around me with a sense of dread. To the side of the rockery, up a small hillock, stood a spare haphazard garden filled with bare cornstalks and broken poles. I am here to tell you that the place looked to me like a baleful footprint. Doited and dark! But where do you find special truffles, tell me—by the waters of Babylon? I rapped, confidently, to show firmitude of purpose.

The door fell open, creaked down an angle—and an immediate squawk.

"*What be doing 'ere?*"

Good God!

"Well, my name is—"

"It be Zaturday. What be 'ee about?"

My throat flexed. The Star that is called Wormwood had the door open the width of a crack, a smile, wide enough for me, alert to such things, to discern a definite and frightful G283.1.2; Tale 21—"Witch Who Raises Wind to Sink Ships"—coupled, this, with your frequent, and in this case obvious H691.1.5; Tale 22: "Test Game: Questioning Stranger at the Door."

Horrifying! She could have been—*was!*—the Witch of Wookey Hole! She was a combination of Wordsworth's Goody

Blake, Yeats' Crazy Jane and Black Annis from Leicestershire.

"It be late, ye kna?"

Nelly Longarms herself!

She raised her nose to smell the air. "Most fwoak be turned in."

I waited patiently for her to assess me, choosing the moment to take a surveying look at the strange garden to my right.

I could well believe this crone on a dark night had shoveled her hubby under with the potatoes, trust me, though I cannot for the life of me imagine that, given the daily alternative, he would have argued. Mrs. Marwood, arthritic, stooping, peered over an inquisitorial trowel nose pinched almost paper white. She was thinly clad. Strands of greasy hair hung, swung, like late tendrils, over the snapping hamsterish eyes of her pumpkin-head, and her ears, which were both pointed, were also a bit flanged, for sharp listening. She looked an obvious pellagrin, the rude claw of the old working hand this side of the door dead, harsh, and roughened with old sharp fingernails that looked like polished horn. I cast around for a precedent in terms of a lead motif. I noticed a detail, the detail became a wen—on her nose. It spoke volumes. Had the thatcher been correct about her murders? All I needed now was a witch, believe thee me.

O Keightley!

"You be down from Nailsea?"

I shook my head.

"No. Cleveland." I waited. "Ohio? Rubber tires?"

"You go back whoame."

"Wait—"

"It's late. Dimmet. Be ye 'ere for books. Wha' odds izzit to

I? Marnen for that. I've got a figgety puddin' on."

Oh, good grief, I thought, no. "No, dear, do let me explain, please. No, listen," I said, "I want to have a look at your books, dear, the books in the house, see, your books. I took a train here. I'm an American book-collector. I took a special train just to get here. Book-collector. Folklorist, really. You know, tales of yore, fairy stories, old fables, bull beggars, ghosts—"

Want to know something? She let me in.

"The wind she blow a whist," mumbled Mrs. Marwood, bumping along, lurching, tic-toc, into a very dark room full of what looked like hoardings. Filling up an old pewter teapot, she put it on the boil, rattling the handle with decrepit fingers that were as white and wrinkled as European asparagus. She wore the spooky colors of El Greco, drawn, indistinct greys and browns. She caught her shawl to her neck and slumped into a chair across the room, somewhere. I could see practically nothing; it was almost pitch-black inside. I inhaled the smell of queer herbs.

"I take it, you are Mrs. Marwood?"

"Aye, Old Mother Ink they calls me," she cackled, coughed, spit phlegm into a soiled hanky pulled from her sleeve, and quoted,

> "Old Mother Ink,
> Fell down the sink (cough)
> How many miles
> Did she fall?"

She coughed quite a bit, hacking up phlegm, and croaked, "Brown titus." Periodically, I could hear little chipmunkish slurps, nips of a cracker, little slurps. "Maybe it be hun-

keypunks. Spunkies."

"Spunkies?"

She cackled.

But I was taking a gander around me. Piles of crackers. Old tins of tea. A corn broom. Putty knives. A gluepot or two. Hand saws. Broken dishes and cups. The place looked like the Old Curiosity Shop. What were those, bottles? Oil of vitriol and sulphur, storax and terebrinth, knapweed, mastics, herb trinity, great figwort, roots of orris, horehound, soapwort and angelica. I saw in a deeper corner piles of wreaths and no end of weird herbals, cloven helms heaped high, sad cypress, vervain, eugh and yew, and every baleful green denoting death, "hoary simples, found by Phoebus's light with brazen sickles reap'd at noon of night," as Virgil put it, and it did in fact immediately summon to my mind with a kind of grisly rebellowing echo, that backstreet witch, half-hag, half-magician, in the Garden of the Hesperides that crazed Dido sought out in the despair of her suicidal intent. Talk of rites obscene, accumulating omens! I thought I could actually smell meat—cold cuts? Hanging from a few low filthy crossbeams were long stems of drying nettles, fennel stalks, and thrum-eyed primroses.

No, it was bad cheese I smelled. There was a brick of hard, Angrywood cheddar sitting on a cold table there, beyond ripe, gamboge, and mouldy. Worse than mousetrap, in its state. Gammers like her in Somerset often made it, I'd heard, using their own cultures and unpasteurized milk.

And, indeed, there in a pot on an old small cast-iron stove sat what I gather was her figgety pudding.

Who was this Hecate of that crossroads?

I thought of Shakespeare's apothecary:

"A beggarly account of empty boxes,
Green earthen pots, bladders, and musty seeds,
Remnants of packthread, and old cakes of roses
Were thinly scattered, to make up a show . . ."

Did the old crone dispense fever cures? Peddle medicines? Was she also an herbalist, some sort of redshank? An actual alchemist?

Wind, howling down, shivered the chimney.

"A white gale be approaching"

"Well, personally, I wouldn't mind wind, if"—I was trying to be, well, I think the word I want here is congenetic—"if, ah, it didn't blow so hard." That was weak but the best I could do. *Slurp, crunch.*

"It run 'avoc wi' me garden, wind," creaked a frail voice hanging in the darkness. "It ruins me beans, carrots, zprouts. Goozegogs. The teddies is aright, for underground they be." *Crunch, slurp.*

Teddies. I smiled, recognizing the word. Potatoes. It was then I remembered the outlandish yarn I had heard and felt a bit uncomfortable. But I wanted the books, you see. *Livres!*

Let's be truthful, that's why I had come.

§

With her claw Mrs. Marwood poured a cup of tea, for herself. She sipped at it. She coughed. She cleared a ball of mucus from her throat, rattling through her like rope running out of a moored boat. "Hoppy cough." I thought I smelled offal and mentioned that. "Parget," she clarified. "Pelm, see. Inside the chimney be plastered wi' cowdung and mingle o' lime. The chimney's lively with it."

"Lime, you say? 'Lively' with it?"

I could barely make out what she said, her voice a combination of a diphtheria cough and the sexual honk of a brent goose.

"Aye. We talk with our mouths shut so's not to let the east wind in."

She talked, solitary reflections mainly. She lived all alone but took care of herself. I managed inadvertently to learn a few of her habits. She drank beech leaf gin and agrimony tea. She made tansy omelets; baked shaggy caps, a ditch fungus; and brewed up arrow and chickweed soups. She nipped tiny Alexanders buds and pignut tubers—she gave me one to chew, which left the hot afterscorch of radish, like a braise, at the back of my throat. She ate bramble jelly. She ground goosegrass seed for coffee. She made sloe jelly from blackthorn and distilled water of Jews-Ears, a fungus which grew on elder trees. I saw jars of dill and bottles of sage and bags of fairy ring mushrooms, drying dulse, and scurvy grass. She told me that she rubbed her chapped hands with elderberry lotion and held up her gnarled fingers—*blecch!*—as visible proof.

Where was the fillet of a fenny snake, the eye of newt, and toe of frog, the wool of bat and tongue of dog, the adder's fork and blind-worm's sting, the lizard's leg and owlet's wing, all the hell-broth boil and bubble?

Without abating, frightful gusts of wind kept tearing down the chimney with an echoing kind of hollow threat.

Mrs. Marwood slowly rose and hobbled over to close a banging door.

I immediately caught a draft of black hellbore, so-called "Christmas Rose," the dominant purgative of antiquity. Once a traditional cottage-garden favorite because it flowers in the depths of winter, the plant was deadly poison. So, what was she doing with it? True, in the Middle Ages it was spooned into ailing children as a remedy for worms, but then how many did it kill? In a ceramic pot, I noticed henbane—hog bean—unmistakably for its stout stems and long, toothed leaves, all covered with pale sticky hairs that had a fetid stink and those hideous tell-tale seed capsules along one side of the stem that when hardened and matured and resembled a row of large teeth. This place was Daggerville!

I felt suddenly cold, the chill of apprehension. I asked about her herbs. She kept mandrake roots wrapped in silk in a special box—for rheumatism, she said, but large doses of it could be fatal! Did she know that?

What kind of had I come to?

Was that foxglove I had seen growing in her garden, its spikes of tubular pink flowers with those unmistakable soft, ugly, wrinkled leaves, the "dead man's thimbles" that Dr. William Withering isolated in 1795 as the lethal herb that also figured in so many ancient German fairy-tale murders? And thornapple with its jagged, daggered leaves and spiky fruit—jimson weed—that grew in the world's waste places? And lily of the valley with its scarlet berries and creeping, creepy roots, all poisonous?

She began coughing again. A purple hacking.

"Wind," she muttered dolefully and hobbled up to turn a knob on a thin black wagging shutter. "Screws, it gi' me. Sexton's bones." She clutched an elbow as if to work it free. She meant rheumatism. "Aye, it run 'avoc wi' me garden, wind. Whips it to a whitpot leavin' but scraggly notlins. Brings down water like rainin' chairlegs." She coughed and pulled tight her shawl. "Drisk. Seafret."

"No, you're correct. Wind cannot be good for a garden, not at all," said I, trying to commiserate but at the same time rubbing my hands in delight at the shelves of old volumes, dusty tomes, and upside-down books of all sizes now standing out more vividly before me as my eyes settled into the darkness of the rooms and a bleak hallway. "But, here, look at these books!"

I made the transition, I can't say subtly.

Mrs. Marwood bent to retrieve fallen books under the table, lifted them, then dropped them. I stepped in to help her. She gave off a breadcrumby odor. I got closer. She also smelled of gorse and horseradish. An old herbalist crone, she began munching pignuts she kept snatching out of a deep latch pocket in her apron. "Me old 'and is warped from toil. Scrammed frae the cold, aye. Room's betwaddled frae neglect. Look-see, no purpose else." I saw skulls, small and large. Animal skulls. Bird skulls. I hesitantly asked, "Is that a skull or a beak?"

"A woodpecker's beak is part o' its skull," replied the old woman. "Mr. Gnoats, aye. I used to feed him."

"Did the bird eat—*cheese?*"

She shook her head, no, no. "Mealies. Or meatwich. I fed 'im by hand, personal," She held up the scrape of a hand.

She creaked backwards and lifted a sharp sickle to claw down from two high shelves above a long red cloth, which she wrapped around her frail shoulders. She held up the sharp sickle. "But that zays nothing—what yeel not I believe of me life in the vields." I almost dared not looked at her bent, arthritic, misshapen hands, that wizened, weather-beaten face. "The grim days o' my choildhood were reaped out o' the cob-wall, I zaye, Aye, the things I've zeeun. I was a silly creature." She eyed the fingers she slowly and stiffly raised to wag. "Drat the dukes."

I gathered that for dog's years old Mrs. Marwood worked a withy bed. The job was, they pushed willow branches—osiers, "sallies" they called them—into the ground, left them to grow, which after three years or so, they cut down to the *stools*—ground level—cutting them with a sickle, making sure they were cut flush. Hard work. A winter activity. Then the branches were stripped, pulled through the V-shape of a brake, to bruise and ruddle the bark—brown withies for rough baskets, buff withies, boiled in their jackets, skinned, stripped, and stained for better ones. Duck nesting baskets, fishermen's creeks, eel hives. Tall baskets for wine.

I pointed to a willow basket. "Handmade?"

"But that were in the old man's time. I reckon to see 'em you'll 'ave to go down Crowcombe way. Ask Relish Woodbead or Fed Porlock, they would know." *Fed Porlock? Relish Woodbead?*

"Ol' Penneythorne Hoarharbor couldst tell you."

What in the—! These were ancient names right out of 1066 and the troops of Anglo-Saxon King Harold Godwinson! Among Harthacnuts and Cnuts and Magnuses wielding medieval bladder axes and long swords!

But I'd no time for that. I was measuring with open eyes the piles of wonky books, entire chimneys of them, rising stacks, across the room. I picked up a huge volume nearby on Roman columns and blew whorls of dust off it.

"'Ave a look-see for yoursel', mizter. I creep about them now, 'mid baskets and whatnot, finding nothin' folks 'twas or 'twill be zeeking anymore, though nobody been by 'ere for years

—ever zince the vire."

She picked up a fire crook.

"Fire?"

She gnashed a pignut tuber.

"Aye, a vlash vire, inzoide. It were bad. Cleered t' shelves of many of the volumes, smoked black and curled." She nodded, gesturing aimlessly to the sagging shelves. "They thowt it were Mr. Marwood's spunkie."

She had used that word again. I peered up at her, musty-nosed, over a stack of stiff old Victorian and Edwardian-age mag-azines.

I swallowed, nervously.

"Spunkie?"

"Ghost," muttered Mrs. Marwood.

I could have sworn she was smiling.

§

No matter to me. I got cracking. Have I told you how excited I get over old volumes? Excited is not the word. You can't possibly imagine, for instance, what finding an old parchment or letter still in its eighteenth-century folds or rude vellum enve-lopes with red seals does to me. I am not, *not*, interested in the usual onmarch of general go-as-you-pleases, mind you, stalls fat with statistical Victorian blue books on sanitation and drains; the millrace of Georgian poetry; badly over-larded novels by women with three names; botanical taxonomies with dreadful lithographs protected by onion-skin sheets; or, you know, the interminable sluice of sleep-inducing Masonica, no, no stuff like that. I wanted folklore—Keightley'd have done no differently. I had not come all that way simply to press a couple of pennies into the hand of some half-witted granny goose and unhappily walk out with a fungoid 1909 *Nada the Lily* or a chewed, if manly, Rider Haggard, or a Twenties edition of Cakebread's *Horn Cookies.*

We sat there in silence. I pretended to yawn in order to get up and stretch so I could get a better look around. I stepped over a worthless stack of musty *Somerset Yearbooks* and threw aside a clammy ringed-sheaf cookbook, compiled for the War Effort in 1917. Who needed them?

I shoved aside a load of novels: Rhoda Broughton, Marie Corelli, Ada Leverson. The plays of Lord Dunsany. There was a Harley Granville-Barker, *Vote by Ballot.* Gertrude Page's *The Pathway.* Berta Ruck. Mary Grant Bruce. Talk about pignut tubers! There was a stack of *Live and Learn* magazines, wrinkled and roped together. I saw stamped envelopes in piles, cracked leather torts, junk journals, family prayerbooks, a few ratty children's books—a copy of Madge A. Bigham's *Sonny Elephant; Johnny Crow's Garden*, with pictures drawn by L. Leslie Brooke; and *Girls and Boys Hurrah!* on antique linen which I had read as a lad—along with a set of Robert Louis Stevenson.

Where were the Belgian psalters?

She reached up and took down a bottle from a doited shelf, uncorked it with her teeth. "A tear o' mastic—droplets. I uses it for me gut. Here," she gestured to her stomach awkwardly with her elbow. Into a small spoon she tapped a small measure of the liquid, then actually began to *chew* it! "Me lights and gubbins aches." She coughed and clawed at her neck with superannuated fingers. "Fungal infections. I takes it for to improve me blood circulation." She was a relic, with shrill chatter and passion for pignuts. She spit up phlegm into a rag, which she unfolded to look upon acidly, peering closely with that aging parrot-face and shadow of a moustache,

I was perspiring. I took off my jacket. I was not making any headway. I stepped here and there over boxes, but the floors were sagging, the old pine-boarded slats, the black wooden flooring, slumping, bulging downward. When was this shriveling old house built, *in Jacobean days?*

"Have you anything in the folklore line?"

Through the shadows came the dirty crunch of a cracker, the slurp of tea predictably washing it away. More phlegm. The sounds of hocking, hacking. Be fair. Could you have stood it? And while Mrs. Marwood sat there like a stone in the darkness— but you could hear her, burbling, like a percolator—I was madly, crazily, swiftly fumbling into her stacks of mildewed magazines, damp books, dank bundles of papers tied with string, and, positively reeking, volumes of all shapes and sizes. Maybe there were treasures to be had here, but how in the hell could you find them? See? I mean, how in the deuce could you *see* them? And, if you can believe it, while I was feeling, groping from one carton to another, I thought I heard someone laugh!

"Volklore?" She frowned. "Is yer bum oot the windae?"

"Come again?"

She snorted.

I prodded her. "Mythology, lore, oral history, tradition."

Her mouth peevishly clamped against my words.

"You know, as I said, fairy tales, legends," I replied, huffing, now a bit impatiently, looking over in her direction with a black smudged nose. "Local, well, yarns, as we say back in the States." I tried to laugh, so help me, but she was beginning to give me the fantods, the bloody creeps.

"Ye mean, on spunkies."

"You say?"

"Zomerzet has'm. Aye, we be whoaome to Gwyn ap Nudd, Land of the King of the Fairies. I m'sel' seen spirits down Yeovil way, Wedmore, Yeovil, Martok. They lives there—inhabits the greensward, they do. Live in the mushroom zwards." She waved a claw. "All over. Catsham. Ham Street. Southwood. Boltonsborough, part o' the hundred of Glaston Twelve Hides, where volks zay good St. Dunstan too' him by the very gob and nailt a horseshoe onto the devil."

I paused, then remembered. "Ghost tales, yes. That kind of thing."

She stood up, in segments, creakily.

"Spunkies," she repeated—it seemed with relish—and poked her way to what appeared to be a side door in a small room off her kitchen (slate-colored sink, black oak butter churn, a pewter teapot). Just before she opened the door, she paused and peered over her shoulder at me.

She hobbled toward me, her wicked black eyes blinking at me, and not without a hint of icy disparagement, she droned, "Greed has a north eye. It be a rafty trait. Tidden good to have. It make for boneshave o' the soul, aye, works a dimpsey there. I've zeen a cauldron o' it in me day, diddiky as dimmet, wot?"

She came scarily close, face a cracked plate.

"Mr. Marwood's family were also grasping, like—piggy. They had an eye for value and went about 'ere peering into the cracks for gold. The tightfisted mother o' him worked 'im for gain, I zay, 'twas awful—and to that he niver oncst said nowt! I abominated the shrew! Maist days, she had niver a guid word for me—nay a bit o' kindness, but cruelty. A ter'ble girt dufferance betwixt them two, ye kna? A widow she were, her dead husband I seen oncet, faculty stricken and no nicer, I wadn't say that nayther. Threadbare cloak, went about the land in a dung-cart, cheapjacks, neither weel-spoken. They wuz all unsavory, ill-mannered, uncouth, common fwoak, she fra' Nempnett Thrubwell, with kin in Ditcheat or Minehead, thereaway. Rapacious be the word!"

Was she accusing me?

"They zay a man can no more separate age and covetousness than a' can part young limbs and lechery."

She slowly opened the creaking door.

Hurry, dammit, I thought.

She turned back to look at me.

"Be ye a gulliver playing hangles wi' me? Meachin' about for gold?"

"Excuse me?"

"To that I answers," she said and quoted,

> "One-cry, two-cry, ziccary, zan;
> Hollow bone, crackabone ninery ten:
> Spittery spot, it must be done;
> Twiddledum twaddledum twenty one.
> Hink spink, the puddings stink.
>   The fat begins to fry,
> Nobody's at home, but jumping Joan,
> Father, mother, and I.
> Stick, stock, stone dead,
>   Blind men can never see.
> Every knave must have a slave,
> You or I must be He."

What was all this jibber jabber about?

"We must go vurther in," said she, producing a bent little candle from somewhere from within her widish cuffs, "zo 'ere, taper up t'candle and catch hold. 'Ere," she noisily exasperated. "You're all bum and parsley!" She passed me the candle. I felt like David Balfour. "*Heid doon arse up!*"

I felt in the greasy subterranean air a hint of malice there, creating a mood in me characterized by a need to escape.

We were halting along, bumping, stepping through a dark muggy cellar, its walls mildewed with steamy condensation. My neck seemed to grow sweatier and more sticky for the impossible, impenetrable darkness.

"I think I should come back in the morning."

"Never 'ee mind, mumper. Zome other volks have been 'ere into the night. Hicken' about. Grockles. Tourists." She poked me. "Thinks I lie? The Choughs Hotel be riddled wi' zecrets. Take a photo of the inverted tombstone there by the vireplace and ye surely die. Galloping 'orsemen. Zpectral monks wearin' snuffy robes like demons. The George and Pilgrim Hotel, aye, built in 1475. Eerie loud disembodied voices frae acrost the rover, urging, 'Come over! Come over!'"

Now what in thee hell did she think I was going to make of that remark, may I ask?

"Before he were took ill, Mr. Marwood drew 'imsel' out to the garden 'ere, a turble zad tale that, zo 'tis, and—"

"Mr.—?"

Oh no, I wasn't going to have any of that.

"And 'twere an old varmer, oncet, coming whoame from Langport Town stopped in 'ere—"

"For books?"

"My zoul, nay. To make inquiry about t' road to Sedge-moor. But it come to 'im as well to ask about spunkies and the little trots that be in the Pixy Vair, as he were told." Riddles, puzzles, equivocations.

"Fancy that," I said.

She coughed phlegm. "Influrmayshin." She spit into a rag. "Jack-o'-lanterns, hanged corpses with traces of the gimmaces. Watch 'ee clavel there, vireplace beams turning to cob." I held up my candle.

Books, I thought, *where are the goddam books.*

"'Where they be tew?' say he to me, wi' a queer glint o' the eyes. "'Where they be tew?' say the ancient varmer." Shadows played everywhere, threatening, their most disconcerting—in the chiaroscuro created by the tiny wagging flame—on the weird little ball that was Mrs. Marwood's head. With both hands she pri-pri-pried the door open. It was dry, swollen, moss-covered.

She was dry, swollen, moss-covered.

The wind in the chimney blew fiercely, as if a couple of expiring infants were caught under the crown, hooked in the black cindery liners, howling through the thimble for death to spare them. Never a word was said, there was never a sound but the creaking of our steps along the floorboards. It was not the silence of tranquility, or of a settled peace, but rather a silence of suppression—of *oppression*, a muzzled or stifled threat, a mousy, muted, cantankerous purdah, an emptiness, that bred fear in me. I shook as I went along feeling terror in my scalp, but my companion, but for her wheezing, only kept mum. I felt like I was having an OBE.

Out of body experience? Right.

My every urge to leave those haunts seemed countermanded. Forlornly the room seemed to pitch, the walls, lop-sided and facing nowhere, giving off a sour dust that in their notes of depletion seem to breed even more queerness.

Unabashedly, she snatched my wrist and directed the candle to be held higher, brought forward. Two original *aperçu* were then mine: (1) a weedy, dank black garden, rotten with plants, set off by a fence with several headstones in it, and (2) a face, hers, curving perceptibly into the aura of the candle before me like a dirty little planet—and looking full and directly at me.

An icy shiver passed over my soul.

I smelled dread.

I saw myself suddenly in an hallucinating instant filled with strange atavistic horror immured in a hothouse burial box, fighting for air and pleading to a terror of a ghost for release. . . .

It was a pumpkin, her face, a pebbled gourd, a squash ghost like the hotel horror she mentioned, its teeth black and jagged (if not missing), and all set off in a sallow oily shine by a round head, lined and creased and almost perfectly orange. It was crooked into a deranged smile as she moved toward me with juddering steps. A frisson ruffled me. My skin went walking. My head was suddenly shivering. I felt a shudder ripple through me like a comb going the wrong way.

Legitimately, too, will you ask what we were doing in that terrifying overgrown garden.

As did I.

And at the almost exact instant I reached the train station, it occurred to me—breathless, leg twitching, pale—that, even if I had left my expensive hacking jacket behind, I had, you know, I had at least stumbled upon something new in the way of motif, which even the great Keightley might envy. It would slot into the G's, I thought: Tale 90, say, in the sub-heading G156.33: "Old Witch Who Wants to Show Strangers Her Teddies."

I made the entry in Cleveland, in my backyard.

St. Malecroix

One Crouchmas night the bells in the tower of St. Malecroix Seminary began angrily ringing, and all the seminarians were roused out of their beds, lined up, and questioned as to whom the culprit was who had dared to write out a sign in bold Latin over the chapel door, *Ubi o ubi est sub ubi.* It was blasphemy, howled the prefect, and all the Carmelite priests, Frs. Myron, Suprenant, Liguori, MacGillivray, and even old Fr. Magaw gathered together to abhor the sort of students they had. The scariest of them all was the one with the pockmarked face.

"Ninevehites," screamed Fr. Facemire, bitterly fumbling with his beads and patrolling the line and squinting volelike into the eyes, one by one, of each terrified boy who stood quaking before him.

At his order all the boys were sent out into the dark woods, in the middle of the night, each to try to find two heavy boulders and bring them back. The punishment was to have the culprits kneel down and to hold the boulders out in their extended hands, crucifixion-wise, for two hours as a penalty. Facemire, who could not conceive that those who differed with him acted from any but the basest motives, had coarse, dead-looking hair and black eyes and was taller than doors. The boys had nasty names for him like "Bullethead" and "Leashlaw" and "Vercundorib the Gallic priest." A school legend had it that one night during a storm that mad priest had been seen by a flash of lightning standing, grim-faced, by one of the seminarian's beds holding up a serrated bread knife, Abraham-and-Isaac style, and that the kid later went completely mental and had to be put in a straightjacket.

St. Malecroix rose grey in the mist the following morning. It was a single puddingstone building near lonely old meadows and fields that always smelled of rain and heavy weather. Writ in stone over the front entrance was inscribed *Aut Disce Aut Discede* (Either Learn or Depart). A sunken garden with a small plunge pool lay there but had decades ago gone dry. An old black barn stood at some distance, with its grid of heavy beams, purlins, and braces that held up the mass of old thatched roof.

J. Hoops, a convert who was fourteen and small and went for walks by himself, loved that barn and dreamed of martyrs (especially St. Tarcisius) and often with the tip of his tongue recited Rogation Day litanies on the top of his mouth. Fr. Facemire hated the boy, who once at morning chapel had forgotten his necktie, and the priest upon spotting it furiously asked the student where it was. Hoops contritely said that it was either in the bureau or on it. "So if it is in or if it is on, it is as it is, be it in or on," sneered Facemire, "no?" Hoops swallowed. "*No?*" the priest vehemed, pinching the boy's ear white. For his penance, Fr. Facemire told the boy that in consequence he had to wear his necktie everywhere, in the shower, on trips, at play, *everywhere*. Finally, he proscribed the use of the barn as being henceforth off-limits to him or anybody.

The way out of a dilemma is to recognize that one of its

horns has, so to speak, no point, thought Hoops, who wondered who had scrawled on the refectory wall—Rudy Insana, who had a face like a Venetian carnival mask?—although he would not believe it. He loved God and badly wanted to be a priest and didn't want to prejudge. He was mocked wearing his tie to bed. It didn't matter. He remembered reading of swallows that hovered over Jesus' cross, squawking, "*Svitka*."

Of all the odd seminarians, certain of them friends of Hoops, by the way, like D. D. ("Doubles") La Cross, Pigga Buoncuore, Paul Nosedocks, with his whitewall haircut, Gummy Pointlaces, Charles Verschneider, Wickie Martello, "Bat Lugs" Bugle who had monstrous ears, avocado-shaped, Al Hatblack, pimpled, dwarfish, nasal Gary Fantagraph, and brandy-glass-chinned Ed Every. Fr. Facemire's personal spy was an overweight kid named Wallace Proops, an extremely nervous sixth-former from Buffalo, New York, with oily cheeks, squeaking shoes, and, by way of the high and overpious estimate of his own self-worth borne up by his seniority, the conviction that whatever he secretly passed on to the authorities by way of whispered mutters and memos could easily make or break his classmates.

Proops, though effeminate, was greatly feared. He followed Facemire's every whim, no matter how odd. And Facemire was odd. He sucked gumballs—he disposed of them, white as paper, in unlikely places—collected books, took photos of forests, and, unheroically, at least to the boys, always wore big back box-toe shoes.

The man was truly disturbed and walked vise-tight in his habit. It was his habit to ferret out the sins and peccadillos of the boys, and he ran his classroom like a prison, his *de haut en bas* pedagogic style being the standard method at the time of seminary teaching, where the process of learning meant simply to shut up and listen, to refrain from putting your two cents in, and to be satisfied to remain simply putty in the teacher's hand.

One day Facemire shouted, "*Piano*"—softly, he thought. But La Cross, who was brilliant—and who played the organ—put up his hand and said, "Excuse me, father. The word *piano* derives from the Latin word *planus* meaning 'plain' or 'flat.' During the Renaissance, for example, a sound was called *piano* only when it was at its *usual* level volume, not when it was softer than usual." La Cross was summarily called up front after class was dismissed and, as a punishment for being bumptious, was told to go buff all of the floors in the building that afternoon.

Fr. Facemire gave odd sermons, like "The Religious Meaning of Pets" and "Death as a Nurse" and "The Perfidious Jews" and one day—it wouldn't be made clear why until sometime later—even spoke on "Famous Historical Lost Things," such as Miguel de Cervantes left hand, the poet Sapphos's poems, the original manuscript of T. E. Lawrence's *Revolt in the Desert*, Euripides' *Alcmaeon in Corinth*, the lost tools of the Incas, the lost continents of Atlantis and Moo, the mysterious writer, B. Traven, and Alonso Sanchez Coello's study in 1585 of St. Ignatius Loyola. The priest was for some mad reason completely and utterly obsessed with any one thing that went historically missing: Giorgione's work for the Doge's Palace; Duccio's *Maesta* for the Siena Town Hall; the 107 lost books of Titus Livius Patavinus—the great historian Livy has been shorn of three-quarters of his bulk—Amelia Earhart's last lost airplane, the Lockheed Model 10 Electra; all the work that the painter Giotto had executed in Naples (1329–33); Isaac Fuller's brilliant altarpiece from All Souls College, Oxford; Wolfgang Mozart's buried bones; the portrait that half-blind Mary Cassatt splendidly rendered of Degas; and, among other things, the abandoned city of Dilmin, whither Noah had directed his ark. It turned out that this was a topical sermon.

A missal had been stolen from a pew.

A connivance plan was devised for teams of two to hide in the choir loft to discover the culprit, as Fr. Facemire insisted that the thief would strike again. Proops made a list of teams to keep vigil. Pointlaces and Summa. Reynaldo and Hoops. Ed Every and Paul Nosedocks used flashlights. Bat Lugs and Burquette took in a tape-recorder. One afternoon Verschneider crept in on tiptoe and with exaggerated shadow action pretended to steal another missal, and Hatblack and Murray hooted with laughter and Leashlaw angrily fake-caned them. Another seminarian, Robert Muzzerole, who claimed that he had once eaten dog's Gaines-burgers when he was in grade school, got fed up, and offered to admit that he took it. The truth was, in fact, that everybody suspected greasy-fingered Rudy Insana.

For months nothing came of it.

Fr. Facemire hated the innocence the boys falsely and hypocritically attributed to themselves simply for having not stolen it, a sin of presumption, he said, for, theologically speaking, all of the wretches that composed mankind were involved in every crime and caper. The priest doubted everything. There was no goodness in humans. To externalize his doubts, he attacked the seminarians, bursting into senatorial and Zolaesque invective many a night after prayers. Ed Every got booted. So did Hatblack, Murray, Verschneider. He slowly walked over to Nosedocks and took him by the chin, "Was it you, Mr. Tricks, who playfully put a hat on my pyx?" Facemire looked at Proops. Proops smiled and imperceptibly nodded. And Nosedocks was forced to spend the night in the dark of a locked linen closet.

The seminarians were all sitting around eating bowls of baked beans as richly full of starch as a dress shirt, with everybody joyfully snickering over these pranks, especially Rudy Insana's writing over the doorway, when all of a sudden Radclyffe, another convert, cried, "Custody of the Mouth!" He later became known for manufacturing a flag with St. Dominic Guzmán's chubby face on it, and underneath in large print the slogan "Dogs of God," which the priests found highly abnormal, and one day, inexplicably, he was asked to leave. Young Radclyffe was resigned, he said, because it was God's will. The night he left, in a dented Ford driven by his father, Hoops had waited with him in the driving rain under an umbrella. He shook Hoops' hand, told him that he knew who had taken the missal, then said goodbye, and from the departing car, cried out, "God be praised!"

That night Fr. Facemire delivered an address, a disorganized sermon about headaches and betrayals like Pilate's and how private decretals could only send you to hell and now everywhere pieces were missing in people and how we'd all jumped out of a rotten potato. Hoops, sitting there, wondered if he was losing his faith or his mind. No longer could he concentrate. What decretals? Whose head? Which Pilate? When missing? Why you? How so? Who said? And where?

The missal was later found tucked in the Leper's Squint, a small vertical notch in the wall near the altar where, in medieval times, lepers and others kept outside the church commonly watched the service. The pranks? It turned out Proops had done them all. Written the blasphemy. Capped the pyx. And stolen the missal. Fr. Magaw had confronted Facemire whose reasoning was that, since any one of all God's creatures could have stolen it, why then whoever did was no worse than anyone else, an idea that came spoiling out of the heretical notion that, since we were all lost anyway with good works not being redemptive, the only hope for the vile sinners was confession of guilt. At least that is what he told the boys. But here Fr. Magaw sadly shook his head. It wasn't only the missal. It was far, far worse.

And then Box Toes confessed.

Radclyffe had seen Fr. Facemire and Proops in an act of buccal coition in the black barn and before he left spoke to the authorities that God's will would work itself out in due time. Hoops thought of Hatblack and Every, Verschneider and even Insana and cried so much that whole week that his eyes felt glued shut. In a last maniacal sermon, Facemire vertically banged his cane and shouted up into the nave of the church that final night that we were all of us wretches, boys were wretches, girls were the worst wretches, priests and nuns were wretches, even the Pope, and from the pulpit he spoke in the blotted speech of undecided consonants that comes to the raving mad. He was then led away. And then in that big dark church Hoops began to sing the "*Adoro te devote*" on the top of his mouth with his tongue and began to weep. He stayed there kneeling in the pew long after everybody had filed out, and old Fr. Magaw, seeing him there, asked him if he wanted to go home. He said, "Yes." "Now?" asked the priest. "Yes," he pleaded with wet eyes.

The next morning Hoops left in a truck, down the turning old road that Radclyffe took, past the sunken garden dead pool filled with algae. He would always remember him playing his ocarina in the tower, with the sweet notes, like the sound of little bird crying "*Svitka.*"

God be praised.

Zoroaster and Mrs. Titcomb

There is an old tale that is told over ale,
In the village of Breadville many a night,
Of a mysterious stranger, darker than danger,
Who once inexplicably came into sight.

He appeared all in black to a vicious old hack
Who sold fish from a shanty down by the dunes,
Some say cursing and some say rehearsing
Weird, uncanny, indecipherable runes.

Looking quite tubby, less wife than hubby,
Oval of face and spinnaker fat
—the floor always shook with each step that she took—
Whenever Titcomb unhooked the slat

On the door of her shop, bidding all stop
Until her pet ferret she punted away
Whose hideous shrieks seemed to come from the beaks
Of gulls by her windows who darkened the day.

A fish-shop in Breadville can be like a treadmill
When winters keep you from walking abroad,
So with footsteps unerring we purchased the herring
That slovenly Titcomb threw in with the cod.

Of our foul little village, harbor and spillage
(A troughway that ran through the center of town),
Old Tits was the bitchiest, by far the witchiest,
Sow who could make the sun even frown.

She was given to farting and endlessly carting
Barrels of sprats to the edge of the quay,
Where tikes without waists pleaded weakly for tastes
But she'd pitch the lot right into the sea.

According to rumor, told not without humor,
She had sliced her old man with a fish knife she wore
In a cold rubber liner swinging near her vagina
Under a smock smeared with entrails and gore.

Old townies still say, stare though you may,
That one night out back by the traps and the mesh
What once thought was haddock out on the paddock
Had the rank fetid odor of real human flesh!

She gossiped, she lied, she cheated, she spied.
For squinting at scales her eyes were adept.
What sort of strapping did she use for wrapping?
Sheets from a King James Bible she kept!

No laws of a mayor nor minister's prayer,
Nothing could stop the hideous fact
Of a malevolence that crushed the benevolence
Of everyone simply by her every act.

She sold grey squid and pike, rockfish and tripe,
Complained that people stole fish from her place,
And during one sale a stranger turned pale
As she wagged a clam rake an inch from his face,

Who questioned the price of fish eaten by lice.
But something was strange in this dark exchange,
The tall man's dark eyes clouded over like skies
And over his face came a terrible change,

Which odd condition, with his inquisition,
Brought from her every invective and curse.
He was a magician and with your permission
Now comes a significant turn in this verse.

A stranger, I say, who came by the way,
Someone whom Breadville had never quite seen,
Wearing jet black from the front to the back
And bearing a raven with uncanny sheen

On his tall shoulder and what seemed even bolder
A long pointed feather stood aslant in his cap.
"My name's Zoroaster," with a voice like disaster
He whispered, his face an inscrutable map,

And said he was needful of fish but, unheedful,
The bitter old hag was typically cruel,
"I am here to perform—by magic, transform—
A miracle rare for those yearning for gruel,

Which I do out of care on this earth once a year,
Gathering all those who for the truth yearn,
Fish multiplying and bread for the dying,
Asking only a change of heart in return.

Always I choose, without bruiting the news
Of what is my mission and what is my hope,
One single creature of no definite feature
Whose acts must determine my annual scope."

He stared at the hag, the nasty old nag,
"But what find I here of worth or of merit?
Here is no kindness, only the blindness
Of a fat and fatuous fool and a ferret.

Is Breadville the world? Evil unfurled?
Are you alone the despair that I see?
Do poor men still labor? Neighbor hate neighbor?
With misery everywhere, mercilessly?"

And then with cold fire he pointed a dire
Finger at Titcomb who exploded in bits,
Like a fragmented moon, a broken balloon,
With a noise like sound itself losing its wits.

Within a mere second, as if he were beckoned,
The snarling ferret leaped but was caught
There in midair by the dark stranger's stare,
Which killed the scarlet-eyed beast on the spot.

Nobody then saw the stranger again,
Though a banquet was held the following day
With much bread and fish piled onto each dish
And peace and goodwill both holding sway.

Decades have passed, but thoughts are still cast
Back to that horripilant hour of fear
When a generous feast followed on the decease
Of two beasts for whom not a soul shed a tear.

One thing is mentioned whenever conventions
Of folk in Breadville sit down to drink,
A tale of suspicion, involving contrition,
As if people fear to say what they think.

Had real bread been threshed from real human flesh?
And fish from ferret, as is commonly told?
Was the strange rumor true that the man somehow knew
What his visit to lowly Breadville would hold?

A very old sentence we hear in repentance:
"From dust man is fashioned and thus unto dust
He soon must return," although we would learn
The final meaning of why it was just

For a phantom so rare thus to appear
In a village of such dissent and disunion,
Kill two useless souls, like emptying bowls,
And serve them up as a kind of communion.

What of the bird who never once stirred
But looked on as if it were having a treat?
It was later repeated it watched smugly seated
With all of the pomp of a black Paraclete.

What can be said of this tale of the dead?
Let me pose to the riddling reader, forsooth.
A story? Some dark allegory so to be read?
A cryptic fable offered to tease out a truth

Where Zoroaster in the form of the master
Of a rare world coming down from the sky
The way a forecaster facing down a disaster
Leaves you a problem to figure out? Try.

Song at Twilight:
A Fable of Ancient China

for Zhou Enlai,
than whom no one was wiser, stronger, or braver

The court under Tsin Shih Hwang, First Emperor of Tsin and builder of the Great Wall, a savage dictator, was devious and filled with intrigue. It was the year 212 B.C. and through the many rooms of the pavilions, with their garish décor running heavily to dragons, wyverns, winged hydras, and squint-eyed basilisks, servants went about their dutiful tasks. "Bring children into this realm," was the Emperor's daily mandate read out in an official proclamation.

It was the Feast of Forty Rings.

Nobles who came that night wore coats of finest silk alpaca, with long billowing sleeves adorned by gold-embroidered medallions and rare jade pendants and hats that told, by their color and button, of their authority and rank. Silk-clad ladies who wore combs of jade flashed long nail-sheaths of gold. At the lavish feast, where they dined with eating implements taken from delicately embroidered cases attached to their belts, they spoke mostly of making good marriages for their children, who were in attendance if they were of suitable age. The feast included rare beggar's chicken—*jiao hua tong ji*—wrapped in leaves and encased in baked mud that, to be freed, had to be smashed apart with a mallet, along with Hangzhou sweet-and-sour pork with four delights, Wuxi pork ribs, lotus root stuffed with glutinous rice, Ningbo omelettes with dried shrimp and garlic chives, galloping eggs with slivered pork, steamed taro with Chinese wind-dried sausage and Yangzhou slivered radish buns.

Between each course the guests wiped their faces and hands with towels dipped in hot water. There followed an interval when they rested, then they sat down to eat again. Once more, it was only of the best foods of which they partook, jeweled chicken, bird's nest soup, roasted and glazed whole pigeons, perfumed rice, extravagant cuts of pork in red marinades, oil-exploded prawns, clear-steamed sea bass, and Shanghai red-braised pork with eggs. Only the best sauces, concocted of oils and rare peppers, were offered. Pots of the rarest vinegars of Zhenjiang boldly strong and a smart reddish-black, were reserved especially for such memorably festive occasions—rich, pungent, peppery vinegars of different colors and degrees of heat and liquid texture selectively appointed for the large platters of delicious glutinous rice.

The mustachioed Emperor, Tsin Shih Hwang, sitting on his throne that was adorned with a large jade disc, symbol of his authority—it was he who created for himself the honorable title of First Emperor (*shi huang*)—presided over the festivities as people gathered in the rooms draped in red. Courtiers knew not to take advantage of the Emperor's offerings of whatever, whose famous declaration only a fool would not take to heart: "Refusal is a part of acceptance."

One family, of which severe, unbending Quang Poo was the father, was in attendance on this special night. He had brought along with him his three daughters: Soo-si, Shao Lee, and Song. It was inevitable that Song, by far the prettiest and youngest of the girls and distinctly of marriageable age, would command the most attention.

Song had jade beauty—slightly slanted lettuce-green eyes, high cheekbones, and full lips as pink as peony leaves. Her face was sweet with the V-shape form people in that country loved—a thin, small face with a delicate jawline that ended in a pert, pointy chin, commonly called 瓜子脸 or "melon-seed" face, which among the Chjnese carried with it the ultimate compliment. She washed her skin in rice water which before any application she stirred to get milky white

She had a vibrant, beautifully modulated voice and faultlessly proportioned feet with the contours of a lotus. Her figure was perfect, her carriage quick and graceful. Her comely demeanor also revealed an inner substance that was both precious and life-giving, and, like many young women from the area of Suzhou, the surpassing beauty of her soft skin the color of glowing marble and luminous brought her much attention. She had attended banquets several times before, for which, always excited, she had washed her hair in ginger water and then perfumed it with a zest of lemon mist, plaiting it with a delicate white ribbon that coiled down her neck.

It was on this occasion that Song first laid eyes on young Chin, a shy but handsome fellow from a poor family in Jiangnan. It was his occupation to provide the special vinegars for the feast. He went from table to table, self-effacing, quietly ladling out the dark heady brew from a lovely blue-and-white jar hung from a wide belt around his neck. Song smiled on him, as with a flourish he dutifully mopped a small spot of the brew that fell on a table. "What is your name?" she softly asked the enterprising young man. "My insignificant presence does not warrant such attention from so kind and gentle a person as you," he said. But he told her. He chastely smiled at Song and, with beating heart as they stood, seeking an opportune but graceful interval to do so, humbly offered the young maiden the gift of a small vinegar pot, which is considered precious in China. Her eyes shone with love for his kindness.

A notion found in the ancient text *Huainanzi* stated those who lived in fertile soil were beautiful, those on level ground were clever, and those in southern soil matured early and died young. Chin qualified in all three categories. No more industrious or hard-working fellow could be found. The young man made his unique vinegar brews from sorghum, peas, barley, and bran, which had a much stronger smoky flavor than rice-based black vinegar. He tested vinegars with different ingredients like seeds, wine, apples, shrubs, and leaves. He tried out various malts. He worked with hops. He experimented with exotic rice brews like Japanese Awamori, which was first introduced to China more than 3000 years ago from Siam by way of the Ryukyu Kingdom (1429–879), Japan's southernmost island. Soon he was concocting vinegars so strong—"fire arrows"—that a single sip of them made one reel.

It is reported that the first written mention of vinegar was made in 1058 B.C. in a book with the title *Zhou Li*, about the rites of the Zhou Dynasty, and a professional workshop for vinegar making appeared in the Chunqiu Dynasty (770–476 B.C.).

At that time, it was very costly, so that only rich noblemen could afford it. Vinegar first became popular with ordinary people in the Donghan Dynasty (25–220 A.D.). Up until the Northern and Southern Dynasties (420–581 A.D., a book named *Qi Ming Yao Shu*, about the essential techniques of farming, written by Sixie Jia, recorded in detail twenty-four different methods for brewing vinegars.

The people of Jiangnan, compared to everywhere else, had a special and particular affinity, a harmony, a deep accord— and to the extent of their relishing it, almost a kinship—with its first-rate vinegars, which in their culture had long been regarded as one of the "seven essentials" of daily life (along with firewood, rice, edible oil, salt, fermented sauce, and tea). It was a tonic, he knew, that could relieve pain caused by sprains and minor injuries. It is also topically used to disinfect wounds and insect bites, and to ease the pain caused by bone fractures. Vinegar held a distinct and important position in Chinese daily life. As it served their needs in crucial ways, it also espoused their values. It warmed the stomach when it was consumed. It dispelled the fishiness of seafood. It awakened the appetite, and cut through the oiliness of food. It comforted women through the toil of childbearing, it brought fire to the loins of men, it eased a heart in trouble and in strife. It got rid of kidney stones. It was a medicine, an energy drink, a pickling agent, and an emetic. It could help as an antiseptic, work as a cleaning agent. It was a condiment and a restorative and preservative. Nothing better than a peerless vinegar could bring such comfort and solace to the costive and the depressed, the listless and the wounded or suffering soul. To the mural of the mind, more than to the palate, it brought comfort, wealth, prosperity, joy, and happiness.

Song fell instantly in love with Chin. It was meant to be. Her physical soul, *po*, she knew, would follow his body to its tomb when it went through a dust cloud and journeyed home. She had vision and sensed a destiny with him. His sense of worth was reinforced by a traveling fortune teller who, pressing his skull, revealed to his parents that the boy's cranium was different from everyone else's and that he was an "exceptionally gifted child." The two of them had to meet in secret, for she was of noble family. Out of devotion for her, Chin sent her small gifts by way of one of her servants—a shadow hand puppet, a cricket in a tiny straw cage, and a pigeon with a whistle that could be tied to its leg, so she could listen to the fluted tones its flight. Soon the two of them were going for long walks through the lush Lingering Garden with its ornate viewing pavilions and to the Crown of Clouds Peak, a striking limestone rookery where together they watched the birds in silence. Lovely Tiger Hill was home to the seven-story leaning Cloud Rock Pagoda at its summit. They loved the woods, all nature.

They took "forest baths"—*Sēnlínyù*, 森林浴—seeking comfort through the greenwood of the dense forest simply by being in nature, connecting with it through their senses of sight, hearing, taste, smell and touch. *Sēnlínyù* is like a bridge. The two of them took time to notice how a tree sways in the wind, ran their hands over its bark, marveled to see how water pumped to such high levels, admired all the patterns of leaves, smelled the flowers and grasses and weeds to inhale their citrusy, sugary scents. As a society, too many suffered from having been removed from such beauty. One day they climbed high over the vast hill. In China, the ninth day of the Ninth Moon is the by far the best day for mounting hills and flying kites. As they looked over the beautiful waters of Lake Tai, they knew that something new had been born of love.

At the Festival of the Harvest Moon, the two of them walked among the lanterns, where under old golden larches families shared nuts in paper cones, purple fruits, and red bean buns. Chin modestly offered Song the indispensable delicacy of an intricately-carved expensive mooncake.

She blushed to take it, but did so gracefully, and in the middle of a small bridge, when alone, he recited to her this poem:

The moon spies on us
near the blue-kissed
lakes of Wu. Pensively
you sit in mingled mist
and on the soft east wind
where moonbeams float
about like kin to kin
my spirit lifts and dandle
in the air where, twinned,
I speak your holy name
and hold a gilded candle
wherein the golden flame
as if from your throat
I hear your gentle note.

Chin tenderly kissed her soft cheek. She blushed and stood aside. Had he been too forward? He asked forgiveness by collecting and with a sincere bow presenting to Song a delicate mass of apple blossoms, cherry blossoms, tender willow shoots, silky magnolia buds, and a nodding daffodil.

There were seven rivals for Song's hand: Wang, Zing,

Hong, Yang, Ding, Feng, and Bung, all of them brothers and as cold as serpents. (Dong and Fang, twin girls, were smothered at birth as being "four-sided" cackling geese.) They were of the rich and entitled Pouchong family who owned a large fish business in Guanzhou which brought them prosperity. To build up good *guanxi* among their neighbors the unctuous Pouchong mother and father did favors for them, gave gifts, and offered services to create obligations and make debtors. They gave banquets, kept eunuchs to fend for them, and drank only the best tea with tiny leaves from the hills of Hupeh, Kiangsi, Fu-kien, and Chekiang, selecting the choicest of every harvest from May to July. They were wily business people and traded strictly for copper cash even with white foreigners with short legs, arms as long as gorillas, wet earwax, filthy armpits, hair that smelled like the reek of rotten turnips, and ridiculous ears reaching down to the ground who had aboriginal sweat glands and hot red faces with bodies that stank of meat or sour milk.

The brothers were spoiled rotten. They were hedonistic and dissolute of heart and would not eat grain that had been damaged by heat, refused rice that was damp, rejected any meat not cut properly, spurned any drink that came from public water, sent away any vegetables that smelled strange, disdained any fish or flesh that was spoiled, and would touch nothing not served on rose porcelain plates. They insisted upon extra long noodles in their soup, to increase longevity, and heartily kicked such waiters who dared to serve them anything less. Chin knew them and told Song, "Beware. They go behind you and harbor wolf hearts and dog lungs—*lang xin gou fei.*" The rude hair of those young men shone like gleaming oil. Brazen Wang, the worst of the brothers who had a tiger tattoo crawling up his neck, once sarcastically dunked a plum into a cup of wine and handed it to Song and winked at her.

What was that supposed to mean? she wondered

He was a boaster, loud, profane, and volatile, and hopping onto a wall by the river once crowed, "I throw fish at people below me. I eat their eyes. I pinch their tails. I cut them up!" And he wildly sang,

> I can sauce a plaice,
> kiss her on the face.
> I can splay a bream,
> infiltrate her dream.
> I can fresh a chub,
> wash her in a tub.
> I can side a haddock,
> steal into her paddock.
> I can splat a pike,
> tell her what to like.
> I can string a bass,
> pinch her on the ass.
> I can chine a salmon.
> gobble her like gammon.
> I can halve a smelt,
> teach her with my belt.

Song knew only that she loved Chin alone.

Chin was poor but handsome and always toiled hard to make his living. He concocted black vinegar. The best vinegar in China, indeed preeminent in the entire world, is created in Zhenjiang and in the little towns neighboring it, where choice black and red vinegars have been barreled and cured for decades and in many cases for centuries and sold at highest prices. Chin, who had learned his skill from an old brewer, worked hard from sun-up to sundown to bring his own vinegars to perfection, adding acetic acid and bacteria to glutinous rice, sometimes to wheat, millet, or sorghum. He tasted with a spoon each deeply colored batch for fruitiness, seeking an *umami* richness. The secret was in the pure water there, although a special knowledge for brewing was necessary as well, as any and all who tasted the product universally agreed. Water was very cold there and benefited from the local dulcet water plants.

Flavor served to promote the circulation of *qi*. To follow nature, not convention, however, was the major rule Chin went by to seek harmony in the making of his vinegars—the word for harmony (*he*) even doubled as a verb for mixing or blending (*huo*). To assist the five flavors, he knew, were the five colors, which paralleled each other: spicy-white, sweet-yellow, sour-green, bitter-red, and salty-black. The venerable old brewer had instructed him, by way of the handy guide, about the *Tao Te Ching:* how the mouth or the palate should comply (*shun*) with its own character (*xing*). When one did not use it in compliance with its character and individual capacity (*ming*), he or she thus perversely harmed what it was by nature (*ziran*).

Green crabs flourished in the region—as did shrimp, seaweed, box jellyfish, conch, clams, all delicious, except for the box jellyfish (*Chironex fleckeri*), which was to be avoided for its poison. Nature could be benevolent or not. Such was the way of life. To protect himself, Chin carried an ampule of the poison around his neck in a pouch in case a black kite, a savage bird of prey, should ever attack him. His design was only his ambition to sell his vinegars. The Chinese revered it. Vinegar coded very well with much oil, salt, sugar, sweet bean paste, and rice ale.

At first Chin began carting about the precious liquid in pots from an unwieldy shoulder-pole. He was underfed, improperly clothed, and poorly equipped. But he was also resolute and had drive and was unswerving in his goal. He rose early, toiled hard each and every day, eventually crossing the Jianglang mountains, and hawking his product from wooden stands on dusty roads and at times formal structures with double doors in front for those of rank to be admitted and single doors at the sides for others. He was always sent out to the back. A group of Chinese bandits, Kujiu, 苦蝤, the Dry Grubs, named for their baldness, roamed the mountains and one night "squeezed" him for free fare, taking the fruits of his labor. But he persevered.

Over the year he traveled as far as Tangjiang Crag and Hangzhou. He slept outside in a cheap burlap bag in the Wuxie National Forest in order to save money. His footgear was paper-soled, or rags, and wore down quickly. He had only a rude brazier in which he burnt scavenged charcoal bricks to keep warm, for he had no *kang*, a warm box-like structure on which to sleep. He ate sparingly of what he could scare up, often a stew of leached acorns and water chestnuts in brown sauce. Sometimes he rummaged under the shore mud and caught eels, stunned them in cold water, banged their heads against a wall, cut them up and cooked them with lemon grass in his wok. He kept with him a bag of oats and barley. Sometimes he found a potato to gnaw. His only illumination at night was a wick floating in a dish of oil.

He had no comprador, or business agent. There was only himself to canvas the area to negotiate sales. Nor had he the keystone of education to help him, the nine books of Kung Fu-Tzu classics, to consult. But one day, for want of money, an insolvent customer gave him instead a scroll of some of the Master's words. One read: "Success depends upon previous preparation, and without such preparation there is sure to be failure." The more that he read, the harder he worked.

Chin devised a larger stove on which to cook and test his increasingly tasty vinegars. Business picked up. Soon he moved on to Zhuji where he hawked his wares in Melon Street, Jade Alley, Medicine Lane, Bubbling Well Road, Chaofoong Alley, Yanktze-kiang Avenue, Shanghaitong Street, Shaanxi Bei Lu Lane. He was often footsore and beleaguered with fatigue but managed to save his earnings. Time passed, and he was able to buy a small vinegar shop, with cisterns. He began drifting toward the south month after month along roads, learing as he went, selling where he could. He met the wise and the foolish. He sojourned in kitchens in all kinds of places to try to improve a chili vinegar. Word now began to spread through many small towns in Guangdong Province of his wonderful vinegars. He ranged widely over the land from north of the Huai River to south of the Yangtze River in East China.

He developed enterprising skills. He was now selling his black vinegar—"fire arrows"—to daily workers in nips, a tonic to those who labored hard. They would come to him sometimes with a copper coin, but they would often barter with eggs. He wanted to perfect teas, as well. One day in his travels, while picking tea leaves by the swide of the road, he met a wise man from the Huai River who taught to make *báichá*—"white tea"—which, when, brewed, he found was typically light gold in color with a delicate floral fragrance. He gathered it and sold it to patrons, packets comprised of young, springtime tea leaves that grew in Fujian province, a dried tea known for its withered small leaves and buds that looked slightly fuzzy. He kept with his vinegar but also sold teas—Silver Needle or Yin Zhen, White Peony, another white tea that also came from the Fujian province, and Gong Mei, another Chinese white tea.

Chin returned from Jiangnang and opened a tiny shop in an off street. The worth of his vinegars preceded him—their rich and fruity and exotic dark blends became famous—and he sold most of what he made. There were also his teas. He sold Pai Mu Tan. He made small vats of Shou Mei, which included fewer buds than Gong Mei, which he also sold. Shou Mei, or "Long Life Eyebrow Tea," is usually darker than Shou Mei, but it was perfect for making white tea blends. Shou Mei was likely to contain much less caffeine than Silver Needle or White Peony. The Pouchang sons once saw Chin on a street corner speaking to one of Chang Poo's daughters. They looked upon him as a peon and mocked him for being in trade.

Surly Wang, one son, of Guanzhou origins, hated Shanghainese food. "All food for dog and black as soot," he protested whenever someone dragged him off to a Jiangnan restaurant. To him the food was sullied with a lot of inky sauces and pestilential glazes—dark, sticky braises, ugh!—made with soy sauce or black vinegar. Whenever one of his roistering bully boys dragged him out to ingest black "lion's head" meatballs or stewed duck in soy sauce Wuxi style or black glutinous rice congee or black *char sui* pork with its dark cooking juices or fermented beans in bowls or grilled salmon head and tofu in gumbo-colored gravy, he would cry, "What is the reward for all the dirty fingers, sticky lips, black spit-out bones, and crumpled napkins in scattered morsels of gelatinous cartilage and the occasional piece of meat?"

A notion also found in the ancient text *Huainanzi* stated

those who inhabited barren soil were ugly, those on hard soil unyielding, and those in northern soil daring but invariably inhumane. Wang qualified in all three categories. No more calculating or duplicitous trickster could be found.

Squeezing his coarse hair, Wang would rise up to scream, "Smell that? That is the stink of wok peasant cultch, the terrible off-scourings of oaf-clown-fool food that has been bruised by ferociously hot cast iron. You ignore!"

Certain of his friends would not have it and argued to the contrary, "When you let rice cook languidly in a not-hot-enough pan, it becomes flabby and heavy. A blistering hot wok keeps the rice airy and light and the vegetables crisp. Good fried rice demands urgency, don't you see?"

Wang would strike them intemperately, and howl out loud, "*You filthy egg! You green hat cuckold! You stink pig, little white face!*"

Quang Poo, Song's intemperate father, disapproved of Chin. So did her two cruel and homely sisters, Soo-si and Shao Lee, who mocked and berated him for his working in trade. They warned their sister that he was a peasant boy as useless and as insignificant as the thin raddled crakes which flew over their tall chimneys every autumn dragging their unattractive legs. Rivals of Song, and invidious, they insulted her with freakish names— "You sing song girl!" "Big feet, you!" "No walk on golden lilies!" "Ugly turtle!" "Idiot, with mental retardation!" and "*Yāoguài* monster!"—and abused her with tight vicious pinches on her arm.

Meanwhile, "Whom should Song marry?" everybody wondered, and even augurs were consulted. One particular augur of high renown, who was paid a great deal of money, bowed to all four earthly directions and over a fire heated a white cow bone and proceeded to interpret the cracks in it, which subsequently appeared. Result? Indefinitive and undefinitive. A further heating revealed an *S* crack, the meaning of which came up, "Red glaze end phase."

Song carried a lotus-flame lamp to the water. She gently placed it into a boat, which floated down the blue stream. She prayed to She, the God of Soil, for Chin's heart to be happy and to be pleased with her. She wore her hair behind in a twisted tail that set off her sun-bright face, which was innocently pure and shone, and to avoid vanity refused to look at her reflection in the water.

The two spoke with each other whenever they could, meeting at the busy street market under the orange-tiled pavilions in Zhenjiang where goods were sold, hawkers at fruit stalls cried out their wares, and lacquered palanquins passed by in the busy streets ringing with commerce and trade. They spoke with yearning of liberty and walking out freely in the open, over the Grand Canal and of visiting Yangzhou to see the shrines and where Chin could find exotic salts to try out in vinegar.

On this one day, Chin gave Song a small *pomelo*, a kind of grapefruit, which she gracefully accepted with both hands and bent to reverently kiss in gratitude. She knew the import of its meaning. It is an old Chinese principle that no one possesses anything until he has given it to another. It is the deep secret at the heart of love. They looked to the sky, to wish. "But do not point to the moon with one finger, for your ear tips will fall off," he said. He chastely took her by her hand. Her love for him empowered him to dare to dream. They together wondered if they would ever come to marry and so consulted the shape of small sticks that they threw down to read. He knew that there were other suitors for Song's hand. It had bothered him, but wisdom told him never to give in to anger or jealousy: *Before you embark on a journey of revenge, dig two graves.* The pattern of thrown sticks augured well. Marry! To celebrate he tendered her a vessel of *"Zhaojun"*—rice wine with a taste of ginger—and, working up his courage, bowed and recited to her lines from Li Po's poem, "Listening to a Flute in Yellow Crane Pavilion," he had learned from a balladeer in Jiangnan:

> *I came here a wanderer*
> *thinking of home,*
> *remembering my far away Ch'ang-an.*
> *And then, from deep in Yellow Crane Pavillion,*
> *I heard a beautiful bamboo flute*
> *play "Falling Plum Blossoms."*
> *It was late spring in a city by the river.*

Meanwhile, Song's father, who fussily roamed through the chambers of his daughter upon spying the vinegar pot, threw up his hands in despair and boomed with anger and execrated his young daughter, shouting, "This filthy turtle! This—" He hung on the aposiopesis, and demanded, "Choose one of the Pouchong brothers for husband, or I will give you sharp hiding."

Song had long feared and hated the brothers.

Clever and calculating, Father and Mother Pouchong knew that she was a good catch for any of their equally deceitful, double-dealing sons. "Song is pink flamingo. Longest, thinnest neck, legs slender high as stilts," said the father. "Does not swoop or dive. Only fly," added the mother. "Curves of a mountain path. First prize for being most astonishing and beautiful bird," added the father, "prance through water softly, Swims through air with restful rhythm." "When standing makes vertical design," snapped the mother, who always got the last word.

But the brothers pursued her. Feng was too short, Zing was too tall, Hong never spoke, Yong had cicatrices on his cheek, Ding had a stammer, Bung, the older of the brothers, was a person fitted with a leather nose from syphilis, and, the worst of all, Wang was a loud and incorrigible boaster who had the vulgar habit of coursing the open streets late at night eating large watermelons and crudely spitting out the seeds. The evil brothers reminded Song of the seven venomous animals (the viper, the scorpion, the scolopendra, the toad, lizard, the stonefish, and the spider), the sole protection against which was a talisman—a button that she kept around her neck—surmounted by the significant character *ch'ih* (Imperial order), comprising the element "strength" (*li*) which is placed above the *t'ai-chi* and the eight trigrams (*pa-kua*).

Song's simple wish was fully to be free of the brothers' attention. She began wearing a wristlet that she fashioned with eight seeds, to bring luck. The family was like a set of weasels. On the one hand, they were wealthy. On the other hand, they were slippery, manipulative, subtle, and unscrupulous.

A wandering persuader who knew well that contentious family, and most specifically Wang, told Chin of that guileful brother, "He paints legs on a snake," meaning he is overreaching, and "He travels by night but he hides by dawn," meaning he is sneaky, and "His nose favors facing north," meaning that he is treacherous. Mysterious without being mystifying, the persuader wrote out on a bone: 纸包不住火. Chin read the words, "Paper cannot wrap up a fire."

Of the guileful Pouchong parents the persuader said nothing, nor did he ask of them, especially Mother Pouchong. It is a great impropriety, when speaking, to speak about the female members of the family.

Meanwhile, Wang had seen the two lovers Chin and Song, and was filled to the neck with poisonous envy. He was a bully and a boaster and had sharp teeth like a trout on the roof of his mouth called vomerine teeth, and there were even brown spots on his body like fish skin. He took opium and, it was rumored, had commerce with foreign devils, *yang kuei*. He always wore a long rat-catcher's coat and had begun practicing the black arts and after suitable deliberation soon jealously devised a cruel but secret plan to implicate his hated rival, Chin, in a devious state plot to have him eliminated and thereby win the hand of Song.

In this devious stratagem, quite typically, he was venomously aided and abetted by his sly and intervering Pouchong parents, the gross and wealthy father who was comically referred to in the village as *chǒulòu* (ugly) and *Fù zhū* (rich pig) and, because he was bald, *Zài tǔdì zhōngjiān dì hǎi* (the sea in the middle of lands), and the imperious mother who was so fat that she was called—always behind her back, of course—*Wan dun ju lun* (a 10,000-ton ocean-going ship).

How to hurt Chin? There was a sudden *qiangda* in that horrible family as to who should be the first to answer the question.

The parents were as heartless as stone. Wily Mother Pouchong had been married once before. One day she had been seen sitting at a graveyard, slowly fanning the earth, beneath which her dead husband lay buried. "What a tender heart she has, that she still endeavors to comfort him with her loving fan," sighed one onlooker. The facts were much different, however. In her cunning, Mother Pouchong had promised her husband not to marry again until the earth of his grave was dry.

"Be like a jade cutter—wear him down," cunningly advised Father Pouchong. "Rock hard, jade cannot be cut or shaped with knife or other metal tool but requires abrasive agent—sand or grit—together with water to polish it." He murderously pushed a thumb into his palm. "Must be ground and worked hard." Baroque Chinese courtesies had their equivalence in baroque savagery. Wang suggested that he be led into a public square to a standing pole and with the sound of drums garroted by a red-hot wire. Zing suggested they throw him into a river with his hands tied to a boulder. Bung said catch him unawares, rub his eyes with ash-hopper lye, and then force him to consume himself by being fed three ounces of his own flesh every day. "Run him through with your Han jian," suggested the cruelly inventive Yong, who relished the pain game, "or willow leaf saber tipped with poison." He sniggered. "Or get a 'knifer'—a *tao-tzu-chiang*—to strip him, truss him up like a sacrificial glazed duck, and have him surgically remove his shaft and testicles and let him carry his dessicated organs about in a sack, called a *bao*, instead of that wretched vinegar of his or we can sell him to the Royal Palace as an attendant in the rump court for servile duty in the Forbidden City!"

Ding suggested, "Bring white frost to his face when by sudden you shove bamboo in ears." Feng jumped up and said, "Behead him with your two-handed *dao* or throttle him with a meteor hammer!" Hong of course said nothing. Their scheming mother, who always urged, "For direction, feign indirection; by pretend no trick, you make trick," had been listening.

331

Others offered their own vile suggestions. The brothers piled in on him. "I boo in disapproval of this white skin pig!" sniped one. "Ox demon!" said another. "Turtle face!" "Snake spirit!" "To me, he rolling egg 滚蛋 (gǔn dàn)," fretted yet another. "*A bàn diào zi* (半吊子)! Half a diào with 500 coins!"

Guile was their goal, shrewdness their plan. The insults bred in them all a rising need to single him out for pain and humiliation. "Hand him broom to hit you with, so bring him bad luck," would have been the parent's ordinary suggestion, but in this case, death must be the outcome.

Mother Pouchong, finding it all too elaborate, said to her son, "*Tuo kuzi fang pi*—"You take your trousers off to fart"—and pointing a long fingernail at him, she upturned it into a hook. "Much simpler." The Chinese way is roundabout—never directly to the goal. She made a *Y* with her fingers and held them to her glittering eyes. "Craftiness learn from crow. Peck! Peck!"

Taking his sleeve, she drew her son closer and whispered, "Curves wind around back again. Go roundabout. Serpent wind in order make twist." Was he listening? "Point at mulberry but abuse the pagoda tree."

His mother took his hair and turned his face to hers.

"Be clever and quiet," she ordered him. "Attract attention give you bad reputation. Knock down enemy with bludgeon not necessary." She breathed in the shell of his ear, "Cut his throat with feather."

Heeding her advice, their son resolved to ensnare his rival.

Delighted, Wang vowed, "I will lead vinegar boy to grave."

At a court assembly the following week, Wang managed

to enter the palace secretly, insinuate himself into the royal kitchens, and pour powdered orpiment into the Emperor's dish of vinegar, which sickened the man almost to the point of death, but he recovered and sought vengeance.

Several likely malefactors from the village were immediately arrested on suspicion. By tradition, saliva was used as a lie detector. Each of the accused abjectly knelt and was forced to chew grains of rice. If he was telling the truth, he would have enough saliva to spit the grains back out again. If any one of them was lying, his mouth would go dry and the rice would stick in his throat.

Calumnies, with bribes, blackened the name of Chin, into whose mouth was placed a wooden bit to prevent him from talking, and after a public trial where scornful fingers were pointed like daggers at the innocent young man standing there in humiliation—"Cane his deceitful face!" loudly bellowed Wang in attendance, "slice the criminal in two!"—he was sentenced to death, to be executed by a sickle, and was duly beheaded and bled profusely. The Great Cymbal was struck at the moment of crisis. Song, who walked to the river, wept in silence with a cherry branch in her lap as the wind blew across her wet cheeks, as she recalled that lovely day on Tiger Hill and the seven-story leaning Cloud Rock Pagoda at its summit.

With an ominous irony, that very same rising wind blew off the talismanic button that Song with great fervor had always kept around her neck out of loyalty and love. Her father, Quang Poo, who assured her of the shame that she brought to her family, scorned her tears and immediately acted upon the situation, stating in no uncertain terms that fealty and formal acknowledgement of loyalty was demanded and admonished her, "Two leaps per chasm is fatal."

What of Chin's ignominious death? Kung Fu-Tzu had taught that the first duty of every individual is that his body be sacredly restored intact to his ancestors. Song had heard that friends of decapitated criminals often sought the privilege of sewing back on the heads of the decapitated bodies before burial. This was a favor never granted, except on condition that the heads shall be attached face backwards. Seeking to venerate Chin's body, she secretly enlisted a cousin from the area of Suzhou to do that honor, in spite of the grim restriction that she would not refuse to accept.

Meanwhile, Wang sought out Song at a tea house. He had exchanged his long rat-catcher's coat for a collarless shirt in white to impress her. So infinitely great was her disturbance, it silenced her, bringing her to the border of fear, of which her conceited courtier took advantage, as he began to stack coins on her collar bone to frame, to prove to himself, her seductive beauty. He slid his reechy hand slowly down her slim jaw, lewdly whispering, "You carry 'first-love' face—goose-egg face 鹅蛋脸—and have lotus feet and tear-sodden eyes, of which I approve."

He boasted, "All tigers share similar markings on their foreheads, which resemble the Chinese symbol *Wang*, meaning 'King.'"

Wang, vain, offered her a red lacquered ornament—it was called a *ju yi*, which means "according to my wishes." If the lady so offered received it into her hands, it signified her willingness to become a bride. Song was revolted. It was refused by the girl, who shrank from his coldness, but, unbending, the domineering father Quang Poo soon made intercession and overrode rejection, declaring with indignation, "Turndown reflect on family.

Discountenancing is knockback. Defiance prove rude mistake."
Again, refusal became part of acceptance.

Quang Poo therewith arranged an alliance between Song
and Wang, and the two were married. The bride-elect, attired in
a full red gown and red veil hiding her lovely features, sat cross-
legged on a yellow satin sedan chair, hidden in a curtained con-
veyance from many curious onlookers. She was handed a tray of
cowry shells and three tea bricks as a gift from solicitous Mother
Pouchong, by which she knew she would surely have to submit to
her mother-in-law. That same woman handed her a traditional
silk wedding quilt, embroidered with a hundred baby boys.

Ancient rules of etiquette always required that any
exchange of greetings or the giving of gifts always be done gracefully by a person standing with full feet on the ground. Mother
Pouchong however chose to sit, stonily, and observe.

Unknown to Song, part of the formal nuptial bargain, a
devious secret in the underhanded plan, was also the fobbing off
of Soo-si with Hong and Shao Lee with Ding. "Crabs should not
be eaten, for they go sideways," gravely warned the smug Quang
Poo, proclaiming, with the paternal wisdom he always assumed,
much obstetrical and gynecological advice, and, reaching ino
a sparkling pile of uralian emeralds, fire opals, golden beryls,
pearls, onyxes, and sparkling moonstones, he ostentatiously
handed each of the three brides and three grooms a large red
tourmaline, a stone notably worn by mandarins but cautioned,
"All expectant mothers in China desire a child be straightfor-
ward. Be certain to remember also to eat black sesame seeds for
shiny eyes of baby."

"And vinegar for good heart," put in Wang with irony,
breaking into loud raucous laughter as he squibbled the cheek of

his wife, flamboyantly offering her a larger pot than the one she had kept in Chin's honor at home. Vows to have children were extracted. Song, who was forced to accept it all, remembering the true declaration that "Refusal is a part of acceptance," let him take her hand in hers with a sorrow so deep in her breast it watered it with tears. Of her secret sorrow she said nothing. One who knows does not speak about it, one who speaks about it does not know. The last words that Chin had spoken to her in his extreme, she kept in her bosom, was to quote the noble Wu Ding, a king of the Shang dynasty in ancient China: "Be to me as the yeast and the malt in making sweet spirits; as the salt and the prunes in making a harmonious stew; as the acid and sugar in making perfect vinegar."

When he then recovered from his illness a week later, Tsin Shih Hwang, First Emperor of Tsin and builder of the Great Wall, smiling on the couples, bothered to throw a lavish banquet for all of them. The venerable Chinese banquet, as established by tradition, provided a venue not only for one to judge human character, hone one's social skills, and foster dexterity but it also presented an occasion to employ trickery, to humiliate, and eliminate political opponents. Corrupt, the Pouchangs, who had paid for it, spared no expense on their cuisine. Their kitchen with its exotic but decadent fare reflected their louche and dissolute tastes. They served snake wine, bottles with curled cobras inside that had been pickled for months in rice wine, for it was a widely held belief in ancient China that such wines boast medicinal properties. There were rows of Balut in silver plates, developing duck embryos boiled and served in the shell. Wang raised a snake wine bottle and gleeped into it, smiling.

A banquet table along a wall had been lavishly set up

with skewers of deep-fried scorpions and octopuses, sea cucumbers and glazed chickens stuffed with nuts. The chefs had prepared an array of cooked larks, turtle meat, fried grasshoppers, long wheaten noodles, sorghum-infused squashes, and soft, rich golden buns filled with hornet honey. Bowls of gelatinous thousand-year-old eggs—*pi dan*—which were a favorite were piled high in white bowls along with accompanying fragrant rice bowls lavish with century egg congee called *pi dan shou rou zhou*. Tortoise jelly, called *guilinggao*, was a popular dessert, fashioned from the bottom shell of the golden coin turtle and mixed with rare green herbs. Servants revolved from table to table—each table decorated with plum blossoms and pepper plants—carrying trays that held rare rhinoceros-horn cups carved with designed of winter stars and filled with warm *baijiu*.

Shao music was called for, and a dragon dance was performed. Music filled the room with special melodies the court loved. Music was always spoken highly of by ancient Chinese sages like the renowned philosopher, Confucius, according to whom its essence was a moral, its humaneness paramount. To Confucius, a man who is not virtuous can never claim to be a musician nor ever have anything to do with music. The great sage, furthermore, never sang on the same day in which he had been weeping, which is why as gentle Song sat there, feeling within such sorrow and sadness that it bordered on despair, abstained from whispering notes of any song.

Deep-toned bells were gonged by small servant boys with shaven heads, all garbed in red, to signify that a second banquet, the main one, was to be served in an inner room, with all new settings. Guests were seated and served their dinners on ancient carved apple-green imperial jade plates with matching jade cups, with lavender jade dragon tea saucers, rimmed with gold. Next to plates on the table sat expensive rose medallion bowls, banded by foliage and butterflies.

At table, Soo-si asked Hong if he loved her, but Hong never spoke and Shao Lee spoke to Ding who could only stammer. Song, who thought to give Wang a pomelo, then waited. He tendered her a smelt.

Vinegar, the rarest of it, was then served.

Song, who had been seated sitting facing the east—the seat of honor—most courteously received her saucer, and, taking it in both hands, gracefully lifted it as high as her forehead, and ceremoniously drank of it, closing her eyes and praying to Pan-ku, the father of the universe, all the kings that succeeded him, and then especially of dear lost honorable Chin. She had been raised with the perfect table manners taught in the *I Li* and was word perfect indeed in all three of the great books of Chinese ceremonial—the *Tcheou-Li* and *I Li* and the *Li Chi*.

Reaching over to her, Wang with urgent thrusts of his head went to feed Song a prized delicacy—a gout of the stomach contents of water buffalo, roasted with hot spices. She demurred; he insisted. "Yang foods, strong like me—spicy, meat-rich, take long time to cook—you must take to understand your husband. Bland foods are yin foods—rice, potatos, porridge—like homely, low-bred grains and vegetables harvested from the passive earth." He crowed, "I make balance!"

Mortified, she tried not to show it.

It is an old Chinese principle that no one has accepted anything until she has received it deeply in her heart, which she did not.

Dominating her was his joy. He opened her mouth and

tipped in a spoonful of rice cake soup. "But you must eat rice, as well. In China, young girl must finish all rice on plate for legend say, each small grain of rice indicate each scar, pimple or blemish on the face of future husband."

He squeezed her hand, masterfully.

"Which is me!"

"Are you happy?" asked a smiling Song, running her fingers along the black tattoo of the tiger running up Wang's neck, patting his hand. His lewd mouth was so wide that when he smiled it seemed to go quite behind his ears. He shamelessly gloated as he loudly slurped up spoonfuls of cherry soup, giving himself airs as, swank with preening, he deprecated his dead rival. Twenty servants revolved around the palace room serving the exotic foods. The imperial banquet was spread out on a groaning table: shark fin soup, dried sea cucumbers, baked stuffed conches, Xiao Long Bao dumplings, and very rare fragrant braised pigeons and doves fried in hand-poured oil, all presented on a service of crafted bronzeware shaped like exotic mini-dragons on banquettes set up with double fish, double lobster, double dessert, double happiness!

As she sat there in the midst of all that splendor, she heard only from a misty distance the echo of a flute from Yellow Crane Pavilion and the words *I came here a wanderer thinking of home.*

"I am happy, now you must obey me," said Wang, leaning over and grabbing her delicate shoulder in an anti-embrace. One hand held her. With the other, he lifted up and flashed his long fingernails. "I have clutch of anteater, tenacious creature whose claws, once hook into you, no power has luck of ever breaking. Very ancient tale is told of puma and anteater. Both found both still locked together. Although ripped open by puma's savage teeth, anteater's razor-sharp ungula still remain stuck in unfortunate puma's back, a clutch that death itself unable to break."

At her shock, he threw back his head in loud burst of crude laughter full of imperious contentment and swaggering self-delight, revealing, as always, his long red tongue, when just at that very same moment, unseen, unobserved completely, Song poured into his porcelain cup in two quick slips—two leaps for him into the blackest chasm—part of the ampule of poison that Chin had carried around his neck in a pouch in case of an attack by a black kite, a savage bird of prey.

Wang slurpily drank, immediately stood up, spat, gagged, wiggle-waggled as he tore at his throat, and pitched over dead.

As refusal became a part of acceptance, Song therefore accepted everything she refused, and refused everything she accepted, immediately drinking the rest of the fatal poison in the ampule, which she to took in one gulp—facing forward, ever facing forward in her brave release—to follow Chin's body when it went through a dust cloud and journeyed home.

Tell Me What Happened

The Sprotts, who lived in remote Grindelwald in the Bernese Highlands of the Swiss mountains until they had their children, were a lonely couple, mismatched in virtually everything they did. Late in life, they were able to adopt two orphans on the day they were born, a baby boy and baby girl who were given the beautiful lilting names of Blaise and Bligh.

Joaquin was a cobbler, a poor shoemaker in the small village who eked out his living as best he could.

His wife, Gullveig—a second wife—had a strong presence and could be very domineering. Sari Heather, his first wife and a strikingly attractive Indonesian whom he had met in Berne, died very young of tuberculosis. A natural desire to share prompted him to marry again, this time upon a decision that turned as much on pity as a need to stem a sense of isolation and remoteness. She was of Latvian origins, and an epileptic, the sister of an unbalanced twenty-four-year-old wood finisher in the village whom she had come to take, after the stabbing of his employer, to the State Hospital for the Criminal Insane in Zurich. It was, in its awkwardness, never an easy relationship between the two. Courtship under unconventional circumstances, like working hard brindle leather to make shoes, imposes its own special disciplines. Love in its mystery speaks a secret language of buried needs and unspoken loneliness.

The Swiss notoriously marry late. It is a trait clearly borne of a national conviction that marrying late is better than marrying wrong.

Gullveig was a tough, intractable woman who, from the very beginning, understood parenting as a competition, a battle for supremacy, one that she flatly refused to lose. Desperately, to prove to anyone and everyone, including herself, of her own self-worth, of her own significance as a mother, of her competence, she sought by skewing facts for framing—lying—to win the children to herself by running down her husband at every possible turn, falsifying faults against him, anything to rationalize her own value, to establish her maternal legitimacy, to substantiate her claim, so to speak, to find herself vindicated as a real, if new, mother, even if by cheap tricks. The country of Switzerland has always been the land of die-hard reformers, happy natural spies, and narrow-minded, rabble-rousing firebrands, and here she felt quite at home!

She took over the raising of the children right away and brooked no argument. The concept of rule she appropriated as proper to motherhood alone. In an ornery and often spiteful way, she would never cede in a debate, yield in an argument, apologize for a mistake, or admit a single fault. It proved that children met her deepest need. Why had she never had a child, she had often crossly interrogated fate, she who had so much to offer, to share? One answer was, her life had been a succession of continual, emotional crises, of intuitions of evil, coupled of course with equal convictions of her own importance. Another answer was that she put men off, for she was highly strung and did little in the way of functioning that was not accompanied by neurotic precision and, far too often, implacable raillery.

She was tall and thin with a sharp pointed nose like a Swedish fid and had long mannish hands which were not only as rough as coir rope but also were always moving, and her walk had the reaching, long-footed stride of Pieter Bruegel the Elder's overly-intense, half-mad, open-mouthed, goggle-faced "Mad Meg" or Dulle Griet. Her gold-white tresses became distressed, even wild, whenever she was infuriated. Frankness was one of her traits. She had been raised a Swedenborgian and believed in devils.

Doctrine was one thing, however, practice another. According to the founder of her Swedish denomination, each co-religionist must cooperate in repentance, reformation, and regeneration. It was an article of belief as exercised by Gullveig, however, that managed to exclude her husband from her care. According to her faith, man is a form of truth and woman is a form of love, and the two make one. But whatever truths she found in her husband seemed odd, arbitrary, and insufficient and put him beyond the pale.

Joaquin always secretly smiled to know that, in spite of his altruism and highmindedness, Swedenborg himself, nevertheless, had remained a resolute bachelor all of his life and was perfectly content to stay that way.

His wife was critical, headstrong, never at rest, extremely efficient, demanded punctuality, disliked the outdoors, and was allergic to sun. She was obstinate, even contrary, and generally hers were butcher-block decisions. She was importunate in all of her habits. She walked thuddingly on her heels, even when unshod, making loud noises, but, whenever she went storming up and downstairs in their small house in her clomping wooden shoes, it created a truly distracting and deafening racket. Nevertheless, It would be to create only a much louder noise to complain about it, as he learned, so he never mentioned it again. In her favor, she knew he harbored fond memories of the years he had lived without her in the life he once led, or so she felt. He kept on a shelf in his working room a bottle of Chambolle-Musiney that he had saved from his first wedding in memory of Sari. It was a keepsake not unknown to invidious Gullveig.

Adopting tiny tots brought out inordinately affectionate, if intimidating and autocratic—and, sadly for her husband, unforeseen—traits in her, surprising even herself. After the adoption, everything seemed to change between them. It so fell out that within a matter of weeks, as her affections began to focus on the two children, she tended insensibly to withdraw some of the warmth previously given to her husband.

He early sensed the estrangement and sought to heal it. Whenever he felt the need to enlarge on any ideas along these lines, however, his companion would respond with an interest that faded more and more day by day.

Joaquin was older. There was a touch of diffidence in his good will. He was given to remoteness and inaccessibility at times and many of the faults Gullveig held against him were legitimate. He was at best modest, at worst meek. He was bony, pinched by the wind, but he had muscles hard as a rope end and bowline. He was a quiet, playful man, up before the sun. All his habits were simple and natural. He economized on candles, never threw out scraps, fed them to the squirrels. He loved burnt toast, always on seeded rye, dishes of roast pork, grapefruit juice, the smell of tobacco. He would set aside his needles, thread, pegs, knife, and leather and make his own meal at the stroke of noon, almost always alone, as if a kind of shelter, while Gullveig saw to the children.

She harbored disquiet on a hundred fronts and had a peasant's fears, the jittery anxiety of the toiler, the yeoman, the haymaker, and was often inspired by a favorite authority of the Swedenborgians, the book of Revelation. Threats, all of them imagined, scared her, when she could hear in her ears: ". . . and I will strike her children dead. And all the churches will know that I am he who searches mind and heart, and I will give to each of you according to your works."

He was non-antagonistic and sought refuge in silence, and although the gravity of it gave him a measure of peace, his wife chose to see it as a confession of cowardliness and lack of strength. "You are weak! Timid!" she would cry at him in full-throated howl. "Everybody who know you knows you would not commit yourself to the time of day, even in a roomful of clocks!" She was unforgiving, stubborn, and had been born into a dys-functional family, the Zugs, one rife with various phobias and disorders touching on eating, panic, and depression. She could be ruthless. One did not converse with Gullveig; one debated— one argued with her.

Joaquin was neither meek, nor weak. Gullveig in her misconceptions simply failed to understand that her husband was simply trying to steer clear of any confrontation. If or when he could not manage to do so, he would try to outface her with patience, if not pity, but never without the certain determination that whatever the opposition, he would hold his ground. The subtlety of a stance does not diminish its efficiency. On the contrary, it makes it only more difficult to oppose.

"You eat eels! I smell shellac everywhere!" screamed Gull-veig with raised arms, whey-faced in mid howl. "The lather in the tin bathtub, your trough, is greasy with filthy soap! A pinkel sausage sits in the sun! The children stumble over your peat spade! A lipped knife sharper than devil claws, along with skivers, are left on the floor with cutting awls to stab and puncture children at play! Have I even mentioned all of the hides you have piled up, accumulated like a monkey its bananas? Hides, hides, hides, and ever more hides! When will you ever clean the root cellar? Potatoes go black! Unsown seeds go sprouting in their packets! Coffee grounds are spread all over the table like so many rat leavings! You wobble on a pushbike! *Tap-tap-tap*, an incessant *tap-tap-tap*, but you bring in no money! You talk in your sleep about hugging fog! You forget everything, and you remember nothing!"

But in all of the criticism Joaquin heard only one note, blown like a flute across a pond: *you love my children too much.*

She would openly accuse him in her wrath of wanting to desert the family. The fact was, it had often occurred to him—leaving her, not the children—but of course he told her he did not, and so he got angry with himself as a way of justifying the guilt he felt for lying to her. A miscalculation had occurred. The strategy of concealing a mistake is not unlike altering the direction of a moving body A sudden stoppage, even stasis, had been called for, a redirecting chop and change—no reversal in between—before switching from one to another. But he had not waited.

Sari, who was an innocent as he when they got married, had been a landscape painter and in the vigorous prime of life. Nothing had prepared Joaquin for the experience of suddenly losing her. She had seemed indestructible before she grew ill. Terror lurked at the very heart of the consternation in all that transpired by his having married again. The fright that he felt over her death had inured him against the chance for, any prospect of, the expectation of a marriage failing. The known seemed to cancel the unknown. Every fear is the fear of loss.

Gullveig had a face-off compulsion, fairly butted heads everywhere she went, and, even if it became the occasion of aggravation, found in clashes and conflict a means of confronting, so conquering, her own fears, of which there were many, indeed, almost all of which were traceable, again, to her own feelings of failure and her own unexamined inadequacies made only the worse by having been ignored for a lifetime. Gifts that Joaquin gave her she quickly shelved—out of sight—or put away. This obviated need and precluded any intimidating requirements to be grateful. What complaints she had of him had long mounted up. There were too many piles of shoes around, he did not bathe enough—the source of her greatest consternation was odor—and the stale cologne he used stank. The fees that he occasionally waived for cobbling for poorer people, just when they needed money, only infuriated her

Her earnestness instilled in him—increased—a mood for incorrectness and an urge to break rules. She avoided anything he made or grew or fashioned for footwear, in consequence. Whenever out of a creative urge he fashioned a creative shoe, she would never look at it. She walked by him from morning to night, breezily and cold, as if he were invisible. When she did turn to him—a long penetrating sharpness—it was with a glare that could outstare death itself.

I am nailed upon a cross, he lamented with accumulating

dejection and no small self-reproach, the crossbar of which are her accusations while the upright is her raucous voice.

Hatefully, she could not bear to see the children exposed to any views other than her own and was always trying to distract attention. She worked part time, several days a week, in a local bakery. Her husband paid the bills. The money she herself earned, never disclosed, was for the children. Spite ruled much of what she did. He foraged, went big for seeds. He had a small garden, of about 12 square meters, grew garlic, squashes, peppers, carrots—the one overriding vegetable that grew best in Switzerland—and loved to raise tomatoes, which he cultivated and even made sauce of, but his wife—studiedly—never ate it. If Joaquin cooked anything, she would be loath to taste it.

Undeterred, he kept at the soil with his hoe around dusk. "A calorie is a currency," he would say, "like printing your own money."

§

Gullveig worked hard and tried to maintain a clean house. She did all the clothes washing and hung it out to dry in the high mountain air. She cooked—serviceable food—and made bread (*zopf*) and meat pies (*pastetli*) and sauerkraut and often for the kids deep fried apple cookies (*kleine apfelküchlein*), which they loved. The children loved Zürcher Geschnetzeltes which was typically served with rösti, the traditional Swiss shredded potato cake, and it was expensive to set out, but she spared nothing they wanted. She had quirks. She cooked everything in one cast-iron pan. She fried everything. She liked to say even a dried boot is appetizing if it is fried. Her advice for maintaining longevity was never to eat anything that tastes good.

The children were her entire life. She bathed them, she fed them, she squired them everywhere, sometimes in a harness or on her back, and she alone tucked them in at night. She indulged the two of them, catered to their every whim. She lavished on them toys of all sorts, stuffed bears, peg-boards, cricket boxes, dolls, tops, balls and blocks, no end of jinglers and janglers. "Have they enough toys?" a slightly perturbed Joaquin would ask, fearing she was spoiling them and just managing to stifle sarcasm. Gullveig would rifle back with spitting derision, "No, but do you know what we *do* have too much of here?" He was always ready for it. *"Hides, hides, and more hides! Stinking hides, animal hides, hairy hides, disgusting hides!"*

One evening, when they were just pre-toddlers, in the midst of a bitter argument, Joachin snatched up baby Bligh, refusing to give her over, and Gullveig, knife high, threatened to kill him. It had been a terrible night, white-faced people in a stand-off. Both stood facing each other in an impossible impasse. Gullveig raced to his room and in retaliation smashed his precious bottle of Chambolle-Musiney on the floor. And in the end, Joaquin gave in and handed over the baby.

What proved to be a central anxiety for Gullveig's was that the children had been adopted, and not having been the children's natural mother created a deep and ongoing unease within her, the deepest feelings of inadequacy and fracture, forebodings of incompetency, a dearth of conscience, severe suspicions of maternal failure—lack, deficit, and shortfall in every direction—and, taken altogether, the full onset of these gloomy reflections set off tocsins of misgivings that as time passed forced her in turmoil to feel that she had to prove and re-prove to herself that she was a force in her own right, and the vehicle she chose was, in her dire hope to reign supreme with the children—to be seen that way, to be honored that way—was to demean the other parent, her husband, Joaquin. But it seemed worse than that.

An expression of low-grade anxiety never seemed to leave her face when she saw the children interacting with Joaquin.

Joaquin, who repaired shoes, took pride in his craftsmanship. He was unswerving and set in his ways and had a penchant for old tools as he applied himself to his trade. He had a favorite workbench that was covered with scattered shoe lasts and, often piled high, was a bit of a mess, which his wife resented. He was slow at his work but took pride in the quality he produced in both the mending and making of shoes. His small workroom set off to the rear of their house was an agglomeration of old awls, a pull-cutter, sets of knives, a large shoe stand in front of a big stool, walls of spare leather, spincers, rotary spools of thread, and all sorts of pig-nosed cobbler's hammers, tack hammers, saddlers hammers, carpenter's hammers, a vintage repair stand, tool boxes, no end of scorpers, hole punches, sewing, carving, decorating and carpet needles, gluing material, a wheel with a foot pedal for edging, grinding, and polishing and other functions for leather craft, stitching groovers, a special copper taper-shank awl with three needles good for sewing or repairing canvas leather, shoes, and soles, adjustable swivel knives, and leather pronged punch a screw driver with a rotation bearing that could be adjusted to change the length of the head, which he loved to show the kids.

Although he did mostly shoe repairs, he took in cordwainer work for a price, soft leather shoes and expensive four-piece boots—vamps, counter covers, front and back tops—for the mayor and some of the richer aldermen. "Take the hard coin!"

Gullveig would warn her husband, shaking a monitory finger at him, as he sat there at his work bench, among his bags of pegs, trimming a sole. "No bartering! You are too lavish in taking time with your '64-stitches-to-the-inch!' It will send us to the poor house."

The small jobs that he took on were done mainly for neighbors, sewing a rip, repairing soles and heels, replacing a worn lacing, adding a rubber lift for Old Mr. Sigg with his ketchup red hair. The customers came by, and he dutifully obliged them—Karl Beerbahn, the butcher. Rev. Lohr Maise from the Lutheran church, for goat farmer Pointko, Herr Marlo and Mrs. Merlo, Signore Dittami the tailor, the laundress Marietta Gemenini, for Pastor Burgler over from the Gerber Canton. Vito Bernasconi the bell-ringer, and pretty Luisa. A very jealous woman, Gullveig would stand back but cagily spy through the curtain whenever Luisa came by with a shoe, suggesting to the children that he flirted with her. "He waits on pretty Luisa like a princess!"

Needless to say, it was a taboo, well-observed, by both, never to mention or allude to Joaquin's first wife, the better to avoid any cause for jealousy that would send Gullveig into extravagant fits of a rage.

§

Joaquin kept to his work room. The upper room as a sort of retreat, or bolthole, used in the desperation of privacy. It was a tall house, and there was an attic. A main preoccupation of his was keeping clear of his wife and the shower of remonstrances that rained down on him whenever she came across the accumulating jumble of shoes and hides he had gathered about him.

There were piles of shoes everywhere, mounds of them, some left behind and others never picked up, frayed pairs left to be re-soled. Vegetable tanned leathers from artisanal tanneries in Italy and England. where the leather is tanned with natural organic matter such as oak bark, chestnut and mimosa, were stacked up everywhere. It was part of Joaquin's eccentricity that the imposing piles, the extent of them, never bothered him. Laughing, goading them, with his silly and slightly superannuated sense of fun, he would call the children over—prodding, beckoning, cajoling—to ask them to come close and to smell the tanned hides, explaining that as a little benison it imparted to the leather a wonderful grace, saying, "It wears well, looking better and better the more you smell it." The bright sting and smell would send them reeling back with screeches of shock. It sorely bothered Gullveig.

His treasured books, like hides, she always found in the way. Books to her were obstructions, impediments, encumbrances and meant nothing to her. To him they were salvation. Gullveig saw them as funerary stones, refuse, blocks stacked up like pyramids of ruin to wall off life in the way of a sarcophagus, to seal in, muffle, and obscure. She kept in bags the children's toys, which took precedence over the books, and with a kind of marshalling delight she would stride forth and shove the bags into the book corner, knocking the piles over and upsidedown, breaking their spines, bending them, often ripping, the pages. Whenever he complained, she would argue, conflicts and clashes that would escalate and so continue because, dug in, aching to duel, head-to-head she would simply never remove herself, standing pat, *maintaining ground*, talking, even through a shut door, talking, endlessly talking.

It was a battleground, warfare, combat, but in its well-defined and inveterate antagonisms war, unlike marriage, has no ambiguities. How words spoiling for trouble, grieviously wounded. The mouth, giving guile its best strategies, engenders program, procedure, and scheme where best to hurt. There where cruelty comes easily, it can lie and deceive either party equally.

"Look at this place," hectored Gullveig, barging from room to room with a broom, whacking it into corners and up to the ceiling joists, kicking aside a pair of old galoshes. "Boots, wing-tip shoes. Old shoes, new shoes. Black shoes, white shoes, wooden shoes, brogans, high-button shoes. You don't earn a living worth its salt," she would nag, "but look how the hides pile up like snowfall and take over the house!" She stamped a foot, her signature move.

"Why must you bring in more and more hides? Look at you! Are you a hoarder? Ankle boots, army boots. athletic shoes, ballet shoes, Alp hikers, boat shoes. Boots, ten-pin bowling shoes. Look at the piles you've made. What good are they? A room full of hides! They could all fall on the children! Brogues, cleats. climbing shoes, clogs, court shoes. cowboy boots, cycling shoes, deck shoes. dress shoes, raised shoes for mentals, espadrilles, figure skates, flip-flops, mountain shoes, gumboots, heels, high heels, low heels, high-top hiking boots!"

It was a like a hard cold rain, freezing and relentless.

"You are weak! Timid people hide in piles. *You belong with my brother in the State Hospital for the Criminal Insane!*"

"No, don't say that."

"It is true!"

"Please, please, Gullveig," Joaquin sorely pleaded.

"The stink of cow hides! It is a stubborn smell! It is an animal smell! It has the pungent, penetrating smell of urine, rotting flesh, stagnant water! It is the smell of the tanneries of Gimmel and Horn, and it splits my nose!"

She who with the ease of a lashing tongue could cast jibes, slights, and insults polished her own wounds until they were regnant art.

Both of the parents had their faults, of course. Joaquin was a bit of a magpie, a grubber, and collected everything, especially tools, ironmongery, and hardware which he kept in the back piled in their barn. An old 19th-century chest they had, a Balkan *kirst* they kept in a shed and whimsically called "Hermenegilda's Trunk," was filled with odds and ends, many things that he treasured: old flags, a kaleidoscope, a stringless lute, climbing chalk, ice picks, a locking carabiner, rope, a medical textbook, an abacus, lead toy soldiers, a clay pipe, and whatnot. He was forgetful, smoked a pipe that gave off reeking tobacco, and hated to bathe. He munched gin-soaked raisins. Whenever he ate from a tin of sardines, she said he stunk of fish oil. He made his own medicines, quaint and questionable herbal remedies and home infusions for cramps and cold and congestions. He kept laying hens, for a time, and even raised quail in the cellar. He stressed the importance of wildcraft to the kids and tried to give them meaningful jobs, like taking care of goats, collecting firewood.

She was confrontational, left candles burning all night, ignored unwashed dishes in the sink, and thoughtlessly disrupted him at work almost always in the middle of conversations she was having with herself that never made sense to him. She was a wastrel, threw away good food the children left behind, and out of a self-justifying but misplaced snobbery patronized the better shops in Grindelwald as if money never mattered. But, above all—the complaint that most bothered Joaquin—was her constantly barging in to interrupt him with cavils and quibbles of a thousand kinds. The windows were corroding, mice were running in the attic, lead paint was everywhere. She banged doors, never shut them softly, and hated the smell of food cooking, one of the testimonial joys to virtually every cook or chef. She was the worst listener and with a pronounced deficit disorder was literally unable, whenever addressed, to let a person finish a sentence without cutting him off, breaking in, interrupting.

Worse than anything, she would at times wake him—shock him awake—when he was dead asleep by grabbing his foot, shaking it with *schadenfreude*, crying, "Get up—now!" It is among the worst things you can do to a person, anyone. When she killed rabbits to eat—processing small game—he hated the sound of bleats, but he knew it was calorically dense food. But his income was so small. And meat—food in general—was expensive in Switzerland. It is a rare Switzer who is fat.

She would shop while he minded the kids, buying from the fruiterer, the grocer, and the butcher with her net basket hanging on her arm, bargaining and fighting over every miserable coin they had. It was he who paid all the bills.

Money was always an issue in their household. Joaquin was not a drunk, but he dearly loved kirsch, the strong, clear local brandy made from cherries, and he harbored a special home-born taste for Pflümli, a kind of plum-flavored schnapps. Different Cantons preferred different beverages. The Valais drank Williamine, which is made from fragrant Williams pears, while the Graubünden preferred a syrupy, cherry-flavored concoction called Röteli. It was this beverage that had been Sari Heather's drink of choice, far and away her preference—they drank it at their wedding in Geneva—and he never failed to think of her with love as he sipped one. They had lived in Geneva and, after she died, Joaquin never again went to that city. As to the drinks, he was not choosy, and would happily consume both, but with the family being in dire straits most of the time, or at least close to it, he would settle for beer.

Whenever he did chance to sell a pair of new shoes that he had made, however, he would always go out and buy red wine. He wished he could have afforded a bottle of TBA, even a half-bottle of it. Trockenbeerenauslese was a dessert wine, deep golden in color and made from individually selected grapes affected by "noble rot," a style of wine meant only for special palates and so rare a vintage that, when being made, merely finding enough of the dry grapes to produce a single bottle becomes a day's work, even for skilled picker. He could almost taste its viscous sweetness, thick and concentrated, but they were too poor for such lavishness. Maybe for another day, he thought, smiling, and settled happily for the red. Most of the wines produced in Switzerland tend to be white, which is what Gullveig herself preferred. So, small although it was, there was yet another impasse between the two of them.

"You have a peddler's pedigree, Cornelius," she told him—using his middle name—seeing him in a leather apron with a mouthful of tacks.

§

They were poor—because of him, she said. The sink taps creaked when they were turned, and the beds were so old and high they felt like pigeon lofts. The small rooms were often as cold as a meat locker, with ice outside chunked high as harvest haycocks or castle doors. A husband who is poor receives no respect from a wife, especially given a shrewish, belittling one. Gullveig with envious disregard had no respect for the time he gave to any project. In his spare time, Joaquin designed and made cuckoo clocks, on the side, oh maybe three a year. He had the requisite tools. She was always interrupting him. Why should a man, and a poor breadwinner at that, have the right to barricade himself into a room? Privacy was for productive people. A shut door to his wife was forever a temptation. A true working artist would have shot and killed her for such intrusions. What sharpened the pain was that his first wife was a painter who loved art. Gullveig, who was the polar opposite, would barge through his workroom door, taking delight in it, breezing past him with neither consideration or regard—*through* him, as it were—like parading down a garden path just to grab a broom or take a shit. She would hurl things in fury. She had hands that could palm a German pancake.

It was maddeningly as if something he had loved in one beautiful creature had turned inside out in becoming another one, a monster whose very presence, day in and day out, rendered him transparent.

He loved his kids. When they were small, on his walks he had to leave them home. It was a companionship he sorely missed, not having them nearby. On solitary hikes, trooping high, he would often go walking into fog-shapes that he went to put his arms around, thinking it might be them. He would feel suddenly elated, but euphoria is thin and ultimately false. At home he would pursue them like a small boy following a marching band. A sense of humor ran through him like a wick through a candle.

A poor man with a rich spirit is in all ways superior to a rich one with a poor spirit. He would often borrow the words of St. Paul to explain to his family that the former is as "having nothing, yet possessing all things," while the reverse was true of the latter. He told them that only the poor in spirit are truly poor.

"Can I hug you?" "Do you love me?" he would ask the kids. It galled his wife. "Desperate?" she would ask him. "Needy?" He looked over. Gullveig, sitting in the next room, had him fixed from afar, monitoring the scene with competitive intelligence. It was a rivalry, as she saw it. Vying. She kept a cold, impersonal eye on him, lest he turn her children greedy, trying to feed them candy and by doing so usurp her. She failed to see it was she who was needy, however, she who was so pathologically desperate. We are all of us past masters at seeing our own vices in another, and in the very act feel exorcised of our own. One sweeps in front of a stranger's door only if there is dust behind one's own.

She would intentionally panic the children. There was a grave indisposition he caught one freezing winter month, an influenza, and the children, whenever near, would either be summarily yanked out of his presence or, as taught, would, go racing past him at great speeds like skittering bed bugs or silverfish, protectively cupping their mouths or pinching their noses. It was, all of it, a dumb show to poke fun at him with simulated disgust. They would trickily open doors but a crack and peer in at him as if he were a leper.

Joaquin had a small window into the self that was remarkable. He could by holotropic breathing warm everything around him. He was also psychic, in a way—"remote viewing," it has been called—but it was only the clairvoyance of a raised intuition, a second sight or creative insight in reading the enemy's mind. He could sense avalanches and was able to read into the inner being of mountains and track and comprehend the spirit—the *atman*—of their weather. On a rare occasion, however, he actually experienced uncanny perception and knew in the end that for all of her stratagems and subterfuges Gullveig would fail—he experienced it as fall or fail.

With his second-sight, he thought it would take place on a Thursday, in the morning, on a rainy day, in a place of ornate white. A hospital?

Clear your mind, Joaquin would try to tell her, fearing beneath the wiles of her unsleeping aggression a potential for epilepsy or some kind of seizure. It is less a meaningless expression than a doltish request. No one can ever wholly unblock his or her mind for anything like a ludic or crystal-clear new beginning, no matter how hopeful a desire for transformation. Tension and the straitened circumstances at home of which Horace speaks—the *res angusta domi*—compelled him to stay scarce. Otherwise, pushed to the limits, he was driven—forced, by having no blessed alternative—to yell at her, and sometimes literally screech, his only recourse, when any and all such profane redresses the scandalized children heard.

Where was the justice? What were the choices when he could no longer reach her with words or meet her with reason? Against her warring compulsion, there was little or no recourse, for striking her was unthinkable. At a point in the middle of one uncompromising argument over her ceaselessly and pointlessly interrupting him at his work—shouting repeatedly through his door—he fought an actual impulse to attack her physically but had been subverted by a heart pain that staggered him. As if by the throw of a switch, Gullveig's hysteria dropped away, and she became a ministering angel. He had prevented himself from doing the unforgiveable and simultaneously transformed his enemy into a steadfast attendant.

It became a muddle to him, all of it. Had the past come forward or did the future back into him? He never knew. So, he forebore. Belayed. The Bible says he that is slow to anger is greater than he that taketh a city. In any case, his trust in Gullveig was not lost, for no man can love what he never had.

Resigned, Joaquin sadly envisioned their natures as chess pieces, each with its own unalterable characteristic, its perpetual moving part ingrained. He kept to his room and played with his children whenever he had the chance. As to his wife, large and bold and fighting like a dogfish, he apprehended her rebellious and unrestrained ability to temporize, to wait out his age, to bide her time, and to outsit her opponent—*Totsitzen*—until he dropped dead.

Or was he himself being unfair? He was worried. He became filled with despairing reflections and in despair saw himself flailing for insight as if beating with impotent wings against his fate and the mystery of God's face. Was he slanted in his mind and cruelly reshaping Gullveig in his imagination, so that by some feeble attempt at transference or reverse substitution he could retrieve something of his first wife and feel less of a betrayal of her for having gotten married again? Were his thoughts a revenge against this woman for making him seem so small in the eyes of the children?

Let what falls, fall. He did not care but only looked to 2nd

Timothy 3: "But mark this: There will be terrible times in the last days. People will be lovers of themselves, lovers of money, boastful, proud, abusive."

It was his vow never to be one of these.

§

Gullveig Sprott made sure the children practiced their flutes every morning before school, even before the sun was up. "It is good for your lungs!" she would insist, waving the silver instruments that she had rented from the conservatory. They took bi-monthly lessons from M. Distruber from Andermatt, paid for by church funds. But no music teacher alive could have been more diligent than the children's mother who, when it came to practice, was a martinet. She drilled the children, harped at them, made them whistle whatever melodies they fumbled on the instrument. He heard every kind of vociferation in her directives, always Gullveig's goose honk voice, a promising plum tone, thick grunts, a barking voice, minatory yelps and jungle barks, steep pitches of a deep 72.5 hertz, followed by a screaming mandrill's shriek, loon calls, bustard's cries, shouts and vents and mutters and roars and yells.

Nature had given her a voice of unparalleled stridency and stubborn lack of reason. We're talking factory horns! Still, that her combative attention had turned away from him was a blessing. No more Junker or Prussian soldiery or hard barking. For he had begun to think of her, disdainfully, as the "Pointed Helmet."

It was a great inconvenience to her husband, nevertheless, that she chose to give these lessons directly next to his small room where much of the day he tried to work. But she cared nothing for what he was up to in there, not a jot, and any and all pleas of his for her to go elsewhere fell on deaf ears. She would stamp a foot. Her voice was shrill, and, as it bore through his door—"Start again with the B-flat major scale!" "Have you not studied the fingering chart?" "Use the trill key!"—as desperately Joaquin tried to think of anything else, even praying to Saint Crispin, patron saint of shoemakers for peace. Anything for quiet!

But there was no peace. He would sometimes take a pull of schnapps to relieve the noise. Gullveig cared not a whit for his objections. He would picture her a loud bullfrog in weeds, croaking, barking wet with a pebbled saurian skin and wide mouth, inflating, deflating. The lessons she gave were exercises in domination, even tyranny. "The flute won't come to pitch! The room is too cold—a cold flute is always too flat!" "Where is that vibrato you used to do?" "Relax your spine!" "Put your feet on the floor *flat!*" She gabbed all day, couldn't hear herself. "Where is your flute book?" After the lessons, she would clap the books shut and turn on her husband with, "*Why must you breathe like stoat?*"

In a very real way, the mad exertions of her instructions recapitulated the incurable habit she had in her arguments with Joaquin of continuing what was intolerable long after it has reached its logical conclusion.

It was less a cross to be married to Joaquin than to have a husband at all. Rather than live a married life of uneasy semi-importance, she nightly dreamt of Xing-out her older husband to win and maintain the primary role of parent. Gullveig had her just complaints with the man. He was not like other people, but set in his ways and a challenge to compulsory conformity. He wore the same drab clothes every day, lackluster shirts all washed out, corduroy pants and lumpy shoes. He was frugal in the extreme, sober, and abstemious. He also had given up talking to her. She also gave him the silent treatment, the *Totschweigetaktik*, a tactic of killing by keeping silent and ignoring someone no longer bearable.

Parenting to her meant who would take command. It was a question of conquest. Plotting and planning led to nothing, only the crazy dream fugues that came to her at night that would disappear in the morning like the snow tails that blew in ghostly sheets off the sharpened tips of the mountain peaks. *Please him just a bit. Shut him off when he goes on talking. Keep our secrets. Tell him of little. Don't go with him on his walks. Say nothing to him of importance. Tell him I have to go. He will not live too much longer.* There were even molestation suspicions of him that she dramatically contrived simply to gain the upper hand. It was a device.

Whenever any accident or incident occurred making the poppets cry out over whatever misfortune it was—a dropped cup, a snap of glass, a ripped shirt, a doll left out in the rain—out of nowhere Gullveig would suddenly appear as if in response to a formal stage direction, an exhibition with technique involved, for she would come flying in from another room, looking daggers at him, and calling forth the children in her imperious way, insistently demanding that her husband stand right there, she would indicate precisely where, sometimes stamping her foot, and then in a big melodramatic way with a calculated and studied look—a cold level brutal stare drilling right into their eyes—scream to them, "Tell me what happened!"

They never said.

§

When Blaise and Bligh reached the ages of seven and eight, a delighted Joaquin would take them on short hikes into the mountains. He delighted in their lively company, little ducks quacking in his wake. They always came whipping about him like a good spring breeze, letting out squeals, jouncing into his room and leaping on him, yelping like puppies, dragging him outside to go running the meadows with rapture, or scampering in the deep snow—sturdy, healthy little folk who were game for anything, sledding especially.

They were biddable children, gentle, innocent, keen to learn. No walk was without its attendant lesson. "Finches almost never eat insects," he told them. "Starlings and grackles crave sunflower seeds. Cardinals—there is one—never migrate. Ground-feeding birds especially love to eat millet. The Golden Eagle—see him up there?—is supreme. Its nest can be two meters wide. This is our royal bird. Its head is mostly an eye! Our national bird is the turaco—'loeries,' we call them. Bright green and red feathers. Crests. Long tails. I love their crazy feet. Their second and third toes always point forward, sometimes conjoined, as well, but their outer toe—their fourth—switches back and forth. I could never make shoes for them!"

"'Live in the sunshine, swim the sea, drink the wild air,'" Joaquin told them, quoting from his favorite philosopher. "'The earth laughs in flowers!'" "'Always do what you are afraid to do.'" They sailed toy boats in their pond and fed trout in a nearby pool and loved to dance and to perform and to sing "*Wäggis zue.*"

> *Vo Luzern uf Wäggis zue,*
> *Holje-guggu, holje-guggu,*

brucht me weder Strümpf noch Schueh,
Holje-guggu, holje-guggu . . .

Hoduliduli hopsassa holje-guggu, holjeguggu,
Hoduliduli hopsassa holje-guggu-guggu.

Fahr im Schiffli übern See,
Holje-guggu, holje-guggu,
um die schönen Maidli zseh.
Holje-guggu, holje-guggu . . .

Joaquin taught them how to draw shapes, glue on soles, snell a hook, stir dough, walk on stilts, fashion hand-puppets, play "duck on a rock," contrive a clove hitch, cut dandelions, pick gooseberries, build peg puppets, make a monkey's fist on a rope, as well as a reliable water knot—also known as a Double Overhand Bend—which is crucial for joining flat tape used by climbers. It was important that they learn safety. He showed them how to climb hills using prusik knots, to bind a sling to the main rope, and how to form a sliding Italian hitch for rappelling in order to control the distance of an unforeseen fall. "But the most important truth of the most important lesson," he told both of them, quoting from Emerson and tapping each child several times on the chest, "is 'What lies behind us and what lies before us are tiny matters compared to what lies within us.'" He had them repeat it clearly and slowly, twice.

He cooked gingerbread for them, He made them leather puzzle cubes. He once constructed a workable glockenspiel with hammered plates from a used metal drum, and he also fashioned colorful slippers for them out of woven braids and sennits, grommeted to the leather soles he cut. He liked to surprise them with something new each morning. He called each kiss he lavished on them an "Alpine butterfly." They daily fed and kissed a pet goat he had bought them, Gilgit. Joaquin told his wife once his toys might make some money. *Was he serious?* Gullveig laughed out loud, scornfully, and covered her mouth in mock apology. She celebrated nothing, reused to commend her husband for anything. The children saw all of this. All the while, their mother's ardent devotion to them, so exclusive in its determination, slowly began to nurture an arrogance in them which would quicky curdle into a precocious cynicism for, and doubt about, their father. In many ways, he felt he was letting a berserker loose on them.

If she had only let them together love the children, equally from the purview of their open and twin affectionate hearts, the children—indeed, the family—would have glowed. But she was too needy to share and too crude to care. The very idea of control, which alone mattered to her, was the one thing necessary.

He loved to read and sought every chance to share his impressions with his family and his friends. One of his few treasures, he kept on a shelf by his bed an old weathered copy of the essays of Ralph Waldo Emerson, that American philosopher who had once on a tour even made a visit to Switzerland. It was all in a balance, life was: "Each of us has all the time there is; each accepts those invitations he can discern. By the same token, each evening brings a reckoning of infinite regret for the paths refused, openings not seen, and actions not taken." It was not by any means that Joaquin was perfect, far from it—he tended to break things, was stubborn himself, resented change, often repeated himself with stories, removed himself in spats.

He told Blaise and Bligh many stories, fables, and colorful tales of old mountain legends. There was much shoe lore in all he said, of course. An old shoe is a lucky object. Putting your stockings in your shoes before going to bed will cause bad luck. A shoe string coming untied shows you are in the thoughts of a friend. He told them that to be traditional in Switzerland it was necessary to throw a shoe at someone whenever he or she was setting out on a journey, in order to wish them luck, and the shoe must be thrown in the direction of the journey.

They constantly made wishes, dreamt fancies, and loved asking their father to predict things, which he happily did to oblige them, although he never further explained his riddles. To Bligh, he said,

"Someday somebody will ask you
a question you'll want to say yes to"

and to Blaise,

"One day someone will teach you
Lessons that sadly will reach you."

When young, Joaquin had climbed the north face of the Sass Rigals in the Geislerspitzen, and he told his kids that back then, when he was strong, he had organized belays and lost any apprehension he might have felt at the prospect of extreme climbing. He told them of his past. He had done small peaks, a training ground—a *klettergarten*—for later climbs, which it turned out he could no longer afford. He had intuition. On a climb, intuition can play as important a role as a person's mental or physical condition. He told them of great climbs like the Laliderer Walls, the Freney Spur on Mount Blanc, and the West Face of the

Dru. "The Eiger Face looks at you, yes, but always remember that there is something behind a face."

"What *is* it behind the face?" asked Blaise.

"That is the mystery. Mountains as they rise are but matter, and matter is but a symbol for spirit, which when you come close to them both whisper their secret, that over every mountain there is a pass."

He knew everything about climbing. They exhilarated over the facts he knew. Did they know that the summit of Everest may be the highest point on the surface of the Earth, but that it isn't actually the tallest mountain on the planet? That distinction goes to Mauna Kea in Hawaii, which is actually 33,465 feet (10,200 meters) in height, a full 4,436 feet (1,352 meters) taller than Everest! The origin of that great mountain, he explained, was deep beneath the Pacific Ocean.

Sitting up on the high hills, looking off into the romantic white mists of the Alpine ravines, they thrilled to hear the many superstitions and traditions connected to the vast mountains that their country was blessed with, especially the names of the royally ascending peaks, all the dramatically imposing "four-thousanders," whether in the Alps or the Jura, soaring as high as golden eagles, many of them crescent-shaped—spiked, ragged, and craggy—whose rough cut, sharp-pointed, snow-covered, mist-shrouded configurations from the Ice Age appeared jagged like the lower jaws of a lynx. He would take them by their waists and, swiveling around like a wild weathercock, point due north, out west, down south, and back east and, quoting Swedenborg, declare, "'The sky is an enormous man.'"

The two children would be enthralled, bright as firelight, hugging his neck and begging him to tell them more and more.

"You must learn to see all sides of a mountain," he explained to them. "Every side. It is not like moon, of which we see only the one side. Did you know that?" When they returned home, he would have them draw little pictures with their mind's eye of what they had seen. He sought examples to give them to drive home his points and told them about Luigi Kasimir, the Austro-Hungarian-born etcher, painter, printmaker, and landscape artist, who famously insisted that one can appreciate the worth of a sculptor's work only if and when you walk around a statue, viewing it from all angles.

"No, I do not mean turn a painting hind-side-to," he added to make the kids giggle, "that does not apply. One must walk *around* the statue to see it correctly and with full understanding," their father pointed out. "To give it its full dimensions. Circle it. All 360 degrees. Do you understand." He would circle his index finger round and round. "A mountain, like a statue, has many sides. You must circumambulate the object. *Herumlaufen.* Revolve around it. As our friend Signore Dittami would say"—and here Joaquin with a spin would pirouette two fingers –"*Andare in giro.*"

The children listened soberly and took in what he had to say.

It did his heart good.

He called them back. "'Wildness is the building block of everything,'" he told them. It was Emerson again. "Do you hear me?"

"Yes, papa," they chimed in together.

They were obedient.

They read their Bible. Both parents were strict about that. Devotions were a nightly ritual, with prayers offered while they knelt.

§

As the years rolled on, as unstoppably they did, Joaquin slowly came to the full realization that he should have never married again. His wife was stubborn in the extreme. She cut him off in mid-sentence whenever he tried to explain anything. He was a loving father, but the worst thing was, she clearly disapproved of the time the children spent with them. "Come, packs on, *kinder,* we'll all clamber up to the Hatbox!" He had favorite climbs. "You prefer to scramble up the Cachalot and see the scampering ibexes? Scale Old Bonaventure? Gooseberry Rock? The Thorn of the White Beak? The dangerous Heretic?" But Gullveig would immediately scotch the plan. He would try to free the children, but she would confine then.

Where he sought to join, she sought to separate. As he worked at his craft, his thoughts as he hammered away on soles and heels, facing alternating moods of expectancy and anxiety, always immediately reverted to the one unalterable fact of his existence: he was caught, pinned in something like a cleft stick. While he adored his two children, and dearly cherished their company, they were constantly being taken from him, sequestered, squired off into alternate or rotating projects, music instruction and practice, snacks and meals, busyness of many different sorts and stripes—it was as if her nose, a weathervane, pointed to exactly where in such instances she wanted it to—rendering him, at least to over-superintending Gullveig, a superfluous man, mere interruption. When he woke up every morning—he and his wife slept in separate rooms—he would find them all at breakfast, sitting at a table set for three.

Whenever he came into the room, she never looked at

him. She would coldly walk by him, as if he were invisible. She threw out several of his old jackets for being threadbare. Consulting no one, she went and got rid of Gilgit, the pet goat, because he shed hair. She flung an old cologne bottle of his out the window because it was stale and smelled of corpses, she said. Joaquin often escaped to the forest, brooded, sitting on a cliff ledge whenever he could, spending long hours walking in the mountains before finding it in his heart to return.

How could he have predicted such an impasse when, young, he had come back from Jakarta, the one trip he ever took abroad, when in Ban-dung he had met Sari Heather? There was no getting over her. He thought that she stamped him like the Pentecost left its stamp on the Apostles. Joaquin's reveries of Sari were plangent and deep—the way they met, her Asian beauty, her talent as a painter, her gentle hand. Could God bring her back by some kind of corrective miracle the way it is said God put right at night the mess that people made by day?

As time passed, the Sprotts spoke to each other less and less. It seemed pointless to Joaquin whenever he returned to register his complaint about her usurpation of the children, coupled with her neglect of him. Gullveig would never, could never, admit that she was wrong—literally could not manage it. Contrition was a foreign tongue to her. It ceded power. It weakened her hold on herself. It took too much away from her, gave too much away. She never listened, they could not talk, he could never finish a sentence. He could never open his mouth to speak without the socially-killing anticipation of being abruptly cut off, after even the merest word or two. She violated the very act, instantly contravened the attempt. Out of a deep need, born of the neglect from her own parents, she had to command. It was her privilege and her priority.

They lived in an old house, one that he himself had built many years before he had married her. At one place on a stormy night, dollops of rain would go leaking through a roof corner. A broken louver with a hole in it dripped. There were broken spouts on the outside of the dwelling. And while Gullveig had taken over, that was only the beginning of her prerogatives. He was soon facing a new set of worries. She never sought to deflect or deny her regrets. "I wanted a rolling boulevard of dreaming, with lights and noise. Your history is a straight line, going dark," she told her husband.

With a smirk and arched eyebrow, she would often address him mockingly as "*Hochseilkundler*," or high-wire daredevil, meaning of course quite the opposite, that he was in fact in his modest and inadequate way a small and indifferent lapworker. The fact of his menial job now seemed newly an embarrassment to the children, as well. But why ever would it? "Are we poor?" the children would ask their father, intimidating him. It mortified the man "Why would you ask that? Who told you so?"

Concerned, Joaquin mentioned this to Gullveig.

"Must you tell them of our troubles needlessly to dwell on in their youth?" he asked her sorrowfully." I am serious."

She gave out with a champagne laugh and walked away.

The old cobbler looked beneath a brow as sad as a sunless twilight.

What on earth was happening?

§

Gullveig had taught the children from an early age to fix

their own breakfast so that she was able to sleep late, it became the morning habit for the family. Joaquin would now rise, eat by himself, and proceed to the cobbler room to get busy. He would call to them to make sure that everything was in order, but they would not answer. The children were awkward and, shaking out a tall box of muesli, would often spill it. It was hefting the milk bottle that became too much. One morning after Bligh overfilled her milk bowl, her father solicitously intervened, but now headstrong and self-directed, the determined child yanked back the bottle, and the milk went splashing everywhere. Predictably, Gullveig came roaring out of her bedroom, slovenly half-dressed, and, glaring at her husband, almost spitting in his direction, stamp her foot and militantly bark at the children, "*Tell me what happened.*"

They never said.

Alarm was her intent, disquiet, a manufactured dread, and fright a way to raise a mountain of agitation from a molehill, for such occasions gave her purchase, a justification to hold him responsible, and derelict.

It was a judge's phrase, a mantra of accusation, a pretentious Solomonic pose giving objective inquiry full weight. The expression, first off, demands something to have happened, in a very real sense instigates it, sets it in motion, inspires it, pouring fuel on the force of the very fracas it creates. An order has been given, too, as the speaker with incontrovertible ego intrudes. Gullveig was virtue incarnate, while infantilizing her husband with her role of contravening sheriff.

It was an ominous cry-out, never pleasant. Something *happened*, you see—unanticipated, forbidding, threatening, adverse.

There was also something subtly horrifying in her tone

of implied alarm, as if in her intercession she were investigating child-abuse, for there was a distinct patina of that threat in her noisy agitation. The children had been taught—raised—to blame the father for everything. It satisfied the logic of the scheming woman, as habitually she would barge thudding in on her heels, ignoring her husband's explanation, to pull little Bligh or Blaise away, ordering them to speak. It was pure theatrics but it gave a context—provided a narrative—for her domineering role.

Roles define action. A part is assigned in such a symbolic way that it can never vary in the defining ferocity fact or expectation. We fall into life as the character we find representing us demands we be.

Gullveig was a good mother in caring for Blaise and Bligh, if the sole yardstick of her attention to them meant anything, but it was an attention she had usurped from Joaquin with an endless array of dissuading, deterring, and diverting procedures that made law, law. The children not only brought out her neediness but gave her the occasion to fill it. Losing that, she would lose not only confidence, but face. Face meant everything to her. A failed person, or so at least she saw herself, what she craved more than anything in life with her new found motherhood was mastery. That alone proved her worth. Nothing else could do it. The children were a living testimony to her worth. Commanding them equally served her sense of self. She reveled in their obedience to her, every spontaneous beckoning to her call. Whenever they heard her even stir, they assembled—*marshaled*—themselves to order.

And her calls were tests to be answered. She would countenance no opposition. Her husband was the odd man out. The kids would often point to their father, whenever he might suddenly appear in his apron with shoe glue on his nose and sticky cyanoacrylated fingers fluttering with string or stitching thread, and screech with glee, *"Clown mit deiner dicken Schminke und deiner grellbunter Kostüm!"*—or, with their hands waving him away, yowl, *"Nano pazzo! Nairn! Zwergwuhsige!"* Once, unsure of himself, with an unsteady hand, Joaquin had dropped an expensive vase of theirs, one that she loved, which shattered. and ever since that time all of them—she saw to it—referred to him as "Crackbowl." Whenever her husband sat the children down to tell them a story, she would interrupt. "Flute lesson time," she'd sing out. Whenever anyone stopped by the house to see him, she would stick her face into the room, refusing to be excluded. They two of them ate separately. The children worked on drawing paper in a separate room. They held nightly devotions without him.

As they grew, they would now parrot their mother at their father's expense. "Bag of bones, bag of bones, bag of bones," they would chant. "There is Crackbowl making a bang with his hammer again!" "Let mommy decide. She knows best." Only then would Gullveig smile. It was more than the smile of pride.

It was the smile of victory.

§

Joaquin was very soon fully excluded from family activities, she saw to that. No single aspect of his temperament other than humbly but ungainful cobbling was so firmly developed that it was possible to use it as a channel to influence her mind. Stubborn, she was immune to persuasion. It was as if she absorbed and gave expression to her fears and ambitions by induction and osmosis. There was an ongoing debate within her she always won.

She swore she could hear him thinking: *You with your nose like the long intrusive beak of an arctic loon!* It only served her purpose in despising him. She was redeeming the time, rectifying her own life, by way of the children. The trouble was, it began to grow worse by the day. She poisoned the children's minds against her husband, fabricated tales about him, made light of his person. He became as a stranger to them, a shadow of aging and complication. It started when they began to repeat, and often, her many intemperate charges. "Mommy's right," they would cry in unison. "You wait on pretty Luisa like a princess!" they chided him.

She said that he smelled, so they said that he smelled. She said that he was deaf, and so the children repeated the charge. She said he was old, and they agreed and said the same. He was a pole without a flag.

To try to catch them and pull them into his orbit, Joaquin imitated a merry-go-round horse. He wanted to tell them about space travel and William Tell and the apple and the twelve greatest men in Europe. But they ignored him. He began to sleep poorly and suffer from shapeless apprehensions.

"We cannot stay here a minute more—we have to go upstairs!" they would cry, standing by the bathroom door, ragging hjm with ridicule. He would feel hurt but laugh. They made silly faces at him and sometimes stuck out their tongues. "There's a man in there at the sink." "Who is that scary person tap-tap-tapping at the shoes?" they would mock. "Look at all these filthy hides," cried little Bligh, as if by rote. "Boots, wing-tip shoes. Old shoes, new shoes. Black shoes, white shoes, wooden shoes, brogans, high-button shoes," they would echo-cackle in derision, singing as they trooped in rogation around the house. "Tell us stories of when you wet the bed and had diarrhea," they would taunt him sarcastically, giggling and jeering and pointing to their little bums. "You're a Crackbowl!"

It would hit a pitch of deafening noise

Instantly, with feigned horror, their mother would appear in her apron with every outcry or outrage, wringing her hands.

"*Tell me what happened.*" she would order.

They never said.

§

Time passed. The children grew. But their disregard of him got no better in their teens. Bligh and Blaise did exactly as they had been taught. Yet whereas they had once joined in the mockery of their father with the mantras their mother had devised, a litany of abuse, it eventually became a matter of ignoring him. He cared, of course. But he was too old to be crushed and not vain enough to be insulted. The curious detail here was that he even began to take their point of view. He began to drink more. He boxed his tools, the old spincers, set aside his rotary spools of thread, clapped into a closet cobbler's hammers, tack hammers, saddler's hammers, carpenter's hammers, and the pig-nosed one that as a little boy Blaise loved, it did not matter. He carted his vintage repair stand into a far corner, along with the tool boxes and all the scorpers, hole punches, sewing, carving, decorating and carpet needles, gluing material, and his wheel with a foot pedal for edging, grinding, and polishing.

Joaquin could not, would not, pressure the children. He fished. He knew how to fish. One has to let the line run. You run the risk of having the line snap if you yank it constantly. Never be forever reeling in, nor drag too tight, for too much tension on a leader can break the fish off. Don't be slow, either, for lack of pressure creates slack in the line, an opportunity a fish will take to spit the hook. Reel when the fish gives you an inch, and hope for the best.

That was all he could do with the children.

He followed pure reason. It seemed the only course. He found it fit in his old age to abandon all reliance on the senses. Ralph Waldo Emerson was right. Reason is God which is omnipresent throughout nature, while understanding is man's grasp and use of the world around him. It was all he had left.

The piles of hides stayed put, a stacked and convenient mockery to Joaquin's insufficient foresight. Mold can permanently damage leather surfaces, discolor white leather, and easily spread to other items. As is well-known, leather of any kind, whether shoes, gloves, harnesses, even clothes—dirndls and lederhosen—and other accessories are prone to mildew and mold growth if stored in any area where moisture levels are too high. It took only one spore to start a colony, and so of course it was important to remove mold as soon as possible. "But where is your father to cart these unsightly cow hides away?" came the predictable wail on many a day. Their mother pausing for an echo seemed to be waiting for a refrain. And inevitably it would come. Bligh would laugh and Blaise would slap his knee, and the two of them would leap about, both crying in comic derision to no one in sight—their father was in the mountains—"*It is a stubborn smell! It is an animal smell! It has the pungent, penetrating smell of urine, rotting flesh, and stagnant water. It is the smell of the tanneries of Gimmel and Horn, and it splits the nose!*"

The older he got, the more withdrawn their father

became. They wanted to go to the mountains, to climb again up to Eagle Pass, but Gullveig who hated hiking always put them off with excuses and empty defenses.

Joachin went to the upper room and stayed there.

An upper room allowed for perspective and for him represented a place of prayer, a shelter, a refuge to prepare for personal communion with God, a secret reserve for quiet time set aside for the habitation of the Lord.

Many things happened in an upper room in Scripture, he knew. The Last Supper—the Cenacle—took place in an upper room in Jerusalem. The Apostles, he knew, assembled in an upper room and prayed there in the confines where nothing profane could enter. Jeremiah, the weeping prophet, referenced the upper rooms as something that the rich have possession of. The prophet Daniel with his windows open in the chamber of the upper room knelt upon his knees three times a day and toward the Temple prayed before his God. David gave Solomon, his son, the plan of the vestibule of the temple, of its houses, of its upper room. The very first Christian hurch services took place in an upper room. It was in an upper room that the Holy Spirit alighted upon the eleven apostles at Pentecost

Soon Rev. Lohr Maise from the Lutheran church no longer came by. Goat farmer Pointko, whose wife was a cousin of Gullveig's, sensed friction in the household and steered clear of the place. Old Mr. Sigg with his ketchup red hair who needed his carriage canvas re-sown and patched was told by Gullveig, standing at the door, that he should go and find another cobbler. "Tell me what happened," asked the solicitous old man, sadly, cap in hand. "*Holtzchopf!*" Gullveig tapped her temple, and mimed a rickety walk with a cane. "*Glon. Löli,*" she said, explaining that her husband had a wandering brain. Karl Beerbahn, the butcher, was owed money and, giving up in the end, simply crossed the Sprotts off his list. Herr Marlo and Mrs. Merlo pitied Gullveig and, when they saw her at Sunday church with her two handsome children, could only admire the mother. Laundress Marietta Gemenini had married Vito Bernasconi and moved away. And Luisa never again came by, not any longer.

Joaquin no longer went up to the mountains. He tried to maintain dignity but kept to himself and acted as the iron bite of necessity dictated. The world became a prison. Solitary confinement was best for him, he concluded, and became his sanctuary. A creature cannot help his age—he can only express that it is doomed.

Pilgrimages had always beckoned him, like fate. One particular morning he arose and took up a stick and inexplicably set off, for no reason that he could think of, walking from Grindelwald to Brienz in a snowstorm.

§

Joaquin Sprott died, at age 86, from a respiratory infection. Pastor Burgler over from the Gerber Canton presided at the funeral, a closed and perfunctory affair. He had died, strangely, with his window unlatched and open, freezing, facing the terrible white peaks of the Jungfrau, 4,158 meters high, located between the northern canton of Bern and the southern canton of Valais, halfway between Interlaken and Fiesch. A single line in a note addressed to Blaise and Bligh had been found under his pillow, "'Be sure of this, that I am with you always, even to the end of the world. Amen. Matthew 28:20." All agreed that his had been a mysterious death. Rumors in Grindelwald had it that Gullveig had been the cause of it. Many repeated that she had suffocated him. Some said poisoned. Some simply said she wore him out.

Weeping, the youngsters took the time devotedly to square-lash two poles to bind and stabilize a cross for the grave with a knot he had taught them to tie.

At the cemetery, Gullveig was resolute and told both of her children not to be sentimental. "He was weak," their mother said. "I was the strong one. Someone had to be." They listened in sorrow, then, and throughout the bleak interim the following weeks, often staring at the piles of hides and forlorn nail-bitten, hammer-scored, scorper-dented cobbler bench. They felt a hollow vacancy not only in the house but in their hearts of someone missing, someone special, a creature whose tap-tap-tapping now was no longer heard. It was a terrible emptiness of a missing someone in whose defense it was too late to intercede.

On their way back from their father's funeral, something memorable happened. Was it a symbol? A sparrow fell from its nest. Blaise stooped to pick it up and said to his sister, "Against the sparrow, rapaciously battered by the wind, thy wageth thy great might, and persecuteth innocent feathers." Both looked at each other and began to cry. Their mother regarding this—what was this in aid of?—prodding them, pressing their shoulders, and directed them down the path home. She sententiously remarked, "Pining for the past does nothing but sully the future."

Tidying up began. Thrown out were Joaquin's hides. Disposed of were his pipes and pots of reeking tobacco and no end of iron barn tools. Gone was a smelly barrel of alcoholic bottles. Out went all of his hats, gloves, no end of bent and rumpled shoes, a mass of stitching groovers, his tweed hiker hat with the brim still pulled down, a special copper taper-shank awl with three needles good for sewing or repairing canvas leather, shoes, and soles, almost his old breviary—Blaise grabbed it from the pile to save it—adjustable swivel knives, and a leather pronged punch screw driver with a rotation bearing that could be adjusted to change the length of the head. He also snatched as many of Joaquin's books as he could, fumbling fast, after Gullveig had carted off a small loaded wagon of them to a midden heap.

Behind their backs, Gullveig had notified a a faraway neighbor and given away "Hermenegilda's Trunk," the chest that had been filled with odds and ends, many things that he treasured, all the ice picks, old flags, the kaleidoscope, the broken lute, climbing chalk, ice picks, and locking carabiner.

Standing in the cobbler room, Blaise and Blight who saw with a glare of despair that there was nothing left of their father also began to see as they looked at their mother that they were looking at one side of a statue. Gullveig could not divine their sorrow. She stood scowling, her long marlingspike nose critically sharpened and pointed in their direction. Her children kept looking at her, so she huffed and walked off.

The young boy and girl, stalwarts to a degree, who were precocious when young, had by now become almost scientific in their reasoning and understanding. It was a Swiss trait. Unity, yes, they reasoned, uniformity, no. A national habit was to be direct, to take things by the horns. Neutrality may have been a property of the country's identity, but it was not a Sprott distinction. It was however also a national characteristic to want to examine matters thoroughly and well, with watch-like precision. It was almost an aspect of thrift and punctuality. Blaise and Bligh with the reconsidering necessity that a change of fate brings came to suspect Gullveig of being a callous and inconsiderate dominant, to see an unabiding awfulness in her uncaring and inordinate dismissals of their father and the way she would hold up a shoe and derisively say, "A hoof!" She had beaten them more than once over the years, with a strap, when they had defied her with arguments of her having being unfair to their father.

Whenever she did so, Bligh would ask, "Has mother gone completely mad?" To which her sagacious brother would reply, "But isn't what we are seeing, what we have always seen?" They seriously began to fear that she had inherited the madness of her brother who before he was committed ate skin scabs, tore up his clothes, and threw turnips at visitors. There was also the possibility of epilepsy. Was their stepmother suicidal? According to Swiss law, they knew that anyone of sound mind who has, over a period of time, voiced a consistent wish to end his life can request a so-called assisted voluntary death or AVD. That person, however, must commit suicide, by his or her own hand, for example, by taking the medication himself. It was obvious she was irrational. But her behavior was such that the two of them also slowly began to see through Gullveig and what they saw they were able less and less able to abide, particularly the rude and unsettling scorn of her insistent plainchant, "Old shoes, new shoes. Black shoes, white shoes, wooden shoes, brogans, high-button shoes."

Lovingly, they could not bear to see their father's memory exposed to any views other than their own and were always trying to distract attention. Gullveig saw with growing anxiety the sea-change within them as they grew. She rued that they had put away their flutes for good and never practiced again. They had often spent time in the cobbler room, sitting in silence. Blaise who had even become religious spent time with his Bible, saying prayers for his father. Their mother feared that they had achieved a new dimension by way of having found out—singled out—some terrible secret of hers, uncovered under a pile of manufactured derision. What she felt was a loss of grip. It was almost a smell. She sensed with every passing week their disappointment in her, their disapproval, even their disgust, virtually *felt* her abuse of their father as if on their skin. She reverted temporarily to her old practice of booming. She tried spending more time working in the bakery now, feeling unwanted by her children.

But even that did not solace her.

Whatever these new ideas were or how they had come into their heads began to render insignificant Gullveig's own sense of motherhood, her identity that way. Her children were reasoning differently and could no longer be prodded, be advised, be directed. Their perspectives had changed. In a manner of speaking, they were trying to take in new dimensions, circumambulating, as their father said, seeing different sides—*they were walking around their lives.* It was like a shoe trek, not unlike one of the many they had taken growing up. Where did they want to go and why? What was all this new business? A new terror gripped her, a sense of panic, of trepidation that she had never felt before, and here she acquiesced and promised to go with them on a hike to the high ramparts of Eagle Peak.

She told them, "I cannot oblige you on Friday or the weekend. I am too busy. We can go the day before."

She was appeasing them out of fear.

They did not want to go with her.

"Do not sit here and mope. A funeral is final. I intend to take charge," she said, angrily. "Someone has to do it."

§

A high mountain with its breathtaking views could never be listed among Gullveig Sprott's enjoyments. It was a windy day for a long hike and a cold front with clouds of squall lines promised in the sky. The young couple had each donned pairs of durable mountaineering boots that their father had made, sleek and indestructible, decidedly strong four-season alpine boots, light insulation, serving both weight savings and durability, quasi-flexible soles, 4 pounds 7.4 ounces with strong durable hand-crafted Italian leather that absorbed water more readily than any of the synthetic boots that modern hikers were using. Joaquin with the care that he had always managed and taken pride in had even added rubber toes.

Although the children remembered throwing a shoe at someone when they are setting out on a journey brought them luck, and that the shoe should be thrown in the direction of the journey, they did neither that day.

Gullveig and the youngsters set out and took a tram partway up the vast Ritlihorn overlooking Handegg in the canton of Bern. It lies on the range east of the Gauli Glacier and north of the Bächlistock, the summit of which with its vistas of sweeping snow has an elevation of 3,247 meters above sea level and is the tripoint between the glacier valleys of Hiendertelltigletscher, Bächligletscher and Unteraar. They all got out of the tram at one point, so that they could hike the rest of the way to a point at Eagle Peak, a favorite spot of Joaquin's. Reaching the place, they sat down exhausted. "I smell hides," said Gullveig. She could be relentless. "Where are the cows? Walking around in clown shoes?" But the so-called stink of cows, their tanned skins, was now perfume to Blaise and Bligh, bearing no longer and never again the bright sting and scandal of shock that had once sent them reeling backwards.

An overlook invites deep reflection, the vast expanse that height takes in inducing contemplation and a long view inevitably composed of memory and regrets. Any panorama with its wide scope becomes inevitably, and seemingly forever, a force field of introspection and thought. But their mother who had hated the ferocious sun of early morning saw the clouds begin to darken in a now enlarging overcast and spit forth a bit of rain, and, irritated, she sat back cross-legged with an exasperation she did not bother to hide.

The penetrating coldness that she felt as they climbed became frozen at the peak of Eagle Pass, a forbidding and inhospitable frigidity, irritated her. She avoided taking in the sweeping views, only gauging the time before they could head down and get back to reality. The youngsters knew they were looking at one side of a statue.

Something was wrong. A hint of dread was dropped into what seemed a hole of silence that had opened up in a sudden sheepish grievance.

Bligh tried to civilize her voice.

"Why have you always hated father?" the girl inquired out of the blue, staring at her mother with an edge in her voice. Her question was like an arrow that ate up the divide between her and her stepmother and in an instant the steel tip went rifling into that cold woman's heart. There came a long pause. "This is what you say to me now? In your insolence, this the question that you can pose to your mother? It is not true," snapped Gullveig, infuriated. On the edge of fatigue, Blaise oddly declared, "'One mightier than I is coming, the latchet of whose shoes I am not worthy to loosen.' Luke 3:16." He added, "But our father is not coming. Not now, not anymore, never again." He was not even looking at his mother.

"He might have been a success had he not committed all of his energies to his job hammering old shoes together," said Gullveig.

"How nice for you," remarked Bligh, dryly.

Screeching, Gullveig struggled up from where was sitting, almost falling on the ice, and wheeled on them. Her entire life was being repudiated. "That is a lie!" She was hiccuping in horror and began defensively moving backwards. "You are conspirators! Both of you! Does this serve you well?" But it was in her revisionist song and dance that proved, only once more, clarified, the way she was, underlining the very kind of deceit that she had all along denied she ever used. An iron silence seemed to ring out with a sinister and portentous promise. "You are lying!"

The strange manner of Joaquin's untimely death had been raised. "Tell me what happened," said Bligh.

They both looked at Blaise.

The young man who had read some of the theology of Karl Barth, a good Swiss, knew from his doctines that His God was not only totally divine, totally supreme, but also totally unknowable through His revelations, the specific times and places for which, significantly, He chooses all by himself.

This was one of them.

With a surveying but unpitying look at the woman, touching the tip of his tongue to a back tooth that signaled a moment of deliberation, Blaise said, "Yes," Maybe there was another side to it."

Gullveig's voice vapored.

They were waiting for an answer.

"There is what is and what there is is fair," Blaise said unsympathetically. Their mother's nose went pointy, essentially an aiming device she deemed for use as a weapon directed at anyone or anything she despised.

She knew exactly what the treachery was she smelt. A dust-blind wind irked her, catching somehow in the pulp of her eyes.

"Don't you know there is always another side? A mountain has many sides," said Bligh. Blaise pointed to the faraway Eiger and the Schreckhorn, and turned his hand hind-side-to. "No one can never comprehend an object unless she can see all sides of it. Walk around it. To give it its full dimensions."

Bligh put in, "*Herumlaufen*. All 360-degrees."

"I do not care to see other sides. This is why I choose never to come up here. It was your father's whim to do so, and he is dead."

But her voice was rattling with dread.

The youngsters' cold silent stares at her had too much in the way of contempt and accusation for Gullveig to stand another second of it, and as she began backing further and further away from them, she clawed the air. "Seeing one side is a mother's job! *I see only one side, do you hear me?*" screamed the cold, betrayed, logically positivistic woman, feeling herself horribly cornered and, for all of the attacking disagreeableness, the sudden and mercilessly oppressive silence, stepped to an even further point, when, sliding in a huff, near the lip of a slippery slope to get away from them, they saw her turn once, a ferocious draft of air whipping her scraggly hair. "One side is good enough for me."

She stamped a foot. Suddenly, they could no longer see her, and heard nothing but wind.

There followed a legal hearing, a required state inquisition a week after Bligh and Blaise had come down the mountainside alone, threading their way down the snowy passes until they got to the Zaik Road, when Luisa, of all people, happened to be passing, and offered them a helpful lift to town through the snow.

During the inquest, the civic probe and inquiries, much seemed missing that remained to be explained.

"Can you tell me what happened?" asked the magistrate.

There was only silence.

"Tell me what happened."

They never said.

They said nothing.

Not a word.

The Enthronization
of Vinegarfly

King Brulatour III, a fat, swollen, dropsical unhappy royal
who had three daughters woke one morning in the dark castle of
Strang, on the Upper Rhine, to find without much remorse that
Olivia, his wife, upon being delivered of a fourth child, had died
in childbirth. It was a frost-jacking set of weeks in which, miserable, because he blamed God, he could find no surcease of pain
or comfort in his sorrow in finding himself mentally alone. He
blamed God. The new baby brought not the slightest comfort to
him as he looked down at the infant in her bassinette. He had
long demanded fealty of that wife whom he made serve him. His
homely daughters, Cipollina, Allia, and Shallotina, depressingly
made him feel even more alone because they were selfish cats
who cared only for themselves with a kind of cupidity that one
only read about in fables.

The young wantons put on sad, wistful faces but at bottom were far too interested in getting married fully to care for
anyone else. The King, who had given short shrift to Olivia while
she was alive, decided to have her ashes chemically resolved into

a stone which he would set in a ring, but then he considered that would not reflect greatly enough on him, for being the cynosure of all eyes was his highest and deepest goal. A far, far better idea suddenly dawned on him.

He decided that he would build a monument that would give glory to his wife—but mainly to him. A thoroughfare of attention, he saw to it, would lead to him alone. A temporal solution was affected. The blue corpse of Olivia was placed in a small plain sarcophagus and, until the fitting memorial could be realized, he ordered it be housed in the castle but kept in a side transept projecting at a back angle to the knight's nave, which had once served as a chapel. The King by anti-clerical fiat had banished all fidelity to the old faith. Princess Pie Cake, the newborn child, meantime, for whom he had no plans, was removed until he could deal with her. Now to his scheme.

The King immediately summoned to court all of his advisers. To put his plan into motion, formulated over and over in his scheming mind, it was necessary to find an impeccable architect and then a great builder who were the right people for the job. Local homely practitioners of the arts were dismissed out-of-hand as incompetent even before their names were mentioned. King Brulatour scowled and screamed, "I do not want to watch apple-headed morons work!"

A royal proclamation was sent out that very day announcing a nationwide competition to determine which architect could come up with the most impressive design to honor the dead Queen. Entries were filled out and duly considered. All of them in the end, however, proved inadequate, which brought about contempt and derision from the intemperate King, who railed against fate. One architect, Henbit, who had a taste for botany, devised a stand of pines in the center of which he hoped to plant a shrine. The King asked with a crocodile smile, "Don't shrines cost gold and give attention to God, to him alone, but not to my wife or me?" Another architect, fluffy-haired Beausejour, a famous designer from France, disappointed the King with an original but blotchy grid pattern that was supposed to represent a sepulcher, but it was an over-tall monstrosity with grinning gargoyles and beak ducklings and frowning dog-faced downspouts that would have only brought about bewildered stares.

"Porcelain! Porcelain!" squealed another architect, hoping to impress the King, "I want to use lots of porcelain! A phantasmagoria of porcelain, one of earth's brightest jewels, and over it float a perpetual fire balloon." But not a bit of this went down with his regal employer. Bellowed the furious King, "A white vitrified ceramic not only the color of—but actually named—for pigs? With an added balloon?"

Each in turn entered the ballroom with a roll of the drums preceded by the lord chamberlain and the lord steward who carried their staves of office and walked backwards, as no one was permitted to turn his back on His Majesty. They gathered in corners and turned away simultaneously as the King waved his hand as though they were executing a well-rehearsed dance.

A hairy-faced Irish landscape architect, bowlegged and halitotic, from the National School of Ballymacktaggart named Henchy, bespectacled, chinless, and thieving—he proved in the end to be a cheat—demanded far too much for all too little. In one of his crazier projections, an urn for the Queen was to be set up in the center of a vast soft green meadow, the grass of which was to be smoothed out every morning by dutiful barefoot serfs. "Did that fool come to us by potato boat?" cried the King and exaggeratedly bulged out his jaw to mock both the tuber and the Irish architect who suffered from two of that nation's common infirmities: physical, a brandy-glass chin, and mental, a crazed penchant for the color green. A person named Droitwitch who hailed from the Balkans—he had a huge square head and huge square hands and a huge square bum—set out plans which took much longer to unroll on a table than it did for the King to have done with him, crying, "I will have nothing in brown!"

Further competitors came forth.

As to taste, value, and size, funerary architecture became a subject on which everyone had an opinion. Cenotaphs. War memorials. Tumuli. Mastaba types of tombs. Some architects referred to the temples of Malta, others to the beehive-shaped *tholoi* found in the remote Cyclades. Still others spoke of Iberian passage-graves, enriched by carvings. A communal tomb accepted here was then rejected there. Proper materials were debated. Copper could be used, no? Were they not used in Boian cultures? What about ceramic masks? Marble sheaths? An Akkanian by name of Nervoo flat-out would have nothing to do with a hated planner from Syria. Gasconaded the invidious Nervoo, sniffing, "It is a travesty, Your Majesty. Consider the seraglio and the scimitars! There are few conventions more deplored, or more depleted, than Orientalism, the depiction of the East as a realm of luxury, sensuality, and violence."

A small bearded Jew named Klitzman presented printed plans for a waterpool which Pudzler, another Jew, enviously declared looked ugly, when another Jew appeared, one Ditchshowitz, saying, "My forename is Slimane, I may charge lots but always give hotz!" and he came up with plans for a huge orange egg-ball to be placed in a full acre of a blooming bamboo garden, an eyesore. All of these vile, reduced, hairy, insolent, over-eager, hippocrepiform-legged creatures carrying filthy bags on their backs came from the unprepossessing rustic town of Ukmergė in Poland.

The courtiers were all revolted by them. "Are you all fashioning something out of anthropomorphology?" queried the indignant King, who swiftly kicked them upside. *Anthropomorphology.* He loved that word which had many O's in it and which made him sound like a scholar and which reminded him of how much he hated God. The little men protested and grew red. Pulling their black beards, they pouted. "Dismiss them," said the King. "I cannot abide ugly men!"

"It is not only impossible to govern these mewling architects, it is useless," said the King, flinging himself off the throne and parading up to a high porch where, overlooking everyone, he advised his ministers, "I want to find one *who knows enough about himself to be appalled,*" for he knew that guilt is the greatest motive for subservience. His daughters, who were eavesdropping, understood what he meant when he said, "I who have the power to forgive alone must have my way." Many decades before, in the earlier years of the Brulatour dynasty, when Roman priests were allowed to be living in the realm, they had all sagaciously warned the kings to take care of their souls. In retribution, they were all exiled to Africa, with the result that all the churches were padlocked shut and laws were passed that forbade anyone to worship.

The King despised the church and the prelates who grew fat on the purses of its tithing fools. "A parade of rouged, insufferable, be-baretta'ed pedophiles leading us through a desert of crockery!" he cried. "A liturgy of bluffing hoodoo shot through with pedantic dictionary adjectives! Nothing but shells, formulas, costumes, magic, and incomprehensible Latin, its enslaving doctrine bilge and bosh, twaddle and tripe. None of them, not one of them with their pulled faces and in their sober bracegirdles not a conniver! No creeping or fawning nun or novice not an antique leperess! No priest not a scheming and conniving butt-pirate waving astrological wands through the air!"

Looking at an old chapel, Pie Cake, now a toddler, even at the age of six, was bewildered by the mystery of it. She asked, "Why have they shopped up god in this dark place—because he was naughty?"

"I spit Hallowe'en pumpkin curses at priests," the King bellowed through the ringing air and let loose a barrage of farts.

Ladies-in-waiting covered their ears in horror. Having heard such things before, many of them dispersed, waggling away in their smocks, kirtled gowns, colored hose, and cone hats that culminated in ostentatious hennins. They flounced up the stairs to the stronghold tower to ask in a dither, "Did that growler treat the Queen so?" Noises from a turret room reinforced their fears, for they soon learned that, subsequent to the Queen's death and an onset of depression, the King had superstitiously sequestered his daughters, none with whom he had ever gotten along, for one had dropped her scissors, another dreamt of old wood, another let a bird fly in through a window, which were, all of them, bad luck. "Send one to the bit hole. Another to the quirt. Yet another to the snubbing post," ordered the angered King. Guards bowed and obeyed. "There was something wrong with them. I was fobbed off with point-headed onions, when they should have been lilies!"

Meanwhile, their dead mother's corpse, which had been infused with wax in the meantime—until the mausoleum was prepared—still remained secluded, very like an afterthought. Young Princess Pie Cake alone mourned for her—in secret, however. She had knowledge of the treatment her mother had suffered under the rule of the raging and unrueful King Brulatour III. Would there be a fourth? No, she divined.

As of now, none of the architects with their propositions had sufficed. Flamand was a fairy, Snipes too expensive, Beatwell too slow, and a stump-short nincompoop named Delphino who with his cartoon mind laid out plans that configured a vast chocolate mausoleum-cum-theater to be built in the manner of some sort of schizoidal edificial fugue with edible balconies for plays to be staged and operas performed in which he suggested, as an innovation, eunuchs in carnival masks and cinnamon, cocoa, coffee, and copper outfits, while munching scenery, could engage in dramatic exchanges semi-spoken rather than sung in logically definable arias. "Innovation is for clucks," screamed the furious King and punted over a whole series of his candy nesting boxes in the shape of bold, poignard-carrying chevaliers.

What had happened to ingenuity with style? Innovation with panache? There was one set of prints, sheaves of spidery ink drawings of a mystical sort that seemed likely until the identity of the artist was discovered.

"Everybody always says my 'creation,'" uttered Capriccioso, an Italian architect who had come all the way from Perugia with plans and prints he had worked on for a year. "But I say that nobody can create except God. Creation is by God. We just assemble things that already exist."

"A crossback?" howled the King when he learned it was Capriccio who had produced the ink drawings. One of the King's minions leaned forward with a pointer to indicate a series of wayside shrines, a typical Roman Catholic entry from a Roman Catholic architect, he said, whose faith walked before him. The King was in a vexatious quandary, for he liked some of the work. To stay on his good side, all the court jawsmiths, lackeys, prats, and obsequious lickspittles, muttering negative things to save their faces, vociferously and universally agreed that the Italian was nothing but a brazen loiter-sack with garlic on his breath, a swarthy Romanish stamp-crab who could not tell a gladiolus from a gladiator. So, he was dismissed. The King spat, "*Coquin méprisable! Le monde grouille de drones, de parasites, et de papistes!*"

Years passed. The Queen's casket had been clapped into a structure of lead, meanwhile. But the mausoleum project stood.

One day, a mysterious stranger appeared in the center of throne room, as if out of nowhere, bowing low. The court buzzed.

A solution at last was found. The King, impressed, beheld the new arrival whose name was Vinegarfly, an architect who haled from no region anyone knew. He was said to be a Pharsee, darkly connected. Nobody had solicited him nor could anyone explain his confident presence or from whence the strange man had come. "Sunlight is painting, moonlight is sculpture, but my design is midnightlight!" softly proclaimed the mysterious stranger and out of a long metal cylinder he precariously slid out drawings that he unspooled to the length of the table and flattened with caressing hands. He was a tall thin piper of an artist with long crow-black hair and a ferret's pointed nose, who, to help him, had brought along three black men, bald-headed, square-built workers with large, powerfully compulsive eyes who seemed to obey him more out of duty than affection for he did not hesitate to cane them on any whim. He wore a pointed archer's hat tapered to a straight front brim, aslant with a purple feather.

Midnightlight! Was he not one who knew enough about himself to be appalled? pondered the King. He realized he was. Midnightlight proved it. It showed that working in the dark, he sought no glory.

But who were these workers of his who so silently slaved away? It was not so much that this mysterious man had uncanny ways about him, which led to all sorts of gossip, speculation, and whispers, but the laborers all went about their business with a robotic, unearthly manner and means.

The strange architect was an enigma. No mention was made of a country of origin. Or anything like a first name. There was almost nothing to go on to identify this tall, elongated man who had a quick but qualified secret smile. There was also no mention of a wife. He would stroke his nose and lean forward with bony hands fluttering in front of him on the working tables. He stood aloof. Chumminess he seemed to avoid in all that he did. The puzzle of this architect was not only in his power to build, to shape, to order, however, but in the baffling hold that he had on the autocratic King (and even his young daughter) who marveled at his racing inventiveness—his hands flew confidently to extravagant corners and spots and sections of his drawn-up plans as if mapping a new world—and was in thrall to the potential glory that, all of it, reflecting his own person, promised the magnificent monument he so long sought. The materials he used, aggregate, boarding, hydraulic lime, esoteric slate, brick, stone and stucco foundation, as time passed, took on the lineaments of what could be called perfection. He employed jewels, as well.

How reward such grandeur? What could the cost be?

wondered the King. One night he heard Vinegarfly in the high black rafters singing,

> No more tears, my soul is dry
> I don't laugh and I don't cry.
> I look alone to reckon your needs
> and judge by what I need I buy.

Meanwhile, the Queen's corpse, which was turning bone-dust white and still preserved in a casket, was draped over with a rhodopsia cope and remained as before out in the vestibule, but one change had been made: a thick dark velour curtain had been draped over the entrance of the knight's niche, where now no one, including Pie Cake, his pretty little daughter, was allowed to approach, never mind enter. The Princess, who had reached the age of twelve and who in idiosyncratic reveries often brooded over the many bad ways that her mother, the Queen, had been treated, watched the architect fashionably cut the many stones to arrange around a grotto he had ingeniously devised high upon the parapet, adding jewels of blue corundum that shone like stars. He lightly tapped with a delicate hammer a pinkish orange sapphire called a *padparadscha* and, kneeling down, gently placed it in the Pie Cake's hand, folding her fingers around it. No stroke of his, no motion, no gesture or maneuver was made that did not please Pie Cake. She was enthralled with his proficiency. "To measure is to know," gently confided Vinegarfly, speaking knowingly to the slim, admiring girl, lessoning her with special attention as reverently she watched him work, heating rare tanzanite to deep blue, polishing the blackest opals, cutting facets into rare Larimar and grandidierite.

Everyone was in awe of his configurations.

"I am constructing manifolds! Much arithmetic can be developed by logicist means. You must pay attention, for I configure in air the way a ballerina pirouettes." He winked at Pie Cake. "Extra-logical axioms are fed by the laws of thought. In set theory—*manniffaltigkeitslehre*—we examine the constructible universe. The domain in which I am working, mathematics, we throw out anomalies and seek the elementhood of membership. A set is a Many that allows itself to be thought of as a One and the cardinality of a set is its size. Do not look to the fingers with which I write, but rather the mind in which I dwell. I have the genius to customize, build, compose, set up, form, pattern, shape, structure, make, and install. We have to house what we need to hold!"

He looked over at the King.

"Every infinite subset of a continuum has either the power of the set of integers or of the whole continuum," asserted Vinegarfly. "Right?"

"Oh y-yes, yes," agreed the vain King,

"I must make an abyss without desolation," announced Vinegarfly. "Space without nihilism or obliteration. Shoes without feet."

This bewildered the watching King and court.

"It is the architecture of paradox. I am exploring a silence to give it voice, transcending a gap of gazing futility to restate it."

"This is counterfactual, I tell you" whispered an older but fearful counselor. "Theory throttling praxis."

He was a philosopher!

"Holes. Gaps. Absences. Voids." He waved a hand. "All are seen to hold forth like demons in the actuality of absence—the queer failure of an undisclosed anxiety. A gaping void, which watches you vanish by its terror, meanwhile preens in the same way silence has a weight to it and proposes extinction. It rustles as it moves, seethes in a way, is awkward as it peers into the maw of its own dinge, and yet it initiates an exploration, which is why I am here. An empty room recedes in deference to the creative impatience of the man who enters it. I stand before you as authentic as the dismal reduction I intend to displace, with the competing claim of genius, waits like a beckoning demoiselle to be filled."

Enchanted, Pie Cake marveled at his magic words.

"Space is a not only a medium of experience but also a materialization of theory. To define expanse—capacity—is to have to determine boundaries. I do not want absence, I do not want lack, I do not want a sense of shortcoming or incompletion. I want to translate the concept of open margin by overcoming the abstraction. Clearance involves a kind of duration. Space and time constitute a collaborationalist narrative. Space must not occlude but allow, as an open mind is a welcoming, not an empty, mind. We infer a specter in a space, in the way the concave implies the convex. I come as a *tekton*, with set square and rule to unlock potential. I am a hybrid, a mutant. Great reparation is in order here. I have come to reshape the canon. I intend to turn space inside out by way of my own magic. Architecture which constitutes the abstraction of absolute truth, while yet that very truth intrudes upon feeling, must never be the expression of void or vacuum. A person cannot experience and yet *think* he experiences. The concept of dog does not bark. The concept of space is not exposure. I hate the space of vacancy and hiatus and cavity. It is not a hole! *My interior must say nothing.*"

"Say—?"

"Nothing, yes!"

The King stood silent, gobsmacked. Courtiers backed away.

"Actually, *say* nothing" explained Vinegarfly, "as if it is something,"

"Why do you not measure now?"

"I am calculating by the rule of opposition"

"Which is?"

Vinegarfly put a finger to the tip of his nose. "If I say it is opposite day today, it is therefore not opposite day, in the way that if you say it is a normal day, it would be considered a normal day. He shuffled his hands. "This seeming strangeness comes from the fact that the definition of validity in architectual logic does not always agree with the use of the term in ordinary language. Suggested improvements to the notion of logical validity include strict implication and relevant implication. I intend to enclose what I will proceed to open, in the way that falling is a way to fly."

Heads were spinning in a vertiginous whirl, and yet some smiled and nodded. Pie Cake who was impressed allowed Vinegarfly to guide her pretty hand over the exquisite sapphires he taught her not to scratch. The older homely daughters, Cipollina, Allia, and Shallotina, all loathed their sister. Their contumacious looks and leers she ignored. The bold ingenuity of the architect—the two were soon seen conversing daily—alone intrigued her. There was a charm about him, a ravishing, almost seductive manner, a bewitching sort of allure in the confident way he virtually conjured the original style of the mausoleum, as if out of his mere fingers.

One of the black slaves, about to slip on a wide two-point

swing on the parapet staging by an outrigger beam, in a desperate reach snatched at the hands of the Princess, and Vinegarfly knifed him dead. "Matter is motion, motion is force," the architect coolly told the Princess, "force is will."

Vinegarfly's wild edifical creation rose slowly, expertly, as time passed. A golden rococo stairway miraculously spiraled up to the height of a lofty balcony that rose seventy-five feet through three floors, to a distant ceiling plaited with jewels and flocks of enchanted birds. An honored showplace, the interior was built of solid mahogany, rare African blackwood and priceless agar. The furniture for the mausoleum was Islamic mainly, much of it a rare pale ash. Vast picture windows which were made of glass bent in Belgium positively shimmered, reflecting an emerald light on walls facing from floor to ceiling with slate of pale green Cippolino marble. Ceiling panels were painted with displays of stars, moons, unicorns, cherubs, and sweeping orange trees laden with fruit. The rich colors of the draperies, violet, crimson, sky and lapis blue, imparted a dazzling magnificence to the vastness of a revolutionary central room. Invaluable Flemish tapestries with gold thread and Isfahan rugs had been purchased and arranged in counterpoint to a surround of rare eighteen-paneled, hand-carved jade screens.

There was a row of cast-zinc peacocks, lemon-yellow, peering in gargoyle fashion from the high surrounding balustrades. It was high up there on the precarious scaffolding setting a unique oriel window into the upper interior that the devoted architect spent much of his work time, fumbling with its brackets and corbels and then painting it black, all of this perplexing the King somewhat with what seemed to him time-consuming contrivances and quirky ingenuities.

Vinegarfly had called for an enormous wall mural with swan-on-lake motifs, and he convinced the King further to fulfill his dreams of grandeur by super-adding rare Tibetan landscapes and Turkish knickknacks. There were wall niches filled with lapis singing lazuli egg-weights, glistering lustres of Bohemian crystal, fat gold birdcages with enamelled birds, long hand-blown glass Venetian lanterns framed in bronze and ormulu, wondrous irandoles and chandeliers of silver and gilded bronze, patchboxes, caskets and étuis of gold, silver, enamel, and lacquer.

What he had shown the King on paper in his detailed plans not only had been realized but had grown into a massive, elegant mausoleum made of blue faience with rare tiles from far Samarkand and rare windows of jewel-colored splendor centered by rubies that had not been seen since the legendary days when the Achaemenid Empire was ruled by Cyrus the Great.

As Pie Cake devotedly watched him work, Vinegarfly spoke to her of great men, like Tibetan seers and Turkish sultans and Cyrus the Great, compared to whom her father was small. None sees farther into a generalization than one with detailed knowledge, and in her short life Pie Cake had amassed all the details she needed of a father who ignored her and a mother blasphemously dismissed. The architect continued to enthrall the beauty—some say ensorcell—with his spellbinding wisdom. Said Vinegarfly, "He who is satisfied with his labor has a reason to be dissatisfied with his satisfaction." His words threw a further darker shadow across her father, for, upon reflection, she realized that, unlike the wise and insightful artist who spoke, her father was never dissatisfied with his satisfaction and, even worse, never even labored.

So grand was the mausoleum and so illustrious in its

splendor that rumors borne of by who knew spread about that it had been designed and built by actual angels. But no cherubim or seraphim were in evidence, only a small army of full-fed, scarlet-faced soldiers of the King with bull-beef eyes in pointed helmets and defiant militialike uniforms. One day, one of the two slaves, admiring the cut, sought to fit himself out in such a uniform to preen before the Princess. In a silent unruffled response, Vinegarfly leapt forward to brutally—and fatally—snap-twist the helmet on his head, which in a single swiveling full turn instantly beheaded the man. "Motion is force, matter is motion," again the architect explained to the Princess, "force is will." It did not seem to matter. The architect simply worked on, while the King's lurid taste for undisciplined and excessive ornament knew no bounds, except that it was met, point for point, exaction for exaction, by the bizarre, mysterious, and unfathomable architect who seemed never to tire and was transfiguring space as if excavating a cave he hoped to inhabit.

Outside was an artificially tiled garden with a drainage system that recycled water into fountains. Priceless ancient Chinese statues of bulls and guardian lions were brought in at exorbitant expense, figures that held the recipe for a rare form of iron oxide, pure epsilon-phase iron compounds that had been unexpectedly discovered in the glaze of silvery Jian bowls thousands of years before. They were set in a staggered row along verdant pathways that constituted a vista leading to a view of the high central arch. Hoists winched in a series of decorative dragon statues made of stone with red jasper eyes, and huge oval wheels of lapis lazuli, of such a blue that they seemed struck from the frozen sea, all of them rolled in by powerful men to act as balancing spans on an adjoining entrance hall. A long imposing entrance floor, with extended edges on both sides trimmed with Travertine noce, was coopered of pure gold.

For a year the workers labored, but still perfection eluded them. There was some fundamental flaw in the design, felt the King, and he conferred with Vinegarfly, growing more diffident as he grew even more greedy. "It is not in the design but in your fears and hesitation about your own project," replied the sagacious architect, whose knowingness seemed more and more obscure and oblique, and Vinegarfly, who cast on him a severe, mesmerizing stare, led the monarch way up, high up, past the parapets to the very highest cloister vault to where part of a segmented dome formed of curved sections corresponded to the section of the polygon on which it rested, and there on a tiny balcony he whispered encouragement. The view from high above the mausoleum, centered inside the dome, seemed only a perch for birds.

A suspension rope going high up had been replaced when the last black slave that Vinegarfly had brought with him broke a thimble made to attenuate wear on the closure where a screw pin shackle had been fit to bear a working load, and in consequence—Pie Cake watched—Vinegarfly, taking the rope, wound it thrice around his neck and strangled him. "Force is will, motion is force," disinterestedly the architect told the Princess, "matter is motion."

No one noticed, no one cared. The avaricious King as he stood there was consumed solely with the material success of the monumental undertaking. Surprisingly, Vinegarfly's encouragement instilled belief in the King's otherwise faithless heart. "Payment seems wholly inadequate," the monarch, hands folded, confessed to his favorite architect in what was surely a rare moment of gratitude, which yet had much of bluster, but of course every bully at bottom is always a lackey. "But what may I give you as a reward in return for your many accomplishments?"

Bowing low, Vinegarfly understood the question and, whispering with satisfaction, quoted from the *I Ching*, saying,

> "The dark force possesses beauty but veils it. So must laying claim to the completed work. This is the way of the earth, the way of the wife, the way of one who serves. It is the way of the earth to make no display of completed swork but rather to bring everything to completion vicariously."

Then he rose. "So, I lay no claim to the completed work, as that is the way of the earth. As to the way of the wife—"

"Yes?" queried the King.

"I desire Pie Cake in exchange," said Vinegarfly directly and without a moment of hesitation. It came as a ragged, jagged bolt of lightning out of a sheer blue day. While devotion had made the uncommonly contentious King servile and obsequious in his greed, he had expected anything but such a stark and unsettling request. It was more than a mere request, it was a revelation, a demand, a solicitation, an obsecration, a stunningly coal-black report—an *exaction*—from the hell of horror. He was stupefied—actually jolted. It was as if a hideous percussion and prostration hit him both at the same time. Astonished, at a loss for words, he stood there duck-dumb. The architect was cold as camphor and said, "Something human to me is dearer than all the wealth of the world." He held him in an enchanted *fascinatio* with a glittering eye.

There was nothing as he stood there that the King could do but acquiesce, as he gazed around at the entirely sumptuous and lavishly appointed mausoleum, fitted with the rarest jewels, marbles, paintings, and screens. The Princess Pie Cake was then summoned, and the King with an indifferent movement handed her over to the architect and, looking about him, needed to sit down. Before she left the King's side, the Princess stepped aside to make room for her father to sit there, not here—a golden throne that he had not seen had been worshipfully provided on part of the parapet—as if in the upper ramparts there she had distinct familiarity.

But he did not sit down, not yet.

The King ogled the throne, its golden oval headrest fitted around with all of the rarest cut stones. Looking down from such a terrible height, he felt fear as he considered the chair. "Is it safe?" "To measure is to know," declared Vinegarfly as he smiled over at the young girl with multiplying movements of his eyes, "I did not design the kingly throne. It was crafted and constructed by your daughter, schemed by your own flesh and blood—pattern, motif, and device—so fear not," said the architect. "She has taken your measure. She has measured you."

"Do not be hasty," said Pie Cake.

"Space accommodates time," quipped the architect, "just as time space. They work together in cold simplicity."

Vinegarfly reached for the young girl's arm which he took with a grice-fingered grip, and as he did so the act of merely clutching the young girl's flesh brought ascendancy into his complicated soul, as if in a cap-sheaf moment, like a real occupation, he suddenly felt the remarkable experience of having a rare, singularly peerless, audacious, immutable, ineluctable sense of ownership. It was uncanny, however. Something still plagued the unsettled King who overlooked the gallery from high above the central aisle of the vast mausoleum, even while he pronounced it perfect. He was so excited he rubbed his hands as slowly he approached the thronal chair with a mime of pleasure, and yet as he looked around at the ever-circling view, taking it in, he wondered exactly what it was that spoiled the perfect harmony.

Cunning Vinegarfly with a smile did not have to be asked who loomed there. He was way ahead of the King. With the eerie prescience characteristic of him, a property less than a trait, a condition more than a fact, he wordlessly pointed down to the dwarfed casket that had been sitting so long there by the side-vestibule below and the body that death had claimed all these years ago but which had glaringly remained there as a rude, indignant fact, unholy and low, neglected, seemingly now an ugly pointless afterthought, so subordinate, so low-ranking, to the central axis of the mausoleum, a lost and forgotten item situated in the insignificant bay or bays of the overhanging nave or transept, that it seemed utterly irrelevant. It sorely offended the King.

The King hated what he thought he had forgotten and screamed at the top of his voice, "Take that hideous thing away!"

It was a remark eerily coincident with the obliging Princess Pie Cake's helping her greedy father, tenuously groping, to sit down for the very first time upon the royal throne, when with a loud crack it suddenly gave way, splitting in two, the almost obscene exploding noise of it suddenly opening wholesale through the glass of the ceiling oriel window, painted black, the corbels and brackets never having been latched.

The ghastly look on the King's face—a mask of paper-white hue, drained of all blood, his eyes lit up and popping in sudden horrifying shock—stepped into nothing as with a silent scream like that of a silver shriek of a eunuch he went plummeting headlong through an endless league of air, crashing to his death into a splatter. It was over. Where he was buried, as time passed, no one could remember, nor indeed did anyone ever try. He would be recalled neither at the solemn annual occasion of the Investiture of Princess Pie Cake nor at any time or in any instance during her long efficient reign as Queen of the Realm. Nor were her homely sisters, Cipollina, Allia, and Shallotina, ever seen again, having been married off, by fiat, to the three Levantine architects who came from the rustic village of Ukmergė in distant Poland—

    —and banished for their entire lifetimes.

    Queen Pie Cake thenceforth ruled the nation.

    And Vinegarfly ruled her.

CPSIA information can be obtained
at www.ICGtesting.com
Printed in the USA
BVHW060931231121
622334BV00002B/62